Cahe
Evidence of Evil

By

Peter Phillips

For all the regrets and upsets caused
That time may heal the rifts.

Published by New Generation Publishing in 2024

Copyright © Peter Phillips 2024

First Edition

The author asserts the moral right under the Copyright, Designs and Patents Act 1988 to be identified as the author of this work.

All Rights reserved. No part of this publication may be reproduced, stored in a retrieval system or transmitted, in any form or by any means without the prior consent of the author, nor be otherwise circulated in any form of binding or cover other than that which it is published and without a similar condition being imposed on the subsequent purchaser.

ISBN: 978-1-83563-299-4

www.newgeneration-publishing.com

New Generation Publishing

Carter and The Evidence of Evil

Carter is the name of the character that forms the main plank of this book. Yes, no forename only, Carter. His mother just loved the name. Having chosen the police as a career, he became a unique officer, not only an officer in the Merseyside Constabulary with one name but the whole of the United Kingdom.

After a recent promotion to the rank of, Detective Chief Superintendant CID, he still retained charge of the Major Crime Unit. Carter returns home after having spent a week's leave with Diane and Martin Sinclair parents of his murdered wife, Helen murdered in their home by agents of a drug baron, attempting to stem the investigation into his illegal drug operation. He was always made to feel welcome there and allowed to treat it as a bolthole when things got rough.

As usual, Diane had washed and prepared all his clothes, placing them neatly into his holdall. After he unpacked, he put his clothes away. He dealt with the accumulated mail he had found on the coffee table and neatly left by Kate Murphy, his domestic.

Amongst the mail, he noticed a very elegantly designed envelope; he found a silver gilt-edged invitation card from his friend and the well-known jeweller, David Robinson, with a traditional RSVP.

Carter attends at his friend's exceptionally prominent house and party. On arrival, his hosts, David, and his wife Beth, warmly welcome him.

Mingling with the other guests, he began to relax. Whilst all the guests stood and sat talking. Carter failed to notice a certain lady was showing a great amount of interest from afar.

It was whilst relaxed and enjoying himself that his pager suddenly activated; he looked down at the caller ID window and recognised the contact number of the force control room. Message passed. He awaits collection.

His lift arrives with blue lights pulsating, illuminating the house and the ground floor rooms. He apologises to Beth and David for having to leave so early. He casually says his goodbyes to the room of guests and leaves.

1

Detective Sergeant Phil Watson received the official message from the duty Inspector in the force control room to attend at 274 Central Drive, Sandfield Park, Liverpool, 12. To pick up his guv. Before leaving, Carter looked at his young DS, "What's all the fuss? Why, for I was bloody enjoying myself."

Phil replied, "Sorry, sir, I've come straight from home and am not up to speed as yet; I only know a body has been found in Walton Park?"

On leaving, when clear of the property, Phil activated the blues and twos. Carter had not envisaged the effect of his early departure on a specific female party guest. She shivered on hearing the claxons.

Abby casually wondered to her friend Beth, "Why the sudden excitement and the early departure of your guest?" David, Beth's husband, mentioned that's only our friend, Carter; he's a policeman?"

Beth, who at that precise moment had taken a drink of wine, began coughing and spluttering, found that her mouthful of wine suddenly evacuated down her nose. Beth looked at David and barked, "Will you please warn me before making such a lame, statement? Now, will you please explain, or should I?"

Abby looked bewildered. David beckoned her to move closer. "Carter is no ordinary police officer; he holds the rank of Detective Chief Superintendent CID, which is no mean feat. In charge of a professional team of all hand-picked officers, known as *'The Major Crime Unit.'*"

Carter informed his friends. "On being a newly promoted Detective Inspector, he received a message. *'Be at Commander Frost's office (Commander CID) at nine am.'* He explained that such a message without explanation, is likely to turn a newly promoted Inspector's blood to water, thinking *'Who's in the shit?'*"

"On arrival, TF fully explained the situation. The boss (Chief Constable) Had attended a meeting at the Home Office. The home secretary wants to roll out a special crime-fighting unit countrywide. To be known as 'Major Crime Units,' working within their home force boundary lines, initially to deal with major crime. To relieve the pressure from off the shoulders of their divisional CID colleagues."

"He was abruptly told he was to head the MCU for Merseyside. He had to go away having cart blanche to hand pick a team from existing personnel in any of the forces' CID offices. When formed, it deals only in extreme crimes, force wide. Being responsible only to Commander Frost and him alone."

David continued, "As a boss, Carter quickly galvanised a team who'd follow Carter wherever he led. He also gained respect from both sides of the fence."

Abby walked over to Beth she whispered with a discreet smile. "Beth, what are the chances of asking for Carter's contact number?"

Beth replied, "One thing you should know about Carter is he is an introvert when off duty; he asks for people who know him to give him space. He shuns the limelight, although as leader of the 'MCU, on successful detections, arrests, and convictions. He has no power over the local and national press. Although he finds his name and photograph plastered all over the news media."

David, standing next to Beth and Abby, turned with a stoic look. "Abby, the incident that had the uttermost effect on Carter's life, which nearly tore him apart. Because of a raid four years ago on his flat, the monsters murdered a Detective Inspector, Ruth Ellis, a duty armed protection officer, plus his wife Helen, and their two babies."

The audacious raid at his address was because of information passed by a bent police officer and a concierge. Both having been given drugs in prison for the information."

"The horror was committed as revenge on the orders of a local drug baron. Allegedly, the tragedy was organised to derail his team's enquiries, but he failed in his endeavours."

Abby stood with both her hands up to her mouth and muttered, "Oh my God! I remember it, for it was covered by all the news channels on the TV and papers; what a loss. It's a wonder he didn't implode?"

David whispered, "He did, and what did we both do. Beth and me? We shrunk back, finding it impossible to approach him; we thought he'd be in so much pain and anguish that contact with him would open such wounds of happier times. We both remembered the selection of their wedding bands and other jewellery items they selected and purchased."

"Finding we were unable to offer our sense of remorse and commiserations, what on earth is one expected to say, except all the old heartfelt condolences, I realised it was futile."

David continued, "The ice was broken when we experienced a nasty raid on our shop in School Lane due to the severity of the case, for CCTV clearly showed that the offenders were carrying firearms. The case ticked all the boxes and landed on Carter's desk. He and members of his team turned up. He was, then, a Detective Superintendent."

"Carter and his team, indisputably over the months and with diligent inquiries, eventually arrested the offenders, and after the court case, all our stolen property was returned."

David looked at Abby, "Beth has mentioned your request; Carter's happiness is paramount; I see it as a positive move, for although a customer, he is a sincere friend. But I only give you the information on the clear understanding that all matters explained here this night will be revered and never mentioned. Unless mentioned by the man himself?"

Phil arrived at Walton Park, off Walton Hall Avenue; at the entrance to the park, a uniformed officer stood holding a clipboard to record all IDs and times of all officers attending and leaving the site.

Phil stopped and lowered his window. "DS Philip Watson, and Det Ch Supt Carter." The officer checked their IDs, saying, "Sir." Carter leaned over and thanked him, a matter often observed and respected of Carter.

Phil slowly drove down the narrow access pathway, the only way to the crime site. Passing all the highly attended lawns, plants, and playing fields. In the distance, they witnessed all the glowing blue lights, illuminating the outline of the trees, hedgerows, and night sky.

On arrival, Carter exited the car to be met by Woman Detective Superintendent Sue Ford, Carter's second in command. She smiled as she presented Carter habitually with his forensic suit. "Sir, sorry to disturb your evening, but thought you should see this one?"

When suited and booted, he walked off with Sue towards the site. He noticed a slight grin on her face. Carter suddenly turned, "Detective Superintendant Ford, why do I detect a certain amount of pleasure when I had my evening interrupted?" Sue, trying to hide her smirk, replied, "What sir, me sir, no sir?"

He suddenly stopped and whipped around; he stooped down and leaning in, he looked her straight in her lovely blue eyes. She turned, "Oh sir, were you having a pleasant evening, sir?" He looked at her. "Yes, until I received the bloody interruption?"

"Well, it always seems to be just so, sir, for we also have Lloydie and a few others in the team." Sue negotiated a path and walked through a gap in a small, well-manicured ornamental hedge surrounding a perfectly mowed lawn, closely followed by Carter.

As Carter walked through, he noticed two obvious matters: a large circular lawn with a raised mound in the middle. Two, a tarpaulin tent was erected over the top of the mound to protect the victim and site.

While Carter was taking in the scene, his ears rang with the bellowing voice of the home office pathologist, Gordon Chambers.

They were instantly met by Lloydie, a DI from the team, who emerged from the tent. Since the formation of the MCU, he dealt with all the death-related issues. The story is that his boss had a gippy tummy when it came to dealing with murder victims and PMs, a fact he thought was a secret...!?

He smiled, "Good evening, sir. This case is a rather bad one?" Carter smiled as he looked at Sue, "Well, boss (the word used when a senior officer teasingly refers to a junior officer), what on earth must Lloydie mean?"

As Sue was about to explain, they suddenly heard the booming voice of the pathologist. "Is that you, Chief Superintendent Carter, and no doubt your trusty colleague, Superintendent Ford?" With utter frustration, Carter replied, "Yes, Gordon, we're not deaf."

The tent flap suddenly flashed open, exposing the eccentric pathologist sprouting, "What, what!!" It also allowed the bright SOCO arc lights to flood into the night sky. "Welcome, Carter, and your trusty deputy, Sue; please enter."

On entering, Gordon stood to one side to reveal the body of a man sitting on his haunches on the lawn, with his head slumped down on his chest. Gordon Chambers walked over and gently lifted his head. The act permitted them to see the victim's injuries, which ultimately affected both Carter and Sue.

Gordon apologised. "Well, there is no beating about the bush?" They both turned with horror as they suddenly noticed that the victim's mouth had been slashed, from ear to ear, the mouthpiece had been forced open, and stuffed with what appeared to be white powder?"

Carter looked at his pathologist friend, "Gordon, with the look of total shock in the victim's eyes and face, was he alive at the time?" He replied, "Yes, I'm sorry to say, observed by the amount of blood at the scene?"

To make matters worse, it would seem that the perpetrator used an instrument, such as a box cutter, to make the initial injuries to his mouth, followed by an iron bar or piece of wood, perhaps in the shape of a baseball bat, either would do the job, to smash both his teeth and jaw, permitting fuller access to his mouth, a matter you can't see from there?"

Gordon continued, "The volume of powder in his mouth, plus his other injuries to his mouth and teeth, are impeded because of his lowered head onto the victim's chest. Carter walked over. He bent down and gently lifted the victim's head, looking up at the pathologist, "Gordon, it beggars' belief the power needed to commit that much damage?"

"Gordon, do you have a TOD. (Time of death) The pathologist replied, "I managed a body temp as close as I can make it, for its rather cold. Say within the last 8 - 10 hours and change. I will probably find more when I deal with him further and better at my place. That if it weren't for the blunt force trauma to his mouth, he'd probably have choked to death from all the white powder deposited in his mouth and throat?"

Looking at Lloydie, Carter turned, "Have you found any ID?" He replied, "No sir, but I'll fingerprint him to ID him when at the mortuary?"

Lloydie smiled, "Sir, I'll follow the body to the mortuary." Carter thanked him. Stating, "Lloydie, we'll meet you there. Lloydie, how is Sam? Do say hello for me; see you later?"

As they left, Carter looked at Sue, "Alright, if I travel with you?" Sue replied, "But of course, sir?"

2

When leaving the park, Carter looked at his watch, "It's 12.30 am; let's drive to the Royal and get a coffee from the chuck wagon?" Sue smiled as it was a particular favourite of Carter's.

On their way, Carter called Commander Tony Frost, head of the Merseyside CID and his boss. All CID personnel affectionately knew him as TF. *"Frost,"* "Sir, it's Carter. I'm not certain if you're aware; members of the team and I were called out to Walton Park, off Walton Hall Avenue, where the body of a Caucasian male was found in a quiet area of the park?"

He continued, "Sir, it's a particularly bad one. The perpetrator or perpetrators have caused terrible facial injuries to the victim by slashing his mouth from ear to ear, using a possible box cutter type of instrument, and then using perhaps a steel bar or a piece of wood similar to that of a baseball bat, smashing his teeth and gums, to enable him, or them, to jam a load of white powder into his mouth, while he was still alive."

His boss screamed, *"Tell me you're fucking joking...*Interrupted by, *"Really, Tony?"* "Up's Sorry, Joan." (His wife) *"Carter, please call me later when you have all the facts?"* Before he closed the call, Carter said, "Sir, what about Wendy Field?" (PR Director)

TF replied, *"Carter, you must be joking?"* Carter replied, "Sir, it's rather difficult with a SOCO tent popping up in the park and members of the MCU sniffing around?" Sue turned and just smiled at Carter.

TF coughed, *"See what happens, brief Wendy, but let's see the reaction of the press?"* Carter replied, "Sir, it's the relatives I worry about. If the press crawl all over this, and it's out there, I'll have a word in the ear of DI Baxter, and he's, her partner. See what I can do?" He heard the growl, *"Fine, sort it."* He closed the call.

Sue looked at Carter and laughed. "Quite the politician, sir?" Carter shouted funny bugger, just drive."

Sue smiled, letting Carter's comment go over her head. On arrival at the hospital, Sue parked in an empty bay. Carter left the car and walked over to the chuck wagon to buy their two coffees. Minutes later, he returned he smiled at Sue, "Coffee white two sugars?" He stayed holding his black coffee, looking down at Sue.

She looked up, "What?" He laughed, "Surely you must be impressed. I remembered how you like your coffee?" She laughed, "Sir, it's only taken 6 years?"

Upon completion, they left for the mortuary, located at the rear of the hospital.

Sue parked up in one of the *'police only'* bays. She locked the car, and they walked over to the mortuary door and the access bell.

Sue pressed the bell, and a tired voice muttered, "Yes?" They both took out their IDs. Sue stated, "Detective Superintendent Susan Ford and Chief Superintendent Carter, they held up their IDs to the CCTV camera on the wall.

The door clicked, and Sue pulled it open. They found Lloydie with a smile on his face. "Morning sirs." Carter laughed, "Okay, Lloydie, lead on."

They found Gordon Chambers standing in his pathology uniform at the end of the cold and dismal corridor. He bellowed, "Officers, will you please follow me?" Carter noticed that he was carrying a file under his arm.

Entering the PM room, they noticed a body shape on the first table, covered by a white rubber sheet, highlighted by the large, blue-tinted theatre light above it.

Gordon Chambers walked up to the body. He pulled back the sheet down to the victim's chest. They both noticed that the victim had been washed, which followed normal protocol. Carter suddenly noticed, *No.' Y-shaped scar?'* Gordon looked at him, "Don't panic; it's first off in the morning."

Carter thought, 'shit, he can read my mind?' Both men smiled with total respect for each other.

Gordon suddenly burst out, "Officers, it's nigh impossible to overt your eyes from the obvious, the big gaping hole which was, once, part of the victim's mouth. You will also notice the number of missing teeth and parts of his upper and lower jaws, smashed, all committed by the powerful use of a hard handheld instrument?"

Gordon finished, "To assist with matters, I've taken blood, body fluids, and hair samples for DNA. Plus, samples of the white powder have all been sent to the labs for identification?"

Lloydie walked over, "Sir, I've checked his clothes. They're of no help as to the victim's ID, but I've fingerprinted the victim to see if he's known to us?"

Carter looked at all present, "Sue, Lloydie, and even you, Gordon, after you put away our John Doe, may I suggest we go home until a better hour in the morning?" They all agreed.

Outside of Carter's address, he looked at his watch, "Look, Sue, it's 2.30 am, Sunday morning. So, let's sleep in…Sue interrupted, "Sir!?" Carter blushed, "You know what I mean? Will you pick me up, say 10.00 am? On Monday morning?" He got out of the car and left for his flat.

As Sue drove off, she thought, *'If only?'*

3

Carter awoke at 9 am on the dot, not having to set any alarm clock. He walked into the bathroom, shaved, and then took an invigorating shower. Upon completion, he dried off and walked to the bedroom to dress.

When dressed, he went to the kitchen to make his traditional breakfast, one mug of black coffee. He sat and thought of the latest incident while toying with his coffee.

During his time in charge of the MCU, the team dealt with some horrific cases, yet Carter failed on many occasions to understand *'Man's inhumanity to man.'* He constantly thought about what drives a person or people to conduct such acts of aggression.

While deep in thought, he suddenly heard the front doorbell and intercom; he suddenly remembered *Sue!*

He placed his empty mug in the sink and returned to answer the intercom. "Good morning, Sue. I'm on my way." From the coat stand, he put on his 'Aquascutum' overcoat, with a fern green woollen collar, and walked down to open his flat's front door.

Walking out into the foyer and closing his flat door behind him, he greeted the duty concierge in the hall, "Good morning, Stephen." He replied, "Morning, Mr Carter, sir." He noticed Sue, who was standing inside the foyer of the flats.

When in her car, he looked at Sue, "I do hope you're well rested after the rigours of the weekend. She turned and replied, "Sir, if I'm not used to the hours we put in, then I'd better quit." Carter, in a serious tone, said, "Don't you bloody dare…?"

On their way to the office, he took out his phone and called Eric. "Morning, sir. Did you sleep in?" Carter could hear the burst of laughter down the phone. "Look funny ass, please do the honours with our coffees, and please assemble the team for a scrum down," "Will do, sir." Came the reply.

On arrival at the office, he and Sue answered to the chorus, "Good morning, sir." And "Morning boss." After signing on duty, they sat by Eric to enjoy their morning coffees.

Carter gave Eric a quick summary of the incident. Eric looked at Carter, "Sir, you'll find that Lloydie has been very busy, plus they're all awaiting your presence in the conference room."

Carter looked at Sue. "Let's go away and show willingness?" They both got up and walked out of the general office towards the conference room, with Eric's laughter ringing in their ears.

Sue opened the door, and they both entered to the noise of chairs being pushed back and the team coming to attention. They all heard a cry of, "Yes, yes, yes, now please sit down." Answered with peals of laughter from the team.

Carter and Sue assumed their places at the top of the room. Sue sat down on her chair next to Carter's.

He remained standing; he turned and looked at the two nearby whiteboards, on which were the SOCO photographs from the scene in the park featuring several of the victims. Lloydie had also obtained mortuary photographs of the victim.

Carter turned to face the team. "Well, late Saturday and the early hours of Sunday morning, your boss and I and some of the team attended Walton Park and dealt with matters at the crime scene, and just in case Mr Morton is listening, hence our late start to proceedings?" There was a roar of laughter.

"You will all be aware that we have a white male victim approximately 35 years of age, found in a quiet section of Walton Park, as shown in photos 1 to 6, giving the impression of our victim sat on his haunches, with his head on his chest." Carter continued.

He then pointed, "Photos 7 to 12 show a quite different picture. You will notice that a SOCO officer has lifted his head, and one can see that his mouth has been slashed from ear to ear, bags of an unknown substance stuffed into his gaping mouth, and signs of white powder on and around his mouth."

"Lastly, photos 13 to 18 show quite a different picture; it is very apparent that the mortuary pictures of the same victim show that considerable damage had been caused to the victim's teeth and jaws."

Our good friend and home office pathologist, Gordon Chambers, states that the gash to the victim's mouth was, perhaps, caused by a box cutter. The damage to the victim's teeth and jaws was caused by some iron bar or a length of wood?"

"DI Lloyd was with the boss and me at the mortuary." Carter asked Jim, "Do we have any results of the blood, bodily fluids, hair follicles for DNA, and fingerprints taken from the victim?"

Lloydie stood up, "Sir, I'm going to the mortuary after your brief. I will keep you informed as soon as I hear anything?"

Carter looked at Sue, "Supt Ford, can you please organise some of the team to return to the park to tie up any loose ends? Who found the victim? He stuttered, "Please, please, don't tell me. I suppose the good old dog walker?" Sue, laughing, said, "Well, I never, sir, must be a mystic?" The team burst out laughing.

As he began to leave the conference room, Carter suddenly stooped down to where Ian Baxter was sitting. Leaning down, and whispered, "Ian, will you come to my office, and please bring your coffee?" Ian replied. "Sir."

Fifteen minutes later, while Carter was sitting behind his desk, there was a knock on his office door. Looking up, he called, "Come in."

The door opened to reveal Ian standing in the doorway, carrying two mugs of coffee. "Hi Ian, never trust a Greek bearing gifts...? No, come in and place the coffees down."

Ian sat adjacent to Carter's desk; he looked at his boss, "Sir." Carter looked at him, "Ian, this is rather delicate; of course, you are fully aware of our latest case; at this stage, should or shouldn't we tell the press?"

"My last question would mean that we inform Wendy. Now, I want you to think outside the box and look at this matter as not being Wendy's partner?" Carter muttered.

He continued, "I do not need to tell you where TF stands on this matter?" He raised his voice slightly, "You know my feelings towards the bosses in the Hallowed Halls, who look down from on high?"

"Ian, my reason for saying my last comment relates to the victim. Does he have a family and relatives?" Carter coughed, "Ian, would it be possible to see if Wendy has been contacted by any members of the press for a comment, weighing up press interest?"

Ian smiled, "Sir, I'm a policeman first, and Wendy, who I love immensely, happens to be my partner. But as in other cases, I've never let one get in the way of the other?" Carter stood and said, "Thanks, Ian. I'm sorry I went to great lengths to get to the point." Ian said, "No problem, sir." And left his office.

4

Eric had entered his office; he smiled, "I did hear your sarcastic comment during the scrum down, yet I still favour you with a coffee?" As he was about to turn to leave, Carter responded, "Eric, you know me, I'm like the Martini Advert on the TV, 'Anytime, anyplace, anywhere.' I, of course, mean about coffee, although the girl in the advert, Christie Brinkley, is very fit?"

Eric turned laughing, leaving for his own office.

Carter's office door had no sooner closed when his mobile phone rang. He took it out of his pocket and, looking down, saw the caller ID, *'private caller.'* He pressed the little green phone icon and shouted, "Okay sunshine, is this a bloody joke, making a private call to my mobile, thinking you can fool me?"

He waited for the burst of laughter when he suddenly thought, 'shit' "Er, er, er, sorry, "Carter." He then heard a polite cough and a lovely soft voice say, *"Excuse me, am I talking to Chief Superintendent Carter?"*

Carter suddenly explained, "I'm so sorry. I thought it was a colleague playing a joke. So now I know it's obviously not him, so whom do I have the pleasure of speaking with?"

The lovely, soft, controlled voice replied, *"My name is Abigail Remington; we met briefly on Saturday at the party of David and Beth Robinson. You had to leave unexpectedly."* Carter felt a sudden flutter deep in his stomach, "Er, yes, Abigail, I do remember?"

There was an embarrassed silence as if both parties wondered who should speak next. Carter coughed,

"Abigail, have you had lunch?" With a sudden lift in her voice, she replied, *"No, not at present?"* He looked at his watch. It was noon. "Yet I know a place that I can recommend?"

"Abigail, how about we meet for lunch at *'Auberge Deli'* on Allerton Road? Do you happen to know the place?" She burst out laughing, *"Why yes, of course."*

"I'll be about fifteen minutes; how about you?" Carter replied, "Thirty minutes. I'm leaving now. What are you wearing?" She laughed; *"I will have a single red rose in my jacket lapel? Sorry, I'm only messing with a yellow dress and a blue jacket."* He burst out laughing and closed the call.

Carter entered the general office and signed out in the office diary, 'Enquiries Allerton Road.' He looked at Eric, smiling. I'm off early for lunch. See you shortly."

Eric stood scratching his head as Sue entered the general office, "What's up? Is that the guv going out?" Eric, laughing, turned to her, still scratching his head, "Er, yes, he's just out to lunch. It's on what one may call a sudden impulse?"

Carter arrived at the deli, affectionately known as 'Toms.' As he opened the door, his entrance was heralded by the tiny delicate bell that always tinkled, on entry.

He walked into the deli and was warmly greeted by Tom. He smiled, "Hello, Carter, how are things?" Carter smiled, "Yes, I'm good." As he spoke, he turned his head, looking about the deli.

Tom said, "Carter, are you looking for someone?" On seeing Abigail, Carter smiled, "No, Tom." He began to walk between the tables in the deli until he stood in front of a table on the upper level, where he recognised Abigail, as she smiled while looking over the top of a menu.

He walked up to the table and smiled down at her, "Well, madam, how did you happen to know of my favourite dining area?" He suddenly turned and immediately looked upon Tom. Who sensitively turned and walked away.

Carter looked down on Abigail, "Madam, I thought your identity was via a red rose. I'd hate to make a terrible mistake?" Abigail smiled, "Why, sir, please take a seat?"

Abigail whispered, "You seem well known in these parts?" He smiled, "Yes, it's one of the few places where I can eat without being disturbed?"

He looked her straight in her eyes, "Abigail, first... He had no sooner started when she interrupted... "Carter, please call me, Abby or Abbs...?" He continued, "Abby, I must apologise for my early exit on Saturday evening, but genuinely it wasn't the company, but my *'lover'....?"*

Abby looked somewhat perturbed; she shrieked, "Carter?" He smiled at her, "No, Abby, all CID officers, when called out, refer to the job as their 'lover.' for it always seems to happen just before or after an intermit occasion. Hence, the inference from the word lover?"

She began to laugh. Carter said, "You think I'm joking? Just wait till you meet one, and you'll end up screaming." Abby looked at Carter, and he noticed her shining gloriously blue eyes. He said, "Shall we pick something to eat?" She smiled, "Why yes, of course."

Tom appeared as if by magic, "Carter, are you ready to order?" "Yes, please, Tom, he looked at Abby. I can recommend cold beef sandwiches on crisp brown bread, a bowl of chips, accompanied by two bottles of chilled sparkling water?" Abby smiled, "Yes, please."

Whilst enjoying their meal, both strived to speak discreetly. Carter suddenly whispered, "Abby, how about we go to dinner?" Her tummy suddenly turned like a washing machine yet trying to remain calm. She looked at Carter, "What about your *'lover?'* He smiled, "I'll bring her with me?"

After paying the bill and saying goodbye to Tom, they stood outside the deli. Carter looked at her, "Can I give you a lift?" Laughing, Abby said, "What, I'm on my lunch hour, for I just work over the road at the NatWest bank, yet I've got my car, for future reference?"

5

On his return to the office, he signed back in. He then walked over and poured himself a coffee from the coffee urn. He smiled and walked through to his office. Eric thought well, sir seems happy.

Later in the day, after an afternoon of trying to concentrate on his work, with files that needed reading, for his comments prior to submitting to Eric for filing. He'd suddenly had enough; he got up and collected all the completed files, leaving for the general office with the intention of handing matters over to Eric.

Eric looked at him, "Well, my word, one has been busy?" He asked Carter, "Do you wish a coffee before you sign off duty?" Carter smiled, "No thanks, Eric, I'm off home. See you in the morning. He signed off duty and left for home.

On arrival, he immediately took off his coat and hung it on the stand in the hall. He turned and walked into the bedroom, stripped off and took part in a wonderful vigour's shower. During such an act, thoughts of Helen, his wife, came to mind, for it was her that introduced him to the sensual act of joint showers and all the extras. The mere thoughts came flooding back.

Such thoughts tended to embarrass him, for he never suffered from amnesia; Helen's thoughts always filtered into his mind from their original sensual blueprint. The mere thoughts he could never remove from the simple act of showering.

After his shower, he dried off and dressed in a T-shirt and sports shorts. He walked through to the kitchen in his bare feet. His first task was a raid on the fridge, where he helped himself to two cans of lager. Opening the first can, it didn't touch the sides. On completion, he opened the second can and walked through to the lounge, where he drank at a more leisurely pace.

He turned on the TV and scanned the newspaper; he let out a sigh, for he'd become bored with both, and he threw the paper to the floor. He got up and went to retrieve his mobile phone from his jacket.

He looked down at his phone and punched in Abby's name and number. Before speaking, he again considered Helen. *'He immediately thought of the following day, after he first met her, and yes, yet again, telling himself to remain calm and not to give way to his feelings. Lo and behold, you're at it again; it's only been three hours. Put your phone away. 'For God's sake?'*

The following morning, Carter got up, shaved, and showered, during which he was fighting the temptation to call Abby. He stood in the kitchen, *'Christ Carter, you've just left her. Do you not think you should leave it until later today?'*

Carter walked into the general office, signed on duty, and smiled, "Looking around you all seem the same people as yesterday, so I must be in the correct place, office, and job. I do hope nothing's changed, no sudden, BOS?" (Ball of shit)

He had just sat down with his mug of coffee when the office door suddenly opened, and Sue entered. She muttered, "Well, I see the early dart suited you yesterday?" He just smiled at her.

He got up and walked over to the break table and poured a mug of coffee, white and two sugars. He walked over and offered it to Sue."

She laughed, "Has anyone got a camera?" Sue looked at Carter, "Sir, I've forgotten something. Do you happen to have a minute?" They both, with coffee in hand, walked through to his office.

When they were both settled, Carter sat behind his desk, and Sue sat in the first chair adjacent to it. He smiled, "Well, let's, have it?" "Carter, I received a message from Lloydie."

Sue leaned over and, picking up the office phone, dialled his number, "Lloydie, can you come through to the guv's office?" She replaced the phone.

Minutes later, there was a knock-on Carter's door. He shouted, "Come in, Lloydie." The door opened, and Lloydie stood in short-sleeve order. As he entered, they both saw that he was carrying a vanilla folder under his arm and a mug of coffee in the other.

Carter pointed to the meeting table, "Lloydie, please sit opposite Sue?" As he sat down, he placed the file on the table; they could both see a file name and the Mer/cro number.

He looked at Carter, "Sir, I give you Terry Wilkinson, with a continuous record in drugs, both using and supplying, in all categories, Class A and B. He is a prolific dealer. As usual, he specialises in running a youth team that sells to children at school gates. He has a web of pushers that deal with the nightclubs. In fact, he is also involved in drug trafficking, *'County lines.'* He has it all sewn up."

"Lloydie, were, was, this gentleman and I use the word reservedly when Michael Hughes was in business?" Lloydie replied, "Sir, he may have been on the periphery, waiting to see how the field played out when Hughes got sentenced to prison. Leaving the field open for Wilkinson and perhaps others?"

Carter said, "Lloydie, do we have a recent address for Wilkinson?" He replied, "Sir, he owns a property off Rice Lane, On Evered Avenue. Like Hughes, it is a possible drug factory where team members prepare the product for sale.

Carter looked at Lloydie, "Look, Jim, let's prepare a warrant for Wilkinson's address. His team may not know he's dead. Which may well give us the advantage."

Carter asked Sue, "Can we organise a scrum down for 5 pm?" she smiled, "Sir."

After they had left Carter remained sitting behind his desk, he entered his jacket pocket and took out his mobile phone to contact Abby.

He thought, *'Now calm down, Carter, and get a grip, for God's sake. Don't sound too eager.'* He pressed her mobile number. She answered politely, *Abby Remington, speaking."* Carter thought well, her voice was business-like and calm, "Abby, it's Carter." She laughed, *"Have you missed me already, Carter?"*

He immediately thought of Helen, for they were the exact words spoken by her at the commencement of their first phone call.

Carter quickly stated, "Abby, I'll have to be quick as my office tends to be like bloody, Piccadilly Circus. I was wondering could we make it tea, perhaps say a takeaway. What's your poison, Chinese or Indian, she giggled, *"I'm not fussy; I like either. I'll leave it up to you?"*

Carter was about to close the call when she screamed, *"Carter, where do you live?"* He laughed, "It's a good job; one of us is concentrating?" I live at flat 2, Keswick Mansions, Sefton Park. He heard a sound, *"Wow."* He replied, 7.30 pm for 8, how is that?" The phone went dead.

There was a sudden knock on his office door; he shouted, "Come in." The door opened, and he saw Sue standing on the threshold, "Carter, we're all ready?" He smiled at her, "Well, that's also taken ages; at last, you've called me Carter?"

They both walked down to the conference room together. On arrival, they entered, and the whole team came to attention. Carter just laughed, wondering how the hell I could get them to comply.

He went and stood in front of the team. Sue stood next to him. He looked at Lloydie. "DI Lloyd, you have the floor." They both sat down. Lloydie recited verbatim the meeting that he'd recently had in Carter's office.

He continued, "I have sworn a warrant for Wilkinson's address; the gov thought that perhaps his Loyal henchmen may not know of his death and could be working away in the preparation of goods."

Lloydie asked Carter, "Guv, do you wish for part of the team to take part in the raid, with others to attend at Walton Park tomorrow?" Carter stood up, "Yes, Lloydie, can we organise for an undercover crew set up in the road, keeping obsies on the operation address? With Wilkinson dead, we'll hoover up the gang. I will call TF and ask for all officers to be armed. Now all bugger off home?"

There was the traditional raw of laughter.

Sue and Carter both signed off duty and left for home.

6

On his way home, Carter called in at his favourite curry house and takeaway. The owner and staff were all dressed in Indian regalia and were always pleased to see him; Carter was a regular customer and was easily pleased.

He loved the ethnic music and the Indian cuisine; his nose was always filled with the smells of all the local spices. The cultural music was always bellowing out from the kitchen area.

The owner's two daughters anticipated his order shouting. "Beef madras, pilaf rice, four chapati's, six meat samosas, and six poppadom's. The two teenage daughters had a sizable crush on Carter.

When ready, they brought him his order. Carter said to the owner, "What do I owe you?" The owner always teased Carter, "That's alright, Mr Carter Sahib." Carter replied, "Do we have to go through all this bloody nonsense again?"

"If you don't take my money, I'll go elsewhere." The owner burst out laughing, saying, "Alright, Mr Carter, sir, please don't get upset." He picked up his change and left.

On entering his flat, he quickly placed the meal in the oven, while in the kitchen, he helped himself to two cans of lager from out of the fridge. He emptied one in a matter of seconds, placed the second on the kitchen table and left for his shower.

He placed some casual clothes onto his bed. He undressed and ran into the bathroom, where he shaved. On completion, he walked into the shower in the wet room.

Carter eventually completed his shower, dried off, dressed, and was ready for Abby's arrival. He dressed in a blue cotton T-shirt with three buttons down the front, washed-out jeans, and bare feet.

He walked into the dining room and laid the table. Placed two table mats opposite each other, a bowl of mango chutney on one and a plate of poppadom's on the other. He looked in on the meal, ensuring he was not overdoing it. He then heard the intercom.

Carter walked towards the handset with a spring in his step. He picked it up and whispered, "Abby, just pull the door?" She replied, *"Thank you, Carter."* He opened the front door of his flat, and looking down to the reception area, he noticed Abby.

He saw Abby as she entered the building; she smiled at the concierge, "I'm here to see Mr Carter." Andy, the duty concierge, replied, "Welcome, madam, pointing, said, "Mr Carter's flat is just up there on the left."

She stood there on the threshold, and Carter, moving ahead, leaned forward and tenderly kissed her on each cheek. He ushered her into his flat. Approaching her from the rear, he slipped off her coat and hung it up on the hall coat stand.

She stood opposite him wearing a beautiful red dress which finished two inches above her knee. The dress had a small yellow pattern of a fleur de lee all over her dress. Wearing black hose and black stilettos.

Carter said, "Wow! Abby, but you look exquisite; as they walked along the hall, he apologised for his casual attire. As they walked into the lounge, he said, "You see, Abby, I love to take off my suit whenever possible, as I see it as a form of overalls."

Abby smiled, "Carter, please, you need not apologise. For Carter, I can't get over your flat from the location and the highly manicured gardens. But it's your flat, and its décor is fabulous.

Carter said, "Abby, would you like a glass of wine?" She smiled, "Yes, please." They both sat and enjoyed their drinks.

Abby sat next to him on the settee, with her two legs slanted to her left at her knees tucked up on the settee.

While both were engrossed in conversation, Carter noticed their glasses were empty; looking at Abby, he said, "Hungry?" she replied, "Starving."

He stood up and gently took her hand, assisting her off the settee. She stood for one minute, please wait but a second to allow the blood to circulate?"

When suitably ready they walked out to the dining room. On arrival, he pulled back a chair on which she sat. He went into the kitchen, returning with their meals. He placed a plate of curry and rice in front of Abby and his plate opposite. He placed three other plates on the table: samosas, chapattis, and poppadom's.

Over the meal, he served white wine from the two bottles on the table.

Carter apologised for not going out for a more sophisticated meal. Abby turned, "Oh! Carter, it's wonderful; when you mentioned a takeaway, I thought it would mean eating with our meal on our knees?" After the meal, they both cleared the table.

He looked at Abby, "I should have told the truth; another reason for our ad-hoc meal stems from the fact that tomorrow, I have an operation with members of my team. It's not so early; nevertheless, it's a fact."

Abby suddenly turned, "Carter! Why didn't you say when you rang me this afternoon?" He frowned, "But I wanted to see you again; my job and rank allow me some slack, as in this matter, it's not a dawn raid."

As they walked through to the lounge, Abby suddenly stopped. She turned and took hold of Carter and kissed him gently on the lips, whispering, "As did I."

She looked up, "Carter, look, why don't I take a taxi home, allowing you to prepare for tomorrow? We can catch up on this on another evening, nothing's been wasted. I truly feel that at least we have the chemistry, and it would be so unfair, as I'll count this as our first date. She smiled if you know what I mean?"

After Carter had seen Abby off in a taxi, he returned to his flat and, after loading the dishwasher and tidying up, sat enjoying a larger when his mobile phone activated. He thought, 'shit, it must be work?'

He pressed the little green phone motive without thinking, for he realised it must be work. "Carter" *"Carter, it's Abby; I'm here lying in my lovely warm bed, thinking, why on earth should I have been so bloody quick and pious, should I have grasped the nettle, but alas, I want us to take matters at a speed best suited to both?"*

Carter sighed, "I'd willingly prepare my work clothes and come over…Abby interrupted, *"And Carter, I'd love nothing more than for you to do just that very thing."* She laughed. *"But unfortunately, you have a heavy day tomorrow, and perhaps we can resume matters?"* Carter whispered, "Good night, Abby, call you tomorrow."

7

The following morning, Carter entered the general office at 8.45am, signed on duty and accepted a coffee from Eric. He turned and walked over, and sat next to him, and chatted with him while members of the team greeted him prior to signing on duty.

Carter picked up his second mug of coffee, informing Eric he was going through to his office. He entered and placed his coffee on a coaster on his desk. He sat down, took out his mobile phone, and called Abby.

"Carter, what a lovely surprise; I thought being busy, I'd have been last on your call list?" Carter replied, "It may be a very quick call, as I'm expecting my deputy to call any minute, but I'll call you later and organise matters." He closed the call.

He had no sooner closed the call when his mobile activated, *"Carter, please take care."* The call ended.

Carter heard a knock on his door. It was Sue informing him that they were already for the pre-raid briefing.

They entered the conference room and were immediately confronted by the usual way. Carter took no notice and continued to the front of the room. He turned laughing, for there in front of him were the team, all displaying such long faces. He looked somewhat worried until they all burst out laughing. Carter was nearly crying with laughter.

He shouted, "Right, let's get down to business. What do we have? Jim Lloyd stood up. "Guv, you can see on the whiteboard several SOCO pictures of Evered Avenue, off

Rice Lane. I was with them and pointed out the house in question, number 38, just after the park."

"Guv, I got a layout of the property. The plan is on the board, although I have no details of any alterations, as like the Hughes property?"

Carter looked at Ian Baxter, "Ian, can I ask you to contact the duty Inspector of the control room and ask if we can have a 'Matrix team.' Do try to get the same team, with our favourite officer in charge of the enforcer?" (Battering ram)

Sue looked up at Carter and whispered, "You're so superstitious?"

Ian, who had left the room, shortly returned. He looked at Carter, "Guv, all is sorted. All they need is the time of the raid?"

Carter sat down, "Lloydie, do we have the warrant?" Lloydie replied, "Yes, guv, we're good to go." Carter looked at Peter, "Can you arrange to have three vans in the yard in half an hour?" He replied, "Yes, guv." He then looked at Phil. "Phil, please check all firearms and that all officers are wearing Kevlar body armour. "Sir."

Carter walked over to the whiteboard. "Right, you will all notice that the property consists of a large three-story terraced building. Now, we all know that drug dealers spend a great deal of money securing their properties. So, things are not always as they seem. The first appearance deceives many?"

He pointed to the plan, "We have a front and backdoor. There is a yard that opens into a traditional entry, that runs parallel to the rear of the properties. So, there are only the two points of entry, and exit to the offending property?"

He looked at the team, "It's a go, so let's hit the property at 11.30 am. So, get everything sorted and leave the yard at 11 am. I want it a blue light job as far as Walton hospital, then plain sailing from there?"

As Carter stood to leave, the team came to attention. He just smiled as he left for his office.

When in his office, there was a knock on his door, he called, "Come in." Eric entered carrying a mug of coffee. As he entered, he saw Carter putting on his holster and firearm. His Kevlar protector was lying on his desk.

Eric looked at him with a serious face, "Sir, at which level of rank do you need to attain, in which you do not need to go on operations?" Carter smiled, "Just leave the bloody coffee and stop playing, mother hen?" He left the coffee; Eric then turned and left for the general office. Carter thought, *'Shit, he didn't deserve that?'*

Carter rang his boss, Tony Frost. *"Frost."* "Sir, it's Carter." *"Well, what can I do for you?"* "Sir, we have identified the victim found in Walton Park. He is no other than Terry Wilkinson, one down from Michael Hughes, perhaps one of his competitors while in prison, which Hughes worried about?"

"In that respect, I'm about together with the team to execute a warrant on his house and see what we may find, for the death has not been in the press, and I feel that his team may be languishing in the property, and we may well be lucky to recover a serious amount of drugs and cash?"

TF replied, *"I want your team to be armed. The raid could be as bad as the Hughes operation. I'll clear it with the Chief. Now bugger off, and you and your team take care."*

Carter entered the conference room. The team all turned and noticed their guv was dressed and ready for action. Sue looked at Carter, "Guv, can we have a chat in my office?"

With a smile on his face, he followed Sue to her office. As they entered, Sue closed the door. Sue turned, "Carter, what the fuck are you doing? How many times do you have to prove yourself? You're the guv, for Christ's sake, and as such, why the fuck can't you let me, as your deputy take the lead?"

Carter slumped in a chair he looked up at her, "It's not me having to prove myself. It's the thrill of the raid, a thing I can't get out of my system. Please remember my replacement in the event…?

Sue sat in her seat, "Carter, Oh! Shit, forget it. Let us get going."

In the police yard, they all entered the three vans. Sue and Carter were both in the lead van. Carter. Prior to leaving, I got on the radio, "All team drivers, please select channel zero; we know it's a closed channel. He heard a simultaneous reply, "Roger." He then informed the control room that they were on their way and to ask for the force helicopter to be scrambled. Plus, if the matrix team were in place?" He got the same reply, "Roger."

They turned left out of Derby Lane towards Queens Drive, and Rice Lane. At Rice Lane, they left the Passover on the drive and turned at the roundabout below to proceed down the A59 towards Walton Hospital. As they swooped past, all blue lights were immediately cancelled.

On arrival at Evered Avenue, they saw the Matrix crew in their van tucked up in a side street off Rice Lane. Sue got on the radio to members of a covert team that Carter had despatched earlier to keep observations on number 38, hoping that all was quiet and none of the rats had jumped ship.

The reply was positive, "All quiet, boss," Came the reply.

One of the blue vans, under instructions, drove to cover the back of the property. While it seemed quiet to all intents and purposes, the remaining two blue vans split up. One parked quietly outside of number 34, and the remainder assumed a position outside number 42, parking two doors on either side of the target address.

Sue then called the Matrix crew to assume a position behind the van at number 34, asking for the officer with the enforcer to stand by.

The Matrix officers dressed in their usual black overalls, with trousers tucked into their black boots and black protective headgear, with Kevlar vests. Were in place, Carter noticed the drug dog van in position, further down the avenue. He gave the order to proceed. The officer holding the enforcer stood outside of the target address, with members of the Matrix crew behind him.

They all heard the words, "Go, go, go; the officer, with the enforcer, swung it at the front door directly on the Yale door lock; it was only after the third swing that the door began to waver. On the fourth swing, it gave way. The officer stood to one side as his colleagues repeatedly shouted, "Armed police, stay where you are?"

As they filed in, sudden chaos broke out as some officers filed in and out of the downstairs rooms and were met with screams from girls in various stages of undress, with claims of alleged heavy handling. Carter, Sue, and members of the MCU remained in the hall, leaving Sue to assist in organising the females, assisted by female team members.

All the present female victims were placed in the two downstairs living rooms, with a female officer standing guard. At the same time, the search proceeded in the downstairs rooms. Carter looked at some of the team, "Let's take upstairs, he began to lead the way while Sue objected. He smiled and led the way.

He was halfway up when a thick, well-built male, dressed in only a vest and trousers, suddenly appeared at the top of the stairs. He levelled a handgun and fired three times at Carter, hitting him in the chest. As he fell back, Phil, who was behind Carter, shouted, "Armed police officer, drop your firearm, or I will fire."

The man raised his firearm again when the sound, bang, bang, was heard. The man fell to his right in a heap onto the upstairs landing. Phil shouted for assistance, and while members of the team busily tried to manoeuvre Carter down the stairs, Phil, with other officers with drawn handguns, continued upstairs.

As Carter was removed in an unconscious state, they all heard Sue, who rushed from a downstairs room, scream. "Carter?" She then assessed the situation: "Get an ambulance, in fact, get three, for other possible victims?" Carter was laid out in the hall.

The drug dog handler was standing in the road outside the house. Sue called, "It's not safe for you and Sally as yet, but it won't be long?"

The first of the ambulances arrived with blue lights and claxon activated. The two paramedics ran towards the house, one bent down at the side of Carter. "What do we have?"

Sue replied, "The victim was shot three times in the chest. He is wearing a Kevlar vest, which took the effect of the three bullets which knocked him out. As he fell backwards, he was wrestled down by members of his team into the hall. We laid him down, as you can see."

There was a sudden raw as Carter sat up, calling, "Holy shit, that hurt." Sue leaned over and whispered, "Perhaps Carter, you'll leave it for others to lead?" The second paramedic stood waiting with a stretcher, folded at hand.

Carter looked at them, "Look, I'm not going to bloody hospital, so get that thought out of your heads?" Sue interrupted and, in a sarcastic voice, said, "Do your worst. The paramedics know best, gentlemen; what do you think?"

The first one at his side said, "I do feel that we should pop you down to the Royal for a check-up, for you may have a broken rib, or ribs at the very least causing severe bruising to the chest, the worst a possible Haemothorax?" Sue said, "Oh! Sir, I do think you should go?" Carter looked at her, "If you wish to remain my Detective Superintendent, do you mind?" There was, a sudden smirk from out of nearby team members.

The paramedic said, "Sir, will you please get on the stretcher?" Sue suddenly called out, "Get on the bloody stretcher, Sir." And he was whisked off to the Royal. After he'd gone, Sue looked at Lloydie and Ian. "Right, what have we got?"

Lloydie said, "We have the body of the victim on the landing. Perhaps when safe, another team of paramedics can review him and confirm his death, to be established at A&E on his arrival. I'll follow up at the mortuary later."

Lloydie continued he smiled, "Boss we've hit pay dirt. As they both exchanged chit-chat, the Matrix Inspector and officers assembled and left the property. Outside, Sue walked up to their Inspector. "Andy, thanks for your support and the use of our lucky traditional *'Enforcer.'*

The Inspector and members of his team burst out laughing. He commented, "Lucky" "The officer only uses the enforcer, a glorified battering ram?" Sue burst out laughing, "Aw yes, but none of your operational officers are as superstitious as our guv, Det Ch Supt Carter?"

It all stems from our first job together. Do you remember the one in Bootle? Well, the officer was our very first enforcer, and look how that turned out?" Sue suddenly stuttered, on behalf of our GUV, many thanks." As Sue walked back into the house, she bumped into the drug dog handler, leaving with her charge, Sally, with a tennis ball in her mouth.

She looked at Sue, "Well, boss, yet another major haul, it's now SOCOS turn to assist you?"

Sue looked at Lloydie, "Okay, what do we have?" He took her into the front room and presented the female prisoners, watched over by Amy from the team. They then walked through to the rear living room, where she saw four men handcuffed and sat on chairs.

DI Baxter, who had joined them, stated. "These four should be five, but one, as you know, tried to kill the guv, and was eliminated. "One of the four shouted, "Murdered, you mean?"

Sue took no notice, and she looked at her junior officers, "Lead on." They left the room, leaving Alex and Geoff of the team in control. Lloydie said, "Boss, will you join us upstairs?"

The three left and, taking the stairs, climbed to the first-floor landing, where they were met by several SOCO officers busily darting from one room to the other.

The SOCO team consisted of photographers, fingerprint experts, and lab officers. Undoubtedly an immense amount of work to complete. A considerable amount of white coloured class 'A' type powder in massive plastic industrial-size bags, eight in all, yet they noticed other items in the front bedroom, thought to be marijuana.

Ian pointed to a door, "Boss when opened, the stairs lead up into the attic. On investigation, we found it to be none other than sleeping areas, like in the Hughes set-up, allowing mixed sexual sleeping arrangements?"

Sue looked at both Lloydie and Ian right, "I'm off to the hospital and speak with TF. Lloydie, will you follow up on the body at the mortuary, and Ian can I leave you to deal with the site, pull in any amount of the team to assist?" There was a collective, "Yes, boss."

8

Sat in her car prior to leaving for the hospital. Sue took out her phone and called Commander Tony Frost. *"Frost."* "Sir, it's Det. Supt. Sue Ford, I'm calling to inform you that the raid was a total success, but on the downside, I have to report that Det. Ch. Supt. Carter was shot three times in the chest?"

Sue waited for ten seconds, and then it came, *"What the fuck? Why am I only hearing about it now?"* "Sir, he wore his Kevlar vest, so I think it's just an investigation into possible rib fracture and severe chest bruising?" I'm on my way to the hospital after finishing this call."

TF replied, *"Ford, keep me in the loop, and next time, please choose your words more carefully."* 'Click.'

Sue smiled, 'Well, he's your boy, you tell him?' She suddenly thought. *'You stupid bitch, you had the perfect opportunity to perform CPR.'* Smiling she pushed the button for the blues and twos, heralding her way to the Royal. On arrival, she packed up and entered A&E. She presented her ID. On admission, she wandered through all the dross until she found Chris Atkinson, the senior duty sister.

Chris looked at Sue, "Have you come down to collect, *'him'* As she spoke, Chris pointed in the direction of a curtained area, where Carter was putting on his jacket as he was about to leave.

She continued, "Just look, he's finding it difficult. The man has badly bruised ribs and should be admitted for a couple of days to check on the severity of the bruising, for fear of other injuries?"

Sue, smiling, looked at Chris, "Has he signed himself out, and is it against medical advice?" Chris looked at Sue, "No, no, but when you take into account his medical record, he should take more care." Sue smiled, "You more than most know how he is; you might as well talk to the bloody wall."

Carter walked up to the two women, "What bloody wall?" Both women burst out laughing. Chris said, "Carter, be off with you, but don't come crying to me if the pain gets worse?" He leaned down and gave her a peck on her cheek.

Chris laughed, "Carter, that may work on some women. Now go and be off with you."

Getting into Sue's car, Carter suddenly winced as he tried to put on his seat belt. He looked at Sue, saying, "Okay, it still bloody hurts." She replied, "It will be for a couple of weeks, so!" Carter looked at her, "Will you please take me home and, on the way, fill me in on the result of the raid?"

As Sue drove, she filled him in with the extent of the operation. "Carter, Phil shot and killed the man who shot at you, for he - levelled his gun again. The offender could have killed you with his new line of fire. After the second official warning, he failed to heed the order, and Phil made the decision and fired twice and eliminate the victim. Lloydie is following up at the mortuary.

Carter looked at Sue, "How is Phil coping?" "He's been suspended, awaiting an investigation with IA (Internal Affairs). I hope you don't mind, but I released Jules to be with him?" Carter smiled, "The very least we can do, for I owe him?"

On arrival home, Carter looked at Sue, "Could you cover for me for about two days?" Sue said, "Carter, only if you make it three days, for I'm sure you'd not spend time off for the proper period, but I'll take three days, okay?"

As he got out of the car, he said, "Nag, nag, nag, you have the helm. I leave it in good hands."

Sue smiled as she drove away.

9

On entering his flat, he looked at his watch; it was 3.30 pm. He thought I must ring Abby. *"Hello Carter,"* An excited voice came down the phone, *"I was wondering where you'd got to? Are we still on for tonight? If so, do you mind if we eat in, as I enjoyed last night immensely?"*

Carter burst out laughing, "Well, when do I get a word in?" Abby, half laughing and half apologising, *"Why, of course?"* He replied, "Yes, and yes, to your questions, if you get here at 7pm, I'll arrange the meal?" Abby interrupted... *"No, Carter, I'll supply the meal."* She took a quick breath, *"Do you like Chinese?"* "Love it," He replied.

"Good, see you then, bye," Abby replied, and she closed the call.

He went through to the bathroom; he felt uplifted by the prospect of seeing Abby yet again. He shaved and took part in an invigorating shower. On completion, he tenderly dried off; he then secured the towel about his waist and strolled through to the bedroom to select some clothes.

Prior to his selection, he decided to lay on the bed to cool down; he gingerly touched his chest and winced with the pain, and then he fell fast asleep.

He awoke at 6.30 pm; he thought shit! Carter, you've nearly overslept. He jumped up and quickly dressed in the casual clothes he'd already laid out. With a blue T-shirt, washed-out jeans, and his leather sheepskin lined (hospital use only) slippers, he so much wanted to be in bare feet, but he thought first impressions. He tidied the bed and placed the towel in the laundry basket.

Sat in the lounge enjoying a glass of lager while he awaited her arrival. He was suddenly interrupted by the intercom. He slowly got up, not wishing to be too eager. He carefully walked over and picked up the handset, "Pull the door?" Abby giggled as she entered.

She acknowledged the duty concierge and continued with her two brown paper bags. Carter stood at the front door and welcomed her into the flat. She walked straight through to the kitchen and placed their meal on the worktop.

Abby quickly turned, letting her coat fall to the floor. He noticed she was wearing a white singlet tank top and white cotton drawstring trousers. She kicked off a pair of loose-fitting trainers. Moving forward in bare feet, she took Carter in her arms; as she was about to kiss him, he let out a sudden gasp.

Abby stepped back, "Carter, what on earth's the matter?" He said, "Abbs, go through to the lounge, and I'll bring in some wine for us." She stood there in front of him, "No, Carter, what's the matter?"

He lifted his T-shirt, and she suddenly looked upon three bruised rings on his chest. The bruising was red because the fresh, oxygen-rich blood had pooled under his skin. He knew it would be worse after a couple of days.

She lifted both her hands to her mouth she shrieked, "Carter, what on earth happened?" He said, "Let's have a drink?" She announced, "Will you at least go and sit? I'll get the wine; now go."

Carter sat on the settee. Abby floated in with two glasses and a bottle of red wine. She placed them on the table. He opened the bottle and poured their drinks. When comfortable with their drinks in hand, Abby looked at him, "Carter what on earth happened?"

Carter told her everything. She placed an arm gently around his neck and kissed him on his lips. She then lifted his T-shirt with both hands and kissed each of his bruised wounds.

When she looked up at him, she had tears in her eyes. He said, "Abby, I was wearing what they call a Kevlar vest, which protects officers who take part in such raids. I hadn't wanted to tell you as I thought that I'd be fine and come through unscathed."

They both sipped their wine. Abby placed her glass on the nearby coffee table. She looked at Carter, "If our relationship is to continue, I wish to ask you to be honest with me, whilst I know you can't tell me operational matters. All I ask is that you inform me of your potential exploits, and I'll join the dots myself?"

She suddenly stood up, "Now let's eat. You remain here while I prepare the meal and call you when ready. Ten minutes later, she called, "Carter, do you wish to attend at the table or eat off a tray?" "The table." He replied and set off for the dining room, minus his slippers.

On arrival, he immediately noticed three tall cardboard Chinese takeaway boxes, with two oval plastic containers with oval tops, all in Chinese designs of red dragons and lotus blossoms, with the name of the restaurant, in Chinese writing, *'The Red Dragon.'*

Abby looked at Carter, "The two smaller containers contain, 'hot and sour soup.' The two of the larger containers hold chicken chow-main, the second, 'sweet chicken and pineapple,' the third box contains fried rice."

He noticed two bowls for the soup and two larger bowls for the other two items.

After their meal, Carter suggested, "Coffees and perhaps liqueurs?" Abby whispered, "Carter, you look so tired. Go and sit down, and I'll bring in the drinks."

They both sat talking and enjoyed their after-meal delights. Abby stood up, "Carter, will you please order me a taxi…?" Carter interrupted, "Abby, there is no need for you to leave. May I suggest that by your attire, other matters were on your mind?"

"Yes, Carter, it was on my mind until you told me of your injuries. Now I realise you have good observation skills that's why you're the detective. But, with a big 'B' under the circumstances, whatever our needs, they must be put on hold?"

Carter took her loosely in his arms; he looked down at her, "I'd love you to stay; I don't want to be on my own. Should you agree to stay the night, we'll just lay like spoons in a drawer?"

Abby, in a serious tone, "That's all well and good until someone messes with the cutlery." They both burst out laughing. After a couple of glasses of wine, Carter stood up and took her by the hand.

He escorted her towards the bedroom, and she looked at him as she pulled back slightly, "Well, Mr. One presumes so much, and I'm hoping that you don't feign injury?"

In the bedroom, Abby suddenly turned and lifted his T-shirt and slowly began to kiss him all over his chest. He pulled away, and when both were naked, he escorted her into the wet room. Carter turned on the shower, and after a brief period the temp level rose to the prescribed temp. He invited her into the warmth of the water.

While in the shower, Carter looked down on Abby. "True life police officer's lives are not like those who play the part on TV. The crimes or cases are not solved in 45 minutes or the odd hour. Real police officers are human and have needs?"

Giggling, she turned to Carter, thinking, Wow! She thought it was such a pity the bruises tainted the picture. While Abby was deep in thought, Carter, holding a soapy glove, discreetly began to soap her body on her front.

He soaped her chest, and lowering the glove to her nipples, she let out a sensual scream.

She placed her arms around his neck and gently pulled herself against him. He bent his head, enabling him to kiss her nipples.

She shrieked Carter, "That's absolutely disgusting, don't stop until I tell you to?" She was nearly hysterical; as he let his tongue play on her nipples, she called, "Carter, stop, stop, please remember the cutlery?"

He stopped the water. Carter took an enormous bath sheet and smothered her in it. On leaving the bathroom, he picked up a hand towel for her hair. He carried Abby, twisting and squirming; she shouted, "Carter, put me down; you're not fit enough?"

He reached the bed and gently lay her down on top of it. As he did, he opened the towel. He looked down on her beautiful body and gasped. He tentatively placed his hand on her chest, "This features the best example of love." He then placed it on his bruised chest. "This, I'm afraid, the worst, yet they co-assist within our midst?"

He kissed her, and she responded in equal interest, with her tongue seeking to penetrate his mouth, attempting to gain access to be allowed to investigate. He eventually did, and it feverishly flitted in and out.

Carter lowered his head onto her breasts and nipples, and she screamed with joy. Abby suddenly said, "Stop, Carter, we're beginning to rattle the cutlery. So please, let's lay as you wish; there is always tomorrow, but no buster, I'm talking figuratively?"

They both ceased and collectively lay next to each other. Carter reached down and pulled up the duvet. She placed her head on his shoulder and whispered, "Good night, lovely." They got comfortable for sleep. A dark cloak fully enveloped them, and they fell fast asleep.

10

The following morning, Carter awoke. He gently pushed his hand over to Abby's side of the bed, finding it cold. He looked over and immediately saw a note on Abby's pillow.

He sat up and leaned on the headboard to read it...

Morning Carter,
You looked so comfortable, and I thought it would be such a pity to wake you.
It's Friday, and I have a meeting first thing. So, I felt so at ease in
Your company, could I come round tonight and cook tea?
We could spend the weekend together. I'd take so much,
Pleasure in looking after you in your present condition.
I'll call you at lunchtime to see how you're coping.
Abby x

He read it and smiled, and he thought at least someone's concerned, other than the team.

Carter got up and walked through to the bathroom. He shaved and showered, and when ready, he dressed in casuals and bare feet. He was, in time, to greet Kate Murphy.

Morning Carter, "Why on earth are you at home, shouldn't you be at work?" He looked at her, "I'm off today after a slight injury at work, and I'll have the weekend off to prepare for work on Monday.

Kate turned, "Coffee?" "Yes, please, Kate, that would be lovely." After he completed his coffee, he looked at Kate. "I'll be out for lunch, so if you don't mind, can I ask you to re-stock the fridge and freezer? I'm expecting company?"

As Kate left for the kitchen, she smiled, looking at Carter, commenting, "Carter, how long have I worked for you? Surely you don't have to ask such a silly question?"

At lunchtime, Carter, dressed in serious casuals, blew a kiss to Kate, and left for 'Toms.' When in his car, he phoned Abby, "Carter, *how wonderful; I thought your call may have been later, allowing you to get some rest?"*

He spluttered, "Rest, pest; I'm okay. In fact, I was wondering what you'd be doing for lunch?" She coughed, *"Why, what are you suggesting?"* "Well, I'm over in *'Toms.'* What's your fancy?" She squealed, *"I'll be with you in ten."*

True to her word, Carter heard the tingle of the ornate doorbell. He looked up and smiled as he saw the vision that is Abby, smiling as she walked over to his table. He stood up and kissed her on her cheek.

Abby was, like an excited schoolgirl, "Carter, how wonderful, what a lovely surprise." As Tom came over, he greeted them both. "Have you decided yet?" Abby said, "Could I have one of your cold beef sandwiches on brown crusty bread?" Carter suggested, "Tom, will you make mine, ham on brown crusty bread, a bowl of chips each, and two bottles of chilled sparkling water?" Tom smiled and walked away.

Over their meal, he looked at Abby, suggesting that she should try one of his ham sandwiches, for there as lovely. She offered one of her beef sandwiches in fair exchange. Altogether delicious.

On completion, Carter looked at Abby, "Have you packed a bag for the weekend, so all you need to do after work is to drive straight round to mine?" She looked at him rather sheepishly, "Yes, Carter, I do hope you don't think it rather presumptuous of me?" He replied, "No, good, it saves time."

Outside of Tom's, he kissed Abby goodbye and whispered, "See you later, and she left.

On his way home, he called Eric at the office, "Look, Eric, please don't make a fuss, but I'm just calling to find out how things are?" He replied, "At present, the raid turned up trumps on a great scale, a massive amount of both drugs and cash recovered. Lloydie is dealing with the fatality, trying to ID the victim?"

I'll think you'll find that all matters will be ready to commence interviews on Monday, see you then, now bugger off." And he closed the call.

Abby arrived at the flat at about 5.00pm; she embraced Carter gently, kissing him passionately on his lips. She stepped back, "Mr, I needed that; in fact, I've been looking forward to it since you left me outside of Tom's?"

He looked at her. Would you like a shower before tea?" She replied, "With you I'd loved one any time." He left her to walk through to the bedroom. Turning, he walked through to the kitchen. He took out two steaks from the top fridge that he'd left to thaw, and he took out a large bowl of pre-prepared salad from the same part of the fridge.

Carter turned and left for the bedroom. He quickly undressed and walked into the wet room; Abby was washing her short blonde hair with her back to him. Carter watched as she had her hands on the top of her head, shampooing her hair. It allowed him to catch the shape of her left breast. He slipped in and took hold of one of the shower gloves.

Without any warning, he began to wash her back, and she screamed, "I hope that's you, Carter, for if not, I have to warn you my boyfriend is a senior police officer and carries a firearm." He just silently placed his arms around her waist and hugged her.

She whispered, "Do you mind if I turn to face you, for your actions last night nearly blew me away." He turned her around and began to soap her chest and breasts, and he began to concentrate on her nipples. She fell back on the wall of the shower, panting as her breathing became laboured.

He switched off the shower and wrapped her in an enormous towel, and he carried her through to the bed. He laid her down, opened the towel, and revealed a perfect specimen of a woman's body. He leaned over her and placed a hand on either side of her, supporting his body weight. Without another word, he softly parted her legs and entered her.

She took a sudden intake of breath, "Christ Carter, what a wonderful surprise, I never thought...?" Carter smiled down at her, "Stop moving." She looked up at him. "But I want to move." He whispered, "Stay still." She screamed, "But Carter, I want to feel you deep in me."

Abbs, looking up into his eyes, whispered. "To tell you the truth, seeing you at the party. I thought, what on earth would it be like...?" Carter, my central feelings began to run amok on seeing such a handsome man, and now I really get to experience and look upon the subsequent sensation. WOW!"

In conclusion, Carter flopped over on his back, exhausted. Abby was the first to speak, "Really, Carter, you have nothing to prove?" But with a serene look on her face said, "Although totally unexpected?" She folded her arms and leaned on his chest. She whispered, "Carter, I experienced my first orgasm, the mechanics of which I've never felt before." She hugged him.

11

On taking part in just a quite hygienic shower, they both dressed, Carter in sweats and Abbs in a white tank top and white cotton drawstring trousers, both in bare feet.

They both walked through to the lounge. Abby sat on the nearby settee. Carter poured her a glass of wine. She looked at him, "Where's yours?" He replied I'm going into the kitchen to prepare tea."

Abby picked up the bottle of wine and the spare glass, "Do you mind if I follow you?" He smiled, "Why, of course."

Carter took the plate with the two steaks to the hob. He salted and peppered each side and placed them both into the prepared frying pan for 4 minutes on each side. He organised a portion of already prepared chips and two portions of the prepared salad.

Abby was sat on a tall stool, with her knees pulled up below her chin, busy watching Carter at work whilst popping backwards and forwards, placing their plates and condiments on the dining table.

Eventually, they both sat down and enjoyed their meal. Abby commented on how the steak melted in her mouth. Accompanied by a bottle of Cabernet Sauvignon, Abby said, "Carter, the wine is gorgeous, he smiled as he replenished her glass.

On completion of their meal, Carter ushered Abby into the lounge, where he served Tia Maria and Cherry Brandy liqueurs, accompanied by cups of coffee. Carter took a sip of Tia Maria from her glass. He kissed Abby, and as they kissed, Carter delicately released a trickle of the coffee liqueur into her mouth.

She suddenly reacted with total surprise to his actions but didn't break the seal between their lips. With her eyes wide open, she took him in her arms, stating, "Carter, how erotically romantic."

Carter took her hand, picked up the bottle and glasses and guided her to the bedroom. He placed the bottles and the two glasses onto his nightstand. He turned and kissed her as they both undressed. He looked at Abby, "Sorry the help hasn't made the bed, do you mind?" "No, Carter, I bet the bed is still warm after the previous occupants?"

In bed, they both kissed and caressed each other, both taking place in the form of self-exploration. As matters intensified, Carter leaned over and took a mouthful of liqueur, and he turned towards Abby.

He kissed her and moved down to her chest, where he released the liquid over her breasts and nipples, allowing the remainder to meander in rivulets down her flat tummy, down to her crotch.

Before she had time to comment, Carter followed up by kissing her breasts and nipples, and he relished the taste of the brandy and the act of sucking her nipples.

After several minutes, he began to kiss her tummy. The net result was total bliss for both parties.

As Abby began to move with desire, he realised that she was beginning to increase in excitement, resulting in her placing her hands on the top of his head, pressing gently to increase desire. She began to shudder and shake; she screamed, "Carter, Carter, don't you dare stop?" She eventually exhaled and lay quite still on the bed.

Carter began to move up the bed, and when level, he lay on top and entered her. He entered ever so slowly, but he felt her respond by lifting her pelvis. She screamed as she threw her arms around his neck, and she kissed him enthusiastically on his lips. Abby placed her head next to his and whispered, "What on earth has just taken place? I've never experienced the like…"

They both lay back on the bed, then Abby turned onto her side facing him, raised her right leg, placed it on his thigh and began to draw around the three bruises on his chest. "Lovely, if that's what it's like taking things easy, God help me when you're better." She burst out laughing.

After they lay relaxing eventually, they both got up and walked into the shower, for due to the liqueur on their bodies, they'd become very sticky. Abby walked closer to Carter and started to wash him with one of the giant, soapy glove sponges all over his body. He responded in kind. She thought how sensually it had all become.

When finished and dried, they walked through to the bedroom. Looking at Carter, she whispered, "I'm so glad you managed to discover *'my start button'* Last night, and yet again this very evening?"

As they both lay in bed, he turned. "Abbs, I totally underestimated you in the way you seem so relaxed, as it's only fairly early into our relationship?" She smiled, "Why, Carter, it's all your fault. You see, I'm still on the periphery of tradition, having come out of the old ages when '*A girl must never sleep with a potential suitor on the first night?*' To the relaxed concept of to-days attitudes?"

"Carter, you have completely no idea, do you, for it was when I first saw you whilst talking with David and Beth. If you hadn't been called away from the party, and if matters developed. I would have made a beeline for you, oh! It would have been very subtle, but please be in no doubt, even at that stage, I longed for you. Please believe if you'd have made the right moves, tradition would have gone out the bloody window."

She laid back on the bed with her arms waving in the air, with her fingers wriggling as she shrieked, calling him,

"Come here, Carter, and do it all again, just in case I was mistaken?" He did, and she wasn't.

Carter leaned down to pull up the duvet. Abby lifted her hand and softly followed the design of his back, feeling his incredibly soft skin, letting it come to rest on his bottom. It then fell, coming to rest on the mattress. He looked over his shoulder and smiled. When he laid back whilst he covered them, she hugged him, placing her head on his chest.

She intended to hear the beat of his heart as it began to calm to its normal beat. Abbs looked up with a devilish look in her delicious blue eyes. "Oh! Carter, I feel such a fraud, knowing that I'm in the hands of an experienced lover. I truly feel the recipient of all your glorious actions. I have no such knowledge of the deeper aspects of lovemaking. On how to make a man happy?"

"Oh! Of course, I've overheard conversations between girls in the staff room, and yes, I laughed and nodded at the right times, implying a sensual knowledge. But as previously stated, an utter novice and fraud."

Carter took her in his arms, laying her head in the nape of his neck. It's not so. He whispered, "Abbs, Abbs, Abbs, we are none of us put on this earth truly proficient in any task; we gain our skills as we proceed through life. Skills are gained, and one does not always become proficient in all aspects and categories?"

"One of my old sergeants once told me that you can be placed on a section (Police jargon for a working group of officers) for, say, two years, after which you may have learned, *'Jack.'* Or you could be put with another sergeant for a week and learn an immense amount. It all depends on who is doing the teaching?"

Abby curled up to Carter, "Well, I think that I have gained an excellent teacher. Whilst I'm a happy recipient of such acts, I'll try to become proficient in all departments. Carter, what does *'Jack'* mean?"

They both burst out laughing, after which he leaned forward and pulled up the duvet. Abbs thought, what a lovely arse. They fell fast asleep in each other's arms.

12

Carter awoke first; he rested his head on the palm of his hand, supported by his elbow on his pillow. He looked down on Abby, who looked so peaceful and surreal while still asleep. He leaned down and brushed a piece of hair lightly from off her face.

Her breath was so light, he thought he'd need a mirror to check if it misted. Her eyes suddenly opened, and he immediately noticed the depths of her deep, startled blue eyes that stared up at him. He thought, God, they're totally unfathomable. Abbs whispered, "What?" He just shook his head from side to side, "Oh! Nothing, I was just looking down on a most beautiful woman."

She suddenly leapt up and grabbed Carter pushing him down on the bed. Abbs kissed him with all the strength she could muster. On completion, she pulled back, "Morning Carter, did you sleep well? Do you feel that you're getting stronger? For I feel that when up to speed, could matters get any better between us?"

Carter got up out of bed; he smiled as he walked towards the bathroom. Abby lay, feigning weakness, "Carter, can you help me, for I haven't the strength to walk to the bathroom, and I need a pee, pee?"

He leaned back as he was massaging shaving foam onto his face. "Sorry, love, but I'm about to shave. She cried, "But Carterrr!" He walked over with his soapy beard, picked her up and smothered her face with the shaving foam as he carried her to the loo.

He returned to his job at hand and completed his shave. He then went and turned on the shower. Abby joined him and when the water had heated, they both walked in. Taking part in one of their erotic showers.

On completion, they both dried and dressed. Carter looked at Abby, "How about a full English breakfast at Tom's, after which we can stroll around the 'Farmers Market' off Allerton Road.

As they strolled, Abby linked his arm, and they walked around the stalls. He purchased some fresh minced beef from one of the many butcher's stalls. There were wooden tubs full of French sticks, and other forms of bread, and fruit galore. Armed with his meat and French stick. She looked up at him, "Tea?" He smiled, "Yes, a choice of 'Spag boll' or 'Chillie, with red kidney beans, accompanied by rice or spaghetti, your choice?"

'Carter lovingly prepared spag boll' and spaghetti in the kitchen, with Abby perched on a kitchen stool with a glass of red wine in hand.

Abby smiled at Carter, "I know you're busy, but can one ask you a question?"

He smiled at her while frying the minced meat and onions, "Why, of course, shoot?" "She smiled. I was just wondering if you'd take offence if I placed my toothbrush in the glass holder in your bathroom. It's the new one. Yours looked so lonely?"

Carter laughed, "Why, of course, for you could always get a stick from off the estate to chew on, a system used by millions of Indigenous Africans?" They use the wood from the *'Salvadora persica,'* also known as *'The toothbrush tree'* or *'teeth-cleaning twig.'* She burst out crying with laughter.

Carter suddenly stopped his cooking and looked at Abby, "How about if you should move some of your clothes in? I'll make space for you?"

She jumped up, "Oh! Carter, that would be so special and practical. It would make a lot of sense not having to go home to prepare for work?"

Their evening meal was exquisite, thoroughly enjoyed by both, and the several glasses of wine went to a good home.

Prior to bed, they both took part in one of the erotic showers. Abby didn't expect what Carter had in mind. Under the torrents of water, they both washed each other with their large, soapy hand gloves.

It was during these actions that Carter let the glove he was holding slip down her body to her crotch. Abby stiffened with excitement. He began to pleasure her.

Abby was enjoying matters so much that she removed the meddling glove to allow Carter's finger total access to her vagina, allowing him to pleasure her. He could tell that she was getting excited. He stooped down and, placing his hands under her bottom, he lifted her. Abby placed her arms around his neck, shrieking in anticipation.

He slowly walked with her over to the tiled edge of the shower and leaned her against the wall. He gently lowered her, impaling her onto his penis. The sudden action took her breath away.

She gripped him round the middle with her legs, interlocking them about his back, finding that gripping him around his shoulders, she could lift and lower herself for deeper penetration.

On completion of their shower, they both lay in bed; Abby looked up at Carter, "Is there no limits to the extent of your sexual libido…He interrupted, "Abbs, I'm no Casanova?" She continued, "For I've never met a man who knows the entire extremes of a woman's sexual compass?"

Carter looked down at her, "Abbs, a man can only do what a woman allows him to do, remembering, *'no means no'* to explain; in the days when we lived in caves, men took it upon themselves, *'Men we're the hunters, and women their prey?'*

"The law, as you well know in relation to the previous comment. *'No means no'* in relation to women and other victims is sacrosanct. But in this case, we're dealing with a woman who willingly presents as a blank canvas; who is a willing victim? Here endith the law, sorry lesson?"

"Abbs, please believe I'm not being sexist, but envisage a man throwing a mound of clay onto a *'potter's wheel,'* instead of making a mug or a ceramic vase, it permits him to shape it by pressing and massaging, it into his perception of a perfect woman's body?"

He continued, "Hypothetically, the whole process if conveyed to a female, the task, allows him by his actions to stimulate her.

Abbs looked up at Carter, "You have no idea how I'm going to enjoy your pathway in developing the blueprint."

Carter leaned down and pulled up the duvet. Abbs said, "To enable me to respond to all that is about to happen, then I'll need my sleep?" She smiled, "That's my boy?" She then cuddled up to him, kissing him passionately, then laid her head on the nape of his neck.

"They both fell fast asleep.

13

Through the mist of Carter's sleep pattern, somewhere in the deep recess of his brain, a sound gradually began to fight through his sleep, the firewall of his mind. He began to toss and turn until he immediately recognised the sound of his pager.

He looked down at Abby, fast asleep. He slipped out of bed, picking up his shorts he quickly slipped them on. He picked up his pager and walked out into the lounge. He looked down and recognised the number 6440.

He thought, 'shit' and taking out his mobile he dialled the number, knowing it to be Sue's.

"Carter." "Guv, sorry to disturb you, but we've got another bad one. Can you please make 'Allerton golf course,' off Allerton Road, close to the junction with Booker Avenue?"

He replied, "Will do, see you shortly." He returned to the bedroom, where he was met by Abby, who was sitting up in bed scratching her head. "Carter, what on earth's happening?" He walked into the bathroom to shave and shower. He turned, and looking over his shoulder, he smiled, "It's my *'lover.'* Remember, I've been called out?"

She leaned over and looked at the time on her mobile, "But Carter, it's only 3.30am?" He replied as he dressed, "Sorry, Hun, but my lover has no perception of time? Three bodies have been found on a golf course. I have no control over the time they are found, but you'd think they'd be a bit more considerate?"

He leaned over and kissed Abby goodbye, telling her to snuggle down and try to catch up on her sleep and that he'd call her later.

Carter got in his car, and he drove off towards Allerton. He drove out of Sefton Park onto Aigburth Road. He only switched on the blues, for it didn't warrant the claxons because of the early hour of the morning.

He continued along Aigburth Road at pace until he came to Aigburth Hall Avenue and Riversdale Road by the Liverpool cricket ground. He turned left up Aigburth Hall Avenue and sped up Booker Avenue, over Mather Avenue, and the continuation of Booker Avenue until he reached the crossroads of Allerton Road, where he turned right. He continued until he reached the lodge at the entrance of the golf club.

It was at the lodge that he could see all the blue pulsating blue lights, with reflections lightening up the tree-lined road.

He turned left and was met by the duty officer at the entrance in possession of the customary clipboard. Carter stopped his car and pressed the window release, "Morning officer, Ch Supt Carter; the officer smiled, "Yes sir, I was told to expect you?" Carter thanked him, a point of respect that they always seemed to remember, and respect.

Sue walked out from behind the lodge, dressed in her forensic overalls, tied off about her waist; she called, "Officer, I hope you checked that officer's ID?"

The officer blushed, "But, Ma'am, it's Ch Supt Carter, you told me to expect him?" Sue replied, "Aw, yes, but you never know. And if you call me Ma'am again, you'll report to the mounted section to brush up all the ..."

Smiling, she leaned on Carter's car, "You can park further up on the right?" She turned and smiled at the uniformed officer, "Goodnight, officer?" He replied, "Goodnight, Mmmm, sorry, boss."

Carter got out of his car, "Do you realise, Susan Martha Ford, you're the bane of all young uniform officers' lives? You more than most know that a female officer, of Inspector and above are all called…" She interrupted, "Yes, Carter, I know, but I hate that bloody word."

Sue turned and handed Carter his forensic suit. He dressed quickly and followed Sue; as they reached the rear of the lodge, he noticed iron posts with police tape looped around them, yet another uniformed officer lifted the tape to enable them both to stoop under.

He smiled and thanked the officer. Sue said, "We're over here, guv, and he noticed a large tarpaulin tent, illuminated from the inside, with flashlights from the SOCO officer's cameras. The iron posts display blue and white police tape covering a large, restricted area about the tent. He noticed the traditional metal forensic trays leading up to the front entrance to the tent.

Carter noticed Lloydie, Ian, Peter, Alex, Jules, and Gill. He looked at Sue. "No Philip?" Sue whispered, "Phil is still suspended?" Carter shouted, "Suspended shit, remind me to call IA in the morning; better still, I'll call TF. It's a bit early to call him presently?"

The next noise they both heard was the bellow of Gordon Chambers, the home office pathologist, "Is that Ch Supt Carter and your trusted sidekick, Supt Ford?" Before Carter answered, he looked at Sue, "How do you like that title, *'sidekick'* would you not prefer…She shouted, "No!"

The tent flaps suddenly opened to reveal Gordon Chambers, "What, what?" Carter replied, "It's okay, Gordon, please don't shout."

He replied, "Yes, well, you'd better come in, but I do warn you, officers. They both walked in, followed by Lloydie. Carter looked upon the sight of ultimate horror, and he felt Sue stiffen as she discreetly took hold of Carter's hand.

Gordon Chambers suddenly called out, "Officers, I want to explain; I see us coming at this from different aspects of a criminal action. Mine as a pathologist and yours as investigating officers?"

Chambers said, "You'll see before you a killing like no other that I've never seen before; please let me try to explain. The three dark-skinned victims take your immediate attention. Each with their hands tied together and placed in an upright position. Leaning back on each other."

"Now we come to the most horrific item. A metal cord has been placed about the victim's necks and fitted to some mechanical device of gismo, which tightens the metal cord until you see the result. De-capitation?"

Carter looked at him in sheer disbelief, "Gordon, are you trying to tell me that they've all been de-capitated?" He let out a loud "Yes, yes." "Now, if you were to get closer, you would notice that their heads are still resting on their shoulders.

Judging by the amount of blood and bone fragments found at the scene, the offence was committed pre-mortem. The cord and the mechanical device are laying in a tight ball between them after their sad demise."

Gordon continued, "Although I stated that I had never seen such a device before, I remember that devices such as this have been used by those who stork in the dark recesses, and shadows of espionage within certain countries of the world?"

Sue gently let go of Carter's hand as he defied all present by walking over to the victims. Gordon was totally surprised to see Carter so close to the victims, For it was a known fact that amongst the team and attending SOCO offers, he disliked gory murders and scenes of crime.

He looked around the tent, "What! Have you never seen a senior officer examine the scene of a crime?" He knew what they were thinking, and before any sarcastic comments, he snapped. "You can all stop staring and get on with your work." To which the reply came back, "Yes, guv."

Carter beckoned to one of the SOCO officers, "Would it be possible to get a close-up of the gadget used before it's caked in fingerprint powder and sent off to the labs?" She smiled and replied, "Sir."

Gordon looked at Carter, "Can we remove the bodies to the mortuary for further investigation?" Carter just nodded his head.

He turned, "Gordon, I'll be down to see you shortly?" He replied, "Yes, yes, Carter." Lloydie looked at Carter, "Guv." He replied, "Thanks, Jim."

Carter walked over to where Sue and other members of the team stood. She immediately stopped talking and turned, "Guv." Carter said, "Boss, will you get things sorted here? Ask for a uniform presence until 9 am; this part of the golf course is to remain closed, and that's no BS.

"At 9am, members of the team will return to complete investigations?"

"When all the necessary is done, follow me to Derby Lane, then we can travel on to the mortuary together. Sue had a look of horror on her face. He smiled and whispered, "Only joking, that's for making me attend at the Royal."

He looked up, "In fact, when sorted here, let's all re-group at Derby Lane for some hot drinks because it's bloody freezing," He looked at his watch, "It's 5.30 am time to call TF?"

14

Carter, as he strode off to his car, pulled his overcoat collar up around his ears to protect himself from the cold. He entered his car, and when comfortable, he called TF. He received the typical gruff reply, *"Frost."* "Sir sorry to disturb you so early, but we have yet another significant case?"

Carter waited for his response, *"Carter, what the f…* Carter heard, *"Sorry, Joan."* Due to the brief silence, Carter got the impression that he'd changed bedrooms. *"What the fuck do you mean, yet another significant case?"*

"Sir, I, and members of my team were called out to a major incident at 'Allerton Golf Club.' On arrival, officers found three men of Asian origin with their wrists bound and placed in a circle behind the lodge at the front entrance to the drive to the golf club.

Further examination revealed that they had been decapitated, caused by means of a single metal loop placed over their heads and necks, attached to a mechanical device, which, in time, reduced the loop considerably, eventually leading to their demise.

After about ten seconds, Carter knew what to expect, *"What the fuck are you saying? Are you telling me that three men stood and allowed some person, or persons alone to commit such a thing and were… Or how the fuck does one get hold of such a piece of equipment?"*

Carter replied, "Sir, I'm on my way back to Derby Lane for a quick hot drink. After a nifty chat with team members who attended, I'll leave for the mortuary and call upon

Gordon Chambers, to see if we can reveal any further information?"

After a short delay, TF said, *"Carter, please keep me in the loop, please excuse the pun, and for fuck's sake, be careful?"* The line went dead.

On his arrival at Derby Lane, he entered the general office to find Eric holding a mug of coffee. "Sir, black, no sugar?" Carter just smiled as he went to sign on duty from the time he'd been called out, of course.

He looked at Eric, "I'm not going to ask?" Eric replied, "Thought you may want hot drinks because it's bloody cold, and you've been mooching around a golf course."

Carter thanked him. He then said, "All officers attending at the scene, my office, all except Lloydie, for he's busy at the mortuary?"

Carter, whilst in his office enjoying his coffee, looked up at the wall clock; it was 6.15am. He thought it too early to call Abbs when there was a sudden knock on his door. He looked up, shouting, "Come in."

The door opened, and Sue walked in, followed by the gang. He called, "Come on in and take a seat." He noticed that they were each holding a hot drink. Sue carried two, placing one in front of Carter on his desk.

He looked at them, "I want to make this quick, for I want some of us to get a couple of hours of sleep. Now I realise that I'll know more after attending the mortuary, especially about that bloody grizzly device used to behead the three victims?"

He looked at Sue, "Can I leave you to organise cover, knowing that we need investigation of the site, and follow up on any inquiries?" Sue smiled, "Yes, sir."

He looked at Sue, "I'm off to the mortuary; see you all later, he got up and left for the general office, signed out and left for the Royal. Sue looked at the faces of her junior officers and shrugged her shoulders. "Which other way can he work?" They all smiled, got up and left.

On arrival at the mortuary, he parked up. He walked over to the door and pressed the button. "He heard a tired voice, "Yes?" Carter introduced himself and held his identification up to the CCTV camera.

The door clicked, and when he opened it, he found Lloydie standing in the corridor. He looked at him, "You look knackered. As soon as this is over, you get off home for some sleep; that's an order."

He followed Lloydie down the cold, dreary corridor to be met at the bottom by Gordon Chambers, dressed accordingly.

"Carter, I'd like to get on, for I'll return later in the morning to conduct the PMs, but this is what I know, and it's mainly the same as explained at the scene. He walked into the subdued atmosphere-filled PM room. Walking over to the three bodies, one laid on each of the PM tables, illuminated by the large PM theatre light.

Lloydie and a technician assisted Gordon Chambers in uncovering the victims. He immediately noticed that each of the three heads had been reverently laid close to their shoulders.

Carter looked at Gordon, "Do you agree that the act was conducted while they were alive?"

Gordon murmured, "Carter, this is the direct result of mechanical decapitation. The equipment used consists of a loop of metal wire attached to each side of the mechanical reducer. When started, it cuts through any or all permitted materials, whatever it's placed around, in this case, the vulnerable necks of the three victims."

"Due to the amount of blood found at the horrific scene. In my opinion. The three victims were alive but drugged. Explained by their wide eyes and swollen tongues."

"Most victims, when choaked, strangled, or garrotted, death is caused by asphyxiation due to the lack of oxygen to the brain. Their faces become contorted, and their swollen tongues protrude from out of their mouths, another source of asphyxiation."

Gordon continued, "A careful examination of the head and neck regions, eyes, and sockets. Scrutiny of the eyes, including the conjunctive on both upper and lower eyelids and photo documentation. Petechial haemorrhages of the conjunctiva are considered markers in the absence of life, due prolonged straining, as found in strangulation, or hanging."

The pathologist walked around the three slabs to a plastic tray placed behind them. With a rubber-gloved hand, he picked up a piece of equipment, triangular in shape, with a narrow black coloured wire tight against the top of the mechanical mechanism."

"Gentlemen, this is the horrific piece of equipment used in the commission of the offence. If one looks closely, it is possible to see remnants of skin, and other body matters, on the surface of the wire."

"On close inspection of the casing, one can see a round small keyhole in the metal casing. In which some sort of key device is placed. I'm of the opinion that when activated, the key controls the device. Removed renders it impossible to be stopped. The surplus wire is contained in the mechanism. Unless one had time to cut the wire, but knowing its use, I feel the wire may be of the sort, rendering it impossible to sever?"

He continued, "That is the end of the lesson; now, is it worth getting any sleep as its 7.30 am? I think I'll have a coffee and then push on with the PMs?"

There was a sudden cough; they both looked around and found Lloydie standing behind them. Carter said, "Why, Jim, what can I do for you?" Carter noticed he was holding two evidence bags. "Sir, one evidence bag contains the victim's fingerprints, ready for comparison. The second is a letter found in one of the victim's clothes?"

Carter said, "Jim give me both items, then you get yourself off home, spending time with Sam, over breakfast, and a couple of hours sleep. No excuses, for I don't want to fall out with my valuable friend, for I may need her help?"

15

Carter arrived back at Derby Lane. He entered the general office to see a look of utter surprise on the face of Eric, while standing in the middle of the office, talking to one of the secretaries.

"Sir, I thought you'd gone home to get some rest. Where the hell have you been?" Carter replied, "At the mortuary together with Gordon Chambers and Lloydie. I've sent Lloydie home for some kip. So, I need this evidence bag with the victim's prints to be sent to HQ. This second one contains a letter found in one of the victim's trousers."

"After signing back in, I'm off to my office. Can you organise a coffee for me?"

Eric smiled, "Guv, I'll see to the fingerprints, and we'll even see to a coffee; now, after reading the letter, get off home for some sleep before you fall over."

Carter turned and left. In his office, he quickly sat behind his desk. At that moment, there was a knock on his door. He called, "Come in." The door opened, and he saw one of the secretaries with his coffee. He smiled, "Come in, Carol, where's his lordship?" "Sir, he's dealing with the fingerprint issue?" She smiled and left.

He took a sip of coffee, complaining, 'Shit, that's hot.' He replaced the mug on the coffee coaster on the corner of his desk. He then took hold of the evidence bag containing the letter. Placing it on his desk, he opened a drawer, and removed a pair of rubber gloves. Putting them on, he opened the evidence bag.

He turned the letter backwards and forwards as if looking for a name or title. Failing to find any other evidence. He picked up a letter opener and slit open the envelope.

Placing the envelope back down on his desk blotter. He removed the two-page letter, checking the quality of the paper and writing. He thought reasonable quality, with neat handwriting.

'To whom it may concern.'
'I realise that if I'm a citizen who is willing to undertake law enforcement in their community without legal authority, typically because the legal agencies are thought to be inadequate' 'By definition, a 'Vigilante.'
'I realise that should I continue in my futile vein, as my first two examples, I may well encounter the wrath of Chief Superintendent Carter, the head and leader of 'The major crime unit' Based here on Merseyside?'

It is only after my first action, the killing of that bastard, Terry Wilkinson, the north-end drug Barron. Subsequently, the three Asian men were found behind the lodge at Allerton Golf Course.
I realise, however much I explain matters of how Wilkinson, a major drug dealer, peddled his wears. He is responsible for the deaths of countless drug victims. A network of users relying on his filthy powder.
His product was supplied on his behalf by poor, unfortunate kids daily, trying to earn a crust. Not only to your typical drug user but to the smart suit-wearing business personnel sitting drinking their coffee Lattes in the smart city coffee outlets. All of which boast that they have matters under control. Yet via driving standards, record increased figures of driving under the influence of drugs.
Wilkinson, via his many outlets, managed to deal with those that sit drinking to both people as private users, frequent club goers, attending clubs in the area, offered,

and sold by his, junkies resulting in an illicit array of choices, on the doors. The bastard even sells his wears to school children at their school gates for their lunch money.

But the area where he makes his money is using young angelic-looking youngsters as mules in cross-boundary line business, up and down the country. Their main task was to supply or collect drugs in two-kilo blocks or other such quantities. Or to collect drug money owed by customers. I do believe that they've also carried guns for the bastard.

The galling matter is that this horror of a man, Wilkinson, had been arrested several times, but when the court date arrived, witnesses failed to appear, and the case was kicked out. Left free to continue in peddling his wears.

The second matter is the three Asians found on the golf course. The title men, I use sparingly and being rather polite. As you'll see, the three victims are slimy sexual deviants with a stable consisting of young girls who, over time, had been groomed for the express purpose of sexual delights.

The girls are either off the streets or girls placed in care, and bent care staff workers would offer likely candidates, tempted by mobile phones, money, and clothes.

Now you, as police officers, know how things go. In investigations of missing girls, social workers say they have conducted inquiries by repeated visits to their home addresses and care homes, only to be false, due to alleged workloads. Placements in care homes that parents and partners, who live miles away, are unable to visit.

The worst thing is the vow of silence. The girls disappear into hell holes, no one seems to join the dots, and when you find a young girl murdered, there is a direct line to social workers and care staff officer's inept duties.

Some pompous ass 'Head of social services' comes out with the usual diatribe, hoping to cover up the cracks stating, 'We've put changes in place to effect new action and work prosses.' You, the police in general, don't come out smelling of roses, and while excuses were being made all round, and such like, these kids are still under the influence *of people like those three bastards.'*

After reading the letter, Carter returned it to the top of his desk. He then picked up the office phone and called TF.

He received the usual curt reply, *"Frost."* "Sir, it's Carter. I attended the mortuary early this morning. Just thought I'd call to inform you and explain that when I joined Gordon Chambers. He explained his initial pre-PM report. Of the three victims from the golf club."

"I must report that DI Lloyd found a letter in the trousers of one of the victims. The author of which is setting himself up as a vigilante, laying claim to both cases."

TF shouted, *"Carter, are you telling me we're in for another serial case?"* Carter replied, "Sir, I can see where you're going with this, suggesting we should tell Wendy Fields (Force PR director). Sir, may I ask that we deal with these matters tomorrow, as I'm on my eyelids, having been called out at 2.30 am."

"I have Sue Ford returning to the office, so I have a senior officer present if I go home?" TF said, *"Okay, Carter, get off home. Shall we say 10.30am tomorrow in the conference room? Get Eric to organise Wendy, Sam, and Gordon to be available?"*

Carter replied, "Sir." He replaced the phone.

He got up and walked out of his office towards the general office, with the evidence bag in hand, when he heard Sue, "Sir, are you still here? I've just returned as requested; why on earth don't you go home before you fall over?"

He looked at Sue, "I've been involved at the mortuary, where after a resume from Gordon on the three victims,' fingerprints for identification, if known, have been forwarded for IDs. But the important thing is that he handed the evidence bag to her. It's a letter found by Lloydie in a trouser pocket of one of the victims from the golf club."

"I've informed TF as the author lays claim to the Wilkinson killing as well, so briefly, I'm too tired to argue the point on a possible 'serial case,' and should we involve Wendy Field?"

"I've suggested that we have a scrum down at 10.30 am tomorrow. Can I leave it for you to arrange an invite to Wendy, Gordon Chambers, and Sam to attend and discuss?" He handed the evidence bag to her, "I'm off; see you tomorrow. Will you sign me off duty, for I don't want to get involved in the general office?"

Sue turned and went to the office door, she shouted "Peter!" The conference door opened, "Boss?" "I need you to take the guv home, for if he drives himself, he's liable to have a TA?" (Traffic accident).

Carter, dressed in his overcoat, stood waiting for Peter. When ready, they left for the yard and home.

Sue walked into the general office. She looked at Eric, "I think he needs a sheepdog?" "Eric turned and looked at Sue, I rest my case?" He turned to continue with his work.

16

Whilst on his way home, with Peter at the wheel. He thought you must phone Abby, for you will crash into bed, and it will be late this evening before you surface. *"Carter, please don't tell me you're just on your way home?"* He replied, "Guilty as charged?"

Abbs replied, *"Right, Carter, I'm leaving my office, see you at your flat?"* Carter shrugged, "Give me fifteen minutes, for I have a chauffeur." He closed the call and relaxed back in his seat, and his mind went blank. On arrival at his block, he noticed Abby's car parked closest to the entrance, for being mid-day, parking spaces were readily available.

Carter thanked Peter and closed the car door. The duty concierge opened the front door of the block, welcoming him.

He felt so tired he looked at Steve, "Steve, please excuse me, but I'm so knackered, I just need my bed?" Steve acknowledged him, "That's okay, Mr Carter?" He continued his wavering strides towards his flat.

Carter approached the door and pressed his fob onto the keyless security lock. He pushed the door open and walked in to find Abby looking overly concerned. "Carter, you look done in. Do you need anything to eat before your shower and bed?"

Carter replied, "No." She looked at him, "So Carter, please don't read anything into this, but just strip off?" He couldn't even raise a smile. When naked, he walked into the wet room, turned on the shower, and walked straight in, not waiting for the usual preferred temperature to cut in.

He just stood there under the torrent of water, and he gently started to sponge himself in a lacklustre way. After 10 minutes, he turned and switched off the shower.

Taking hold of a towel, he dried himself off, placed the towel about his waist, and returned to the bedroom. To find Abby holding up a pair of clean boxers and a T-shirt. While he dressed, Abby picked up his working clothes.

He walked over to the bed, pulled back the duvet, tumbled onto the welcome mattress, straightened his legs, pulled up the duvet, and was asleep before Abby returned from the bathroom.

She looked down on him, bending down, and kissed him on the lips. Standing over him she could hear his light breathing, tidied up the duvet, and left.

On leaving the flat, she bumped into Kate Murphy, his domestic. Abby knew about her but had never met her. Kate had a concerned look on her face. "Is there a problem?"

Abby smiled, "No, only a man that looked as if he was running on empty?" Kate burst out laughing, "Young lady, do you happen to have a minute and join me in a cup of coffee or a cup of tea?"

Abby followed her back into the flat and into the kitchen. Sat at the kitchen worktop. Kate turned well, excuse me, "What do I call you, for please don't take exception, but you're not here to read the gas meter?"

Abby smiled, "I'm Abby, please call me Abbs. I recently met Carter at a party, and our meeting was cut short. Unfortunately, he was called away. Abby blushed; he invited me to tea after his discharge from the hospital."

Kate laughed, pointing her chin at Abby, "Yes, I can see why he'd invite you, for your beautiful."

Kate mentioned no more information on Carter. And Abbs never asked. All Kate mentioned over their hot drinks was the story about how her husband, Tom, had been Carter's probation sergeant when he first joined the police. Sadly, Tom died six months after his retirement.

"On hearing the news, Carter, in such a subtle way, called one evening and put the offer to me, to become his domestic. The proposition suited both parties, and I eventually became part of the family. The man is a true gentleman. Anyone who gained Tom, my husband's total respect, must be special?"

Abby looked at Kate, "Well, I need to get back to work. Aby gave Kate her card, "Should Carter wake before 5.30 pm? If you're still here, will you tell him that I'll quickly visit to see him?"

As she turned to leave for work, Kate called, "Will steaks and salad suffice? I have a French stick to snap and lavish with butter?" Abby replied, "Lovely, what about his nibs?" "Leave him to me, Abbs…?" Kate laughed, saying, "Goodbye." She turned and headed back for the kitchen.

While Abby was preparing to leave after work, her mobile activated; she looked at her caller window and saw 'Carter.' *"Well, hello, sleepy head; Mr. is obviously awake. Are you firing on all cylinders? If so, remain in bed, for I'm on my way."* And closed the call.

Carter, in a naked state, answered the intercom, letting her in. He called, down the handset, "Ask Steve to let you into my flat." He turned laughing as he ran back to bed. He pulled up the duvet and feigned sleep.

Seconds later, Abby entered the bedroom, and she stripped off in seconds. Abbs then ran into the wet room and took a quick shower. She frantically dried herself and walked naked towards the bed. She pulled back the duvet and looked down at Carter's naked body.

Abbs thought, 'Wow.' She slipped into bed, lying next to his warm body and placed a leg over his right thigh. "Oh, Carter, I've thought of nothing else since I returned to work?"

Carter took hold of her and turning her onto her back, he kissed her passionately, after which, when pulling back, Carter heard a low, long sigh, "Aw, pal, I needed that?"

After which, he moved a gentle hand down her chest, "You know what, Carter, if asked to make your top ten list of women's parts, how or what would be at the top of your list? Carter burst out laughing, "I'm rather greedy, for I love the lot, unable to put them in any list." In utter frustration, he fell on his back, shouting forgive me."

He raised a single finger and gently traced the contours of her body. He brushed her neck and lips, passing it over her breasts and nipples. During this time, Abbs relished the merit of such actions. But his inevitable deeds on reaching her crutch sparked her maximum reaction. She whispered, "Don't you dare move that beautiful finger." After which, she softly crossed her legs, trapping it.

With Carter's endeavours, Abbs realised she was about to explode and decided to stuff the edge of the duvet into her mouth to subdue a scream.

Carter's next action was inevitable. He tenderly opened her legs. She suddenly let out a cry of anticipation as he entered her. Abby then lifted her pelvic hips to gain better penetration; she placed her arms around his neck and drew him down to her; she kissed him with such a passion.

"Carter, that's so wonderful; if I could, I'd want to keep you there all the time." She then placed her legs around his midriff and crossed them behind him. Tightening and relaxing them in time with his thrusts.

After their arousing sexual activity, Carter invited Abby to join him in the shower; they both walked into the wet room, taking part in an equally splendid erotic sequence of events.

On completion, they both dried each other. When dry, they dressed in casuals and walked through to the kitchen. Carter asked, "Hungry?" She smiled up at him, "Starving, isn't it funny how hungry one gets after sex."

Carter began to prepare the meal left by Kate earlier. While busy, he looked at Abbs, "Are you thinking of staying tonight?" Abby replied, "Well, over the last couple of days, I've transferred some clothes, so it's not essential to go home before leaving the office?"

After spending time over a leisurely tea, accompanied by a couple of glasses of wine, they cleared up and retired to the lounge to enjoy their coffee and liqueurs.

They eventually retired to bed, both wondering who was to make the first move. Although they both cherished each other's bodies, they weren't quite at the time factor when one just rushed into action. Carter thought I'd shout, *'Geronimo.'* Perhaps tomorrow?

Abby laid on Carter's chest; she began to kiss it with lovely butterfly tender kisses as she moved down to his crotch. She looked up at him. "Carter, you are the most generous man I've ever met with your sensual acts towards me, and yet I'm quite happy knowing it's not always on a reciprocal footing. So will you please lay back and relax, for I realise perhaps I must try?"

Abby continued and eventually began to pleasure him in such a way that Carter derived so much gratification. On completion, Abby returned to Carter's side.

He took her in his arms; it was in such a way that Abby turned, "Should we continue, the inevitable will happen, although a matter that I'd normally accept with open arms, but Carter, you need your rest, so Mr. There is another day or night?"

She leaned down and pulled up the duvet, where she noticed that Carter had fallen fast asleep.

17

Carter awoke to see Abby with her head resting on the palm of her hand, supported by her elbow on her pillow. Looking down at Carter, she whispered, "You know, for the last ten minutes, I've been pondering with the idea of disturbing you, accidently of course, ha, ha?"

He smiled at her, "Well, madam, we need to decide, either bed or shower?" She looked down at him and, with a sly look, "Can't we make love in bed and shower after? I promise the shower will be just hygienic, with no afters?"

He looked at her, "There are a lot of people who would believe your promise, but alas, as a seasoned police officer such as I, no I, don't believe you, madam?" Abby spluttered, "But Carter, please believe me?"

Carter took hold of her. She screamed, "Carter, what on earth are you doing?" He held her up, "I've made a Presidential decision. It's the shower?"

While he had hold of Abby, he turned on the shower, and so it began; they experienced one of their most erotic showers; it was like a gentle water fight, soap suds abounding. Arms and legs flailing abundantly about, everywhere, trying to gain the best purchase and influence on one or the other's body.

Eventually, Carter pulled Abby down onto the rubberised floor of the shower. She screamed, "Carter!?" He laid her down, supporting the weight of his body by placing an arm on either side of her shoulders. He gently made love to her, and she responded, expressing her delights in the proceedings.

On completion, laughing, she shouted, "Carter, am I going to have design marks on my bum?" They both got up. Carter leaned down, kissing her bottom, saying, "OMG." Between tears of laughter, they showered most appropriately.

When dressed, they entered the kitchen; Abby looked at him, "Carter, can I prepare you some breakfast?" Carter replied, "Well, I'm easy; it's just a mug of black coffee, no sugar?" Abbs replied, "I Know, Carter, but what do you want for breakfast, bum, bum?" They both burst out laughing.

After breakfast, before leaving, Carter walked over to a roll-top desk, opened it, then went to a small drawer, one of three on the left-hand side of the desk; pulling it open, he took out two oval-shaped plastic fobs.

Turning, showing his open hand. "Abbs, the blue one is to gain access into the block; there is a keypad placed on the left of the door. The green one is to the flat and is placed on another keypad on the left of the door. For convenience, put them on your keyring, allowing full access?"

Outside in the car park, he noticed Peter parked up. Carter kissed Abbs. "I'll call you later if I'm going to be late?" Abby left for her car. At the same time, he left, walking towards Peter's car.

He opened the passenger door and got in. Peter turned, "Morning, guv?" He smiled and replied, "You didn't see that; all will be explained in time. "Of course, guv."

On his way to the office, he called Eric. "Good morning, Guv. I hope you feel rested." Carter replied, "Yes, Eric, thanks for asking. I was so tired yesterday, and I'm unsure if you know that TF, Wendy, Sam, and Gordon Chambers are invited for a scrum at 10.30 am?"

Eric replied, "Yes, guv, no worries; Sue mentioned the fact after you'd left for home?" Carter replied, "We'll be with you in 15 minutes."

On his arrival at Derby Lane, he thanked Peter and left for the general office, saying good morning to all gathered here. He signed on duty, turned, and retrieved a mug of coffee from Eric. He thanked him, saying, "I'll be in my office if needed."

He entered his office and noticed the evidence bag left on his desk by Sue. As he sat down, there was a knock on his office door. He called, "Come in." The door opened, and he saw Sue standing on the threshold. He uttered, "Come in, Sue." Which she did, with a mug of coffee in hand.

She sat at his meeting table, "Carter, you look rested; you look a lot fresher than yesterday's lunchtime. Are you ready for today?"

Carter looked at her, "Sue, this is a funny one, but after reading the letter from the author, I feel we may have others. Another Gainsford, on our hands, but in this case, it may seem that he has a grievance with authority and the system, and not priests?"

While they were talking, there was yet another knock on his door. He called, "Come in." The door opened, and they both looked up to see Eric standing in the doorway. "When you're both ready, your guests await your pleasure."

Carter collected the evidence bag from his desk and handed it to Eric, "Can I trouble you for copies of the letter to hand out to our guests and team members?" He replied, "Yes, guv."

Entering the conference room, the team came to attention; continuing to the top of the room, Carter said, "Thank you. Now, all be good children and sit down. There was a roar of laughter, but they all complied.

Carter welcomed his guests; he walked in front of TF, Wendy, Sam, and Gordon Chambers, followed by Sue, to the far right of the room. Sue sat on one of the two vacant seats; Carter remained standing.

There was a sudden knock at the door; Alex stood up and answered it. He took the copies of the evidence letter and handed them out to one and all.

When sorted, Carter looked out for the team. "You have just been given a copy of a letter, found in the trouser pocket of one of the victims, from the golf club killing. In the letter, the author also admits to the killing of Wilkinson."

"Well, people, we may be on the cusp of yet another serial case, but a different subject matter. Judging by his first letter, our predator has a grievance against authority?"

Carter turned and looked at Tony Frost. Who stood up, "Yesterday I received a call from your guv concerning the letter, and if he wasn't so knackered, he may have gone on to mention a potential 'serial case'?"

"Your guv has a famous mantra, 'From little acorns, big oak trees grow,' well, are we in the foothills of such matters? He turned to Sam.

"As your resident criminal psychologist, I have been called upon to assist in several 'serial cases.' Although we all know not all psychopaths are murderers, and not all murderers are psychopaths. Psychopaths are a hallmark of 'serials' Who consist of frequent killers in their various guises; in other words, her, or she, doesn't give a dam.?

"In the past when we've had more than two or more victims. It's an unwritten rule; the definition of a serial case is three or more victims."

"Now, the author of this latest letter would seem to wish to blame the system or lack of it. He feels that offenders are arrested, and due to the lack of evidence or witnesses, the accused just walks. If by any chance it should go to the nth degree, and they receive a custodial conviction, witnesses suffer."

"With the condition of the victims, do we have a psychopath on our hands? Is he a lone wolf, or works with another? One thing I must say, he has or holds the playlist?"

"In this matter, it's against the system, a lack of detection and punishment, and all its consequences; I foresee an enormous amount of hard work ahead of you, similar in all your other cases. For you'll be working blind?"

"I feel that if I were to suggest a possible playlist, one should look at the following categories of potential victims; drug dealers, paedophiles, stalkers, rapists, domestic assaults, indecent assaults on pupils by teachers, vicars, priests, of either denomination, the list is endless."

"If matters escalate, then beware, for your predator, or predators, have a wealth of information presented by the press, TV, and worse, the internet in all its formats." Sam sat down. Sam received a round of applause from the team and guests.

Carter looked at Gordon Chambers. He stood up with his usual enthusiasm and began with his bellowing voice.

"Ladies and gentlemen, your two initial cases have issues that prove the offender, or offenders, have committed two horrendous crimes unrelated in subject, or MO."

"The first identified as Terry Wilkinson, a drug baron who deals with the supply of drugs to victims in the north end of the city, hoped to expand on the arrest of Hughes.

"Wilkinson's body was found in a display stance in Walton Park. He was sat on his haunches, with his arms tied behind his back. The offender, to prove Wilkinson participated in the supply of drugs, slashed his mouth from ear to ear with a parcel cutter, using a metal bar or a piece of wood, such as a baseball bat, demolishing his front teeth and gums."

"He, or they, then began to stuff his mouth cavity with white powder and bags containing white powder, underlining the drug issue. The powder used is high-grade cocaine; blood samples reveal that although a user, he had been drugged by means of a date rape drug and was alive at the time of his death; apart from fingerprints, he had been identified by DNA hair follicles."

"Our second case, I have to say that I haven't seen anything like it in all my years as a pathologist. The three victims were garrotted by means of some mechanical piece of equipment attached to a wire noose. When the loop, in this case, is placed about the neck of the intended victim when switched on, it eventually begins to garrotte them— cutting through the victim's necks and de-capitated them. The item was found lying on one of the victim's shoulders. It was so tight, there was barely a gap in the loop?"

"I found a mark on the inner arm of each of the victims; samples reveal each had been subjected to the date rape drug and alive at the time of the offence.

"You must realise that in this case, the culprit needed them seated, leaning against each other. He or they then placed their heads together, allowing the culprit or culprits to place the steel noose over the victims' heads. The gadget switched on, causing the inevitable." Gordon Chambers took his seat and received a round of applause.

Carter seemed to look at Wendy Field and Tony Frost simultaneously. He said, "Sir, the floor is all yours." There was a raw of laughter, for they knew what was coming.

Tony Frost stood up, immaculately dressed in a grey-coloured double-breasted lounge suit, a Royal blue shirt, and a maroon-coloured tie. He looked over the team and smiled, "Well if I have to keep your guv happy?" He looked at Wendy, "Miss Fields, where do we go from here, from a PR point of view?"

She stood up and smiled, "Well, as ever, it's the protection of the public and the force. At present, we have two offences; as Sam mentioned, it normally takes three before we have a serial case, yet we have technically four victims, but on paper, two offences?"

"But one cannot stop the unusual crime scenes being reported to the news and social media networks."

Wendy said, "I haven't had any direct approaches by the news hounds or any mention on social media networks. Can I suggest that the first time I'm contacted, that I report back, and a decision made on the way forward?"

18

After the meeting and all the valued guests had left, Carter, who entered the general office, took his coffee from Eric, stating, "I'll be in my office." He turned and left.

Sue was the next to enter the general office. She looked at Eric, "Was that the guv leaving for his office?" Eric, with a smile on his face, replied, "Yes, boss." Sue also smiled, "Do you think he's hooked a fish?" Eric replied, "If you wish to retain the rank of Superintendent, I suggest that we wait to be told and not to second guess." They both burst out laughing.

As Sue left the general office to walk back down to her own office, she thought, "If only?"

In his office, Carter took out his mobile phone and called Abby. *"Carter, what a lovely surprise, but is it a courtesy call, or will you be late?"* He laughed down the phone, "I know it's like a roll of the dice, but I'm leaving within the next fifteen minutes; I've been in a meeting most of the day, and I was wondering if I could impose on you for some TLC?"

Abbs laughed, "TLC, before tea on your arrival home or after tea?" He then heard a low sexy voice say, *"Carter, bugger it, why not all evening?"* He replied, "Well, I'll wait and see your mood. See you shortly?"

Carter replaced his phone into his trouser pocket, tidied up his desk, put on his suit jacket and light overcoat, and left for the general office. As he entered, he noticed Sue and Eric each enjoying a coffee.

Sue looked up, "Hello, guv. Have we got somewhere to go?" As he signed off duty, he turned, saying, "You don't, but I have?" Sue was just about to say something when her guv, with a serious voice, continued, "I'm off home early for once; see you both tomorrow. He turned and left.

Eric looked at Sue, "I warned you unless you keep your nose out of his business?" Sue replied, "Well, I just wondered, for he is usually the first to tell us of his trysts?" By this time, they were both on their own. Eric said, "Susan Martha Ford, if I didn't know any better, I'd think there is a jealous streak in your voice?"

She batted it back with, "Me, I was just thinking?" Eric replied, "Yea, yea, yea." She got up and left.

On his way home, Carter laughed, *'Well, the rumour mill must be working overtime?'*

Carter arrived home and noticed Abby's car in a nearby parking bay, and he smiled, beaten to the punch.

He locked his car and walked into his block. He smiled at Steve, the evening concierge, "Good evening, Steve; how are things?" He replied, "Evening, Mr Carter, sir. Are you aware you have a visitor?" He smiled, "Yes, Steve, it was last minute, and I gave her my security access. I appreciate what I've always told you in the past?" He continued walking, Steve called, "No problem, sir."

He continued, opened his flat door, and walked in to be suddenly hijacked by Abbs. She peeled back and pushed off his overcoat and jacket in one move, letting them both fall to the floor. She looped her arms around his neck and pulled him down; she kissed him passionately on his lips, after which she called, "WoW!" Carter, that was fantastic; I needed that?"

After which she reached up, placing her hands on his collar, slackening off his tie, abbs, then opened the top button of his shirt collar; she gently used his tie to tow

Carter through to the lounge; she lightly pressed him down onto the settee. She looked down on him.

"Well, Mr., do you wish the gradual TLC to work up to a crescendo or start with the full hit?" She smiled down on him. "Your choice?" He placed the heel of the palm of his hand under his chin, curling his fingers around his mouth, "Um."

Abby picked up a cushion and threw it at him, "That's it, all matters are off the menu?" She turned and left for the kitchen, feigning a huff. She returned five minutes later carrying two glasses of red wine. "You're forgiven."

After their usual erotic shower, tea accompanied by yet other glasses of wine, they retired to bed. They slipped out of their sweats and, when naked, snuck under the duvet into bed.

Abby placed her head onto Carter's chest and cuddled up to him. She began to move her hand down under his boxers and began to lightly massage him, and within minutes, she whispered, 'WoW.' She leaned up and kissed him on his mouth and over his chest.

She moved over Carter and straddled him, leaned forward, and gently placed him inside of her. As she slowly leaned back, taking Carter into her with total penetration.

Abbs leaned back, placing a hand on either of his thighs, allowing her support. Then Abbs quickly realised that by increasing her pelvic movements backwards and forwards, it began to build up a heightened bout of continual sexual feelings and desire never experienced before.

Abbs began to fill with an eye-watering reaction to her sexual fervour. She suddenly began to shake, letting out screams of derision. As she increased, it built up until she fell forward, her head coming to rest on top of Carter's chest.

She placed her arms around his neck, gently lowering her head to the nape of his neck and began to cry. Carter comforted her by holding her safe in his arms and whispering, "Abbs, let it all out." She looked up to him, "But Carter, what about you? It's been all me, for Christ's sake." Carter pulled up the duvet, stating, "Abbs, the actions by you gave me the same enjoyment and satisfaction."

Abbs moved her head and looked at Carter, and with excitement in her voice, "Do you not realise how much I tremble when we meet? I often wonder if you could see how the blood rushes through my veins excitedly. For I feel it so strong, I fear it could be noticed?"

19

Abby leaned over Carter and kissed him on his forehead. Looking up, he stared into the brightest pair of shining blue eyes, so deep in colour, the depth of which he truly felt unfathomable.

He looked up at her, "Morning, Abbs. Is there anything I can do for you?" She leaned down on his chest and looked up, "Well! I was wondering if we have time. Carter pulled her on top of him, to which she called out, "Why, Mr! Carter, it would seem the decks are cleared and ready for action?"

He rolled her over and began to kiss her breasts, eventually kissing and nipping at her nipples. She shrieked with delight, then realised that she'd gently opened her legs, and he slowly entered her. Abbs cried, "Carter, you feel so worm inside of me. She gently placed her arms around his neck, realising that she could raise herself to increase full pleasure.

On completion and covered in sweat, Carter picked her up and carried Abbs, shrieking, to the shower. "Carter, where on earth do you get the strength? For Christ's sake, we've been at it like demons; I couldn't stand it if my life depended on it?"

He replied, "Stop waffling on and concentrate?" She did, and yet again, they took part in one of their many erotic showers."

When dried, dressed, and stood in the kitchen, they chatted over their early coffees when his mobile suddenly rang. Carter commented, "Dam, it's early?" He looked at his watch to see it was 8.15 am.

"Carter." "Guv, sorry to disturb you; it's Gill. I'm 'on call' and just had an early call from the duty Inspector in the force control room. A member of the public called, saying that he'd found the body of a man in a disused building of an old coal yard on Rudyard Road, off East Prescot Road. Uniformed officers are in attendance."

"The witness taking his dog for a walk before leaving for work. Explained it being a favourite location. On his arrival, it's his habit to release the dog from its lead to roam around the old yard and buildings. He then noticed it disappeared into an old garage?"

"On hearing the dog's sudden incessant barking, he followed the sounds, and going to retrieve his dog, he found the naked body of a man stood up against a wooden beam part of the derelict garage, secured by barbed wire."

Carter thanked her, saying, "Gill, activate the team, plus SOCO and Mr Chambers, if possible?" He got a soft reply, *"Will do guv."*

He looked at Abby, "Well, that's my day sorted. Odds on, I'll be home late tonight?" The phrase gave Abbs a sudden warm feeling of security.

She looked at Carter, "Is it a bad one, love?" Carter thought it was a bit soon to offload on her, so he just replied, "It has the makings of one, but I will call if I'm going to be late; by the way, have you moved all of your gear in yet?"

Abbs smiled. "We must chat, say over the weekend if free?"

Carter said, "Well, I must go, you have a key?" He smiled and left, leaving Abbs in a state of wonder.

He activated the blues and twos in his car and sped off toward Queens Drive to head for East Prescot Road. He leaned down and switched on the force radio to monitor the situation over the air.

Although it was rush hour, Carter benefited from the police warning systems, permitting him to cut through the early morning traffic. It was while driving that his phone suddenly activated.

"Carter," *"Guv, it's Eric; all systems have been put in place. Sue will see you at the scene?"* Carter replied, "Thanks, Eric. I will see you later." He closed the call.

He eventually turned into Rudyard Road, where he immediately turned off the claxons and decided to proceed on the blue lights. He was met by all the emergency vehicles, with their pulsating blue lights. He drove to the coal yard gate to see a uniformed officer holding the traditional clipboard.

Pulling up, he lowered his window. "Morning officer, I'm…The officer interrupted, "Yes, sir, I was warned of your attendance; please turn left and drive down the yard, and you'll see your colleagues by some large, dilapidated garages."

Carter smiled, "Thank you, officer," And slowly drove off in the correct direction. He hadn't driven far when he saw a small road on his right. He turned in and noticed all the emergency vehicles.

He drove up to Sue's car and pulled up behind it. As he exited his car, he noticed Sue walking out of the garage, dressed in her forensic suit, with her hood up, mask, rubber gloves, and booties.

As she turned to face Carter, she casually pushed her hood back from off her head and, in the same motion, pushed her mask down under her chin. He immediately noticed the red pinch line on the bridge of her nose and the red lines made by her elasticated mask secured on either side of her head, close to her ears, on the side of her face.

She gave him a weak smile as she passed him on her way, heading towards her car to retrieve a forensic suit for him from her car. Carter said, "Sue, stop; I can get the bloody suit myself; I can see from your face that things must be bleak?"

She looked at him, turned towards him, and began to cry. He pulled her close to shield her from prying eyes. After a few minutes, she looked up at him and whispered, "Sorry, Carter." He replied, "Nonsense, why don't you take a break and have a seat in your car?"

Sue pulled up her mask and hood, "No, get suited; I'll wait." When ready, he turned to see Lloydie standing at the entrance; he looked at Carter and lowered his eyes, "Sorry, guv, but it's another bad one."

Lloydie turned, allowing him access; as he did so, Carter heard the bellowing voice of Gordon Chambers. "Ah, Carter, please, a rather bad one, old man, I'm afraid, do come in."

As he walked in, his eyes fell on a naked male, approximately 6.2" ish, but that is where the symmetry ended. Gordon walked up to him. "Chief Superintendent Carter, you see before you the body of a white male, naked, standing with both his hands, arms, and ankles secured by means of rope around the beam behind him. He is also impaled by means of barbed wire."

"It's very apparent that it is one single continuous length of wire, worked around his naked body from head to toe, impaling his eyes, mouth, hands, and fingers."

Gordon looked at Carter; "It is rather obvious that our offender wished to make a personal and private statement by the way he concentrated on the three specialist areas of the victim's body; I trust you've noticed the ferocity in which he carried out his task, for there is blood everywhere?"

He continued, "Carter, it is obvious by the amount of blood streaming down his body via those important areas that he was alive during the commission of the crime. Blood samples have been taken for comparison to identify if he was drugged, and if so, the name…?"

However polite Carter had been on his arrival at the scene after his apparent inspection of the victim. He turned and left; Gordon Chambers cried, "What no good-byes. Carter made no comment, except he pulled his mask off his face, "I feel that I can't breathe."

Sue walked up to him, "Carter, come and lean against your car." The next thing he heard was a "Cough." It was Lloydie; he smiled, "Mr Chambers compliments." Carter saw Lloydie carrying a leather doctor's bag, which he handed to his boss.

He looked at Lloydie, "Do me a favour, Jim, please do the honours?" He did and let Carter look inside, for it contained a bottle of scotch and a tower of plastic drinking containers. Carter burst out laughing. He positioned the bag to enable Sue to have a glance.

He turned and resumed a position in his car. He took out his phone and called TF. *"Frost"* "Sir, it's Carter, and he began to explain the crime scene to him. TF, in a raised voice, shouted, *"Carter, what the fuck are you saying? The bastard is sick; did he leave a letter or an ID of the victim?"* Carter shouted, "Sir, give me a fucking chance." And closed the call.

He placed the phone into his pocket and sauntered over to Sue, who offered him a tot. "Sir, it's doctors' orders."

Carter walked over to Lloydie and Sue. He continued walking to the garage entrance, "Do we have his clothes, and if so, is there a letter?" Lloydie replied, "Not yet, guv, but I have the team on it, for you never know, he may have stripped him elsewhere?"

With the doctor's bag in hand, Carter walked over to Gordon, the welcomed benefactor and supplier of the pick-me-up. The pathologist, together with SOCO officers, was, of course, terribly busy.

Gordon looked over, "Hello, old man, I do hope it helped, for you see, we medical and scientific chaps take matters such as this in our stride..." Carter interrupted him in mid-flow. "No, Gordon, you are part of the team, and I failed to acknowledge you when I left the garage in a rant; it was unforgivable of me."

Gordon stood up, "Carter, good friends understand and needn't have to apologise?"

"Carter, I need your permission to remove the body; I intend to remove it, as is, and unshackle him in the mortuary before his PM?" Carter nodded, "I'll inform Jim to assist, and I'll follow on. See you at home." Gordon whispered, "Are you sure, old man, for it will be rather gruesome?" He nodded and walked away."

As he left, he saw Jim standing at the entrance; he only needed to look at him, "Sir."

20

Carter returned to Derby Lane, closely followed by Sue. He entered the general office. Eric looked up in surprise, "Guv, morning, what a start to the day?" As he walked over to the diary to sign on duty, he turned, "It couldn't have been worse?"

Eric prepared him a coffee; he was just about to sit down to enjoy it when in walked Sue. One of the secretaries stood up, "Coffee boss?" Sue smiled, "I'd loved one, please." She continued and signed on duty.

Carter looked at her, "When ready, will you come through to my office?" He then turned and, with his coffee, left for his office.

Sue, when ready, got up to leave when she noticed a sad look on Eric's face. "What?" He started to sing, "Who's in the ssshit?" Sue looked at him, half laughing with him and his team. "Mr Morton, please get on with your work." And left.

Carter had left his door open, and Sue walked in. He looked up, "Hello, Sue, come in, come in." Sue continued into his office and sat at the meeting table on a chair nearest his desk.

He said, "Sue, thanks for your concern earlier; it was appreciated, in fact, the smidgen of Vick inside of my mask even more so. Now I'm off to the mortuary. Can I leave you to consult with the team? I know you'll run matters to organise the site and ongoing inquiries; I'll be back ASAP?"

Sue smiled, "Carter, can't you leave it with Jim and with Gordon's report to follow?" "No, Sue, I have a feeling about this, so see you when I get back?"

He got up and left. As he signed out, he looked at Eric, "Can I ask you to contact Gordon Chambers, asking him not to touch the body until I arrive?" and left for his car.

After he had gone, Sue walked into the general office with her empty mug. Eric looked up, "Well, what's got into the guv? He was out of here with a briar up his arse?" Sue smiled, "He seems to have a query on this one but never explained a thing and was just not leaving things to Jim?" Eric hunched his shoulders, "Well, we'll soon find out?"

Carter arrived at the mortuary and followed protocol by presenting his ID to the CCTV. The door clicked. He pushed it open and was met by Lloydie. "Guv, are you sure about this?" He smiled and patted his junior officer on his shoulder, "Lead on, Jim."

They were both met by Gordon Chambers, who stood at the open door of the PM room in his usual pathologist's garb. He bellowed, "Carter, please put on the PM forensic uniform about to be handed to you. He obliged. Gordon said, "Got your message, so let's not delay matters." And he turned.

Carter followed him and immediately felt the room's sudden cold and vista. All issues he was beginning to come to terms with, but in the past had caused him such concern. He loathed the whole process.

He then saw the covered body of the victim under the large theatre light, and two technicians, one with camera equipment, stood at the head of the PM table. When ready, Gordon nodded his head; the man stepped forward and removed the white rubber sheet while his colleague began to take photographs.

Carter took a deep breath through his mouth. He then looked down on the state of the victim. Gordon looked at Carter, "Okay, old son?" He nodded.

Before commencing, he reached up a gloved hand and switched on the above static microphone. He recited the time, day, date, and persons present. He continued. I have here on my PM table an unknown male victim, recovered from the disused coal yard in Rudyard Road."

He continued, "The victim was found tied and still attached to the old beam, for the perpetrator had wrapped the victim additionally by means of barbed wire.

He continued, "When looking down on the body, it is very apparent that he has been bound by his hands, arms, and ankles to a derelict beam, secured with barbed wire. I've decided to cut the wire at the middle of the victim's body, all the way from his head to his toes, which will permit me to remove him from the beam, for not wishing to disturb the outer epidermis of the victim?"

Gordon stated, "I have two sets of wire cutters; I'm offering one pair to my PM technician, who will assume a position on the other side of the body. DI Lloyd has volunteered to collect the lengths of barbed wire for evidence."

Both men began gingerly dealing with the wire about his head; they snipped at each side, and Gordon, gently with his colleague, began to lift each strand away from the pierced body, leaving indentations from the barbs of the wire.

He continued, "I'm handing DI Lloyd each strand he is placing on a table." The technician was busily engaged in taking mortuary photographs.

As they continued, they eventually came to the area of the victim's eyes and mouth. He looked at Carter, "The perpetrator would seem to have concentrated on these two areas, forcing the barbed wire deep into the crevasses of his eyes and mouth as if to make a statement. That causing a problem in the removal of the wire?"

Gordon continued, "We now come to the victim's penis; it is here that the perpetrator has passed the wire over and around his penis several times as if making a statement; in fact, the degree to which he conducted this part of the process, has partly dissected it. So, I must be careful not to cause any more damage to his penis in my effort to remove the wire?"

The legs of the victim posed no further problems.

Eventually, it was time to turn the victim over and continue from his back. It was while they moved down the victim's body, on reaching his bottom, that Gordon let out a gasp. He reached for a large pair of tweezers and began to remove a clear plastic bag from his anus. On completion, he placed it in a metal kidney-shaped dish.

He looked at Carter, "If I were a betting man, I'd say your victim may be a paedophile?"

On completing the task, Gordon invited them to his office, where he poured three nips of Scotch into three plastic drinking containers. While they chatted, there was a knock on his office door, he shouted. "Come in."

A female technician walked into his office, still wearing a forensic uniform, with the top tied around her waist. She handed Gordon an evidence bag containing a folded white piece of paper. Gordon thanked her, and she smiled and left.

Lloydie stood up, "Guv, I'm going to fingerprint him, so we may get a positive ID and his form, if any. Carter looked at his watch; It was 3.30 pm.

He looked at Jim, "When finished, you're to book off duty with the control room and go home. "We'll have a scrum down at 9.30 am tomorrow. Carter smiled, "And that's an order, got it?" Jim replied, "Got it, thank you, guv." "Love to Sam." Jim smiled, "Sir." He left the office.

Carter stood up he shook hands with Gordon, thanking him for his hospitality. He turned and left.

21

Upon arriving at Derby Lane, he entered the general office and signed back in. Eric suggested a coffee. Carter flopped down on a chair opposite Eric's desk. It didn't take rocket science for Eric to realise it must have been grim at the mortuary, for he could not help noticing the pastiness of Carter's face.

Eric thought yet again, you've pushed yourself just to set an example that if needs be, he will stand shoulder to shoulder with his team, and yet he had their respect in spades. Eric made the coffee and handed it to him.

Carter mumbled, "I hope you don't mind, but I'm taking my coffee to my office. As he was about to leave, Sue entered, "Hello, guv." Carter was standing in the middle of the office with his back to Eric. Sue immediately noticed Eric shaking his head from side to side; it was only a couple of times. But she got the point, for she noticed that the blood seemed drained from his face.

He continued leaving for his office; on arrival, he immediately sat at his desk and called Abby, *"Hello, Carter. I thought you'd forgotten all about me?"* There was a noticeable silence. *"Carter, are you still there? What on earth is the matter?"* He replied quietly, "It's been a shit of a day. Could you come over, for I'd hate to be on my own tonight?"

"That bad Carter?" He replied, "You have no idea; I have a dedicated officer to deal with such issues who'd volunteer to take on certain duties at an instance. I only

had to ask. Yet I decided to subject myself to the terrible event, and I am such a fool at times...?"

She replied, *"Are you leaving soon?"* "As soon as it takes me to sign out and drive home, Carter, say 30 minutes?" "She whispered, *"Carter, please be careful, driving when so upset, I'm leaving myself for home."*

Carter stood up, putting on his suit jacket and a fawn-coloured light raincoat. He wasn't worried about his appearance, for he had slackened off his tie and opened his top shirt button.

He walked through to the general office; Sue was still there, and with a weak smile, he said, "I'm off home. Can you arrange for a scrum down for 9.30 am? He signed off duty and left.

Sue looked at Eric, "Yet again, he's running on empty; how the hell do we tie him down, suggesting that it's not necessary for him to respond to 'call out'?"

Eric laughed, "Why, boss, who will tell him?" Sue sat with a blank look on her face. She uttered, "He needs a sheepdog?" Eric replied, "He's already got one...?" He then looked down and continued with his work.

Carter got into his car and left for home. He felt that he must have driven on automatic pilot, for if asked, *'What did you witness on your way home?'* He'd be unable to comment. Couldn't answer a single question on what he remembered of his journey.

He parked up at his resident block of flats. He locked and secured his car. He let himself in, and after a quick hello, he continued to his front door. He used his security fob to gain access.

On entry, there was no acknowledgement of Kate. Although he was so tired, he had no idea of her rota. There was no sign of Abby either.

He kicked off his shoes and walked into the bedroom and to the wet room. He turned on the shower and slipped off his raincoat and jacket, letting them fall to the floor.

Without a second thought, he walked into the shower, fully clothed, and dropped to the floor, sitting directly under the torrent of water. He lifted his face from time to time; he thought it would allow all the disgusting experiences he had witnessed. To wash over his face and pour down the grid. It was after one occasion when he heard, "Carter?"

Abby received no reply to her call; she thought that was strange, for she'd noticed his car parked in a bay close to the block. She continued her search when she suddenly heard the shower.

Her immediate thought was to strip off and join him; she peered into the wet room and found Carter fully dressed and sitting on the shower floor. She stood back and raised both hands to her face, in complete shock.

She knelt on the edge of the rubber floor of the wet room. Leaning forward, she took hold of his hands. Smiling, she said, "Come on, love, stand up; let me take off your water-sodden clothes and dry you off."

He stood up, turned off the shower, and walked towards her. She walked over to the shelf with all the different sizes of towels and picked a bath sheet. She hung it on a hook at the side of the shower.

Carter just stood there like a drowned rat, totally dishevelled. Abbs took him in her arms, leaving herself soaked by her gesture, but she didn't care. Abby stripped him; it had no sexual connotation to it. She placed the towel around him and vigorously dried him off. When dry, she took hold of a towelling dressing gown hanging up behind the door, placing it around him.

She knew he liked walking around in bare feet. She gently escorted him to the lounge and sat him down on the settee. When comfortable, she stood up and walked over to a glass cabinet, took out a crystal Brandy decanter with the ornate stopper and poured him a large measure into a crystal glass.

She returned to Carter and gently offered it to him; he took it in both hands, taking a swallow. He then sat with the empty glass on his knee; Abby refilled it, suggesting, "Same again?"

Abby sat beside him and, in a sympathetic voice, whispered, "Was it that bad?" He smiled, "Yes, I'm afraid, so you see, I can't ever understand man's inhumanity to man. This morning, the simple act of kissing you goodbye after a special night and morning of delight, a matter so normal, why not? But I'd been instructed and attended at a murder...using the word so liberally, for it was a horror."

"Now, Abby, in the day-to-day scheme of things, we've only known each other a short time, and as such, if I were to explain my job to you, with all its various foibles, such as the issues of today's events, it may chase you off?"

Abby sat back, "Well, Carter, that bridge has to be crossed, either now or later in our relationship; you can't hide behind it, for you'll make yourself ill; you need a release mechanism."

Carter was silent for a couple of minutes; he took a slug of brandy and began, from being called out to the events in the mortuary, explaining the process, but downplayed the details.

On completion, he got up and poured Abby a drink; he offered it to her, and he noticed that she was shaking.

Abby looked at him, "Carter, this hasn't been the first in your career, and it won't be your last horrendous case, but I do hope they're not the order of the day?"

Carter burst out laughing. My pathologist, Gordon Chambers, is on record as saying to members of my team, why on earth did Carter pick the police as a career? I have a hatred of dead bodies and horrific murder scenes. A matter unbeknown to my team. Alas, it's crap, for they all know, but too polite to comment?"

He got up and hugged her, saying, "Abbs, we're dealing with a serial killer?" "Thank you, Abbs, but just let the dust settle; whilst I don't want to pour scorn over the issues, it's my job and career; I'm classed as a senior line officer who leads a team of handpicked officers, and it comes with the package."

"You may have heard of the 'Major Crime Unit' Well, that is my unit. In all the macabre cases, we deal force-wide, taking the workload from off the shoulders of divisional CID officers, leaving them to deal with the more moderate crimes."

Abby was full of respect for Carter, realising the pressures he must be working under. After several hours of talking, Carter decided that Abby had shown a committed attitude to his career, showing no bad effects but the opposite, laying a firm foundation for their relationship.

After an in-depth conversation, Abby decided to make a light tea for Carter. He welcomed sandwiches and a bowl of crisps. During this time, they both enjoyed two glasses of wine.

After their tea, she took hold of him, "Well, Mr It's bad for you, and I'll join you after my quick shower.

Abby walked through to the bedroom with a towel pulled up under her arms and secured in her front. She walked over, busily drying her hair with a hand towel.

She stood at her side of the bed. Letting the towel fall to the floor, Carter pulled back the duvet and got into bed. She snuggled up to him and lay her head on his chest, placing her right leg over his right thigh, pulling herself closer to him.

After several minutes, Abby heard the shallow breath of Carter, who had fallen fast asleep. She remained in a place like a statue, and eventually, the cloak of sleep slowly drifted over her.

22

The following morning, they woke still in each other's arms. They kissed and hugged, lingering, basking in the warmth of their love, enabling them to spend the maximum time before jumping up to take their shower. Eventually, they got out of bed and left for the bathroom. It wasn't to be their usual exotic episode, and both realised that a general shower would suffice.

When dried and dressed, they walked through to the kitchen, where Abbs made two mugs of coffee. It was over their coffees that Abbs looked at Carter. "Carter, do you mind if I ask you a personal question?" He smiled, "Was it my sleep pattern during the night?"

Abbs, in surprise, answered, "Why, yes, you frightened the life out of me with your kicking and squirming about the bed, with continuous verbal mutterings, while soaked in sweat. I wrapped my towel that I dropped at the side of the bed around you, then when you began to relax, I wrapped myself around you, hoping that the warmth of our bodies would eventually dry you?"

Carter, in a serious voice, commented, "Yes, I know it's rather disconcerting on the first occasion, but when under pressure or a particular case similar to yesterday, I tend to suffer night tremors."

Abbs placed her mug on the kitchen worktop. She walked over to him and hugged him tenderly. "I understand love; now I know they won't frighten me ever again?"

Outside by their cars, Carter kissed Abby goodbye, promising to ring her later in the day, particularly if he would be late.

When Abbs was driving to work, her mobile activated; she pressed the hands-free button, "Carter, are you all right?" He laughed, *"Yes, I'm fine. I just thought I'd call you to thank you for all your concern and understanding. Plus, to mention how remis it was of me for not commenting on how beautiful you looked on leaving for work?"*

Abbs laughed, "Why, Carter, you're such a generous man with your comments; thank you, speak later?"

Carter continued his journey to work. He nodded his head up and down, commenting, *'Yes, yes, Carter, that will earn you some brownie points?'*

On arrival at Derby Lane, he spritely ran up the back stairs to the general office. He entered the office with a smile, stating, "Morning, everyone, how are things?" He continued his path towards the desk diary. He signed on duty, then suddenly turned with enthusiasm. "Yes, Eric, if you're asking, I'd love a wonderful mug of coffee?" With a wide grin, he slapped his hand on Eric's desk and deposited himself opposite.

"Eric stood up, "Help, help call the police. Who is this man, and what have they done with our guv, having replaced him with this look alike?" All present in the office, team members and office staff alike, all fell about laughing.

Sue entered the office at that precise moment, "Well, morning, everyone, we all seem ready for yet another day at the coal face?" Eric interrupted, "Alas, boss, we seem to have lost the guv and have this specimen as a replacement?"

Carter was still laughing when Sue looked closely at him, walking about him, looking him up and down simultaneously, "I think you're right, for this model is far too happy. let's get rid and try and find our old Mr.

Grumpy?" The place was in an up raw. Carter stood up, "Enough, enough; I feel that some people don't have enough to be getting on with?"

He stood up, and with coffee in hand, he said, "Susan Marth Ford, will you please oblige me with your presence in my office?" He turned and left. Sue stood up to hear Eric singing in a jovial voice, *"Who's in the ssshit?"* Sue frowned, "The guv meant you, Mr. Morton?" She turned and left.

When in his office, she sat at his conference desk adjacent to his desk. "Sue, do you have the letter retrieved from the victim?" She replied, "Yes, Carter." She leaned down and took out an evidence bag from her briefcase.

Carter put on a pair of rubber gloves; opening the bag, he retrieved the letter. He placed it flat down on his desk and began to read...

'Due to the lack of coverage in the news media, I do not have the designated name of any senior officer investigating these proceedings...?'

My victim: Bernard Rollings - Paedophile

To whom it may concern: I presume by now that you've found my latest victim; due to stripping him, I left no place to hide this latter, yet the eventual location, which I found somewhat appropriate, leads you to the type of sick bastard this excuse for a man was...?

Carter looked at Sue, "Precise and yet to the point, suggesting the man's sexual preferences?" He looked at his watch, "It's 9.30 am. Are all present for the scrum down?" Sue replied, "Yes, Carter, Jim has been busy, and I've had Eric make copies of the letter for the team."

Entering the conference room, it all started with the team standing to attention. Without any reaction, Carter continued walking to the front of the room.

He suddenly stopped in his tracks, looking at a series of photographs on two whiteboards. Sue sat on one of the vacant chairs. He looked down at her and whispered, "Oh!

no, you don't, this is your show." Carter turned and waved his arms and hands forward, "Superintendent Ford."

Sue stood up; she coughed. "I see Lloydie. You've been busy before I call on Lloydie. The information to date, the body of a male was found secured to a beam in a derelict garage in Rudyard Road, coal yard."

"Now I know you all have a copy of the letter provided by the offender, which implies the fact that our victim may be a paedophile?" She smiled, "Lloydie."

Jim stood up, "Thank you, boss." He walked over to the whiteboards. "I know that certain team members had a direct part in the initial investigation, and the SOCO pictures are second nature, but for the remaining team members, I will explain."

"<u>Photograph one</u> - "This is the actual way that we found the victim's body—a white male tied and secured to an old wooden beam wrapped in a continuous length of barbed wire. Before the wire, Mr Chambers found that the victim was initially secured to the beam by means of his hands, arms, and ankles tied behind him. The victim was alive but perhaps drugged at the time?"

"<u>Photograph two</u> – This shows the victim at the mortuary, the retched post removed by Mr Chambers's assistants at the mortuary. The likes of which were witnessed by the GUV. Mr Chambers obviously needed to remove the barbed wire from the victim. Now, it is understood that he couldn't just pull it off.

"Mr Chambers decided that together with a colleague, to commence, armed with wire cutters, they'd cut halfway up the side of the victim to cause less damage to his skin. Working in unison while the victim was lying on his back on the PM table. Cut the wire, thus lifting the wire from off the top side of the victim's body.

"<u>Photograph three</u> - A process repeated when the victim was placed on his front. All pieces of wire were placed on a nearby rubber-topped table for possible D&A evidence if needed."

"<u>Photograph four</u> – Reveals the victim after the wire had been removed, clearly showing the victim exposed."

Before he sat down, he continued, I wish to point out, in case you have not noticed, that the offender placed several layers over his eyes and mouth, making a special point of causing damage to the victim's penis so severe it was nearly, please, excuse the pun, dismembered." (Police gallows humour)

"Mr Chambers has taken blood to seek if the victim had been drugged before the commission of the offence, to prove the same MO.

The mention of drugs relates to why a 6'-2" well-built white male remains standing, allowing some sick bastard to overpower him, then tie him up and wind the barbed wire about him. We await the results?"

"I fingerprinted the victim, and results from MER/cro identify him as Bernard Rollings; he is on the SOR (sexual offenders' registrar) and a gobsmacking point; he was one of the paedophiles, mentioned in the 'Evil Room's ledger?"

"In closing, I 'd like to point out that the guv attended at the mortuary and didn't flinch once."

Lloydie sat down to a round of applause.

Sue stood up, thanking Jim as she walked to the front of the team. "Right, let's just look at matters, Wilkinson, a well-known drug dealer in the community. The three victims at the golf club, working as pimps, known in the community?"

"Now, Bernard Rollings comes to the fore, due to the series of sexual offenders dealt with in The Magistrates court, and committed to the Crown Court, for a plea., He pleads guilty and sentenced to four years, possibly out in two, the contents of which are fully mentioned in the national and local press."

Carter's face became profoundly serious, "It doesn't take rocket science to home in on the fact that we as a team dealt with 40 plus paedophile offenders, all of whom were recorded in that *'Ledger.'*"

Sue continued, "I will leave all the evidence on the boards, for we now have three cases. Dr Sam Watson specified the needed quoter to declare a 'serial' offence.' We have a total of 5 victims. The offender sees himself as a 'vigilante' should maters continue to multiply, the press will have a field day."

She smiled over the team, "Now I wish for inquiries to be continued on all three cases but be prepared to drop matters should we receive yet another case. Now be off with you, I think; lunch is the order of the day?"

23

After the scrum down, Carter looked at Sue and smiled. He left, returning to his office. While sitting behind his desk, he looked at his watch; it was 12.30 pm. He took out his mobile phone and called Abbs.

"Carter, what a lovely surprise; I hope you realise that you've just interrupted my perfect dream with a gorgeous hunk of mankind?" Carter initiated an urgent excuse, "Ring me when finished, as I'm ringing to invite you out to lunch?" He waited a matter of seconds, *"Carter, Carter, wait..."* It was too late he'd gone.

A matter of seconds elapsed when his phone rang. "Carter," *"Yes, Carter, I'd love to join you for lunch?"* "Are you sure, for I'd hate to interrupt your dream with your hunk?" Carter replied.

Over lunch, Carter looked at Abs; it was while they were sat in Toms that Carter muttered, "Well, who is this hunk? Did you tell him that your poor excuse of a boyfriend is a police officer?"

"Abbs blushed, "Actually, Carter, I don't know if I've known you long enough?" She whispered, "I was experiencing a perfect wet dream about you and that you're the hunk, and you bloody interrupted me?"

They both laughed; Carter muttered, "Abbs, at home tonight, do tell me where you were up to, and we'll complete matters?"

Abbs looked at Carter, "Well, how were matters at the office? Do you feel better?" He breathed, "Been involved in a scrum down all morning…" He noticed a blank look on her face?"

"A *'scrum down'* is an affectionate term used as a meeting held in a special conference room. In that place, 'what's said in the room remains in the room.' We, 'laugh together and cry together, no question of rank, in any formal sense, even in respect of my boss, Commander Tony Frost?"

Abbs looked at Carter, "I can well imagine that all of that was you're doing, and your team respected you all the more for it?"

While both enjoyed their lunch, Carter looked at Abbs, "Have you moved all your clothes and personal items into the flat? As I'd like to make matters permanent?"

Abbs replied, "Yes, Carter, I wanted to explain to you that senior bank members of single marital status are given a flat until they find a permanent residence. What is the main purpose behind living in the bank's property? Why? It's convenient. So, you are asking me to move in with you; I have no property matters; I just inform the bank of my new address?"

"The bank has this policy, such as when either promoted or moved to help in a senior management problem, you're told, and they pay all the moving costs, so you see, I have no restrictions?"

Back at the general office, Carter signed back in. Lloydie was in the office at the time. "Guv, have you a minute?" With coffee in hand, Carter smiled, "Of course, Jim, ask the boss to join us?"

Minutes later, there was a knock on his office door. He called, "Come in." His door opened, and Sue and Jim walked in. He looked up, "Please take a seat."

He looked at Jim, "Well, Jim, what do you have for me?" He looked at them both. "Mr Chambers sent his regards and has supplied a verbal resume in relation to the Rollings matter while we await the formal report."

"The victim had been tied and secured to the bean. The victim was a reasonably tall and well-built man who would not just stand there while being secured at the beam. It is thought that he'd been drugged, which the necessary blood sample will confirm?"

"Fingerprint details have identified the victim, as previously explained, but more importantly, Rollings is a known paedophile and on the sexual offender's register."

Jim looked at Carter, "Guv, I think we're going to have a problem for all the accused parties dealt with in the Maggie's and or the Crown Court. The accused's names and addresses were mentioned in the press, what if?" Carter interrupted Lloydie.

"Jim, you more than most know we don't play the *'what if'* game; it's all or nothing; if our culprit has in any way got hold of details from the ledger, then yes, we're in the proverbial shit."

"I know it's a waiting game, so for that reason, I'm about to ring TF, and I'm putting the phone on speaker."

"Frost," "Sir, it's Carter, *"Well, what can I do for you?"* "Sir, it's rather like this: our latest victim has been identified by fingerprints as one, Bernard Rollings, you know, the victim of the barb wire case, "Yes, Carter, *get on with it?"* Carter thought to himself, well, you impatient bugger, you'll like this.

He smiled to himself. "Well, Sir, Bernard Rollings is one of 40 paedophiles arrested during the 'Evil room case.' He was named in a ledger as being someone who paid St Vincent's Catholic school money for services involved with children. As you know, the case received full coverage by the press at your instruction?"

Carter looked over at Sue and Lloydie, who sat opposite in total shock. The next noise the three heard was a sudden growl, *"Carter, get your arse down to my office and bring Ford with you."* The phone went dead.

Sue noticed that Carter had a smirk on his face. She looked at him, "Why me? What the fuck have I done wrong?" "Sue, remember the famous adage, *"When you fall in the shit, always try to cover as many people as possible?"*

24

Carter mentioned to Eric his intended destination. As they signed out, Eric looked at Carter, "Guv, do you remember in earlier times, when on receipt of such a command, it was suggested that you stuff blotting paper down your trousers?"

The whole general office was in tears of laughter, including the culprit, Eric. But most of all, Carter and Sue immediately remembered earlier days in which Carter informed people of his days in school when the blotting paper was used to deaden the pain from the cane in days gone by so fondly.

They both decided to go in the same car, Carters. Sue looked at him, "Carter, are you, or we, both in the shit?" He smiled, "Sue, how often do we get to tell TF he's in the wrong?"

"We were both present in TF's office when the Gainsford case had finally been dealt with and the court proceedings completed. TF jumped up, stating, "Well, Carter, do you mind if we now go to press?" He had not thought of the defendants, the majority of which received punitive jail sentences, all being placed on the sexual offender's registrar."

He continued, "Say our perpetrator got his hands on any of the information relating to the paedophile offenders, then he'd just wait, for even after their pilfering jail sentences and their home addresses mentioned in court. All out there for all to witness."

"Now, there is no way that TF will hold his hands up due to his over-exuberance of the press release?"

On arrival at HQ, they both showed their IDs, proceeded to the lift, and continued up to the top floor. The lift doors opened, and TF's secretary, Jane, looked up at Carter and smiled but was rather disappointed to see that he wasn't alone but with Sue. After recognition, she gestured for them to go straight in.

On entering, they both laid eyes on TF, standing leaning against his desk, with Wendy Field, the police PR director, sitting to his right. "Come in, you pair." He snorted, "And sit yourselves down."

He looked at Carter, "Now, what's all this about your latest victim and the connection with the Gainsford case?" Carter re-iterated all that he'd previously mentioned before receiving the official command. TF blurted, "Well?"

Carter thought, is this going to result in my resignation? Carter looked at him.

"Sir, it is self-evident that Rollings is a paedophile. His name and details were recorded in the ledger as a regular customer, kept by those despicable staff members at St Vincent's Roman Catholic school."

Carter continued, "As you're aware, we recovered that very ledger, consequently arrested some 40 offenders. "Now, sir, your good self-wanted the whole business opened to the press. To Herold, yet another result for the MCU (Merseyside), the need to prove a consistent conviction record, above all the other MCUs in the country?"

Carter sat down, but not before noticing the total look of horror on the faces of Wendy Field and Sue.

All three sat back, awaiting the toxic splurge.

They were all surprised when TF walked to his office door. He opened it, "Jane, can we have four coffees, one black for his Lordship?" She replied, "Certainly, sir."

The wait for their coffees was spent in uncomfortable silence. Eventually, they received their coffees.

They all looked at TF, and he interrupted, "Okay, okay, but you must admit it's not just my over-exuberance for press coverage for the MCU. But it was, surely, the arrests of the paedophile offenders mentioned in that disgusting ledger. All of which received varying custodial sentences, making it exceedingly difficult to record their release?"

Carter, using a rather sarcastic tone of voice, expressed, "Sir, what you fail to recognise, the press pack, having been granted carte blanche, itemised the full details of the paedophile offenders when in court."

He continued, "All their details were exposed. All quoted in the press. In one case, in the judge's submission, he implied that they'd all become pariahs in the community. Now some may have moved after their release, and others may have returned home, to blatantly re-locate, under the radar of shame, after their release from prison?"

TF looked at Carter, "Did the offenders appear in groups, for I seem to remember that the CPS tried to object to the number of prisoners appearing before the Maggie's and the Crown courts?"

Carter just stared at him, "Sir, because of the listings and the time to deal with each prisoner, it was decided to proceed in groups."

TF said, "Christ, please tell me that this bastard hasn't all the offender's details?"

Carter looked at his boss, "Well, sir, we only need to wait for our next victim, or victims, for your reply. Identification of the victim will answer your question?" He coughed. "But we can't second guess, as our protagonist may choose a different prey?"

TF looked at Carter, "Are you declaring a serial case?" Carter replied, "Well, we have three cases and some 5 victims; you were present when Dr Sam Watson gave her lecture on what constitutes a serial case?"

TF looked at Wendy and Sue, "Ladies, what is your impression of all of this?"

Wendy looked at him, "Sir, I was at the crown court on the first day of the Gainsford trial. I can only say that both Chief Superintendent Carter and Superintendent Ford needed all the protection offered by DI Charlie Wilson and DI Kate Davies, mainly from over-exuberant members of the press; it was a near riot?"

"One such reporter was so defiant that he was forcefully removed for his violent actions. The problem is a total lack of information on the case. Now I know Gainsford only killed priests, teachers, and a social worker, all of whom worked at the terrible school."

Wendy continued, "It would seem our latest serial killer is indiscriminate with his victims; the only common denominator, they are all males. Our problem will occur when witnesses keep on finding the bodies, not just dog walkers?"

TF asked Wendy Field, "Miss Field, off the record, which is the least line of resistance, a press release explaining matters to date, or to do nothing and wait to see what happens?"

Wendy turned quite serious as she looked at TF, "Sir, such decisions are for the Chief and you to make; I can, of course, type up a press release and show it to the Chief, yourself, and Carter. And await your decision?"

TF threw his arms in the air and then rested them behind his head, "You're no use to me...?"

He suddenly looked at Sue, "Det Supt Ford, what are your thoughts on the subject?" She took a deep breath, "Sir, my job is to support my guv, to deal with whatever the MCU undertakes, but always be aware of what effect an issue like this will have on the community."

Carter suddenly interrupted, "I know it's impossible to have a clear answer. For that's the circ's in which my team works?"

"I understand you won't accept it, but that's hard shit, for it's the *'what if'*s game that you don't like. Mistakes have a habit of covering the likes of me and my team in shit, which never seems to rise to this floor?"

As Carter finished, he failed to notice the look of horror on the faces of Sue and Wendy, for he was looking ahead at TF.

Tony Frost suddenly stood up; his face was crimson with rage. He quietly, under great control, mentioned, "Det Supt Ford and Ms Wendy Field, do you mind waiting outside? Ask Jane to make you a coffee?"

On leaving, Sue looked at Carter out of the corner of her eye, showing concern for Carter.

Outside TF's office, Jane looked up, expecting Carter to appear to be subjected to her sexual innuendos, but alas, he didn't appear. She looked up at both Sue and Wendy, "What, no, Carter?" Sue said, "No, but could we both have a coffee, please?"

At that precise moment, they heard TF's raised voice, even though the closed door. "Well, Mr., before we start, I wish to remind you of matters earlier this morning, your reporting of another victim, and my reaction to the information. If I ask you a fucking question, I expect a fucking answer, and not to have the phone put down on me?"

Sue turned and explained matters to Jane, who covered her face with her hands, saying, "Shit?"

Carter coughed, "Well, sir, if the gloves are off, I should perhaps contact you at the time of my visiting a murder site and not respect the time, particularly at 2.30 am."

"Sir, you were a seasoned detective and should realise that wishing to convey the circs to your boss is just relaying your urgent matters, for you're not in full command of the information. And not to be barked at by you on your reaction to yet another fucking murder is not my fucking fault. You must think I go around looking for shit jobs just to ring you up in the unearthly hours for fun?"

"This last one was the shittiest of all. The victim was bound naked to an old beam in a disused garage, then bound in barbed wire from head to toe in one single strand of barbed wire, concentrating on his eyes, mouth, and particularly massing about his penis, making a personal statement. The victim's body was leaking like a colander."

Seasoned officers showed utter revulsion. You should have seen my team's faces; even Gordon Chambers was suffering?"

"Now, over this present matter, we're not supplied with crystal fucking balls, and you are constantly asking for impossible answers is nothing short of fucking impossible. Now, sir, you may want to return to me, but I'm tired, and it's getting late. I, therefore, will leave matters in your capable hands for the way forward in these matters?"

Carter got up to leave, hearing TF shouting and bellowing, "Don't you dare leave, I'm not fucking finished with you; Carter turned, "Well, it's up to you, for sir, I'm fucking off?"

Outside in Janes's office, he was met by three women in a total state of shock. He turned to Sue, "Det Supt Ford, are you ready?" Sue, in a gliding motion, seemed to follow him to the lift.

25

The journey back to the office was in total silence, and Sue was in complete shock. Neither were aware of the force radio crackling like mad in the car.

A recognised message suddenly flashed over their car radio. *'Ch (The Home office call sign for the Merseyside police, control room.) to members of MCU attending at 'Jones's DIY' yard on Long Lane, Fazakerley, cadaver dog unit on the way.'* 'DI Baxter to CH, "Roger.'

Sue asked Carter, "Are you thinking what I'm thinking?" He looked at her, "Call Eric and see what you can discover?"

Minutes later, Sue closed the call and looked over at Carter. "Well, Eric received a phone call from the duty Inspector in the control room. He explained it's a case of suspicious circs?"

Sue continued, "Baxie, Julie, and Phil, who has eventually been re-instated, *'No case to answer.'*

"Baxie (DI Baxter's nickname) fielded the call; on arrival at the yard, they were directed to the open area at the back of the yard, which holds retail building supplies, to a location giving off a pungent suspicious smell that, showed a point of interest with the company security dogs?"

Carter leaned forward and pressed the blues and twos. He headed across the City towards Scotland Road and the A59, which, although rather busy, with Carter's driving skills, he managed to cut through the malingering traffic. Cutting through to Fazakerley. It took 20 minutes.

On arrival at the location, they pulled up short of the yard. Carter leaned forward and switched off the warning alarms. They quietly drove in and pulled up, displaying blue lights only.

Ian, with a look of surprise, smiled at his two senior officers, "Guv, how did you hear about this, he replied, "Fielded it on CH on our way back to the office; it raised a red flag with us both?"

Carter and Sue in their forensic suits. The team members were already suited and booted.

Carter looked at Ian, "Well, were, are we?" Ian replied, "This way, guv." They walked across the large outside courtyard full of the building equipment, with metal shelving holding concrete garden flags in different sizes and colours, concrete garden edges, and rolls of roofing felt. Around the walls were different styles of wooden garden fences and fencing posts, in both wood and concrete. There were three divisions, holding building sand, shale, and roller crushes.

Uniform officers were on the doors leading out into the yard of the main building and yard gates, acting as a deterrent to customers.

Ian stopped at an area at the back of the yard; it was untidy and used as a tip for returned purchases. Carter suddenly stopped, "Wow! yes, it truly honks?" He pulled up his mask and was equally grateful for Sues's habit of putting a smidgen of Vic in his mask.

At that very moment, the cadaver unit arrived. The officer, dressed in his forensic suit, went to the van's rear. Before opening the door, he said, "All officers in the suspected area, please move into the store area. As I want the search area to be as sterile as possible?"

He removed from his van with the most beautiful looking, 'Cocker spaniel' tan and white with a white chest, with a snub tail, wearing a harness. The dog obediently sat at his handler's feet, waving his tiny tail like mad, distorting his hind legs with excitement.

When his handler clipped on the lanyard, the dog knew he was about to start work. In a low voice, the officer said, "Jenny find."

The dog began to run around the yard, running up and down the shelf areas, sniffing like mad, as she made for the rear of the yard, Chris crossing as she went. The area of the returned items' tip suddenly heightened her attention. Jenny suddenly stood motionless, her nose pointing to the floor like a statue.

The officer called Carter via his mobile phone. "Carter." "Sir, Jenny is giving off a very positive vibe in the area of this tip, at the far end of the yard?" Carter replied, "Officer, is it alright to leave our location, in the shop, and come to join you?" The reply was, "Sir."

Carter looked at his team, "Come on, we're needed at a possible ID area?" They walked across the yard to join the officer and Jenny. On arrival, the officer said, "Guv Jenny showed a great deal of interest around this area. He waved his arm over the designated site."

He pointed to an area covered with several lengths of raffia matting on top of each other. Carter shouted for a member of the SOCO team to come over.

Carter turned to the dog handler, "Thanks for your help. Will it be all right to say hello to Jenny? The officer smiled, "Sir, when off duty, she's anybody's." Carter bent down and ruffled her short coat. The handler unclipped the tracer and threw Jenny her tennis ball, the usual payment for a good job done.

He heard, "Guv," One of the SOCO officers called. He walked over to where the request came from. On arrival, he turned, "Officer, are you not DS Wilson, a friend of DI Peter Wilkins, who's a member of the MCU?" He noticed a sparkle in her eyes, for she was wearing her elasticated hood and face mask; she replied, "Sir." He whispered, "Thank you, Lisa."

Sue walked over to meet him; with a grey pallor on her face, she whispered, "Carter, this is a really bad one?" and gently touched his arm."

The female SOCO officer pointed down to the tops of what appeared to be three old-fashioned grey-coloured tin baths parallel with each other. He noticed the elongated handles at the top end of each bath.

The officer removed some discarded matting to reveal the three baths, with what appeared to be three victims, one in each of the baths. He looked down on what was left of their faces, for each victim's face had been obliterated.

Carter whispered, "Has anyone been sent for Gordon Chambers and DI Lloyd?" Sue, who was leaning down by his side, again gripped his arm, "Yes, guv, they're on their way."

When Carter stood back, he pointed to a length of concrete. 'H' fencing post was laid across the first two baths, partially covering the victims. "A possible weapon used by the predator?" He noticed that at one end of the post bore what could only be described as an abundance of blood and bone fragments.

Carter suddenly stood up, pushed back his elasticated hood, and then pushed down his mask. He took in a big breath, eternally grateful to Sue for the usual...

He placed his hands on his hips and, in frustration, whispered, "The yard is locked and has security dogs to prevent theft, so how the hell does our perpetrator place three victims in those awful baths and commit such an audacious, God-awful offence?"

Ian, who had been standing close to Carter, said, "Guv, the delivery drivers could not get into the yard for work this morning; they found their key would not fit the lock?" Carter suddenly turned, "He, or they, cut the chain and replaced it with a new chain and lock. But what about the dogs?"

It was then that he heard the sudden outcry of Gordon Chambers's voice, "Ch Supt Carter, are you there?" Carter looked in his direction; he threw up his arms, "Gordon, we're over here." He then heard a sudden, "Ah, there you are, old son." The pathologist walked up to where the SOCO officers were working.

He winked at Carter, "I'll call you in after I've had a quick shifty around." Carter coughed, "Well, Gordon, I happen to know most things, for you see, because of the repellent smell, which had begun to interest the two-yard security dogs. The team cleared most people out, and DI Baxter sent for the cadaver unit."

"If you look over there by where the SOCO officers are working, you'll find three bodies identified by the cadaver dog. Found one in each of the three old-fashioned grey tin baths; we haven't moved anything until your arrival.

But I can further inform you that we found an approximately 5ft length of concrete fencing post laid across two of the three baths and victims. Potentially used to commit this horror?"

Carter walked alongside the pathologist; on arrival, nothing had been moved; he saw Lloydie standing close by. He acknowledged him.

Carter looked at Gordon, "Could I possibly prevail on you to allow Lloydie to take the relevant fingerprints, for we must identify the three victims; we need to know if they are on the sexual offenders register?" Gordon replied, "Certainly, old man, if it helps." Carter thanked him and walked away.

He returned to the group of officers and stood talking with Sue. He suddenly turned when he heard a call from Lloydie, "Guv, can I ask for assistance? We need to remove some of this discarded rubbish to remove the metal baths."

All present, even Carter, walked over to the site. On arrival, they all noticed that pieces of raffia matting had covered the victims in each bath.

Carter looked at Gordon Chambers, "Well, Gordon, how do you wish we should proceed? Gordon looked at Carter, "We've placed some lengths of plywood timber over the site to support any accidental falls of equipment, which may fall on the victims?" Carter sarcastically said, "They couldn't make matters worse?"

Gordon replied, "I need for the items, were possible, to be removed so we can get at the victims, before removal to the mortuary?"

Carter looked at Lloydie, who was attempting to gain the victim's fingerprints. Gordon stated, "As you are no doubt aware, Rigor Mortis enters the body at or about four hours after death, an important hint to establish a time of death?"

"Now let's, please get the poor victims out of those awful coffin-like enclosures so we can get them home, where I can stop second guessing?"

Carter looked at the pathologist, "Gordon, it's essential that I have a TOD; you see, why the hell didn't the dogs start barking when the perpetrator arrived? Why, I think they must have been drugged. He or they waited for the dogs to fall asleep. Cutting the padlock off the chain that secured the gates. Get in, do the task, and get out. Replace the chain with a new padlock and drive off. I need to know if it could be done in the time frame.

Gordon gasped, "I'd say that you're flying by the seat of my pants, but I'll be more certain on completion of the PMs?"

Carter looked at Ian, "What time do the drivers begin work?" "Guv, they start early at 8am to load up and get out on their rounds?"

Carter stood for a minute thinking he suddenly erupted, "Let's just think a God darn minute, "If the dogs were drugged, say at 8 or 9pm…Ian interrupted, "Guv, the manager found that the place was in darkness; when he came to work, all the yard lights were out."

Carter looked at Ian, "Get SOCO to search under the positions of the yard lights to see if they find any shards of glass. I also want you to ask the manager if we can arrange for the security dogs to be drug-assessed. Organise a vet to obtain blood samples; I want everyone on it?" He replied, "Yes, guv before you ask, they knackered the CCTV."

26

Carter walked over towards Sue; he smiled, "Gordon has allowed Lloydie early access to the victims, permitting Lloydie to obtain their fingerprints, plus suggesting a possible TOD at approximately 10pm.

"Let's leave matters with SOCO and return to the office; on our way back, I'll call TF." Sue looked sheepishly at him. He said, why the sorrowful look, I'm a man, not a mouse?"

With the help of his hand's free equipment, he punched in TF's name. *"Frost."* "Sir, it's Carter." He heard a sudden raw, *"Well, what do you want?"* "I thought I'd inform you of yet another case. Three victims have been found dead, each in an old grey tin bath, covered over by returned stock."

"The use of the cadaver unit identified the actual victims."

"I've asked Gordon Chambers to allow DI Lloyd to obtain the victim's fingerprints, for we must identify if they're possible paedophiles. If so, it makes 4 such victims. But in this case, he has increased the anti, as he has obliterated all evidence of their faces, using a concrete fence 'H' post."

TF whispered, *"Well, he must know that we have the wherewithal to identify not just the victims but their sexual addiction, so why not remove their hands as well?"*

There was a silence, and he coughed, "Sir, I believe the security dogs were drugged, and the searchlights and the CCTV were crippled." *"Carter, your perpetrator seems to go to any lengths regarding the site; I can only assume that the conditions were horrendous; please offer my respects to all participating officers."*

Carter closed the call. Sue screamed at him, "Carter! you've just put the phone down on him?" He looked at Sue, "He's a supercilious bastard; he bollocks me for calling without all the info while I'm just informing h him of a job? Now he states that this present job must have been awful, and please offer my blar, blar, blar. He was getting on my nerves."

On arrival at Derby Lane, he parked up in the police yard. They both made their way up to the general office. After saying their hello's, they both signed back in.

Handed a mug of coffee, "Eric looked at them both, "Well, it doesn't take rocket science, for I can tell by your faces that conditions were diabolical at the site. I received an update from Lloydie, who is on his way to the mortuary."

Carter took hold of his coffee and, prior to leaving, asked Sue, "Why don't you inform Eric of the result of our meeting with TF?" He turned and left for his office. Sue looked at Eric, who in turn said, "Now, Susan, less of the suspicious looks." "Oh! Eric, are you not interested?" He replied, "No, no, no, you'll get your fingers burnt."

Sue then set about telling Eric of the meeting with TF. And how Carter dipped (slang for closing a call on someone) the phone call with TF.

While in his office, Carter looked at his watch; it was 3.30pm. He thought, 'Christ, Abby.' He used his mobile, *"Well, hello, I was beginning to give up hope, wondering if you'd lost my number. Have you been busy?"*

Carter replied, "Yes, Abbs, and it's not over yet; while I realise my call is rather late, there is a reason, matters due to a meeting with my boss, when leaving his office in a temper, for Derby Lane. On our way, we fielded yet another job in relation to our present case, and the days are not over yet. I have an appointment with the pathologist."

Abbs sighed, *"Please don't worry, Carter, just phone on leaving, and I'll have a surprise waiting for you?"* She giggled, *"Love you."* and closed the call.

Carter sat back, looking at his phone, and he spluttered, "Yikes." His phone suddenly activated. He looked at the caller ID and noticed, 'Lloydie.' "Hello Jim, what can I do for you?" *"Well, Guv, it's Mr. Chambers who wishes to see you?"* "On my way."

Carter got up and left for the general office. On his arrival, he looked at Sue, "Well, Susan Martha, did you tell him?" As he went to sign out for the mortuary, he noticed Eric's face. He looked at Carter, "The man's a loon?" Carter, with a degree of benignity, looked at him, "Yet still, he's, my boss."

Eric replied I hope you're that understanding when he calls about you putting the phone down on him?" Carter replied, "I can't stand irregularity."

"I'm off to the mortuary, Susan Martha. Do you have a problem, for you look as if you've just been told off?" One of the secretaries suddenly snorted down her nose.

"I wonder if, Susan, you may wish to join me?" There was a sudden deluge of excuses from Sue, "Guv, I'm good; I have reports to read and see to?"

As Carter signed out, he smiled, "Depending on my time at the mortuary, I'll sign off duty with the control room." He turned and left.

Eric laughed, "If he only knew what you're up to, he'd have insisted on your company." The office burst out with laughter.

27

On arrival at the hospital mortuary, Carter parked up as usual and completed the necessary protocol with the entry system. He received the usual curt reply, *"Yes."* He replied, "Ch Supt Carter, and held up his ID to the CCTV camera.

He heard the usual *'click.'* He pulled on the door to be welcomed by Lloydie, dressed in his scrubs and white coat, with a mask resting below his chin. "Guv, Eric called, informing me of your visit." He followed Lloydie down the mind-numbing cold corridor. No matter how many times he walked the same corridor, it never ceased to upset him.

A female technician handed Carter a set of scrubs, a white coat, a mask, and rubber gloves. He turned and thanked her, readying himself to greet Gordon.

At the end, he saw Gordon, dressed in his usual pathologist uniform, with a file under his arm. He shouted his usual greeting, "Carter, pleased to see you, old chap. "Walk this way, and Carter, before you say anything, I was a medical student for 5 years." And he roared with laughter.

In the PM room, Carter noticed the three covered bodies, each illuminated by the large overhead theatre light. He also noticed there were the usual body shapes under the rubber covers, except no shape for where their heads should be.

Gordon looked at him, "Are you ready, old man?" Carter just nodded. Gordon, together with Lloydie and a technician, removed the white rubber sheets down to their chests. He noticed that green cloths had been placed over the victims' despicable injuries. Carter knew what to expect, for he'd had prior notice. Carter looked at Gordon, "Please remove the cloths?"

With a belligerent look on his face, Gordon removed the three green cloths. After a couple of minutes, Gordon coughed, "Carter, the victims have truly little or no trace of their faces. You will notice that there are certain evidential characteristics and indentations on parts of their epidermis that we found. Left by the concrete oval shape to the top of the posts?"

He explained, "The top of the posts, looking from the top, you'll notice a square, with an oval top, with two inlets allowing fences to be held in place, giving the 'H' post look. Looking down on the victims, you will notice partial indentations on their remaining epidermis."

Carter looked at Gordon, "Yet again, we have victims found in locations where one does not just lay in a discarded bath and allow their faces to be battered? Can one state that the offences were committed in the baths, or were they killed elsewhere and placed in the baths?"

He then lifted the left arm of the first victim. With his rubber-gloved finger, he pointed to what appeared to be a black-coloured needle site, it's the same on all three?"

"I've taken blood for traces of any similarity as to the drug used for matching on your other victims. Body fluids, as usual, but whilst at the scene, I was unable to make the usual examination from their eyes, etc.; I will know a lot more after their subsequent PMs?" He coughed, "Death was at about 10pm. and change?"

"Carter, I feel sure that due to the state of the murder scene, the copious amounts of blood found inside of each of the baths, all three were alive prior to the impact of the murder weapon?" Carter looked at Gordon, "I have a theory the perpetrator, or perpetrators, rigged the yard gates, possibly drugged the dogs, and dealt with the CCTV and lights?"

Carter could see by the clock in the PM's room that it was 6.30pm. He looked at Gordon, "Have you finished with me?" He smiled," Yes, Carter, you have your work cut out; how about some post-visit medicine?" He then roared with laughter.

Carter smiled, but he reneged, "Sorry, Gordon, I've other places to be. Will speak again tomorrow undoubtedly?" And left.

Gordon Chambers smiled at Jim. Your guv has other matters on his mind; I do hope I haven't messed things up?" They both burst out laughing.

28

On his way home, he called the control room and booked off duty from the mortuary.

Carter arrived home 20 minutes later; after his acknowledgement to the night concierge, he continued his way to his flat door. He was about to enter when the door suddenly opened. Abbs greeted Carter. After closing the door…

Carter walked up to her; Abby felt his arms draped around her like a large blanket under which he began to caress her. Her breasts, although over her clothes and her bottom manipulating her body, began to start a wonderful feeling of sexual delight.

Abby leaned her head on his shoulder and whispered in his ear, "Oh, Carter, that's totally disgusting; you do realise if you continue, I will come here in the hall. Stop, and let's strip off and continue in the shower?"

She stood in front of him and began to undress him. It wasn't frantic but slow and deliberate. Carter reciprocated, his warm hands set about the task; he pondered on the removal of her bra, concentrating on her breasts and nipples. She screamed, "Carter, did you not hear what I said…

After their shower, in which they both derived so much up built sexual feelings, they both felt like a pair of pressure cookers that if the pressure were not released in the normal way, they'd both explode. With a heightened breath, Carter leaned down and whispered in Abby's ear,

"Do you wish to continue to deal with afters in bed tonight?

After their shower, Carter, who Abbs had nearly drowned, said, "It's a good job we continued; what we do in bed will be equally as enjoyable." Later, dressed in shorts and a T-shirt, Abbs, dressed in a small white tank top and white cotton drawstring trousers, both walked through to the kitchen in bare feet.

Abby said, "Carter, why don't you sit at the breakfast bar said, "What would you like for tea?" She immediately noticed the glint in his eyes. "Carter, that is on another menu for later."

Due to his day, Carter was in no mood for food. Abbs challenged him, stating, "But Carter, you must eat, perhaps a cold meat sandwich, with a bowl of either chips or less filling crisps?"

Carter whispered, "Whichever is the quicker, for Abbs, don't think I'm desperate, but all I want is to lay next to you in bed or anywhere. I feel that any mere point of contact would help me forget my overview of this bloody awful day. The shower helped, but I need contact with you?"

After tea and after a couple of glasses of wine, Abbs stood and left their used dishes and glasses on the coffee table. She took Carter's hand and led him off to the bedroom.

In the bedroom she undressed Carter, leaving him in only his undershorts, and after pulling back the duvet, placed him in bed. Abbs quickly slipped out of her clothes and popped into bed next to him.

At their point of contact, Carter let out a long sigh. "Abbs, if I go through life never having experienced such delights, I'll be the poorer man for it, for one can lie here and mention plaudits of adjectives relating to your good self. But at the end of the day, I don't care, for it's me that looks upon you?"

Abbs looked up at him, "Carter, please, you do not need to worry on that point or show signs of vulnerability. For it's what you and only you see."

He whispered, "Abbs, these similar thoughts I do hope are replicated throughout my team, for I would so much hate for them to return home alone after the issues witnessed today. Each having partners who offer such valuable support, for at times under such conditions, one would be lost."

He leaned down and kissed her passionately on her lips; after several seconds, she pulled away, taking in a deep breath, "Wow, Carter, kisses such as that are welcome all day long. Now, please lay back and let me hold you and comfort you. Carter fell fast asleep. Abbs pulled up the duvet, placed her right leg across his thigh and right arm over his chest, and fell fast asleep.

The following morning, Carter awoke and, looking down on Abbs, noticed the lightness of her breathing. She was on her back, normally the recipe for snoring, but not Abbs.

He lightly began to blow onto her face; her mouth began to swivel quickly from left to right, causing her nose to twitch. He stopped for a couple of seconds and began again, which repeated the same reaction. He thought, 'Carter, you're a bloody nuisance; stop it.'

Carter noticed that Abbs started to fidget about in reaction to his messing around; he immediately noticed that the duvet had slipped down to reveal Abby's shapely breasts.

He leaned down and began to kiss her nipples; at first, there was no reaction, and then suddenly, her two hands came up, clasping each of her breasts. He quickly drew back in surprise.

There was a sudden cry of fright, "Oh, Carter!" Followed by a sudden cry of relief, knowing it was only him. "I'm so sorry, for I was half asleep and it was such a surprise to me.

Now that I'm awake, you can help yourself, and she pushed the duvet down to her waist.

Carter returned to the job at hand, knowing he was an idiot. He lowered his head onto her breast and nipples and, with his tongue, made circular movements, with the occasional nip and pull.

In retort, the more he did it, the more Abbs began to wind up to such a sexual passion that, in the end, she took hold of one of their pillows and placed it over her mouth and face. Enabling her to avoid sudden shrieks of delight.

Carter pushed the duvet down and off the end of the bed. While Abbs was getting over the effect of Carter's sexual attack on her breasts, his next action resulted in total sexual chaos.

Carter eventually placed a hand on each side of her body to support himself as he entered her, so naturally, it was like fingers fitting into a glove.

Abbs, muffled sounds of delight resounded into the pillow until, in the end, she lifted her legs and clasped them about his waist to increase penetration. Abbs placed her head on the nape of his neck and began to cry while kissing him profusely.

On completion, they both fell back to their side of the bed, out of breath and covered in a thin film of sweat. Eventually, Abbs pulled herself up and over onto his body, and the action was made all the easier by the abundance of sweat.

She looked up at him. "Carter, I've never met such a person like you, on the one hand, a very senior police officer, who leaves in the middle of the night when called upon to deal with the most infamous of crimes and then has to continue, via attending at the city mortuary, before leaving for home."

She continued, "On the other hand, you're a man that totally appreciates a woman. I can't get over how well you know your way around a woman's body. Therefore, when asked, during one of our sexual episodes, I told you of my intimate thoughts, you weren't troubled by my honesty?"

Carter looked down at Abbs, "Women have rights, equal rights not only in the workplace but in a relationship. Even more so in the bedroom or shower, where we behave like mirror images?"

It was later in the shower that, as usual, they found it so natural to take part in all their encompassing mannerisms. Realising it was not one-upmanship, feeling never having to prove oneself.

On completion, they both dried and dressed for the day. When dressed, they went through to the kitchen; Abbs prepared their breakfast and two coffees.

"Abbs, I'll try to contact you at least sometime during the day, but please be patient, as I'll be walking into an office. Unfortunately, I can't use the 'Q' word. Outside, they kissed each other, and he left for the office.

29

On his arrival at the general office to sign on duty, he quickly became aware of a degree of excitement. He looked at Eric, "Why are matters ratcheted up a couple of degrees in the excitement stakes rather than the sloth-like usual first thing in the morning attitude?"

Eric looked at him, "Guv, I think you need to speak with Sue when she arrives?" Carter took his coffee and thanked him. "Please tell her to come through to my office?" He turned and left.

Within minutes, there was a sudden knock on his door. He called, "Come in." Sue, together with Lloydie, stood in his office doorway, both holding their mugs of coffee; they entered. He looked up, "Morning, Sue and Lloydie, "Well, there would seem to be an early morning buzz about the place; please explain?"

They both sat in a chair adjacent to his desk; Sue placed her coffee down and looked at him. "Sir, first, Lloydie has news for you?" He looked at Lloydie, "Jim, the floor is yours?"

"Guv, fingerprint evidence of the three victims appears to reveal we have the bodies of ex-Councillor Warren Brown, Doctor Malcolm Jones, and Matthew Jenkins, the care staff officer." All three had been placed on the sexual offenders register." Carter sat gobsmacked, "Well, although the three of them were disgusting members of society, no one deserves to perish in that way?"

He continued, "Did we find the usual evidence as in other cases?" Sue smiled, "Yes sir, Lloydie found a blood-stained plastic bag containing a letter. He has it and is going to explain matters in the conference room."

Carter smiled; now, Susan Martha, what can I do for you? Sue stood and squirmed. "Please don't go mad, but last night we got a call from the duty Inspector in the control room; I made the conscious decision not to disturb you?"

She took a deep breath, "A man, whilst walking his dog, at about 10.30 pm. Last night, called the three 9's, his initial comments, that he'd found a man tied to a concrete lamp post, alive, covered in copious amounts of writing, all over his head and naked body?"

"Uniformed patrols attended, and due to the subject matter or the theme of the writing, it was decided to call the 'on call' MCU officer. It was Jules. She called me, and due to your previous day's inquiries, and while this victim was alive, I made a Presidential decision?"

On arrival at the conference room, the whole team came to attention. Eric was standing in the general office. He waved his hand for silence. He placed a cupping hand over his ear. A hush came over the office. He leaned over towards the dividing wall of the conference room, listening to the sudden sound of the team. He turned, nodding his head, "Respect." He smiled as he sat back at his desk.

A new secretary to the team looked at Carol, and she whispered, "What on earth does he mean…?" Carol replied, "You'll see in time?"

Carter took his place at the top of the room, with Sue at his side. He said, "Please sit." He walked over to a series of SOCO photographs pinned on two whiteboards.

Photo 1: The picture of a white male tied to a street concrete lamp post. He noticed in black ink on the victim's forehead: My name is Paul Burke. I'm a 'STALKER.'

Photo 2: Showed the victim's name – Amanda Jenkins.

Photo 3: Showed in note detail; Ex-partner Jenkins finished with me after two years. Retaliated; Followed her in her car to work; Loitered outside her work address. Followed her home. Sent obscene photographs messages, all obtained as an ex-partner to social media, Facebook, Twitter, Instagram, Snapchat, and TikTok. Sent taxis, pizzas, and other meals. Deliveries of builder's sand, manure, smashed windows and put dog faeces through her letter box.

All the matters were written about his body, like tattoos, all evidential of the alleged offences. Carter looked at Sue, "If he was alive at the scene, where is he now?"

"Guv, the victim was taken to the Royal; he's in major obs." Carter looked at Sue, "We'll go in your car, but before leaving, I want to see Lloydie."

Lloydie walked over to him. He smiled, "Guv." Carter smiled, "Lloydie, can I leave matters with you in relation to the three paedophile victims and letter? I'll be back soon?" Lloydie replied, "Guv, call me, for I may be with Mr Chambers." Carter turned to join Sue.

In the general office, they both signed out, 'Now to the Royal' and left.

Carol, looking at the new secretary, whispered, "He's the boss, we all know it, but as a man, he shows so much respect from the loneliest constable on the beat to the Chief Con, and it's known the force over, the queue is round the block of officers wishing to join the team."

The A&E department was as chaotic as ever, with disgraceful bouts of swearing from the regular customers, constantly complaining of timely delays. Carter looked across the mayhem to see Chris Atkinson, the senior duty sister.

On seeing Carter and Sue, she smiled and raised her arms in the air in total frustration. They both walked over to Chris, who on arrival, welcomed them. Chris pointed to her office; when inside, she closed the door to all the abuse and mayhem.

She sat down behind her desk, letting out a large breath, at the end of which she stated, "Hot drinks?" Not wishing to open her office door, she lifted her phone, "Two coffees, one white with two sugars, one black with no sugar?" Chris heard a "Coo, "Ch Supt Carter, must be with you?" Chris whispered, "Nurse!"

Chris replaced her phone and smiled in Carter's direction. "Well, I may suggest that you're here to see 'Tattoo Man'?" At that very moment, Sue's mobile was activated. "Yes, Lloydie, what can I do for you?" "Boss, just to let you know, tattoo man is known at MER/cro as Paul BURKE, 30yrs. 21.11.92. 117, Menlove Avenue, Allerton, Liverpool L18."

"Sue thanked him. Lloydie, text me a copy of his form?" "Will do, boss." Sue looked at Carter, "Tattoo man is known to us."

Carter looked at Chris, "Where is Burke being kept, and is he fit for an interim interview?" Chris smiled, "Well, Carter, this must be unusual for you to have a live victim. Normally, they're land with Gordon Chambers?"

"Medically, Burke shows signs of having been drugged; we found a puncture wound high up in the creases of the skin of his left arm; we also found a trauma wound to the back of his head. Bloods have been taken to identify the drug used."

At present, he has been omitted and is languishing in 'major obs.' He is under uniform protection." Carter smiled, "Can we see him?" Chris replied, "Fifteen minutes?"

Both Carter and Sue followed Chris to 'major obs. On arrival, it was quite clear as to Burke's location, as they both saw the uniformed officer sitting outside his bay.

On arrival, the uniform officer, in recognition of Carter, immediately stood to attention. Carter smiled, "Relax, officer. Are you from 'A' division *(Uniform officers used to have their division letter on all their shoulder epaulettes of their uniforms, but in 1975, matters changed, and now have a number commensurate with their joining date, which made it difficult to identify their divisions?)*

Carter looked at Sue, "Will you please contact the office and have a member of the MCU relieve this officer?" She smiled and left to make the call.

Carter and Sue stood at the foot of Burkes, medical trolly. Carter realised it took both Sue and him an immense effort not to burst out laughing. It put Carter's mind in recognition of a medical study head, which showed and named segments of the brain, yet in Burke's case, his alleged area of complaint.

Carter coughed; Burke looked over. "Well, who are you two, for I'm sick to fuck in talking to everyone. He looked down at Burke, "Well, I'm Chief Superintendent Carter, and this is my colleague, Detective Superintendent Ford, both of the 'Major crime unit.' Burke laughed as he leant back on his arms behind his head, "Am I meant to be impressed?"

Sue thought, "Oh shit." Carter took out his phone and began to take photographs of Burke. He screamed, "What the fuck, I've had countless photographs already?" Carter turned to him, "Well, Burke, those will have been taken by SOCO scenes of crime officers?" He lied, "I'm not in receipt of them at present, and I'm leaving for a meeting." He whispered, but loud enough for Sue and Chris to hear. "After my time spent here with a little shit like you?"

Burke spluttered, "You can't talk to me like that?" Carter replied, "Like what, now, shut up and tell what you remember of this matter.?" Burke replied, "Fuck all, all went black, and I found myself tied to a fucking lamp post, bollock naked, and eventually your lot arrived."

Sue knew what was coming; Chris, who was standing next to her seemed to cringe and whispered, "Oh dear."

Carter walked closer to Burke, "If you wish to receive approval from any of the nursing staff and any of my officers, you will stop swearing and treat everyone with." He shouted, "Respect." He stood looking down at him, "You see Burke, I can also shout?"

He continued, "Burke, your use of obscene language doesn't impress or frighten me, for you see, I can get down and dirty with the best, should you wish it. If I had my way, I'd have you transferred to my office, for I only hope you're not trying to say you're the innocent party in all of this?"

Burke was about to complain about his situation but saw Carter's face and decided against matters.

Outside in the corridor, Carter looked at Chris, "As soon as he's fit for custody, will you tell my officer, and we'll take him off your hands?" Chris looked up at Carter and smiled.

"We're just awaiting the blood results; the trauma wound to his head, I think, was serious enough to stun him, laying him out to enable the suspect to drug him. The result of which you can see for yourself?" Carter and Sue thanked her and left.

30

Outside in the hospital car park, Carter, who was sitting in Sue's car, telephoned TF's office. Jane, his extremely attractive but outrageous secretary, answered.

"Carter, what a lovely surprise. Can I expect a visit from that lovely body of yours, and better still, will you be on your own, or will you have that lucky lady who spends an excessive amount of time in your company?"

Sue leaned over, "Sorry, Jane, I'm in my car all alone with my guv in tow." Jane whispered, "Carter!" He smiled, "Is he in? If necessary, can I speak with him?" Jane splattered, "Carter, I need a fix to see me through until the next time I see you, please?"

Suddenly, a coarse voice said, *"Is that you, Carter? What on earth is going on?"* "Sir, I'm outside the Royal. I've just been to see a prisoner by the name of Paul Burke; he was found naked, tied to a lamp post, with a black marker pen allegations tattooed all over his body. Inferring that Burke is a stalker, and what he's done to his victim?"

TF shouted, *"My office, Carter."* He smiled at Sue, "Do you think I'm in need of blotting paper?" Sue replied, "Carter, it's not your fault; the offender is varying his crimes, and we happen to have fielded a live one. The problem is we're getting closer to Wendy Fields, territory?"

On arrival at TF's office, Carter could see Jane pouting with petulant annoyance, observing Sue walking next to him, linking his arm, and smiling as they walked past. Carter leaned over, handing Jane his phone, "Can you take photo prints from off my mobile phone and bring them through to TF's office?"

Sue suddenly gasped, "Guv, do you trust Jane with your phone?" Jane hugged it to her breast, "Oh, Carter, do you trust me?" I could disappear to the lady's room and take some personal prints.?" He replied, "I'd lock you up under the Indecency Act?" Jane just looked at him, "Mmmm, "The very thought of it?"

Inside TF's office, the three waited for the customary coffees, after which Jane returned with his phone and a copy of the photographs. Tony Frost looked at Carter, "Are you mad? Please don't tell me you're not going soft, giving Jane your phone?"

When all was calmed down, TF began to look through the photographs. He looked up at Carter, "So we have a male covered in marker pen, setting out potential evidence of his actions?" Looking at Carter, TF blustered, "Well, has he any form for stalking?"

Carter stated, "Sir, this man is known at MER/cro. He has considerable offences of harassment, has been in breach of restraining orders, has spent two periods in prison for harassment, so he is well known to the police."

He continued, "Sir, all of this is going to put the police under the microscope; why has this man got away with so much? So, is it the locals who have fallen on this, and why?"

Carter looked at TF, "Sir, I feel if nothing is done on this matter, the next time we see Burke, he'll be found murdered in some terrible way. I'm setting a couple of the team to find the complainant, Amanda Jenkins, to interview her, to get her slant on the matter?"

He looked at his boss, "Sir, I feel that we need the help of Wendy Field, perhaps to think along the lines of a press conference?" Carter sat back to await the fallout.

Tony Frost did not follow his typical reaction but remained silent, eventually, "Carter, let me run it passed the Chief, for you can imagine the fallout?"

Outside of police headquarters, Carter looked at Sue, "Do you think the penny has finely dropped?" Carter took out his phone and called Lloydie, "Guv, can I help you?" "Lloydie, I have a scrum down later this afternoon, but I'm round the corner from you. Do you need me before I leave for the office?"

Lloydie stated, "No guv, I'll see you at the meeting?" Carter said, "5pm." and closed the call.

While Sue was driving back to the office, Carter took out his mobile phone and pressed the necessary button. *"Carter, what a lovely surprise. Are you going to be late?"* He turned to his left, looking out of the passenger door window.

"I have a meeting at 5ish, but should be home for about 6.30pm, will call if the wheel falls off?" Abbs, in her innocence, whispered, *"The wheel falls off?"* "Yep, police jargon, but I'm not going to tell you for fear of invoking the crime Gods, in case we evoke a ballacher?"

Abbs, with a sexy voice, replied, *"Carter, if you need any massaging in that department, you've only got to ask?"* She burst out laughing and replaced her phone.

He returned and looked straight out of the front windscreen window. "Well, Susan Martha, I can feel the vibes; the answer is, yes, we met at a party on the night of the Wilkinson matter?" Sue remained concentrated on her driving yet felt the sudden knot in her stomach.

On arrival at the office, they both signed back in. Carter thanked Eric for the coffee and left for his office. Sue just sat in silence; Eric looked at her, "Boss, is there a problem?" Sue seemed to jump out of her daydream. "Er, no, I'll have my coffee in my office." She got up and left.

Sue was sitting in her office, moving paperwork around her desk, totally unaware of what she was doing. Again, she was brought out of her daydream by a sudden knock on her office door. "Come in."

She looked up and noticed Eric standing in the doorway. "Eric, come in. What can I do for you?" He smiled, "Is there a problem? "She smiled, "Yes." As he tentatively closed the door behind him and sat opposite her desk. "It would seem by your reactions that one of two things have happened: one, another serial victim, or two, you've found out something in relation to the guv?"

Sue looked up at him, "The latter." Eric looked at her with a sympathetic look on his face. "Oh! Sue, Sue, Sue, you're not only a senior detective who not only detects serious crimes, but you're capable of detecting psychological signals in criminals or members of the team if there could be a problem?"

"Now, I've told you more than once to leave matters alone, but no, you had to sniff about trying to detect matters in the guv's personal life. Hence you have a face like a smacked arse?"

"Sue, please do not think that I just sit here with my thumb up my arse, not noticing what goes on. I notice that when a certain guy, who will remain anonymous, enters the general office, a certain person's eyes light up?"

Eric smiled, "Sue, I've known you've carried a torch for the guv, from day one. But you're both top bosses within the unit and the force. Should Carter show you any signs of affection, and should a tête-à-tête transpire? Can you imagine the amount of shit that would hit the fan? Umbrellas alone wouldn't cut it?"

She looked up at him through watery eyes, "Eric, it wasn't me sniffing about? It was a phone call made by the guv to an obvious female recipient?" She coughed, "He admitted it was a lady that he'd met when he was 'called out' over the Wilkinson case?"

Eric let out a protracted breath, "Oh! Yes, that David Robinson party. Well, now there you have it, the reason for him leaving for his office, carrying his mug of coffee with him instead of talking with the likes of us? Sue, I am sorry, but you've got to grow a thicker skin."

31

At exactly 5pm, Carter walked into the conference room for the arranged scrum down. As the team came to attention, he noticed Sue had already taken her place in the room. He acknowledged both her and the team, calling for the team to sit.

Sue stood in front of the empty chair next to Carter's. He remained standing, and eventually, Sue sat down. Carter turned to face the team.

"Right, the boss and I went to see the tattooed victim, known as Paul Burke. He has an attitude problem. You see, he has a background, and the last thing he wanted was for it to be as such, advertised?"

"Burke apparently has form for *'Stalking.'* He is at present in 'major ob's' in the Royal, under guard. He originally presented in a drugged-induced state, suffering from hypothermia, having been found naked in the cold, hugging a lamp post. There was a sudden raw of laughter. "He also received a blow to the back of his head."

"The medical team have dealt with the hypothermia; they do not think the (Carter said in a French accent like Jack Clouseau) "Bump," the team fell about laughing. To the back of his head, it is not too much of a problem. They've taken blood, so we'll eventually find out if we have a possible match with the other victims?"

Carter continued, "Chris Atkinson will let us know when Burke, can be released, suitable for custody. I want the officer guarding to arrange transportation to Derby Lane. I also want Amanda Jenkins interviewed and obtain a statement, get some background on the situation?"

Sue stood up, "Guv, Phil, and Jules have details of Jenkins's address and have made arrangements for an interview tomorrow."

Carter looked at Lloydie, "Jim, do you have anything new?" Jim stood up, "Guv, I'm dying to tell the team the identities of the three victims found in those terrible baths?" Carter interrupted... "Pray, tell Jim."

Lloydie reiterated. "By fingerprint evidence alone, we have the identity of the three victims in the baths; they are no other than Brown, Jones, and Jenkins. The three paedophiles. In the 'Gainsford case,' involved in that awful 'Evil room' in St Vincent's Roman Catholic school, like that of Ronald Rollings. Each received an injection in a crease of skin in the under-arm area, awaiting the verdict from the labs?"

Jim Lloyd said, "Plus the report from the hospital on Burke?" He coughed, a total of eight dead, and one found alive."

"Guv, I have the latest two letters from the accused, which I've put on your desk for your attention."

Carter looked out over the team, "Your boss and I were present in TF's office; I had photos copied directly from my phone, showing the tattoos, or the writings, on Burkes, face, and body, an indication of offences committed."

When the subject arose in relation to the public and the press, we both waited for the fallout. Quite the opposite, TF is going to see the Chief Constable for advice on the matter?"

Carter looked at Sue, "Boss, do you have any comment?" She looked up at him, "No guv, whilst we await any decisions. The interview with Amanda Jenkins will be of interest, for it will corroborate the evidence written on her stalker's face?"

As Carter turned to leave, the team came to attention. He smiled and left, followed by Sue.

When in the general office, Eric looked at them both, "Just to let you know, Burke is on his way to Derby Lane, passed fit for custody, plus the drug used was scopolamine."

Carter immediately turned and shouted up the corridor towards the conference room, "Lloydie, do you have a minute?"

Lloydie arrived on the trot, "Guv?" "Lloydie, the hospital labs have confirmed that the drug used on Burke was scopolamine. Will you mention the matter to Mr Chambers?" Lloydie replied, "Yes, guv." Carter also mentioned, "Jim, will you chase up our labs re the three victims found in the baths? I know it's a knocking bet they're the same?"

On arrival at his office, Sue sat opposite him. Carter picked up the two see-through evidence bags, each containing one of the letters. He put on a pair of rubber gloves, passing a pair over to Sue.

On completion, they both exchanged letters; Carter looked at Sue, "Through all of this, our defendant is looking for someone to blame, for all of his arguments refer to the lack of action by the necessary authorities?"

Carter picked up the phone on his desk and called TF's office. It was instantly answered by Jane, who immediately detected the tone in his voice, knowing that he wasn't in the mood for any verbal acts of bravado.

"Commander Frost's office." "Jane, is he in?" *"Yes, putting you through." "Frost."*

"Sir, it's Carter. Scopolamine is the favoured drug in all these matters. Officers tomorrow are attending at the address of Amanda Jenkins, the complainant, for an interview in the Burke case. The alleged stalker case. All his assumed actions, the apparent evidence tattooed or written on his head and body?"

"I have Superintendent Ford in my office; we've both read the latest letters from the accused; by the contents of his letters, he is looking for a figurehead, someone to offload on?"

He continued, "Sir, please remember that Burke was found in a public place, totally naked; he must have been seen by one and all, and by picking his victims, he wishes to point out to society the total lack of commitment in dealing with such issues?"

"Sir, before I finish, I wish to point out that we are currently dealing with three out of eight of Dr Sam Watson's catalogue of possible victims; I therefore suggest we need, at the very least, a press conference?"

Carter received a curt reply, *"We'll speak tomorrow."* And closed the call.

32

Carter arrived home at 7pm. He had no sooner tapped the security fob to gain access to his flat when a beautiful blonde lady attacked him, suitably dressed in a white tank top and white cotton drawstring trousers.

She looked at Carter, "Now, what on earth is a *'ballacher,'* and if you have one, can it be dealt with by any form of 'hands on assistance'?"

She threw her arms about him and, in doing so, stripped off his raincoat and jacket all in one, at the same time spouting. "Carter, you beautiful specimen of a man, get here front and centre while I see to your ballachers?"

He stood in utter amasement. Abbs said, "Shower first, with all the trimmings, then on completion in bed, then tea, if hungry?" And burst out laughing, then we start all over again."

Carter stripped off, but before Abbs had moved a muscle to comply with his actions, he picked her up and carried her into the wet room and shower; she screamed. "Carter, Carter, what the hell are you doing? The initial temp of the shower, as you well know, is freezing until it gains the required temp?"

Knowing such a fact, he took no notice of her pained expression. Carter increased his grip on Abbs to seek any heat from her body.

She spluttered, "Carter, what! Why, on earth?" He smiled, "Just wanted to see if you were wearing any underwear?" In utter frustration, she screamed, "All you had to do was either feel me all over or strip me off. Not to be so cruel?"

On completion of their *'touchy, feely'* shower, both decided that bed would be their main area of sexual expertise.

Carter lovingly wrapped Abbs in a large bath sheet and carried her through to their bed. She felt like a servant girl in the *'Arabian Nights'* rolled up in a carpet, to be thrown down, unravelled at the fee of a handsome Sultan.

After opening the towel, Carter looked down upon Abbs; he took in a deep gasp, for he thought it was like looking down on perfection. He bent down and kissed her on her lips. She placed her arms around his neck and pulled him down.

While she lay on her side facing him, he casually traced a forefinger over the silhouette of her stunning body from the contours of her face, over her shoulder, down to her hip. He then returned his finger to her chest and breasts.

He noticed from all their foreplay in the shower and now in bed. Both he and Abbs were so aroused that the next step was inevitable. Carter realised that Abbs, had lay back smiling up at him with anticipation.

The initial action was met with squeals of derision. Abbs seemed to dig her heels into the mattress to gain leverage in raising her pelvis to determine total access.

At the end of a truly sexual encounter when both lay drenched in sweat. Abbs, excitedly, leaned over and raised her leg onto his thigh while she lowered her head onto his chest, allowing her to hear his beating heart eventually return to a normal rhythm.

Abbs looked at Carter, "You do realise that the night of the party, I fancied you like mad. I experienced pangs of joy in my tummy, which I have to admit never experienced before. But I assure you, in my wildest dreams, I never imagined it would lead to the likes of this?"

He looked down at her and smiled, "Why?" Abbs replied, "I thought I needed to make tentative inquires with both David and Beth as to who was the handsome man that offered his excuses, having to leave after only a matter of minutes, for he'd only just arrived?"

Abbs suddenly twisted in their bed and pressed down on his chest while she kissed him tenderly on his chest tummy; she continued down his body. She hovered, looking up at him, "Carter, when you first saw me, did your radar instinctively tell you that I was this type of woman, for it's my first…?"

On completion, she noticed that Carter lay comatose, absorbing all the delights of her actions. Until he heard, "Carter, are you hungry?" He placed his hand and fingers under his chin like a wise old man in thought, like the statute of the 'The Thinker…' "Umm!! Starved." She pulled herself up, took hold of a pillow, placed it over his face, and pushed down on it.

Pushing her up, he placed his arms around her, "Madam, do you realise that you're assaulting a serving police officer? Stop and desist, get up and feed your man…"

The meal constructed by Abbs was nothing short of magic special, but after such an evening of passion, it didn't have to be but just completed the evening. Choices of cold meats and a side salad. Accompanied by a bottle of Sauterne, each glass alluded to its rich nectar.

After which, they retired to bed, where Abbs rested her head on his chest. She smiled up at him, "Carter, I don't know if you realise how much I love you, both as a person and a man; I never thought that I could ever love anyone as much as I love you?"

She continued, "Carter, it's so difficult for a woman; I often wonder, do men have a poor reaction to a female or partner that shows poor sexual esteem? I admit to the fact that prior to meeting you, my sexual experience was in the basement."

Carter looked down at Abbey, "The problem in any relationship is however much couples love each other, the sexual orgasm rate between men and women is miles apart. Take a man. He has an orgasm or ejaculates every time during sex. A woman may experience an orgasm, so infrequently it's proved a problem in most relationships."

Abby looked at Carter," You do realise I experienced my first-ever orgasm with you, and Wow, I'd never thought matters like that ever happened. Am I not a poor cow? And although I understand there are significant differences in the bodies of men and women. I will willingly take what I've got."

Abby suddenly inhaled, letting out her breath and slowly whispering. "I've now met a man who doesn't make demands. You are so gentle and patient with me; it is so natural to want to commit to you and our wonderful sensual actions."

Carter took her in his arms, "Abbs, I feel the same; we have laid down a sexual blueprint, a sexual foundation, which refers to all our feelings and actions, appropriate in every way." He sighed, remembering his long conversations with Sam, for his thoughts instantly reminded him of his days with his wife, Helen.

The following morning, Carter leant down over her; she was on her back with her arms above her head. He gently kissed her nipples. Her eyes flashed open like that of a toy doll that had been lent backwards by a child.

With surprise, she looked up at him and laughed as she noticed that he'd left, leaving for the wet room. She shouted, "Carter, you're a spoilsport; you, more than most, should finish what you started?"

As he entered the shower, he called, "Sorry, but I have an early meeting, will finish off matters this evening?"

After his shower, he dressed and was met by Abbs, dressed in a brief cotton see-through dressing gown. She looked up at him with a mug of coffee in her hands. "Morning, Carter. Is there anything you fancy for breakfast?"

He smiled, "That's the last thing that you need to wear to attract my attention. For its time, that's against me, and not lust, so whatever mood you're in, hold that thought for tonight?"

33

It was while he was languishing in peak hour traffic his mobile activated. He pressed the hands-free gismo, "Morning Eric, what's up?" *"Where are you, guv?"* "Where am I?" You know where I am, you stupid bugger, on my way to the office?"

He then heard a cough, *"Guv, I hate to say it?"* Carter suddenly said, "Boss (Carter's affectionate name for his old DS), please don't say another...?"

"Yes, guv, I've just put the phone down with the control room; a body has been found in a warehouse on the Wellington Dock estate, off Regent Road. I've informed Sue, who activated team members, SOCO, and Mr Chambers. They'll all meet you at the scene."

Carter whispered, "Sorry, Eric, I shouldn't have been so rude." And closed the call.

He realised that he'd just arrived at the gates of Sefton Park, with the junction of Aigburth Drive, knowing to expect a formidable high-pressure journey, mainly due to the rush hour traffic.

Carter, through bouts of swearing, suddenly saw a bad-tempered driver give him the finger while another driver tried to adjust her make-up. Carter leant down and smiling activated the blues and twos, their faces drained of blood as he shot off.

He finally arrived at Regent Road and Boundary Street. He leaned forward and switched off the claxon. He proceeded on the blues only. Turning left and coming to a halt at the dock gate.

A uniformed officer carrying the typical clipboard walked towards him. He lowered his window. Carter smiled, "Morning, officer." On seeing Carter, he stiffened to attention, "Sir, I was pre-warned of your arrival; good morning to you." Carter took out his ID; the officer began to say, "Sir, there is no…" Carter waved it in front of him and smiled.

The officer, on completion of the usual record, noting his arrival, looked at Carter. "Sir, if you turn right and drive along to your first left and follow the dock warehouses, you will no doubt see the emergency circus. He smiled and drove off.

He turned first left and immediately set eyes on all the vehicles. He slowed down until he arrived at the obvious location. As he came to a halt, he noticed all the SOCO officers mingling about, darting in and out of the warehouse, all dressed in their forensic overalls.

He was just about to get out of his car when he noticed Sue walking from the warehouse. She acknowledged him.

He walked over to her; on arrival, he noticed that she had pushed her forensic hood back and lowered her mask. She offered a weak smile and the fact that she'd been crying.

She turned, "Carter, it's a nightmare; I often wonder if we should travel together to the scenes of crime, witnessing the vista at the same time; for now, I have to take you in and do it all over again…?"

Sue walked over to her car parked nearby and took out a forensic suit for him. A tradition emulated from day one. He thanked her, saying," Sue, that's the least of your jobs while so upset? He quickly dressed, thankful for the smidgen of Vick that Sue placed in his mask.

She looked at him, "Carter the Vick won't cut it; you'll notice a sick bucket nearby, used by seasoned officers. I just don't know what to say; I happen to know you don't have a traditional breakfast prior to setting off for the office, thank God. I'll leave it for you to see for yourself?"

Carter followed Sue into the giant Cathedral-like warehouse. It had huge sliding doors on both sides of the building, giving access to the loading and unloading of ships on either side of the dock in days gone by. Sue happened to walk through the gaping entrance nearest to all the vehicles and personnel.

As he followed Sue, he noticed that she was walking towards a large wooden structure in the style of a self-contained room within the massive warehouse, where he could see all the investigating officers walking in and out of the structure.

On his arrival, he was met by Lloydie, closely followed by Gordon Chambers, who in his indomitable voice called, "Ah Carter, there you are, old son." Without making his usual fuss, he took him to one side, onlookers presuming he was updating the senior operational officer with all the facts.

They couldn't be further from the truth. Gordon whispered, "Now look here, Carter, you've gained immense strides in dealing with recent events, but this one, old son, is off the scale. I can attempt to explain it to you, or do you want to see for yourself?"

"Carter looked at him and, while he still had his mask under his chin, replied in a low voice, "Gordon, you have broken all police protocol in your efforts in the past of shielding me from any such grizzly events; you even conducted, Helen, and our children's, and Rab, my best friends PMs without my attendance?"

Gordon gripped his arm if you insist?" Gordon looked over his shoulder at Sue and Lloydie as if to be available.

Carter looked at Gordon, and he gestured with his chin. Gordon moved off, followed by Carter. As he entered the special room, originally used as an office for dealing with all the ship's cargo passing through the city.

Prior to entering the room, the waves of the vile smell had begun to permeate his nostrils and stomach and began to cause a churning effect with his intestinal gases. After trying to control his natural reaction to spew, he'd only had his usual black coffee for breakfast, yet enough to exit his body.

His eyes immediately fell upon what could only be described as total carnage. Such a putrid smell hit him. He noticed what was once a body with its wrists and ankles pulled up some 45% to the floor, secured by ropes tied to rings in either wall of the structure.

The body was pinned to the floor by a pile of concrete slabs on top of each other. As Carter got closer, he recognised due to the mass of concrete, the torso of the victim's body seemed flattened on the floor.

Parts of the victim's face, arms, and legs were the only remains of what was once a normal human being. Carter realised that if it weren't for the victim's clothing, due to the crushing weight, body parts and liquids of the body would be seeping onto the floor.

His attention was drawn to four large arc lights, one in each corner. Plus, the busy, incessant flashes from the cameras of the SOCO officers.

He felt someone close to him, who took hold of his arm. When he turned, he noticed Sue, who whispered, "Carter, pull up your mask, and she squeezed his arm.

Carer realised that Sue had made a tentative request, but he was unable to conduct the simplest of tasks. He was unable to move, as he was frozen to the spot. He looked at Sue, "Sue, I can't move."

Carter looked down at the victim, a mistake, for he suddenly felt his stomach churn, for his eyes fell on the pitiful casualty. He hadn't had any formal breakfast, only his usual black coffee, but that was enough, for he felt whatever was in his stomach, perhaps the remnants of last night's meal, was making its way up into his throat.

He turned to Sue, who pointed to a large filing cabinet, which had a Castrol 20L plastic oil container, with the lid leant next to it. He also noticed a large roll of paper towelling to wipe one's mouth and a pile of clothes if one didn't make it. Plus, the inevitable roll of black plastic bin liners

Carter made it just in time. He leaned down and just managed to remove his mask before all his stomach contents were evacuated. The amount of vile, putrid liquid contained in the oil drum was evidence of other users, which made matters worse. After several minutes, Carter stood up and taking two pieces of paper from the roll, began to wipe his mouth. He placed the used pieces of towel into the drum.

He ran his hand down the front of his forensic overalls and walked over to where Sue was, standing talking with Gordon Chambers and Lloydie. He looked at the three of them, "Well, you can tick another thing off the list?"

Gordon moved forward, "Well, Carter, all empty as I need you to move over and view the body?" He looked at him, "Gordon, let's not drag our feet, and let's get on with it?" Carter looked at Sue, and he noticed her face displayed such a poor pallor. How do you feel?"

She sighed as she looked at him, "Sir, the same let's just get on with it?" They walked over to see the body lying in a once-hanging position, mainly due to being suspended by the wrists and ankles. At first sight, the body gave the impression that it was in a curve position, as the victim's clothes dangling down made the square look of the body.

Gordon Chambers walked up to the body, and he suddenly turned, "Now, Carter, please don't ask for the TOD, for as you can see, I have truly little to go on. Carter replied, "Will you know more when I get him home?"

Carter remained focused on the vision in front of him; he coughed, "Gordon, is there any way that we can compute, measure, use a piece of bloody string, if necessary, to work out how far the victim was off the floor before the slabs were placed on top of him?"

Gordon Chambers, the pathologist, looked at Carter, and he smiled, "Old son, that's a bloody good question and nigh impossible to answer. You see, there are too many variables. For instance, there is no such thing as a standard human body, thus unable to use a standard equation to enable such matters?"

He continued, "It's a question of physics and calculus. He coughed, "One must consider the strength and type of rope used to secure the victim. From what I can tell, there is no give in the rope. Therefore, you have the weight versus the strength of the human body?"

Gordon uttered, "It's rather like the old saying, 'What happens when an impossible force meets an unstoppable object'?"

Carter looked at Gordon, "Then obviously, we must remove the stone slabs." He looked at Jim Lloyd, "Lloydie, can I leave that with you, for you'll need the help of the SOCO officers?" He coughed, "Arrange matters with SOCO to take sequential photographs, as each slab is removed, for there may be pieces of evidence; if possible, line them up in order, mark them if necessary?"

As he went to move forward, Sue discreetly took his arm, and she whispered, "Carter! leave it with Gordon and his team?" He turned, "Sue, there is nothing left to bring up, so I need to be seen, looking about the scene as if interested?"

Carter walked forward towards the body, and he immediately realised due to the weight placed on top of the victim had resulted in a mass of blood and human excrement running from the mass.

Although he wore a mask, he mistakenly took an immense intake of air through his nose instead of his mouth, taking in the aroma of the Vick at first, but alas, he couldn't block out the odour, for it was so intense.

He looked at Gordon. Can we start to remove the slabs from off the victim and cut the retaining ropes but make sure we keep the knots. I noticed that the first slab had partially obliterated the victim's face, causing considerable damage, the remainder covering the torso down to his thighs.

34

Carer looked at Sue, "Superintendent Ford, will you come with me?" Carter walked away from that disgusting room, quickly followed by Sue. When outside, she looked at him, "What's your problem?" He looked at her and smiled, "I'm about to call TF, so I thought you could do with some fresh air?"

He continued to walk to his car; Sue followed with a smile on her face, "Well, guv is this for me to function as your backup." He turned, "Do I need a reason?"

Carter leaned against his car next to Sue. He looked out over the dock inlet at the ink-coloured water, overlooked by hostile-looking redundant cranes, again used prolifically in days gone by. Loading and unloading of merchandise. He could well imagine the workforce needed, thinking anything would be better than the sight that he'd just witnessed.

He took out his phone and called TF. Jane answered the call, "Carter, what a lovely surprise, my first caller of the day, and it's you; you've set me up for the day…" He interrupted, "Jane, please, is he in?" "Yes, Carter, just let me milk it…?"

"Frost." "Sir, it's Carter. Well, we have another; whilst on my way to the office, Eric told me of a call he received from the information room, telling him that a body had been found in a warehouse on the Wellington dock, off Regent Road."

Tony Frost shouted, *"Carter, what the fuck is happening? Please tell me we're getting somewhere, anywhere, in your attempt to catch this bastard?"* Carter coughed, "Well, sir, it's as previously discussed, he's a lone wolf, just look at his field of operation; if not the fucking City, he has the total force area. Whatever this victim has done, he seems to have upset our offender to warrant such a punishment?"

TF, in a low voice, just said, *"How?"* Unbeknown to Carter, Jane was listening to the call... Carter coughed, "We found the victim, where the offender had tied the victims' hands and ankles with rope to large rings on the opposite walls. We have no means of knowing how high from the floor he aggravated matters by laying about 30 large concrete pavement-size slabs on top of the victim."

Further examination found that the body of the victim, due to the weight placed on his chest, was crushed to the floor, with assorted body fluids leaking out onto the floor.

At this point, Jane nearly dropped the phone as she tried to stifle a shout on hearing the horrific description.

The call continued. "We are at present beginning to withdraw the slabs to remove the victim to the mortuary, and I'll follow up and keep you in the loop?"

TF whispered, *"Christ Carter, unfortunately, it's necessary, but please...*He closed the call. Carter had no sooner closed the call when his phone activated. "Carter." *"It's me, Jane. I overheard your call with TF; what an awful task for both you and your team. Please be careful?"* She closed the call. He looked at his phone, and after several seconds he replaced his phone in his pocket.

Carter heard the sound of a motor; he looked in the direction of the sound, and he noticed a SOCO officer dressed in forensic garb driving a forklift truck.

Both he and Sue followed. He drove to the location of the body and the concrete slabs. The officer slowly positioned the truck in front of the 30 flags, standing approximately 5ft in height. Four of his colleagues, two at the far side and two on the nearside, were all dressed in forensic overalls, wearing their hoods up, with masks in place, rubber gloves, wearing black wellingtons.

On a given single, the truck moved slowly forward, the four officers raised the top slab, the truck was moved into position, and the flag was lowered onto the forks.

The officer driving reversed; he then took the single slab to the far side of the area, where, joined by the same officers, it was removed and laid on the floor. And so, it went on.

Carter stood in the middle of the room. Sue and Peter stood next to him. The procedure was repeated. Each slab lay side by side on the warehouse floor, numbered for possible items of evidence.

Jules and Phil both walked in, with Phil carrying a tray of coffees, as it was bitterly cold. The warehouse had its doors permanently opened, and the wind around the dock blew straight through the building.

Carter shivered with the cold as they removed the slabs. He looked at Sue whilst he pulled up his small overall hood and stuffed his hands deep into his pockets.

"I'm off to the mortuary. Sue, can I leave you and the team to deal with matters here? With each slab marked one, to... Please ask SOCO to go over the slabs with a fine-tooth comb. We need to ascertain any possible ID marks?"

Sue looked at Carter, "Guv, you've seen the state of play; can't you leave it with Lloydie?" Sue coughed, "Guv, no one should have to witness such things, and now you're driving yourself to attend at the bloody mortuary?" Carter looked at her. He smiled, "Why, Susan Martha Ford, anyone would think you showing concern for me?"

He turned to face Sue, pointed his chin towards the slabs, laughed and left for his car.

Sue looked on, whispering under her breath, 'Carter, you can be a right shit at times?'

35

As Carter got into his car, he looked at his watch. It was 1.30pm. He called Eric, "Eric, I'm on my way to the mortuary…" Eric interrupted, *"Guv, why don't you leave it with Lloydie?"* Carter exploded, "Not you as well; I've had enough with Susan Martha." Eric replied, *"Guv, I got the full works from Lloydie. Shit, we're only upset for you because of the state of the victim?"*

Carter whispered, "Boss, it's taken a while to get my head around such things, but would you have cringed when we worked together? No, you bloody know you wouldn't; I'll see you later."

His second call was to Abs, *"Carter, what a wonderful surprise, I do hope all is 'Q,' I remember never say the word."* Carter coughed, "Well, Abs, it couldn't be worse. It seems I ran into a brick wall at 9am, and I can't get over, under, or around it…Abs whispered, *"Well, Mr., if you want me, then you'll have to cork it, laughing Carter, Carter…* But the line was dead.

Carter arrived at the mortuary; he parked in one of the police parking bays, got out and locked and secured the doors. He walked over to the main door and pressed the bell.

Following the correct protocol, he gained entry, the door opened, and Lloydie met him. "Look, guv. I've got this; why on earth don't you return to the office?" He smiled, "Jim, you've covered for me long enough, nearly as long as we've worked together, even Gordon Chambers, for Christ's sake. Now, let's get on with it?"

Both turned and walked along the cold mortuary corridor to be met by the home office pathologist, Gordon Chambers. Gordon, in his usual manner, blurted out, "Carter, old son, why-o-why when you have both Jim and I to assist in such matters?"

Carter just pointed with his chin towards the PM room. Prior to progressing forwards, Gordon Chambers insisted that both officers dress in full forensic clothing. Eventually, all three walked into the room. Carter was fully aware of the situation, the three PM tables, the two large theatre lights, and the adjustable recording mic poised over the tables.

Carter's eyes initially gazed at the first table, with a white rubber sheet draped over it. The fact that it wasn't completely flat, for there was a dip in the middle where the victim's chest should be. Due to part of the victim's head, arms, thighs, and feet, matters he had seen earlier.

Gordon nodded at one of his technicians, who walked forward to remove the sheet. Prior to his actions, all three pulled up their face masks. Carter immediately missed the inevitable aroma of Vick, always placed in his masks by Sue.

Carter looked down on the remains of the victim. He grimaced, and due to his mask and the rubber hood pulled down, his colleagues failed to notice he'd closed his eyes.

He knew he had to open them, open them he did. He immediately looked down on the pathetic remains of the victim.

Gordon Chambers coughed, "I know that one saw the remains of the victim while his body was compressed at the scene by those obscene concrete slabs. Now let's press on."

He looked down at the victim, "Jim, I can let you obtain his fingerprints to try and identify him, but you'll both notice that his shoulder joints just attach to his arms, and thick layers of ligaments attached to remaining muscles, covered by remaining thick dermis. They have precariously placed on either side of where his rib cage and torso should have been, for there is evidence of bone?"

"You will both notice that the ropes were cut to enable removal of the victim. The original Knots are in place around his wrists and ankles?"

He continued, "Now one can see the whole of the damage caused by the concrete slabs, times thirty, that had been placed on top of the victim." With a rubber-gloved finger, he pointed to the lower half of the victim's head. He stated, "One can see from point 'A. Below are parts of the victim's head to point 'B.' His two thighs, legs, and feet. All in between flattened, showing the odd residue of bones."

"The victim was lifted by his clothes, which assisted in keeping what there was of the body in place. He was laid on the table as is. Items of his remaining body parts were placed in a cloth sack.

The sack was then emptied onto the neighbouring table. One could see parts of rib bones and remains of the victim's essential organs, heart, lungs, and kidneys, all in some offal-like soup. Lab samples taken will help identify the organs?"

Carter looked at Gordon, "We'll await to see if the victim is known to MER/cro; it may help not only to ID him, plus give us his background?" Gordon replied, "Good luck."

Carter looked at his friend and colleague, "I suppose you didn't happen to find an injection site or letter in all of this mess?" Jim was the next to reply, "Guv, I have what one could class as clothing; I'll search them and get back to you."

He looked at them both, "Well, I'm going to change and head off back to the office." Gordon, smiled, "Perhaps can I suggest a post-op nip?" Carter replied, "Old friend, the way I feel, I couldn't keep anything down." He suddenly turned, "Gents, please retain the knots in the ropes. "Speak later." And left.

Gordon looked at Jim, "I know how close you are to your guv; in fact, the whole team are, but I have to say he has nothing to prove?" Jim smiled, "The guv is no ordinary guv; you must have realised that he has galvanised himself, unlike when the unit first formed?"

"He thought that no one knew of his plight, for he tried to act the part, but it became self-evident, yet we never let him know; Sue saw to that. But the guv has this drive, he's self-driven, never to just let us deal with the awful stuff, he'll join us, and so he's managed to come to terms with matters."

Jim continued, "I always remember your passing comment, '*What on earth made that man pick the career in the police, knowing full well that in the CID he'd come face to face with death, in all its frailties?*' You even commented on the fact, '*He was the only man that could lean 45% to the ground without falling over.*'

Jim, while still laughing, looked at Gordon, "It is widely rumoured that our guv has a new friend; he is going through the '*nipping through to his office routine*' when returning to Derby Lane. He has only made the one call while on inquiries in the car, and that was in front of Sue."

They both burst out laughing, but deep inside, both men knew he'd gained their utter respect.

36

Carter arrived back at Derby Lane; he walked into the general office to sign back in. The first thing they all noticed was his dishevelled appearance looked like he'd been on the piss. He presented with his jacket and overcoat open in a drooped off-the-shoulder fashion, the top button of his shirt was open, and his tie slackened off.

Without a word, he just turned and left for his office. Sue looked at Eric, and whilst trying to stand up, Eric just smiled, "Sue, give him some time, for you should know what state the body was in and how gruesome it must have been at the mortuary?"

Entering his office, he just flung his overcoat and jacket over the coat stand in the corner of his office. He then slumped down into his chair behind his desk. He flung his hands up suddenly, screaming, "Oh! fuck." His way of letting off steam. What he didn't realise was that Sue, Peter, Philip, and Jules, closely followed by Eric, entered his office at a rush.

He looked up from behind his fingers, which he'd interwoven and clasped over his eyes and then his forehead. On seeing his team members, he stood shouting, "Hell, wow, what's up?"

It was Sue, with hands on her hips, who cried," Christ guv, we thought someone could have come up the back stairs to get at you?" Carter apologised, "I 'm sorry, I was just letting off steam after my recent visit to that bloody mortuary. I forgot the door was open, ops!"

While Carter fell back into his chair, he noticed that Lloydie seemed rather concerned, for he had missed all the action. He remained standing behind the group. He looked at him, "Jim, welcome; all we need now is the other twenty-five members of the team?"

Jim had such a blank look on his face, as not being privy to the original reaction by his colleagues. After laughing, they all turned to leave except Sue and Jim, for Sue, noticed that Jim was carrying an evidence bag. He held it up, "Guv, I found this in the remnants of the victim's clothing?"

He handed it to Carter, who on examining it, noticed a white piece of paper contained inside. He opened his desk drawer and took out two pairs of rubber gloves, handing one pair to Sue, and he put on the remaining pair. When ready, he opened the evidence bag, letting the paper fall out onto his ink blotter.

Opening it, he found a neatly typed letter.

'I'm getting sick to death typing, 'To whom it may concern.' Hasn't anyone got the bottle to stand up and take responsibility for all my actions? I also noticed there are no press releases; perhaps I should contact the likes of the Liverpool Echo, addressing my letter to the crime desk.

Well, our friend is no other than Andrew Matthews. Does the name ring a bell? Yes, you've got it; in 2000, arrested for the murder of a 10-year-old schoolgirl, Jenny Wilson, abducted by him whilst she was on her way home from school.

The police got information that he'd shown an unnatural interest in young schoolgirls; they searched his house with a legal warrant. They found items of interest under his bedroom floorboards: a pair of girl's knickers, 2 hair clips, and neckless, suggested trophies.

He was arrested, D&A was taken from the knickers, hair clips, and the hairbrush used by Jenny, offered for comparison by her parents. Her body was never found.

Over the years, the police held several press conferences, where her parents pleaded with Matthews to enable closure for them, but the bastard just sat in his cell and remained silent. He must have thought that he'd get parole and where he'd buried her would be his trump card.

Well, time has come and gone, and he was released from prison ten days ago. I have to say that I now realise that he'd take the information to the grave, so on behalf of Jenny's parents. We all knew he wouldn't cough, so he got his just deserts.'

On completion, Carter looked up at Jim, "Does he fit the bill?" Jim smiled, "Guv, his form elevates from concern shown as a child to offences reported as a teenager; there are several cautions and fines. But Jenny, I believe, was a culmination of pent-up feelings, rather like a pressure cooker. Of course, it's a fact Jenny's body was never found."

Carter looked at Jim, "Do we have his home address?" Jim replied, "Yes, but after the case and his conviction, the family moved; after his release via the probation service, he was in a hostel; the perpetrator must have snatched him literally off the street. I found no other details in his clothing. I intend to contact the probation service to find a potential address, to see if he has personal belongings such as a comb, hairbrush, or toothbrush for DNA comparison."

Carter looked at both his officers, "Should we tell Jenny's parents of Matthew's demise? Along the lines, he's been found dead. It may give them closure?"

Sue looked at Carter, "Guv, what on earth will you do about the author's frustrated threat?" He looked at her with a face that may have passed for a smile. I'll phone TF and report matters to him."

A low scream came out of Sue, "Well, we may as well start the collection for your resignation right now, as the fallout will be felt throughout the land?" She burst out laughing.

He looked at her, "Jim, come in, and you can join us by witnessing TF's reaction?"

After they had all received fresh mugs of coffee, Carter set about ringing TF's office; as usual, Jane answered the phone, *"Carter, what a lovely surprise…"* He interrupted her, "Jane, if he's in, please put me through?" She whispered, *"Is it that bad? Just wait?"*

The next voice he heard was a growl, *"Frost, yes, Carter, what do you want?"* He could see the look of anticipation on their faces.

"Sir, I've already explained to you our recent case and all the horrific remains found at the scene?" He then heard, *"Well, get on with it."* With Carter having put the call on, *'conference setting,' Sue* thought shit and awaited a reply.

"Sir, is there any way that you could come and join us in a scrum down at 9.30am tomorrow?" He heard a cough, *"Yes, see you there."* The phone went dead.

Sue was the first to speak, "Guv, is it your plan to quote, 'what is said in this room remains in this room?' He looked at her, "Well, Sue, by tomorrow, I may have calmed down, for I quote Nietzsche, *'Battle not with monsters, lest you become a monster, and if you gaze into the abyss, the abyss gazes into you.'* "Sue, this day, I feel that this has taken place, and I didn't like what I saw. Plus, the lack of lustre remarks of TF, I wondered, even if I explained matters, he'd not the faintest idea of the ball of shit that is coming his way?"

"I believe that you have witnessed on more than one occasion my advice, and latterly demands, that we have a press conference. Yet again, TF has remained so stoic, knowing if it all went tits up, he has me to carry the can?"

He looked at Jim, "Now Jim, how are matters at the mortuary, having identified the victim by his fingerprints, matching the details portrayed in the letter submitted by the accused?" Does the victim happen to have any tattoos or scars, which may prove his identity?" Jim replied, "Unfortunately, no." Carter continued, "Jim, did you find a needle sight?" He replied, "Yes, guv awaiting results of bloods?"

Jim replied, "Guv yes, you're right; identified by his prints alone, unable to use dental records as corroborative evidence due to the injuries to the victim's face and mouth. As you well know, to prove beyond any doubt, we can use another possible source, for I've taken samples of the victim's hair for possible D&A analysis, subject to comparison. We can only hope to find his digs, allowing us to potentially ID the victim from items found, such as a hairbrush or comb. We can also use his toothbrush. We have a full pathology report, giving the cause of death and the condition of the victim."

Carter leaned back in his chair, "Can I suggest that you contact the coroner's office, suggesting the possible ways we can prove the identity of the victim? In similar events, as in plane disasters, we ask that the relatives, due to the state of the victim or victims, not be allowed to view the body, and suggest could we make an application for a *'closed coffin?'*

Carter looked at Jim, "Can I leave the situation over informing the Matthews family? But please wait until the coroner's people have cleared matters?" He replied, "Sir."

At the conclusion of matters, Carter looked at his watch; it was 4.30pm. He looked at both Sue and Jim, "Look, let's take an early dart, for I've had enough, and I need to get my head around matters for tomorrow, pass matters along to the rest of the team."

After they'd both left, he turned and called Abby. *"Carter, what a lovely surprise; I hope matters are panning out fine, and you won't be late?"* He replied, "Abbs, I've had one shit of a day, and please, I only want to have a quiet evening, as I need to get my head around matters for tomorrow?"

Abby replied, *"Carter, I'm leaving now; see you at home?"*

Carter adjusted his clothing and left for the general office. On his arrival, all in the office looked up to witness Carter in his usual smart attire. He walked over to the diary and signed off duty.

He turned and looked at Eric; he said, "If things are, you know what I mean, you and your team can also leave for home; cheers, see you all tomorrow." And left.

37

As Carter walked into their flat, a rather lacklustre Abby met him. As she slowly walked up to him, and tentatively kissed him on his lips, subsequently she gently corralled his face by placing a hand on either side of his features, so different from her usual excited reaction on his arrival home.

Abby walked behind Carter and removed his overcoat and jacket. She placed them both on the hall coatstand, on removal of his coats, he slowly moved into the lounge, where he just flopped down onto the settee.

She left for the kitchen and returned, armed with two cans of Larger. She handed one to him, placing the second on the coffee table. He pulled on the ring pull of the can. It made the usual, woosh!

After a long slug, he let out a gasp together with "That'll stop them farting in church?" On completion of the can, he placed it on the low coffee table. He was about to open the second can when Abbs whispered, "Was it that bad?"

Leaning back, he placed his head onto one of the cushions behind him, on the rear of the settee, while looking up at the ceiling. "Abbs, Abbs, Abbs, where on earth does one begin? As you well know, we are dealing with some psychopathic serial killers. In his effort to bring social faults to a head?"

"Not seeing any response to all his killings and letters, getting frustrated by the day, caused by the several community departments, who have failed in their commitments."

He continued, "Abbs, the killer, or killers, are choosing a subject matter to highlight a lack of response by the authorities yet underlining them with horrific examples."

Carter thought to himself, how does one explain matters to a partner? How far should I go in this present case? It doesn't seem just enough to say one has had a shit of a day?"

Carter suddenly found Abbs, had walked over, and sat next to him. She took him in her arms. "Carter, I can see by your face that your mind is in turmoil, playing the 'what if' debate, or 'should I tell her, or not'?"

"Well, Mr. For you to admit, 'A shit of a day' that's good enough for me?" She smiled, "So this is the order for the evening. Shower alone, a quick meal, then bed, and sleep, with me offering genuine TLC."

Matters panned out as Abby suggested for when in bed, she insisted that he should lay with his back to her. She snuggled up close to him, placing her right arm over his right shoulder and neck, with her right leg over his right thigh, pulling herself close to him.

Carter turned his head and, with such a pitiful voice, whispered over his right shoulder. "Abbs, if you think that I'm capable of lying here with you squeezing and moulding the shape of your gorgeous body against me, please accept my so inevitable reactions?"

Abby leaned over him and, after kissing him on the nape of his neck, whispered, "Shush lovely, now try to go to sleep?" He smirked, "I'll try?"

38

The following morning, Carter woke up to find himself in the same restricted grip. He lifted both her right arm and right leg from off him. She began to stir, "Carter, Carter, what are you doing?"

He looked at her, "Abbs, thanks for your acts of concern, but due to my early commitments, I must try and get my head around a meeting that my boss, Commander Frost, is to attend."

Smiling at her, "Going by his reaction to a comment made by me, if he had remained on the line, it would have ended in disaster. I decided to invite him to a 'scrum down' an off-the-record meeting with myself and my team." He coughed, "Not being too dramatic, it all could end in my giving in my notice?"

Abby suddenly gasped, "Carter, surely, as the head of the MCU, it's a trusted position; you have all your team and others depending on and looking up to you."

Carter burst out laughing, "Correct, but even in the police, the higher you climb the tree, there is a great wedge of career politics. I not only function as a police chief dealing with serious crimes, but when we have a serial case, such as my latest, once the invisible line is crossed, *'Should we alert members of the press and public'?"*

"My immediate boss knows should the shit hit the fan, he realises that he has me to take the blame, but I have always mentioned for him to involve our public relations director, but as usual, he'd go mad and demand my appearance at his office. Abbs, I have so much evidence of my requests, yet he shoots me down."

Abby leaned over and hugged him while kissing him passionately on his lips. She pulled back. "Carter, it would be so easy for us to ardently fall into a sexual mass. But no, you need to prepare for your council of war?"

Carter got out of bed and walked into the wet room; switching on the shower; he waited until the correct temperature. He strolled in and began to soap himself, thinking how much bloody time she needed. Reluctantly, he completed his shower alone.

Abby had laid out his clothes; he stood in the bedroom with a towel around his waist. She looked at him, "Carter, I told you that you should shower alone, so change your face and stop looking so miserable?"

He dropped his towel and just stared at her; she left the bedroom saying, "Carter, get over it, and come through for your morning breakfast.

When dressed, he walked into the kitchen; she held out the mug. She smiled, "Well, Carter, isn't it unbelievable how quickly men can resort to being little boys when they don't get their way?"

On completion of his coffee, he handed his mug to Abby. Thanking her, she replied, "Carter, subject to your meeting, and you still hold a job. Then, when you come home tonight, there may well be something on the menu to your liking?"

He kissed her goodbye, left for the front door of their flat and continued to his car.

39

As Carter drove to the office, he called Eric, "Morning Eric, not wishing to use the 'Q' word." Eric burst out laughing, "Sir, all have gathered, and I've been informed by TF's secretary he's on his way." Carter replied, "Is Wendy there?" "Yes, sir." Came the reply. Carter replied, "Fine." And closed the call.

He arrived some fifteen minutes later, booked on duty, and received his welcomed mug of coffee from Eric. He was about to thank him when TF walked in. "Morning everyone. Is there one of those for me?" One of Eric's young secretaries jumped up and completed the quest.

He thanked her, then looked at Carter, "Right, lead the way and let's get this over with." As they left, Carter looked at Eric, waving, indicating for him to join them.

On entering the conference room, the team came to attention. Eric filed right for the back of the room, leaving TF and Carter to continue their way to the front of the room. It was there that they met Sue and Wendy. TF sat in one of the empty chairs.

Carter looked out over the team. "Good morning to you all. I'd like to welcome Commander Frost and Wendy Field, the force PR director."

"Before we start, I'd just like to go on record, for the mantra born out when in this room, plus there is no consideration of rank, just good manners?"

He continued, "Yesterday, I was on the phone with TF, and the subject arose about organising a press conference in relation to our most recent case?"

Sue noticed TF began to fidget in his chair.

He suddenly stood up, "Well, there you have it; your guv wishes to open it up to the press; now, why should he want to adopt that attitude?"

Carter noticed Sue and Wendy, for all the blood seemed to drain out of their faces.

He suddenly turned, "Well, sir…" TF stood, "When in this room, there is no rank; it's TF."

Carter turned, "You more than most know the senior rank structure of the force the Chief, who is three places, and TF, who is one place above a serving Chief Superintendant, and if this case goes tits up, I see my head on the block, and the shit falling all over both me and my team?"

TF stood up, "Utter nonsense; I see that it is the responsibility of the police to protect members of the public, under certain circumstances, when confronted by such issues that may cause dissent?"

Carter, who remained seated while TF made his statement, stood up, "Well, TF, I and certain others feel the longer it goes on, the worse it will be both as a public and press issue?" He coughed, "At present, we have a death toll of some 13 victims, as you are aware, 10 above the specific number of a serial case…?"

He glanced at his boss, "I feel that we're at the damage limitation stage, and in the victim's latest letter, his next will be to the Echo's Crime desk."

TF stood up, "Wendy, have you had any news hounds sniffing around?"

Wendy stood up, "Sir, I do feel we should wait until the reporter sniffing stage; it's too late. Do you remember the 'Rule of four case?' The force decided to keep a lid on things (She was careful not to point the finger directly at TF)

"I assure you that I was present in the CPS office, inside the Crown Court building, when Carter and Sue were both manhandled into the office by their protection detail to avoid all the hordes, and the free-for-all with members of the press."

"A loud body of the press met them, "Why were the public never told of these matters?" Another called, "Why are we just learning of the fact that four of the defendants are, or were, top-ranking police officers in The Merseyside force…?"

"Some of the press shouted in such an annoyed way that they just shouted, in their tempers, and so it went on, together with the torrent of profound accusations. Matters descended to a level needing one of the reporters to be escorted from the building."

Wendy continued, "Sir, I hope I've been able to give you an insight as to what happens if we exclude the press when dealing with another serial case, which could affect members of the public?"

"Sir, in conclusion, I must point out that we're always quick to involve the press when in need of their help, as in the 'Gainsford case' you must remember another serial case. The local press assisted in the preparation of a glossy insert, re the long and forgotten schools of Liverpool, with photographs, most importantly the one of St Vincent's catholic school."

"The photographs continued, showing the old school picture, with the offender's father, Godwin, as possible bait to lure out the serial killer, Gainsford. Resulting in the brave antics of Carter and his hospitalising as a result." Wendy turned and sat down to a vigorous round of applause.

Carter stood up, and he looked at TF, "There lies the case for the defence; I now await your case for the prosecution?"

TF stood up, "I realise that you all think that I'm the villain in all of this, but you all must realise that I'm accountable to a higher plane, namely ACC Crime and the Chief Constable, who has a direct line to the home office, plus other members of the 'Marble Halls'''".

TF continued, "Before we start down the BOS (ball of shit) road, I'd like to mention two points, 1. It's been mentioned on so many occasions by Wendy that the PR director's main responsibility is the protection of the home office, force, the Ch Con, and, of course, you all in this room and the public. 2. That in certain cases, we have the invisible line, how far do we go in which we put lids on matters, that in certain circumstances how do we deal with the fallout, in telling the press, and the public?"

"We look at items, is the job at fault, if so, how do we deal with it, are other agencies involved, do we throw them under the bus? Now, in the latest case, it would seem that our predator is seeking retribution on several fronts, so in my position, how do we proceed?"

Carter stood up, "First and foremost, we have an identity problem, not just in seeking the offender, but most of the public know that all serious cases are investigated by the MCU, so while the shit hasn't hit the fan when it does, it tends to fall on us. He looked at TF, please don't say that's why we get paid the big bucks?" The room roared with laughter.

He looked at TF. "It is plain to see that the predator wants to hang all of this on someone. In his letters, he has begun with, *'For whom it may concern'* he has also mentioned, *'Dear DCS Carter'* with the reason for his actions against the victim. He, therefore, sees that under certain circumstances, such matters should fall under the remit of myself and the MCU?"

So, prior to his threat of escalating his letters, addressing them to the crime correspondent of the Liverpool Echo. In a press release, perhaps we can leek a brief resume of the crimes and matters being dealt with by me and the MCU; in that case, he gets me to moan at the respectable MCU team on all the reported matters?"

Sue suddenly stood up and, in a raised voice, said, "No, guv, why do we have to clear everyone's shit up, for which she received a loud round of cheers and applause.

TF stood up; by the look on his face, they could all see he was annoyed. "Ford, while your thoughts are commendable, please take stock of the situation. At times, there is no running away from such situations, including all present here?"

Sue jumped to her feet, "TF please, you must be fuc…Carter leapt to his feet. "Yes, Ford, we all get your point. At that precise moment, one could hear a pin drop, for there wasn't the raucous laughter from the team acknowledging their bosses' thoughts.

While the room remained quiet, Eric coughed; perhaps this would be a good time for a well-earned break; there were refreshments at the back of the room. Carter stood up, "Say fifteen minutes?"

Most started to drift to the back of the room for their refreshments. Sue, who found herself walking at the side of Carter, looked at him and smiled, and Carter, in a low voice, and through his smile, muttered, "Look, please, you do not need to defend me; it's a well-trodden road, and we've both come through matters as in the past." He broke off and headed for his coffee and Eric.

Upon receipt of his coffee from Eric, Eric looked at Carter, who, through his smile, said, "Guv, please don't let them fuck you, for you know you're getting fucking nowhere; please, please do not make it a resignation job?" Changing the subject, but still smiling, "How is the coffee."

Before he had time to reply, TF, who must have heard the end of their conversation, interrupted, "Yes, Eric, I keep on reminding myself to ask the name and blend of your coffee, as the coffee served at HQ is woeful."

  Minutes later, TF said, "Are we ready to resume?"

40

When all suited and booted, TF stood up; he looked at Carter, "Right, how do we proceed, for its blatantly obvious that both you and Wendy Field wish to include some type of press involvement? Which in turn could have such a catastrophic effect on the public alike. Although we keep the perpetrator on our side, which overall allows us to control what we tell the press?"

He looked at Carter; Sue could see by the look on his face that he was about to explode. Carter shouted, "Well, fuck me if this is not a rose by any other name. It's nothing but a watered-down admittance of what should have been fucking dealt with on day one, and it would appear that me and my team will take the shitty fallout."

Carter turned as he walked towards the office door, "Mark my words, when the press and the public find out that we have a psychopathic murderer in our mist and had been about for the last, say, two months, there will be shit, and we'll all need umbrella's?"

TF shouted, "And where the fuck do you think you're going to?" Carter spun round, "To the fucking gents, you don't mind. Or do I have to put up my hand?" Sue immediately put both hands over her mouth, and Wendy's face looked completely drained, awaiting a typical TF broadside.

Carter continued with his intention. Alex stood to open the door and, with a weak smile, said, "Guv."

TF returned to his chair and sat down in a huff, folding his arms and mumbling, "Ha! All stops for his Lordship to nip to the loo...?" From within the body of the room, a voice said, "Why don't you get off his fucking back.?" A second voice commented, "If you could do any better, why don't you have a fucking go...?" The room erupted in rapturous applause and laughter.

Carter happened to re-enter the room, and the whole team came to attention; he burst out laughing as he walked over to get a glass of water, "I only went to the loo, for Christ's sake?"

When all settled down, TF suddenly stood up, "No, Carter, we seem to have two bloody comedians in our midst. Carter looked at Sue, who, it was obvious, had tears of laughter in her eyes. She just shrugged her shoulders.

Suddenly, Peter and Philip stood up. Peter said, "If one has the immunity afforded by this room against any rank implication, or punishment, for a comment, then we're the comedians. Carter looked completely gobsmacked.

TF said, "Can we please agree to move forward that Wendy prepares a press brief, with a copy for yourself? I'll take it to the chief and let you know. He looked out over the room, and will all accept that you lot?"

As he turned to leave, the team all stood up, calling, "Goodbye, Tony." They could all hear him laughing as he walked down the corridor.

After the meeting, and when standing in the general office, Eric offered Carter a mug of coffee. Carter thanked him and then looked at both Sue and Eric. "Right, do I have to ask, or is one of you going to tell me of the remark about comedians?"

Sue smiled, "It was after TF made his sarcastic quip about your need for the loo that the obvious offenders were the 'Chuckle brothers,' Peter and Philip. Peter chirped up, "Why don't you get off your fucking arse?" The second, Philip chirped up, "If you could do any better, why don't you have a fucking go?"

Carter smiled, "It's a good job they're protected by the anonymity that's held in this room?" He turned and armed with his coffee, left for his office.

Sue looked at Eric, "I thought he'd have commented?" Eric just smiled, "Boss, did you not see it in his eyes?"

When he sat in his office, Carter looked at his watch. It was noon. He called Abby, *"Carter, what a lovely surprise. How did the meeting go? Did you get your way? As like with me. Sorry, I forgot we're talking about work-related issues?"*

Carter coughed, "I was ringing to invite you to lunch, but on second thoughts, it may be dangerous to let someone out with such naughty thoughts?" Abby screamed, *"Please, Carter, I promise to be a good girl, oh! Gosh, I've done it again..."*

Through his laughter, he spluttered, "Tom's 12.30pm. Now, please try to concentrate." He closed the call.

Entering the general office, he walked over to the diary and signed out, 'Enquiries Allerton Road, crime file number to follow.' Eric, who happened to be standing by the table looked down, he smiled, "You little liar." He looked at Eric, "Will you let Sue know? And I have my pager and phone with me. Will you please ask Peter and Phil to be at my office, say 2.00pm?"

He walked into Toms; the little brass bell activated; it always seemed to herald his arrival that fellow diners looked up like a grazing herd of animals that suddenly heard a noise.

Carter found what he was looking for. As he passed Tom on his way to Abby's table, Tom said, "Coffee?" Carter smiled, "Why, of course, Tom."

Carter smirked as he moved between the tables. Apologising to a nearby diner, he happened to catch he squeezed into the cramped space. The lady looked up at him, and she smiled, "Why, that's okay." Her smile lasted until he turned to sit next to Abbs. After navigating the reduced space, he managed to lean down kissing Abbs on her cheek, prior to eventually sitting down.

He let out a sigh, "At last, pew, it's like being at a football match." Abby took hold of his arm, pulling him closer to her, "Come here, you gorgeous man; I do miss you even though it's only been some four hours since I last saw you?" She leaned over and gently placed her lips onto his cheek but pressed significantly, prior to returning to her position.

Tom acknowledged them both, took their order, and fifteen minutes later, one of the young waitresses brought it over to their table. They were both deep in conversation yet trying to eat with dignity during their meal. Abbs listened intently to Carter as he explained the vigorous meeting with his boss and the team.

Not realising that Abbs had just taken a sip of water, Carter resighted the two quotes made by both Peter and Phil, two members of his team, after he'd left the room. Abbs suddenly snorted with reaction, and all the residue ejected down her nose. She squealed, "Carter."

It was while Abbs was tendering to her blouse, and her fellow diners embarrassed sniggers could be heard. That Carter's pager activated, again the finger of embarrassment pointed at them both.

He looked down, and while he pressed the button to stop the constant noise, he noticed the telephone number for the general office. He apologised to Abbs while she was still dealing with her blouse. He decided to make the call at the table, for the place was packed.

He pressed the contact number on his phone. Eric answered immediately, "Sir, please return to the nick. There has been yet another incident, but you won't have time to come up to the office for DS Watson. Your designated APO will be waiting in the yard to explain matters?"

He looked at Abbs, "I'm so sorry, but I must go. The wheel has fallen off. I will call you, but it's a knocking bet that I'll be late home tonight. He kissed Abbs and left. On his way out, he paid their bill and quickly left for his car.

41

On his arrival at Derby Lane police yard, he noticed Charlie stood leaning against his car with his arms folded. On seeing Carter's car arriving, he stood up. Carter locked and secured his car. He quickly walked over to Charlie.

He opened his car, saying," Hello, guv, sorry for the drama?" Carter got into his car, and prior to securing his safety belt, they were off. Charlie pressed the button to activate the blues and twos.

Carter shouted, "Charlie, why the fucking rush?" He coughed, "Can we not calm down? Where the fuck are we rushing off to, and why?" Charlie replied, "Sorry, guv, but two important things happened while you were out for lunch. One, the duty Inspector in the control room activated the MCU, informing Eric that the bodies of two men had been found, query drowning. In Queens Drive swimming baths, Walton, close to County Road."

Charlie continued, all while he was trying to negotiate his way through the traffic on Queens Drive.

Guv, and two, The ACC crime, and TF, agreed to a press release to catch the lunchtime edition of the Liverpool Echo."

"The important thing is that, as mentioned in your scrum down, to comply with the perpetrator's wishes, he wanted the details of both the police department and the officer given the task of making the necessary inquiries. Guess what, yes, you've got it?"

As they were speaking, Carter's phone activated. He took it out of his jacket pocket, "Carter." "Guv, it's Sue... he interrupted, "Yes, Susan Martha Ford, I have just received the news if that is what you're calling about?" She shouted, "Yes, guv, what a fucking cheek by TF; you'd have thought he'd have given you the heads up, as he allegedly promised?"

Carter stated, "Sue, we're almost there. See you shortly?" And closed the call. Charlie continued driving, heading towards the flyover of Queens Drive and County Riad. He took the off-ramp for County Road. He then turned immediately left into Church Mews, opposite Walton church, which leads to the public baths.

On arrival, Charlie noticed Sue standing by her car outside of the building. He pulled up and parked next to her as Carter was about to leave his car. Charlie coughed, "I've also been ordered to give you this?" Carter turned to look at him, and he noticed that Charlie had his gun and holster in his hand.

Carter looked at him, and he burst out laughing, "Where, pray tell, did you keep that while we were hurtling down Queens Drive?" Charlie replied, "Why, here in the interior door panel, until such times as I could give it to you?" Carter just laughed.

Sue walked over and handed Charlie his forensic suit. She then suddenly came to a sudden halt, "What the fuck...?" And in utter surprise noticed that Carter was standing with his holster in one hand and firearm in the other.

She whispered, "Please take care, Carter, for the dogs of war have been released?" Carter laughed, "Why, it's okay, Sue, Charlie has informed me."

Carter took off his overcoat and jacket. He leaned against the car, saying, "Charlie, will you please take these items to the car?" He replied, "Yes, guv." On his return, Carter laughed, "Will the pair of you stand in front of me looking outwards while I adjust my holster and firearm?"

When ready, Sue bent over and picked up his forensic suit, which she'd placed on the bonnet of her car. She turned and placed it onto his chest as usual.

While walking to the building, Carter took out his mask, placed it up to his nose, sniffed, and immediately took in the aroma of Vick. Sue looked at him, "Guv, what on earth are you doing?" Replying, he smiled, "Oh, nothing?"

42

On arrival at the Victorian-style building, they noticed all the emergency service vehicles parked out front, consisting of two ambulances, relevant paramedics, SOCO vehicles and staff with a police uniform presence, as well as MCU team members.

All three walked up to the proverbial uniform officer with the wooden clipboard to record their IDs and all the comings and goings. They offered their police IDs, and within minutes, the officer said, "Many thanks' sirs and ma'am." Carter quickly took hold of Sue as she tried to whip around, about to let rip.

He said, "Just leave it." Charlie, Ian, and Lloydie. We're laughing, looking upon two forensic-clad figures in what looked like turmoil at Sue's antics.

Eventually, normal service resumed, and all parties ascended the 10 stone steps to the entrance hall. The ticket office was on the left-hand side, with a glass frontage with a semi-circle cut at the bottom, which allowed the bathers to purchase and collect their tickets.

Carter noticed the typical Victorian-style decor, for the whole entrance was covered in green- and white-coloured tiles. On the hall walls were glass-fronted display cabinets with adverts for swimming costumes and lessons. Others displayed opening hours and applications for season ticket membership.

Facing Carter and colleagues, a uniform officer stood in front of four doors, two of which allow entry clearly marked, and the remaining two doors for exit clearly marked.

Sue walked up to the officer, who greeted her and opened one of the doors. They all passed, thanking the officer. They climbed a further three tiled covered concrete steps. At the top was open access to the splendid pool and the typical smell of chlorine. They also noticed access to the individual changing lockers that ran the length of the pool. Males to the left side and females to the right.

Carter noticed halfway down the pool a set of steps, with the same opposite, each placed on a raised wooden stand, with a chair-like seat on the top. He thought were the duty life savers perched. Behind the steps on the left was an arch with a notice, 'TODDLERS POOL' on the far side was the same except the notice read, 'SAUNA AREA.'

The whole area was painted in green and white colours to match the wall tiles. While Carter walked along the poolside, he noticed that all the changing locker doors were colour-coordinated individually, painted green doors for males and white doors for females.

All the locker doors were pushed open. In the lockers was a wooden board across the middle of the locker for a seat to assist changing, with two metal-shaped hooks on the walls on which to hang items of clothing.

He saw the two bodies floating face down in the water. He again observed the typical colours used in the pool. Only the floor of the pool had a large flower-shaped mural.

Carter walked up to where Gordon Chambers, the pathologist, and some of the SOCO officers were standing. Gordon in his typical loud voice which echoed around the pool. "Ah, Carter, welcome. I see you have some of your trusted senior officers with you?" Carter immediately interjected, "Gordon, Gordon, please, you do not need to shout?" He replied, "What, what, why yes, of course."

Gordon lowered his voice. "You will notice in situ the two bodies, still in the pool, as found and untouched."

Carter looked around and noticed a tall man dressed in a blue vest, white tracksuit bottoms, and trainers. "Excuse me, can you please tell me who you are?" He replied, "I'm the duty manager, who happened to find the two bodies when we opened. Other members of staff are in the staff canteen." Carter smiled, "Well, I'm Detective Chief Superintendent Carter of the 'Major Crime Unit'."

Carter looked at Gordon, "Our next move is to remove the bodies. Any ideas, apart from me designating an officer?" As he looked around, he noticed that all his officers made to look as if they were busy. The manager coughed, "Er, we have a large metal pole with a large plastic-covered hook, used to assist swimmers in difficulty and to remove any discarded clothing which may have been thrown into the pool.

Carter looked at him, "Can you fetch it for us to look at?" He turned and walked to the top left-hand corner of the pool; he returned carrying the described item. Gordon walked over and examined it. "Yes, yes, Carter, that will suffice. It will not cause any harm to the victims."

As Gordon got on with the matters at hand, Sue walked over to the manager and introduced herself, "I'm Detective Superintendant Ford of the MCU." Sue commented, "Please make yourself and members of staff available for interview by one of my officers."

Carter looked at the manager, "I must ask you to leave while matters continue. Please be aware that this is now a crime scene, and the premises will remain closed.

He replied, "Yes, of course." And left.

Carter and Sue both turned to see Gordon Chambers, standing holding the large pole in a vertical position, like some large ancient Venetian gondoliere. He looked at Carter, who smiled and nodded. Gordon leaned forward and, with the pole, gently hooked it under the armpit of the nearest victim and gradually pulled him to the edge of the pool.

He then placed the pole on the poolside while two of his staff lifted the victim from the pool, laying him on a black body bag. Gordon repeated the same for the second victim.

While this was being accomplished, Carter looked at Gordon and Sue, "Has anyone checked the male lockers to see if we can find their clothes? Philip approached his boss, "Guv, I've made a check and found nothing." Peter chimed in, "Guv, I checked the ladies' lockers just in case?" Carter smirked, "I thought as much."

Carter looked at both of his junior officers, "Gentlemen, please come to my office." He gestured to the steps leading down to the junior pool. Both, with a sheepish look, followed their boss.

Sue smiled at Lloydie and Ian, "One thing they won't need is the blotting paper?" Charlie looked at Sue, and she smiled, "It goes way back to the days when if the guv were to expect a bollocking from TF, he'd make the statement. It stems from his time at boarding school together with Rad. If they got the cain, it deadened the blows."

Sue was right; Carter, who was sitting on a bench at the side of the junior pool, looked at both his junior officers. "Welcome to my office?" He smiled, "Right, you two, you're both incredibly gifted officers, but what you're both not, you're not my mouthpiece. When making such statements on my behalf, please don't get me wrong, I'm profoundly grateful, but the mantra for that room only lasts to a certain level of decent.

Phil went to say something, but Peter gently touched his arm. They both stood to attention, "Guv." And left to join the others.

Back on the poolside, Sue looked at Carter, "Is all correct guv," He smiled, "Why yes, of course, were ever so…

43

Carter and Sue walked over to Gordon Chambers, who at that precise moment was on his hands and knees, examining the victims. He looked up, with his unusual crimson face due to his size and effort to get to the floor.

"Ah, Carter, our friend tends to make my job easy. I've found the tell-tale needle mark in the armpit area of the victims. He lifted each arm and pointed to the suggested marks, "Death by Asphyxiation. If you look closely, there are signs of light bruising and evidence of a choke hold around the necks of each victim, I'd go as far as saying that their hyoid bones have been crushed, as they say in the NYPD. *'I'll bet dollars to doughnuts that there is no pool water in their lungs?'*

I will know a lot more when I get them home; before you ask, TOD, between 8pm and 4am this morning, one should look for a possible break-in. Do we have your permission to remove the bodies?" Carter nodded.

Carter called over Lloydie. Before a word was uttered, his DS smiled, "Yes, guv, leave it with me?" He then looked at Peter and Phil, "Gentlemen, can I suggest that we set some of the team on a possible search of the premises for a possible source of entry? Plus, inquire if the building is alarmed when locked up for the night?"

Sue, Carter, and Charlie stood talking when they both noticed Wills walking towards them carrying a tray and three white plastic-type drinking containers, with what looked like steam residue wafting out of the drinking vessels.

Wills looked at his boss; he laughed, "Guv, please don't shoot the messenger, for I have no prior knowledge of the quality or taste of the coffee from the vending machine?" Carter smiled at him, "Wills did you not taste one yourself before serving your bosses?" The young DC just blushed, "Sir I just thought…"

Carter looked at his young DC. "Son, it would seem if it present's that bad, HR will be looking for replacements for three essential officers?" Wills burst out laughing, "Guv, I'm just pleased you don't have an official food and drinks taster?" Carter just smiled, "Son it's the thought that counts."

All three burst out laughing, yet after their first sips, they all turned, looking for a receptacle in which to discard the liquid and throw in their drink holders.

Carter put his hand into his pocket, taking out a note, "Wills, please nip round the corner to Monas café; they do *'take outs,'* purchase two white coffees, with two sugars and one black only. His face lit up, "Guv."

While they awaited their hot drinks, Sue called, "DC's Jules and Emily, can I ask you both to search the female cubicles, and DC's Alex and Elliott, the gents? She heard the echo reply, "Yes, boss."

Carter took a sly peep at his watch; it was 6.30pm. He thought the bodies had been removed, duty pool staff being interviewed, and a search of the premises was underway for a possible break-in. Perhaps home for sevenish??

He walked away from his colleagues, took out his phone and called Abbs. *"Carter, are you wondering what is on the menu for your tea, both on the real and erotic menus?"* She burst out laughing.

Carter coughed, "I'm just wondering, am I hungry, for there is a topless restaurant just opened, and the lads are wondering, should we pop in and satisfy both our needs?"

There was silence, then a sudden tirade, *"Look pal, I know you only have one bloody name; it's such a pity for one can put so much power behind a normal two-word name when blaspheming in making a point?"*

"I suppose guilty of killing a police officer, they tend to throw the key away?" She could hold her antics no longer, and she shouted, *"Okay, I forgive you. See you at home shortly?"*

After the call, he returned to the matter at hand. Sue informed him that they found signs of a break-in at the rear of the building, gaining entrance via the boiler room, the water heating, and chlorine until. But giving access to the pool's building?" She continued, "SOCO are in attendance."

Carter said, "Okay, let's finish here, leave matters to the SOCO officers to secure the premises, and regroup tomorrow, scrum down at 9.30am. Good night, all."

Charlie dropped Carter off outside of his block. He looked at Carter, "See you tomorrow, guv, early, he smiled, and after Carter had left the car, he drove off home.

44

Carter placed the security key fob on the reader and opened the door to their flat. He looked up the hall, and like breadcrumbs, he followed a line of discarded clothes in the hall leading to their bedroom. It started with shoes, stockings, skirt, blouse, bra. He thought, wow!

He took off his outer coat, suit jacket, shoulder holster and firearm. He placed his coats on the coat stand in the hall. He entered their bedroom to hear the shower. Placing his holster and firearm in the floor safe in the wardrobe, he undressed and stood at the entrance of the wet room.

He could hear lar, lar, lar, coming from the shower. He suddenly heard, "Oh! Is that you, Carter? I've been waiting in the shower for ages?" As Carter entered the shower, he was immediately met by Abb's beautiful body; with the soapy sponge glove in her hand, she had a look of utter surprise on her face.

Carter smiled at her, "You little liar, for a start, your clothes were still warm, and where are your panties? She had such an embarrassed look on her face, "How silly of me, I should have realised, forgetting my item of clothing, trying to fool you?"

Bursting out laughing, he shouted, "Me detective, you the predator, you gave it all away for it was rather like Hansel and Gretel, except in clothes and not breadcrumbs. And where are your panties.?"

Abbs burst out laughing, "Please don't worry, Carter, I'm no sexual deviant; I did it on purpose, for you'll find they are the first item on the top of the laundry basket?" He looked at her, "Yes, that's what they all say?"

Carter joined her in the shower, and battle commenced, a battle that they both genuinely enjoyed. They both fed off each other, taking their erotic behaviour just short of the dam-busting line.

Carter wrapped Abbs in an enormous bath sheet, and he took a small hand towel for her hair. He carried her, giggling and squirming, towards their bed; on arrival, he unrolled her onto the bed. Carter took hold of the hand towel and began to gently move the towel up and down her body. He lingered on her breasts and nipples.

It was while in that area that Abbs suddenly screamed, "Carter, it's either you on top of me, or me on top of you but stop lingering as if we don't complete matters; I'll get off this bed. Go and retrieve your firearm and shoot you; now, for all that you call Holy, will you please screw me?"

Carter got on top of Abbs, leaned down, and whispered, "Was it the thought of wearing no panties that turned you on?" She smiled up at him and suddenly took him in a vice grip, placing her legs around his torso, and just as she placed him inside of her, she suddenly squeezed.

She screamed, "Wow, Carter...yes, yes!" Abbs, reaching down, placed the corner of the duvet into her mouth. He smiled, "Yes, I should think so, for my night APO, may think an attack is taking place?"

Abbs looked up at him and, whilst trying to talk with the edge of the duvet in her mouth, laughed, shouting, "Carter, will you please shut up? Concentrate on the job at hand. He did, and on completion, he fell off her and back to his side of the bed.

He looked at her, "You do realise it will mean another shower?" She rolled over towards him, laughing, "Carter, do you mind if we leave the shower until after the last component of the day?"

Carter dressed in shorts and a T-shirt, and Abbs is wearing her drawstring cotton hipsters and one of Carter's T-shirts. He looked at her, for the garment fell so differently over the top of her body than his. Both walked through to the kitchen. They sat and enjoyed scouse, cabbage, red pickle, and portions of French stick with lashings of butter. Washed down with two glasses of lager each.

On completion, they cleared away, and both decided to leave the dishes until the morning in the lounge, ending the evening off with two glasses of Remy Martin and traditional coffee.

It was during this time that Abbs leaned over onto Carter's shoulder, "Isn't it funny how tired one becomes after a good meal, during which she looked up at him with such Devilment in her amazingly blue eyes, "I feel a yawn coming on?" She looked at Carter, and jumping up ran off toward the bedroom.

Carter strolled through to the bedroom, and his mind split between the present case and the aberration that is forever Abbs. As he entered his eyes immediately fell on her discarded clothes, and to be met by muffled screams of excitement. He looked in her direction to see that she was under the duvet, with it pulled up to her chin.

He stood at the foot of the bed with his clothes on. "Abbs, I was thinking, due to my recent case and an early scrum down in the morning, I thought that I'd sleep in the spare bedroom?"

There was a sudden silence. Abbs suddenly snorted and stood up completely naked, "So, Mr., You'll forego all of this whilst you retreat to the spare room to play mind games for tomorrow. Well, so be it, and she fell and entirely cocooned herself in their duvet, turning away from his side of the bed.

Carter burst out laughing, "Abbs, Abbs, Abbs, I was only joking. Nothing, complete silence. Carter went through to the bathroom to complete his ablutions. He returned ready for bed, entirely in the nude, after leaving his clothes in the laundry basket.

Walking across their room to bed, he fell onto his knees at the foot of the bed and slid under the duvet. On reaching her toes, her legs gently opened.

Abbey squealed, "This is far better than all of that mental turmoil; now, why don't you take it out on me?" He did, but it was passive on her behalf. The whole event eventually settled with their usual exotic shower.

45

Carter was awoken in receipt of tender kisses. All raining down on his lips and torso via Abbs. He slowly opened his eyes to witness the glorious face and the unfathomable depths of her radiant blue eyes looking down on him.

He sat up, taking hold of her, smiling, commenting, "Abbs, you do realise I could get totally lost within the atmosphere of your eyes; I'd have to wear my inflatable water wings, should I drown."

They both burst out laughing. Yet Abbs, who suddenly became serious, "Carter, please go and prepare for work alone, as you must get your head around your forthcoming meeting. While showering, I'll prepare your clothes for work."

When dressed, he walked through to the kitchen. Abbs turned around to see Carter. She smiled, "There's my man. You look gorgeous and seem none the worst for all of last night's capers?"

Carter finished his coffee, and when offering Abbs his empty mug, on receipt of it, she kissed and hugged him. At this time, she felt his holster and firearm; although she never stiffened, showing her distaste, she felt it all the same.

Carter left and, at the hall reception desk, met up with Charlie, his APO, for the journey to the office. Charlie smiled, "Morning, sir." Carter duly replied," "Morning Charlie." The journey to the office was in silence, and Carter read the morning paper that he'd collected from the reception desk.

On arrival at the general office, Carter wished everyone, "Good morning." And received a salvo of replies. He walked over to the daily diary and signed on duty. After which, he received his first and most enjoyable mug of morning coffee from Eric.

He then went and sat next to Eric, giving him a quick thumb sketch of the swimming pool murders. Eric said, "Guv, they are all awaiting your presence in the conference room for the scrum down.

Carter got up and, with his coffee in hand, left the general office, it was while he was walking towards the conference room that he bumped into Sue, "Morning guv, we're all waiting for you?"

Sue opened the door, and they both walked in. As the team shuffled their chairs, they came to attention. Carter said, "I'm not saying it, I'm not saying it, I can't be arsed, as you take no bloody notice?" He didn't and continued his walk to the front of the room. Hit by a roar of laughter from the team.

After normal service had resumed, he turned to notice that Sue had sat in one of the vacant chairs. Carter remained standing with hands in his trouser pockets. He looked over the team. "Right, most if not all of us were at 'Queens Drive baths' Walton yesterday evening. Two bodies were found floating in the pool."

The door to the room suddenly opened to reveal Lloydie, who stood looking rather tired, offering his apology. Carter turned, "Jim, please come in, please help yourself to a coffee, and take a seat."

Eventually, Lloydie sat and completed his coffee. Carter looked at his junior officer, "Lloydie, can I ask you for a thumb sketch of matters attained by Mr. Chambers."

Jim stood up, "Guv Mr. Chambers, sends his respects." Lloydie coughed as he slipped a hand into his inside jacket pocket, removing a plastic police evidence bag containing a white piece of paper within a plastic bag.

Looking at Carter, "Guv, the initial letter in the plastic bag was recovered from the swimming shorts of one of the victims." Carter smiled, "Jim, you have the floor."

Jim removed a pair of rubber gloves from his jacket pocket, putting them on. He opened the evidence bag and then the letter from the original plastic bag. Jim placed the two original bags on the floor next to him. He coughed.

> Dear Detective, Chief Superintendent Carter,
> Well, now, after several weeks and incidents, I've been given your name and title as a potential figurehead. After my threat to contact 'The Echo' the authorities didn't want matters spread to the press.
> DCS Carter, I know that you are the senior officer in charge of the MCU. Your reputation and that of your team are respected on both sides of the fence. I, therefore, realise that you have been hung out to dry by your bosses. I say this in two ways, 1) should you fail to resolve and bring the various parties to book, as requested in my previous letters, then it will be truly your head in the block if you know what I mean, and 2) I will go to press, I bull shit you not.
> Getting back to my latest victims, they are both rapists. Their MO, a figure of speech used in your circles, is quite appalling. They abducted three women, all teachers, who'd been on a night out in the City Centre.
> On leaving a club, they saw their victims walking up the street. They stopped, and with windows down, they chatted them up,

offering them a lift. At first, they declined their offer. Unfortunately, alcohol muddied the waters, and eventually, they relented and accepted the offer.

During their journey home, the two bastards offered them a glass of wine. Each glass was subsequently drugged. The girls found themselves in a warehouse. Well, they were repeatedly raped, and on each occasion, they were throttled to near death as the perpetrates derived sexual satisfaction.

The three girls were eventually found like some discarded rag dolls, suffering from severe bruising to their thighs and evidence of strangulation to their throats. The police found fingerprint evidence, and those two bastards were arrested but walked, due to insufficient evidence, due to a fuck up by your lot??

So, I thought I'd give them a taste of their own medicine. I feel that the MO will record not death by drowning but death by asphyxiation. Please remember DCS Carter, either fIx matters or else??

46

At the completion of the letter, Lloydie coughed with some caution prior to sitting down. Sat placing the letter back into the respective bags. Removing his rubber gloves, placing them inside each other as if like a pair of socks, placing them in his jacket pocket.

Carter looked at Jim, "Lloydie, have you had the letter dusted for fingerprints?" "No." Came the reply. "I'm just about to organise matters, guv?"

Carter turned, "Yes, Lloydie, for I need for you to remain, to fill us all in with Mr. Chambers report, but when completed your off home no arguments, you look done in."

Lloydie stood up, "Guv, Mr chambers sends his respects. Both victims showed signs of trauma wounds to their heads, and a puncture mark is hidden deep in their armpits, suggesting that both victims were rendered unconscious and drugged. Bruise marks to their throats no water found in their lungs suggests death was by asphyxiation."

"Guv, as you are aware, this is a brief vernal account of his findings; a formal report will be forwarded to you, with photographs, in due course."

Carter thanked him and, in doing so, said, "Now Lloydie, get off home, for I do not wish to upset Sam and thus lose the services of a top criminal psychologist." Laughter rang out around the room. Lloydie looked at his boss, nodded and left the room.

The atmosphere in the room remained buoyant until Carter turned to look at Sue. Because he was standing, his eyes fell, and he noticed she had such a stoic look on her face. He said, "Why, Superintendent Ford, whatever is the matter?"

She stood up, looking around the room she suddenly vented. "Am I the only one who picked up on the bastard's threats made in his letter? He is now aware of the guy's name, title, and the fact that he is the boss of the MCU. Plus, the threat in his closing paragraph, *Carter, fix matters or else?"*

A cloak of silence fell upon the team as they began to fidget in their seats. Carter shouted, "Enough, enough, why, Superintendent Ford, will you please refrain from upsetting the children, for you must realise I needed to give him a name, a point of reference, save him running to the Echo, revealing he's a serial killer."

"You all know my feelings on this. TF refused to involve the press, save a public outcry. Failing to understand that burying your head in the sand only makes matters worse."

At the completion of the guv's explanation, Sue turned, "Well, wait until TF hears about his threats. In his latest letter, you'll have APOs six deep around you; under no circumstances will he cough an apology?" She looked directly at Carter, "Guv, I feel you need to tell him not only are you at risk, but it's all the shit that will fall on you and the team?"

Carter suddenly turned, "I want a sub-team made up of a DS and four team members. You'll collect all the original letters, copy them, and replace the originals in their files. I don't want Eric upsetting?"

"Trace all the crime file numbers, source the names of the officers dealing, for our friend mentions mistakes made by the job?" (Slang for the force)

Carter left the meeting for his office. Eric must have seen him walking past the general office, for within minutes, one of his young secretaries knocked and entered with a mug of steaming black coffee on a tray.

He looked up, took the coffee, and thanked her. She smiled, saying, "Sir." And left his office.

It was some minutes later that there was yet another knock on his office door. He called, "Come in." The door opened and in walked Sue, carrying a mug of coffee. She walked over and sat on one of the chairs adjacent to his desk.

He immediately noticed the stern look on Sue's face, "Well?" Sue placed her coffee mug down on the table and spluttered. "Well, is that all you can fucking say, Sue pointed out a potential problem with his personnel security. Now that this bastard knows of your name, rank, and position in the police, fed to him by fucking TF. Overall, the inevitable would cause such a shit storm?"

Carter looked at her. "Sue, I know that you have my interest at heart. At this point, she stood up and dashed from his office in tears. As she quickly walked down the corridor, not wishing to draw attention to herself, through her tears, she whispered, 'You'll never know Carter?'

47

After Sue's reaction to his inevitable lack of concern for the threats made by the perpetrator in his latest item of correspondence, Carter smiled inwardly and set about dealing with the hoist of paperwork that lay in a pile on his desk.

Matters had continued, and during the afternoon, Carter suddenly realised that he hadn't spoken with Abbs. He relaxed back in his chair, took out his mobile phone, and dialled her number; within seconds, he heard her dulcet tones.

"Well, Mr., it's about that time of day, for time is slowly ebbing to an end, and still you hadn't called. Are all the wheels on or off?" He burst out laughing, "We at this end of the phone do not wish to second guess the Gods of crime quoting the 'Q' word, so I'll expect a hug and a cuddle at my usual man cave at the ebbing of the sun?" Abbs replied, *"Well, for one, I can't wait."* Laughing, she closed the call.

At that precise time, there was a knock on his door; he thought, 'shit, now you've gone and done it?' He replied sharply, "Come in."

The door opened to reveal Sue stood with Peter, and Phil stood behind her. Carter smiled, "Come in, come in; by the looks on your faces, it looks serious?"

The three entered and assumed seats at the meeting table adjacent to Carter's desk. He asked why the long faces. Sue looked at both her junior officers, "Well, who is going to tell the guv?"

Peter looked at Phil, "You might as well start as you heard most of the conversation?" Phil looked at Carter," Guv Pete and I had reason to attend at the CPS office about a matter due for hearing in the crown court, for a plea?"

"Guv, It was whilst in the general office waiting to see our case solicitor that I happened to overhear a couple of secretaries commenting on information that they were downloading, details of offenders due for release from prison, and their convictions."

"One paid particular attention to offenders having served time for serious offences such as rape, serious assaults, domestics, paedophiles, in fact, guv such matters dealt with by our predator?"

Carter leaned back in his chair he raised his arms behind his head. He took in a big sigh. "Information of due, or immediate release of convicted prisoners, that information of their release date, is passed to the CPS to suggest the terms of early release. Perhaps on parole or license, the sexual offenders register, such matters recorded due to limits on their behaviour?"

He shouted, "Hurrah for the White hats." Sue looked at the blank faces of her junior officers…"Urm, never mind, your guv loved cowboy films?"

Carter smiled, "If so, not so important in the normal run of things, but in the wrong hands, names of such offences could be very interesting if passed to a certain person?"

Carter looked at Phil, "Now, this is particularly important. Did you, Phil, mention such matters after leaving their office, say on your way back to the nick, or whilst in their office in a discreet manner?"

He continued, "Please, don't think your guv is cracking up, for it goes to the nub of the matter. Did you both see the secretary or just one of you? It gives credence to your evidence?"

Phil replied, "I mentioned it to Pete whilst in their office, mainly from the point of view that I wasn't hearing things?" Carter smiled, "Good lad, two pairs of ears and eyes are better than one where evidence is concerned."

"This may be a rhetorical question; did you see the girl make any notes…?" Sue interrupted, "Our friend may well run off a copy at the end of play today?"

Carter said, "Right, Pete, Phil, get yourselves off home to your bat cave; we'll pick matters up tomorrow, as I'm about to ring TF, for I fear a shit storm is about to descend? Perhaps we should all live in a bat cave, as they are all full…? Now, will you both please keep matters to yourself? Until we're certain…?"

After they left Carter looked at Sue, "Well, what do you think?" Sue, with a concerned look on her face, stated, "Carter, we have for ages kicked this round, and the most important question has always been, 'Where is he getting his info from'?" And yet it couldn't be simpler: have a friend in the CPS office?"

Carter stated, "Hang on, let's pass it up to TF?" He moved over, dialled the number, and pressed the *'conference call'* button. Jane answered as usual. Before she could get into gear, Carter interrupted, "Jane, this call is on the conference, and Sue is present." Jane replied, *"She gets all the luck."*

Jane, as if on second thoughts, mentioned, *"Oh Carter, how disappointing; I so look forward to my sexual-innuendo chats?"* Carter snorted, "Jane just put me through."

Click, "Okay, Carter, what do you want?" The rough voice of TF sounded. After Carter's explanation, after several seconds came the verbal salvo. He growled, "For fuck's sake, Carter, do you realise what sort of shit storm could come from all of this? We'll all get covered in it."

Carter, in a droll voice, said, "What, sir, surely not enough to get to the fifth floor?" And closed the call.

Sue put her hands to her mouth and shouted, "Carter?"

48

Carter arrived home at 6.15pm. That evening, he had pre-warned Abbs that he was running late via a quick call on his way home. Carter said good night to Charlie, his APO, turned and left for his block.

After his usual chat with the duty APO and the duty concierge, he left for his flat. Placing the door fob on the security door system, he entered their flat to be met by Abbs, stood smiling, dressed in her cotton drawstring trousers and white cotton tank top, revealing her firm midriff, and the contours of her braless breasts, pressed against the material of her top.

Smiling, she looked at Carter, "Love you look dun in, now go take a lone shower, tea is about to be served, beef curry, and all the works." Carter smiled, "I'm starved?"

They hugged and kissed. Carter slipped out of his coat, jacket, and kit, removing all and placing them in their prescribed locations. Peeling off to their respective destinations. Carter, the bedroom, and shower, with the aroma of curry in his nostrils, and Abbs, to the kitchen.

Carter entered their bedroom and felt a slight breeze. He thought that Abbs had left the window open in the bedroom to help eradicate the partial steam from the bathroom after her shower. However, the ceiling extractor fan dealt more than adequately with the situation.

Stripping out of his work clothes down to his boxers. He was about to move for the safe in the wardrobe...That was the last action, as everything went black. Due to a solid blow to the back of his head, causing a severe head injury.

Carter was not aware of the four well-built men hiding in the bathroom and a fifth hidden behind their bedroom door. All dressed in black, wearing balaclavas, overalls buttoned to the neck, gloves, and boots with their trousers tucked inside.

They quickly went into action like a well-drilled team. One man placed a hand towel over Carter's head to stem the bleeding. Another man took out a hypodermic needle and injected Carter with a clear-coloured substance. A third man brought out a dressing gown from the bathroom, and they quickly placed it on him; the fourth man stood at the threshold of the bedroom door to stop possible detection.

Prior to leaving, one of the men covered his head with a black hood, and another hoovered up all his day clothes, placing them into a prepared plastic bag. When completed, he tired the bag and threw it through the open ground floor window.

Three of them lifted him up and gently raised him through the window. One man had gone through first assisting with the manoeuvre. Taking hold, Carter under his armpits and pulled him through. It took all of ten minutes.

Carter and Abbs shared a ground-floor flat, and the master bedroom window overlooked the side of the estate, allowing access to allotted garages. It was dark, and the area was packed with rhododendron bushes.

The abductors had parked a dark blue transit van in the darkest area of the garages, out of reach of the shafts of light given off by the high-intensity security lighting. The beam of the lights overlapped, causing a blind spot.

When ready, they picked Carter up and carried him through the bushes over to their vehicle. He was placed in the back, covered by a black sheet of tarpaulin. Three got in the back with their quarry. Leaving one to get in via the driver's door. The fifth quietly checked and secured the doors, leaving him to get in the front passenger door and seat. They removed their balaclavas and slowly drove out of the estate, not wishing to draw attention.

Abby, wondering what was keeping Carter, walked down the hall, calling, "Carter, Carter, how long does it take you to have a shower? I could understand if I were with you?"

She walked into their bedroom. She was about to call Carter but only got as far as, "Carrrr." She immediately noticed the draft from the open window and could not hear any sound of water running from his shower.?

But what suddenly brought her to an abrupt halt, turning her blood to ice, was the large amount of blood on their bedroom floor. It was everywhere.

Abby, with a bloodcurdling, screamed as she ran out to the front door of their flat. The duty APO ran from behind the reception desk, calling, "Abby, what on earth is the matter?"

Replying, she cried, "It's Carter, I think he's been taken?" The officer ran past her. On entering their flat, calling, "Sir, sir." She called, "Check our spare bedroom on the right."

Abby had caught him up and witnessed the APO as he came to a sudden halt. It was as if he had suddenly turned into a statue. He eventually came around, turned, saying, "Excuse me, Abbs, and rushed back to the reception desk; he called over his shoulder, "Don't touch a thing."

On arrival at the reception desk, he picked up the phone and dialled the force control room.

49

The mobile phone placed on Sue Ford's coffee table suddenly activated with her call theme. She snorted, looking at her date. With a devilish look in her eyes, she said, "Please, not tonight of all nights?" She picked up her phone, "Ford."

A tearful voice said, *"Boss, it's Jules, I'm 'on call.' Can you attend at the guv's flat immediately?"* Sue screamed, "Why?" The floodgates opened, and through her tears, she spluttered, *"They think the guv's been abducted?"*

Sue apologised to her date, "Sorry, I have to go." With a weak smile on her face, she said, "Mind if I take a rain check on our date?"

Outside her house, she kissed her friend, then jumped into her car and activating the blues and twos, she sped off for 2, Keswick Mansions, Carter's designated address.

While she carved her way through the traffic, her force radio continually spewed out information, "To patrols and controls, patrols and controls."

On arrival, she saw the circus, blue lights flashing, illuminating the whole of the night sky. The glow silhouetted the outline of the trees on the estate and the nearby park. The force air unit helicopter noisily hovered overhead like some giant agitated bee. It kept circulating, also illuminating the scene and park with its immensely bright front-mounted searchlight.

Sue ran from her car and entered the building to be met by Martin, the duty APO, who was standing talking with

Charlie. Also present were Jules, Phil, Peter, Ian, and Lloydie.

Sue turned to her team, "What the hell happened?" Lloydie walked over, "Boss, SOCO are all over this, like shit on a blanket. Working in the guv's flat and bedroom. Martin, the night APO heard a sudden scream. He looked up and saw a lady by the name of Abby Remington coming from the flat in a distressed state and running towards the reception desk.

Sue looked at Lloydie, "And where is this lady now?" He replied, "Sat in the guv's lounge, with a uniformed policewoman for company. We were all awaiting your arrival."

Sue turned, "Jules, Lloydie, and Charlie, come with me. Will the rest see to the investigation in and outside of the block, get the dog section out?"

In the flat, Sue stood outside of the bedroom, looking in. One of the SOCO team walked over, "Boss, we're still dealing with the scene inside and out, but you can have a quick look-see."

He walked Sue closer to the window, and he said, "The cheeky bastards removed the double-glazed unit and lent it against the wall. Allowing complete access. Sue noticed the metal trays on the floor to preserve the scene. She immediately took in all the blood on the carpet. There was the usual flashing of the SOCO photographer's camera. Sue looked at the officer, thanked him, and left.

In the hall, Sue turned and walked into the nearby lounge. The policewoman stood up, smiled at Sue, and uttered the usual, "All correct, boss."

The lady also stood up, and Sue said, "I'm Detective Superintendant Ford, DCS Carter's deputy. The attractive lady shook hands and replied, "I'm Abby Remington… Before she continued, Sue interrupted her, "Yes, Miss Remington, I am fully aware of the situation.

She looked at Abby. Can you please explain what happened here this evening?" After Abby's full and detailed explanation, Sue looked at Lloydie. "I'm just going to go outside and call TF. While I'm out, can you see to some hot drinks? I'm sure we could all go one or something stronger?"

Outside at the reception desk, Sue called Tony Frost; the phone answered in seconds, and a growl came down the phone "Frost." "It's Ford, sir; I must report that DCS Carter has been abducted. They gained entry by removing the guv's ground floor bedroom window."

On the guv's arrival home…TF shouted, "Call him Carter, for Christ's sake." "Carter went for a shower before his evening meal. It was only when Miss Abby Remington, a friend of Carter's. Called him for his tea, and why the delay? She went to their bedroom. Found the open window and all the blood over the carpet. She went out screaming into the reception area and reported matters to the duty APO."

Tony Frost shouted, *"So we know fuck all, except him missing from his flat. There is no need for me to come down; I'm sure you'll have things under control?"*

He continued, *"Now look here, Ford, whatever you need, you only need to ask. I want you to organise a meeting at 9.30am. Tomorrow at Derby Lane, with Wendy Field Sam Watson. Right, I'll see you then."* And he closed the call.

After her call, Sue returned to the lounge. Where she found Abby sitting with a glass of brandy, Jules and the uniformed policewoman had hot drinks.

The policewoman turned to Sue, "Boss, can I get you a hot drink"? "Please." Sue replied, "Coffee, milk and two sugars." *'Sue's mind drifted into overdrive, for she knew exactly where everything is kept, but alas, that was when he was married to Helen, his wife.'*

Hot drink in hand, Sue, sat opposite Abby, sat on the settee. "Miss Remington, no doubt WDC Fry has taken a full statement. Abby nodded in agreement. Sue continued, "Miss Remington, I would like to have a chat…Abby interrupted, "Officer, please call me Abby."

Sue made herself comfortable; she took out her mobile phone, "Abby, do you mind if I record our conversation? It will only be used as an 'Aide-memoir' and not used in any legal capacity?"

Abby smiled, "That's fine."

Sue leaned down and switched on her phone to record. "Abby, how long have you known DCS Carter?" Abby looked Sue straight in the eyes, "I met, or should I say, I was a guest at a party. He was a fellow guest. We were never formally introduced?"

"I had no idea who he was. Until his pager activated, and he offered his apologies and left. It was only afterwards that the hoist informed me. That he was a senior police officer."

Sue coughed, "Abby, how did you get to know DCS Carter?" Abby again looked straight at Sue, "DS Ford, I've given WDC Fry a full statement as to the circumstances of the recent events."

"I feel that legally, I have complied with police instructions, which is my duty. Legally, I feel that I don't have to tell you anything about my relationship with DCS Carter?"

Abby stood up, again looking Sue straight in her eyes, "Officer, have you now finished with your inquiries? I realise that the bedroom is a crime scene, I will lock the door, and as such, I will sleep in the spare room, not disturbing matters. So, if done, will you please leave."

Sue looked at Jules, and she nodded; she then looked at Abby. Miss Remington, thank you for your time; I assure you that we'll keep you up to date with our inquiries." She smiled, turned, and left.

As Abby was about to leave the lounge, Sue suddenly called, "Abbey, were you aware if DCS Carter had removed his firearm? Abby replied, "He'd removed his coat and jacket. He removed his firearm and walked into our bedroom.

Sue looked at Lloydie and others, "I want a full search of the bedroom; the last thing we want is a police firearm on the loose. If locked and secured, Phil, call out the duty locksmith to make sure. For the guv may have done the business before he got abducted?"

50

Sue arrived home at 10.30pm. She took off her coat and let it fall to the floor in the hall. She walked into her lounge and placed her bag onto a nearby armchair.

Looking around her lounge, realising that her intended evening had gone up in smoke, and her expectations for the night, had all dispersed into the either, on receipt of her call from Jules. She secured her firearm.

Walking up the stairs to her bedroom, muttering as she undressed, thinking it had been ages since she'd last been laid, and oh! How much she was looking forward to such a night.

In the shower, she vigorously washed herself with her sponge as if she were trying to wash away her thoughts. Dried off, she dressed in her, PJ's and dressing gown, and Woolly slippers, departing for downstairs.

Entering her lounge, she walked over to the drink cabinet and poured herself a large scotch. Returning to an extremely comfortable armchair. She took an excited swallow. As the warm, yellow-coloured liquid went down her throat, she ex-hailed, whispering as if she didn't want anyone to hear. "Then she screamed, "It's just like you, Carter, it's as if you wanted to fuck my night up?"

On completion of her drink, she swanned into the kitchen to make herself a sandwich. During the process, she nibbled at a radish, a slice of cucumber, and other salad components of her snack.

Returning to the lounge with her much-awaited sandwich, a bowl of crisps, and a can of lager, she placed them on her side table, opened the can, poured the content of the beer into a glass, and took a drink, in fact, several. She suddenly thought, if I'm going to sleep this night, I'll need the assistance of alcohol.

After yet another scotch, leaving all the vestiges of the evening, Sue retired for the night. Discarding her dressing gown, she removed her PJ's top, went to the dresser, opened a drawer, and removed a sweatshirt belonging to, of all people, Carter. Placing it over her head, she smoothed it over her breasts and slipped into bed.

Sue slithered under her duvet, making herself comfortable. In doing so, she cuddled the sweatshirt close to her; it had never been washed and held the faint sweat, smells, and used cosmetics of himself. The aroma of Aramis, his favourite aftershave, but alas, it was getting fainter by the day.

It was a garment that Carter had left after one of their surveillance jobs in which they'd both been soaked. Carter being the usually organised sod, had spare clothes for such an event, kept in a holdall in the boot of his car. The garment had been left by accident by Carter. Sue had conveniently failed to remind him.

Her mind was working overtime; with all the events of the evening, she just continued to hug the garment to herself, smiling. Then suddenly, she burst out crying. It was not only the pressure of Carter's abduction but the love she held for him; it was unbearable.

It all began when she was posted to the CID as an aid (usually on six-and twelve-month secondments) at Eaton Road police station. On her first morning in the CID office, she found she was working on Carter's state (duty schedule). She knew him when she was in uniform and remembered all the jaw-dropping tones which spewed out of the mouths of the divisional WPCs describing Carter.

Sue suddenly, while still crying, pushed her head into her pillow and bawled. Through her tears, remembering all the conversations mentioned by Carter, when from time to time mentioned a date, he'd been on, and witnessing all the different girls on his arm, at promotion and retirement do's. And now, bloody Miss Remington.

She thought. What is the point of living if you have such a shitty life?

51

Carter was harbouring no such thoughts, for he felt he was starting to awaken from a black haze; nothing was making any sense; as the black mist was beginning to dissipate, Carter realised that he was on a bed, bound by his wrists, behind his back, and ankles.

He felt cold and began to shiver, for as much as he could tell or make out, he was wearing a dressing gown, 'T'-shirt, trousers, socks, and loafers.

Eventually, Carter realised that he must have been drugged, for he was affecting matters he'd once experienced before, resulting in that feeling of slowly reconnecting with life, and yet secured, unable to move whilst laid on a bed. Each time he moved, he could feel a sharp stab of pain in the back of his head and right arm.

However, much Carter blinked his eyes, he could not make out any impression of where he was. The place, or room, was as black as pitch; there were no shafts of light from ill-fitted doors, no noise, total silence.

He had no sense of time, no windows permitting him to tell day from night. He could feel his watch, but also being secured, could not move his left arm, for if he could, his watch face was luminous. On one occasion, when he moved, he felt his lanyard and ID gently on his face.

On beginning to feel somewhat better, he thought, Carter, it's totally useless to try to work things out. Just lay back and wait to see what they have in store, thinking there must be a reason behind all of this.

Not knowing of time, Carter suddenly felt his shoulder being pushed and a bright light in his face. He squirmed away, shunning from the light. Unable to protect his eyes, he turned away.

A voice, through a voice distorter, told him to sit up. On doing that, he noticed via the light the outline of an adult, dressed in black from head to toe, with the voice distorter against his mouth.

The intruder cut free his ties. The distorted voice said, "Sit up, Mr Carter, now, through the light, you'll see in my other hand I'm holding a revolver, so let's be sensible?" He told Carter, "Now stand up, get your balance and follow me?"

Carter could see the light cutting through the darkened room. He saw nothing but his bed, a fridge, and a door, which he thought maybe a bathroom.

Carter smiled inwardly; his first thought, at least he could obtain light when opening the fridge door. His thoughts had no sooner taken root when the intruder stated. "Carter, I'd just like to point out that the illuminating bulbs have been removed from both the fridge and the en suite bathroom. Alas, unable to offer any source of light on the subject, so to say." He burst out laughing.

The intruder turned and, through the insidious voice distorter, explained, "Carter, inside the fridge, you will find assorted sandwiches and cold drinks for your consumption, re-stocked every three days. The bathroom has adequate supplies. Now, you're quite a fit man, so no need for a medical?" He turned and left, leaving Carter in complete darkness.

52

The following morning, Sue awoke; she felt completely drained; she lay back and, looking up to her ceiling, screamed in temper while kicking her legs and pushing her duvet off the bed at the same time.

She got out of her bed and shuffled off into her bathroom, stripped, and took a shower. It was during her shower that Carter came to mind. She thought, "Oh! Carter, if you were only mine?" And she began to cry. Her tears streaming down her face joined that of water from the shower, all disappearing down the drain.

Sue, when dressed, walked downstairs to the kitchen. She prepared her minimalist breakfast, one round of toast, buttered and spread with peanut butter and black cherry jam, white coffee and two sugars.

Sue walked into the general office to be met by a concerned-looking Eric. Looking at Sue, he whispered, "Any news boss?" Sue, with a weak smile, whispered, "No."

After Sue signed on duty, she accepted a coffee from Eric. Coffee in hand, she went and sat opposite him. During this time, members of the team filed through to sign on duty. It seemed very surreal, none of the usual bluster or banter, with shouts of morning guv, morning boss.

After they had all left for the conference room, the door to the general office opened, and Wendy, together with Ian, followed by Sam and Lloydie, walked in. Wendy and Sam attending at the request of TF.

The next person to walk in was TF himself, and all went to stand, and he muttered," Please sit." Armed with hot coffees, they all walked down to the conference room. On arrival, the team came to attention. TF called, "As you were." they all sat down.

TF, Sue, Wendy, and Sam, all made it to the top of the room and sat behind the desks which showed their names. Sue noticed Charlie, Carter's APO, and Martin, the duty APO, from Carter's apartment block. Stood at the back of the room.

When settled, Sue looked at TF and nodded, suggesting that he should make a start.

As immaculate as usual in his civvies, he stood, and at that precise moment, one could hear a pin drop. He coughed, "Right, we all know what happened last night, and I'm sorry to report that I have no further news to give you?"

He looked at Wendy, "Where do we stand over the press?" Wendy stood up. She looked at Sue and TF at the same time. "Well, while the investigation was going on at Carter's flat. As requested by the Chief Cons office, I spent most of the night placing a temporary 'D' notice on the press. So far, it's holding?"

TF looked at Sam. As usual, as she stood, she busily looked over the team to find Lloydie. She smiled, then looked out over the team. "There is not much I can say, in this case I fear by naming Carter in the press, you've played into the perpetrator's hands. He threatened to spill the beans by informing the press?"

"Our man, I understand, has not been threatened at this stage of the proceedings. No imminent sign of arrest. Carter and team were not breathing down his neck, so unlike the case of The Evil Room, in which the perpetrator drugged Carter for fear of closing in."

"No, in this case, we're dealing with a character showing possible Histrionic personality disorder (HPD) boarding on a psychopathic nature. In his way, he is trying to draw attention to the failures in society. I do not need to go through his crimes, or the information in his letters left on his victims at the scene." Sam sat down.

TF looked at Sue. She stood up, "You all know the guv's mantra, when in this room? So not being too rude or discourteous. I feel like Sam, the information mentioned at the time of the meeting, releasing to the press, the guy's name, title, and location, gave the bastard the information needed?"

Sue continued, "In relation to the guv's abduction, a matter you may not all know is that the abductors removed the glass from the bedroom window without any trouble, which gives us some information of what we're up against?"

"Yet we may have a positive note. Literally, just prior to the guv's abduction, two members of the team, Peter, and Phil, whilst both in the CPS office. Phil, corroborated by Peter, noticed that one of the secretaries was making a note of all prisoners due for release. Names, addresses, and most of all offences committed." The room was so quiet; the only noise was that of people breathing.

Sue said, "TF is aware of the circs and the delicate course of action needed in any possible investigation?"

"Now, until this information came our way, we had not a, Scobie of detecting the offender. So, looking into this, it may be our way forward?"

"Lastly, before we go any further, most, if not all who attended at the guv's flat, realise that he has a very attractive friend staying with the guv, the informant, Miss Abby Remington."

In her statement, she mentions where she works and her phone number. I intend to keep Miss Remington up to date with matters; it's only fair."

Sue had just sat down when TF stood up; he coughed, "I owe your boss, guv, and yourselves an apology. I just failed to connect the dots, plus should the bastard conduct his threat, to directly inform the press, I didn't have the bottle to withstand the shit storm."

Sue suddenly stated, "It's rather like 'Lions led by sheep.' In this case, the lions get covered in all the shit." TF stood and left.

53

Later that afternoon, Sue had mentioned that she wanted Lloydie, Ian, Peter, Phil, Eric, and Charlie, to attend at her office.

Sue was sitting behind her desk dealing with some of her accumulated paperwork when there was a knock on her door. She called, "Come in." The door opened, and they all strolled in. Her office was set out like that of Carter's. Except the meeting table was not as long, or the number of chairs.

Sue looked out at them, "Right, I feel that I should point out the reason for this meeting; I need to either write things down or discuss matters face to face."

"I have arranged a meeting with Simon Patterson, head of the CPS, at 9.30am. Tomorrow. Charlie smiled, "Boss, I've been appointed your APO?" Sue smiled, "That was bloody quick; who?" He just smiled.

Sue coughed several times, "So be it."

"When asked by Simon Patterson the reason for such a meeting, she mentioned an old case, where the accused was seeking an appeal; I, we needed legal advice, I need to discuss our way forward?"

"After I drop the bombshell, telling the head of the CPS that he has a mole in his office. I will want to know who is responsible for logging, offender's release, dates, and details. Is it an assigned task, or is it on a rota basis?"

"Should it be a designated job? We know that all CPS staff have IDs via a lanyard around their necks, so?" She looked at her assembled officers and Eric.

Lloydie said, "You're right, boss. All CPS staff will have been photographed, with their names and departments printed on their IDs, etc., prior to commencement of employment?"

Sue called, "Exactly."

Ian, with a grin on his face, said, "Boss, after all the shit storm has settled. Simon Patterson must realise that such actions will be with the knowledge of TF and the Chief Con?"

Sue said, "Um… Yes, but being a legal bod, he'll want to cover his arse?"

Eric, who was sitting in the corner of her office, immediately erupted, "For Christ's sake, boss, it's for the guv?" "Eric, like you, I feel the same, willing to run at or through any doors to find him, she coughed Carter. As always, TF walks the line of damage limitation?"

Peter chimed, "But boss, can't we discreetly run off the photos of the CPS staff working in that office? We ID her picture, and you'll have her name up your sleeve prior to your meeting in case Simon Patterson coughs and farts, putting up fences?"

Sue looked at Peter, "Well, that's as may be from a police point of view, but Mr Patterson has a foot in either camp; he represents the police from a legal point of view and is in charge of a very large and prestigious department?"

"Now, the former is fine, but to find he has a mole in his camp, we need to tread carefully. So, based on the latter, I intend to keep the appointment tomorrow."

Looking at Lloydie, "I'm taking you, Jim, with me, she smiled, and I will also have the company of Charlie, so yes, let us proceed with back channels, continue with looking into running off the IDs of personnel in that department, if it can be done, see if you can have copies by the end of play today?"

They all stood up, said their goodbyes, and left. In the corridor, outside Sues's office. Eric moved his head, gesturing for them to come to the general office. On arrival, he said to one of the secretaries, "Sandra, please take a mug of coffee through to Sue."

Eric looked at Ian, "Can you get Gill and Jill, to contact their friend in HR and again by the back door, see if they can run off copies of the ID photos needed? But first things first, coffees…"

Sue called out, answering the knock on her door, "Come in" The door opened, and she saw Sandra standing holding a mug of coffee. "Oh! Thanks, Sandra, that will hit the spot."

After Sandra had left, after taking a sip of the hot drink, Sue picked up her office phone and called a private number. "Abby Remington." came the reply, "How may I help you?"

"Abby, it's DS Ford from the MCU office. Just thought I'd give you a call, although I'm sorry to say we have no further news in relation to DCS Carter's disappearance."

She heard a long sigh, "I thought, with your initial introduction, that you may have had some positive news?"

Sue apologised, "Sorry, in matters like these, we're dammed if we do, and we're dammed if we don't when we try to deal with investigations. A case of no news is good news, and how long a gap between leaving without calling the complainant/informant?"

Abby replied, "DS Ford, I will leave information updates with you. I know you are busy, for he is a high-ranking officer, so it must be all hands…No, you call me when you have something. I don't care how long it is." She closed the call.

Sue just looked at the handset and slowly replaced it on the cradle.

There was a sudden knock on her door. She called, "Come in." The door opened, and she saw Eric standing with a mug of hot coffee. "Thought you could go one of these?" Sue replied, "Yes, I'd loved one." He walked in and placed it on her desk.

He sat opposite her, "Well?" She replied, "Well, what?" He replied, "Don't give me that shit?" He had hardly gotten the words out... when she burst out crying. Through her tears, she spluttered, "It's having to hold all things in when we're talking about him?"

Eric replied, "I know, I know, how long have we all worked together? I've seen it every day when you come into work, how your face lights up. "Sue, can you tell me how bad you'd have to be to miss work? You've held the torch for him since your appointment to the CID. I did try to warn you?"

"Sue sniffed, "Eric, you're the only one who knows, for it has briefly come to the surface in the past, and you have been there to warn me. Do you remember when I tried to find out if the guv, had a friend, and you told me to drop it? Well, I have, Miss bloody Remington."

Eric looked at her, "Sue, you're going to make yourself ill, together with all the luggage you're carrying in your feelings for Carter. You have the team to run, a team of highly trained police officers, who, if you give so much as a crack in your fascia when around him, you're dead."

"On top of everything else you now have to cope with, Miss Remington, who without knowing may drop personal information, background facts, matters that will drive you mad, and yet you will have to put on a veneer at all times?"

He continued, "Yet you being like the proverbial duck swimming in the water, all is well above board, and yet under the bloody water, the ducks' web feet are going ten to the dozen."

There was a sudden knock on her door. She called, "Wait one." She looked at Eric, "I must look awful. What with all the blubbing?" He looked at her, "Boss, you're splendid." She walked from around her desk to open the door. Before leaving, she raised and pecked Eric on his cheek, "Thanks, boss, for understanding (both Carter and Sue called Eric boss as he was their ex-DS)

Sue opened her door she looked at Eric, "Thanks, Eric. Will you please give Charlie my home address, for he'll need it for his APO team?" Eric smiled, "Will do, boss, see ya later?"

Sue said, "Come in, Lloydie, Peter, and Phil; what can I do you for?" Lloydie took an A4 folder from under his arm. When Sue was seated, he placed it on the table. He opened it, and Sue immediately looked down on lines of coloured photographs depicting male and female prints.

She smiled, "Well, is that what I think it is, pictures of our friends from the CPS?" Lloydie replied, "Yes, boss and we have a positive result." Sue looked at both Peter and Phil. "Okay, you look as if you're both about to explode; who is it?"

They both pointed to a dark-haired, attractive young lady with a pleasant smile on her face for her official ID. Under the picture was the typed Hazel Combes, CPS. Lloydie said her DOB was 17.03.98, making her 24yrs. We have her home address for future use, nothing known with MER/cro."

Sue looked at them both, "Gentlemen, I know I don't have to say it, but for fuck's sake are you both sure?" They both replied, "Sure, boss."

She looked at all three of her officers and smiled, "Leave this lot here. I'll deal with it for tomorrow, now be off with you."

Sue walked into the general office and saw Charlie patiently waiting. She signed off duty and left with Charlie in tow.

54

The following morning, Sue awoke, finding herself in the same body position as when she first fell off to sleep. In a tight curl, the duvet and Carter's sweatshirt pulled up under her chin.

She stretched out with both her arms above her head. In doing so, she pushed the duvet down. She turned and got out of bed, and she pulled at her dressing gown, which lay within the creases of the duvet.

Sue pulled it on, tied it about her waist, and placed her feet into her slippers. She strolled around to her bedroom window, pushed open the curtains and looked down upon all the various cars and people scurrying off to work.

Biting her bottom lip, she thought if only life were like that of the ebb and flow, as per the rush hour, that without knowing other people's problems, studiously take part in their rush for work.

Looking down, she could see her security detail, transfixed, looking at all the drivers on their phones and all the women still putting the touches to their make-up.

Thinking about her situation. She felt like a boat that had slipped its moorings adrift in the water, away from the safety and security of that which is Carter. She stepped back from the window, stripped off and screamed, "All this is yours, Carter." Sue walked to the bathroom. "Just seeing you at the commencement of the day sets me up, giving me the inner strength to cope with the battle of keeping my feelings for you under control?"

After her parental chat with Eric, she is not convinced. Although, at times, she thought she had matters under control until you bloody walked in... As always, it was Wiley's old fox, Eric, who saw through her…

She stood in her shower, only allotting five out of her ten minutes duration to her usual sensual thoughts of Carter.

Breakfast. Two rounds of toast and marmalade, coffee white with two sugars. On completion. She walked through to the hall cupboard. Prior to taking out her jacket and raincoat, she removed her pistol and holster from her wall safe. Clipping her holster onto the waistband of her slacks, she was ready to face the rigours of the day. Her doorbell sounded.

Opening her door and saw Charlie standing at the side of the car. "Morning… Boss, you know your one IC what on earth do I call you for ma... is out?" Sue blurted boss or guv."

He took in a deep breath, "Morning guv, is it the office first, before our trip to CPS?" Sue went around the car, opened the front passenger door, and climbed in. "Yes, Charlie."

Charlie looked to his left, "Guv, I thought of holding the door open for you, but knowing the similarity between you and the guv, thought better of it?" Sue just gave him a look, enough to turn him into a pillar of salt. He thought. 'Wow.'

Sue smiled, "Charlie, are you well?" "Yes, thanks, guv…" Sue interrupted… "Charlie, there is only one guv, so please make it boss." The journey to the office was uneventful. On arrival and after parking in the police yard, they both went up the stairs to the MCU office.

Entering the general office, both Sue and Charlie faced the daily torrent of "Morning boss, and morning Charlie." Sue turned and courteously replied as she signed on duty. Looking at Eric, who produced for, Sue his traditional cup of morning coffee. She walked over with her coffee and sat next to him. She smiled and whispered, "I'm alright, thanks; after this, we're off to the CPS."

Sue sighed as she self-consciously walked across the office and signed out for the CPS. She looked at Lloydie, "Are you ready, Jim?" "Yes, boss." He replied. Sue said, "I have the photo with me, so let's go and possibly set off a giant BOS (Ball of shit) all burst out laughing.

The journey to the CPS offices in Dale Street went off without any comment; the only interruption to their journey was the force radio, which punctuated the occasion.

Charlie parked up, and they left for Mr. Patterson's office. They took the lift to the first floor. The lift doors opened, and before them, they saw a large oak door with a brass plate showing Simon Patterson's name.

Sue knocked on the door, and a female voice called, "Come in." Charlie pushed the door open, and Sue noticed an attractive woman sitting at a desk. She looked over, "Morning, Superintendent Ford. Would you like to take a seat? And I'll inform Mr. Patterson of your arrival.

Sue looked around the room, and there was a window in the middle of the wall overlooking Dale Street. The walls were adorned with legal photographs showing various figures dressed in legal gowns and wigs.

The phone rang on her desk, and the secretary picked up the phone, "Yes, Mr. Patterson, will do." She looked over, "Superintendent Ford, you can go through."

All three stood up and walked towards the large oak door, with yet again Simon Patterson's name on a silver plaque. The secretary interrupted, "Err! Excuse me, Chief Inspector, but I thought it only applies to you?" Sue turned, "Sorry, but I have my colleague and my APO, we're all going in?"

Sue opened the door without knocking. Simon Patterson looked up from a mass of legal files littering his desk. "Err!

Superintendent Ford, the appointment was with you. Prey, tell me, who are these other officers?" Sue smiled, pointing, "This is DS Watkins, my APO, and the other officer is DC Jim Lloyd, from the MCU."

Patterson looked at her, "Well, you might as well all sit down now, Chief Inspector; what can I do for you?"

Sue took in a deep breath, "My Chapman, may I ask, how do we record the names and details of released prisoners? I realise there is a need to categorise and list the different offenders to pass on for MER/cro?"

Reluctantly, he looked at her, "Why, Superintendent Ford, I thought your reason for your appointment was to discuss a pending appeal?" Sue looked at him, "Mr. Patterson, I'm sorry for the subterfuge, but the less people know, the better; please, may I refer you back to my original question?"

He spluttered, "The task is given to a permanent employee; please don't expect me to know her name?" Sue smiled, "No, but just a simple task by your secretary, you can easily find out?"

He replied, "Yes, I suppose so, and went to reach for the intercom. As he was about to speak, Sue gently touched his arm. "Mr Patterson, I trust your secretary can be trusted to deal with confidence?"

With a look of absolute disdain on his face, he blurted out, "Why, of course." Sue removed her hand. Simon Patterson continued. The courteous voice of his secretary, "Mr. Patterson."

He replied, "Heather, can I trouble you to inquire who is responsible for the collation of information on released offenders?" Heather replied, "Mr. Patterson, it will take but a minute."

On completion, he looked at Sue, "Please excuse me, officer, but what the fuck is going on?" Sue replied, "On receipt of your secretary's information, I'll explain matters."

The intercom on his desk suddenly activated, "Mr. Patterson, the process is the responsibility of ..." Sue held her breath..." Hazel Combes." Patterson said, "Thank you, Heather."

Sue looked at Simon Patterson and dropped the ID photograph on his desk. He looked down on the smiling face and the name. He stared up at Sue, "Again, officer, what the fuck...?" He looked at Sue, "Officer, I have used the 'F' word twice this morning; the last time I used it was while having a conversation with your boss."

Sue looked at her two colleagues and could see the pained look on their faces. She then turned her gaze to Patterson.

Mr Patterson, you'll be one of a handful of personnel who are aware that DCS Carter has been abducted. Sue went on to explain matters, after which she seemed to flop back in her chair.

Patterson said, "First things first." He pressed the intercom, "Hazel, will you please bring in the coffee thermal, the milk, and sugar? When all had received their coffees, Hazel smiled and left his office.

With a coffee cup in hand, Patterson smiled, "Sue, why all the subterfuge?"

Sue turned, "Sir, you are no doubt aware of the current serial crimes that the MCU team are dealing with, until recently, and prior to Carter's abduction. We had no clue as to the offender. No prints or clues left at the various scenes, only a letter left, secreted on or under the victim."

Prior to his abduction, two of my officers attended the CPS general office on the ground floor. They were there to discuss a remand case due for sentence in the crown court."

She continued, "It was while in the office, that they noticed one of your young ladies, had the task of recording all the information on released prisoners."

Patterson suddenly gasped, "Christ, the girl has the keys to the parish...name, address, offence, and release dates?"

Sue whispered, "Exactly." Patterson looked at Sue, "Superintendent Ford, do you suspect Miss Combes is the conduit to the offender?" Sue replied, Mr Patterson, there must be a system. These matters just don't manifest themselves. Why Combes?"

"Mr Patterson, this is purely an impromptu opinion, imagine. Combes meets a man and during their relationship, mentions her job. Unbeknown to Combes, this man has form; he also has a friend who is fed up with society. The poor response and responsibility to actions shown by social workers, community workers, and even the police service.

"He wants and demands action, from the same frustrating replies, 'Yes, we must learn from our mistakes?' He sets out to even the balance of punishment and become a vigilante, a one-man killing machine."

Not stopping, Sue continued. "How does this mess develop? Combes falls in love with someone, not knowing, she tells him her Job. He tells a frustrated friend. He demands information. Combes is persuaded by means of subtle persuasion. Initially, nights out presents, and, of course, love and sex."

"Primarily after all of the grooming she succumbs to the increasing intimacy brings out the necessary information, which is secreted in her bag, gives it to boyfriend, he passes it on...?"

"That Mr. Patterson is truly a broad outline of the conspiracy. Commander Frost is fully aware of this appointment with you here today. I intend to instruct certain members of my team to make delicate inquiries into the background of Miss Combes. You will be kept informed of our every move?"

"I'm returning to Derby Lane to complete my inquiries?" He stood up and shook hands with Sue. "I hope you don't mind if I call you Sue, but goodbye to both you and your officers; I do hope it may assist in your inquiries?"

55

On their return to Derby Lane, Sue partially turned and looked at both Lloydie and Charlie, "Well, gents, how do you both think it went?"

They both, in unison, exhaled. Lloydie was the first to speak. He smirked, "I thought it went quite well?" Charlie spluttered, "No disrespect to the guv, but I don't feel he could have done any better. Whatever the problem, the MCU is never short of a leader?"

Sue looked at Charlie and just smiled. Lloydie said, "Couldn't have put it any better?" They all burst out laughing.

It was during this that Sue discreetly produced her mobile and called Eric. "Well, boss, how did it go?" Sue sighed, "I have to say that it didn't turn into the intended BOS; in fact, after the initial hick-up, the feigning of my true reason for my visit to his office? Mr. Patterson helped accordingly."

"When told my initial reason and the abduction of Carter. I have to say that Patterson was astonished?" Sue continued, "Admitting one of the last times he'd used the 'F' word was, in fact, whilst talking to Carter, funny enough?"

Sue coughed, "Look, I'll tell you the rest when we get home, or else we'll have fuck all to say?" They all burst out laughing.

It was 12.30pm as they walked into the general office while they all signed in. Eric and a couple of his secretaries began to make coffees.

Sue looked at Eric, "Have you eaten? If not, can I ask that you organise drinks and sandwiches in the conference room, my treat? Also, give Pete and Phil a call. I'm off to my office to update TF."

Twenty minutes later, Sue entered the conference room. There was a shuffle of chairs. She looked at them," What?" No, please, let's keep this in the family?" She smiled as she picked up a plate, taking advantage of the working lunch.

Two tables had been pushed together and chairs put around them; she looked at the group. After spending time taking advantage of the break, she looked at her team. "Well, TF is on board, so how are we to proceed?"

Peter said, "Boss, while at your meeting, Phil and I ran Miss Combes's details through MER/cro, as we thought, due to the career selected, she has no previous convictions?"

Sue looked at them, "Well, that may as well be, but this is such a positive way forward. Yet, we must look at the argument: could there be someone else in the office who is aware of her job? Piggybacking it as a sauce of information gathering?"

Peter smiled, "We've identified Combes and her job. I feel. We need to follow the breadcrumbs. Say, she was intending to pass the information to a third party, how is it done?"

Eric replied, "Well, we know how the information is passed to the CPS; it is via computer. Picked up by Combes at her terminal. If bent, then she must make a copy, again knowing computers the process is logged. If she needs all or certain information, then her only way is to make a written note; this is open to detection?"

Lloydie smiled, "It may sound daft; how about an excuse to carry out a discreet bag search, a BS story about increases in stationary loses, or reports of theft of personal property, for the accused thinks they'll get caught?"

Phil smiled, "The person taking the risk, don't forget, has been getting away with matters for months; they may even write down the alleged information from their console. It may look quite a casual act, thus drawing little to no attention to herself. Therefore, as we know, the information collected seems he is selective with his victims?"

Sue sat back and pondered, "Lloydie, I think you may have something. The culprit can't download the information onto a USB due to the DPA, its primary intelligence, and the CPC will have the necessary protection set up?"

56

Carter had lost all aspects of time; he decided from the outset that he could rule out time, that due to the conditions and the lack of windows, he didn't know if it was morning or night. The room and place wherever he was constituted one black hole in complete silence.

He had come to terms with the sandwiches and, whilst hostile to his present surroundings, had come to accept all the provided facilities. He had quickly worked out. Use the bed as a guide. Walk along the edge of the mattress; the bed was a divan and headboard. At the end, he gripped hold of the mattress and took a couple of steps.

Then he'd reach out into the inky blackness, and with his arms acting as a foil, waving out in front of him, he'd contact the cold metal exterior of the fridge. It was the type that fit under a worktop in a kitchen.

He knew the door was on the left-hand side. He'd move his hand over the top and, feeling the seal of the door, would open it. Thus, enabling him to reach the contents.

Two important facts: his aggressor informed him via that terrible mouthpiece, "No interior light in the fridge, the bulb removed, plus the food, would be changed when he saw fit.

Carter realised that there were countless negative effects on isolation, and even worse on extreme isolation, such as his conditions, relating to the effect it can have on our minds and bodies.

He recalled the issues undertaken by Terry Waite, who was captured for some 5 years in a Beirut jail. He remembers that to keep his mind and memory intact, and he drafted short stories and even a potential book that he eventually wrote on his release.

Carter smiled to himself, 'It could be worse. I'm not tied to a radiator and made to sleep on the floor.' With both hands, he pushed down on his mattress to convey the comfort of his bed.

He lay on his bed, with his hands behind his head, and immediately thought of Helen and their two babies, who the henchmen mercilessly killed, Michael Hughes.

Carter's eyes began to fill up as his mind drilled down into a futuristic time he envisaged of his family's visit to Helen's parent's farm. Consisting of Carter, Helen, and their two children, Lizzy, and Martin, at their birth, the news had been so warmly embraced that her father had kept his promise and bought the children a pony each.

On arrival, the first thing the excited children always did was to search for Jimmy, a herdsman on the farm, who just loved to hear, "Uncle Jimmy, where are you?"

He'd reply, "Now look here, you youngen's, have you?" They'd both scream, "Oh! yes, hello nan, and grandpa." And run off followed by Pippa and Bruce, Helens two Labradors.

Carter and Helen tried to insist on a proper greeting but were always met by roars of laughter from Helen's parents, "Oh! Stop, for we just love to hear their voices of excitement on arrival ..."

Deep in his thought, Carter's fanciful memories were having the correct effect, although he had to fight to retain such reflections, as he was constantly battling with the facts, and although life had dealt him the ultimate blow, with the total loss of his beloved family.

He eventually dropped off to sleep, for again, he had no way of knowing what was up or what was down.

Suddenly, the door to the room opened, and he awakened with fright. All he saw was a narrow beam of light. It moved towards the fridge, for he could clearly see the dark shadow of a person, all in black from head to toe.

The intruder opened the fridge door, and he heard cellophane caused by the exchange of sandwiches. He immediately sat up. The intruder, with the voice distorter, burst out laughing, "See, you're still with us?" Turned and left.

Carter instantly calculated that three days must have passed... 'He thought, shit, how long is this going to go on for?" Exhausted with all his day or night dreaming, for he'd lay awake for what seemed for hours, he lay back, and just prior to nodding off, his mind suddenly filled with thoughts of Abby and all the beautiful memories.

With such vivid imagination, Carter's mind visualised all the striking women with whom he'd had flings and affairs. The commencement of such actions had hit him with such unfathomable desires that, over time, he eventually met Helen.

On that first date, after dinner, we returned to her flat. The following morning, Helen, had got up, leaving him in bed. He got up and walked into the kitchen. He saw Helen's wet hair and realised she'd already bathed like a prude and asked if he could shower.

When in the bathroom, Helen showed him the shower controls. It was then that he noticed the white towelling bathrobe hanging from a hook on the shower wall, apparently man-size. It was such a blow, with the significant thoughts that flooded his mind. The three words, 'Who, when, and were, filled his head with instant jealousy.

Helen left him to shower; he was tentatively bathing when he suddenly felt a soapy glove sponge slither down his back and Helens, head resting on his back. She explained, in case of your housed and suspicious thoughts.

Pressing her head, she whispered, the dressing gown is my brother's; he sometimes flat sits for me when I must work away. Carter sighed on receipt of such a simplistic explanation…

57

Sue telephoned Simon Patterson, "Patterson.?" Sir, It's Superintendent Ford, on return to the office, I had a meeting with selective members of my team. Commander Frost is fully aware of my decision."

Simon Patterson replied, "How may I help?" "Sir, we want to attend at the CPS general office, in Dale Street. I intend to commit a search of your staff, as they leave the office for home. I can assure you it will be completed with the least amount of inconvenience."

Patterson replied, "Superintendent Ford, the staff leave at 5.30pm. I suggest that your officers assume station at the office door and explain your actions as staff leave at the end of the day."

At 4.50pm, Sue entered the conference room to be met by her team consisting of. Pete, Phil, Jules, and Jill. Sue looked at them, "We'll take two cars; I'll be with Charlie and Lloydie, looking at the others; you leave in the second car?" There was a sudden reply of "Sir."

Sue sat and, looking at them, said, "Clearly, with our frequent visits to the CPS general office, we're fully aware of its layout; it is a large office, windows on two walls, with one door in and out."

"Obviously, Jules and Jill will cover the office door. I'll go in and explain matters to the office manager. Pete and Phil, you'll both have a roaming brief in and about the office as the staff leave. To be aware of Combes and her actions. Just in case our friend Combes, realising what is going on, may try to discard any evidence?"

They all left for the general office to sign out. Sue deliberately recorded the location and one of the crime file numbers that refer to the matter. Eric looked up; he smiled, "I wish you all good luck, boss. I'll remain in case needed?"

Downstairs in the police yard, they left in their two vehicles; there was no need for blue lights or horns; to all intents and purposes, they were going to town.

On arrival, they entered the main entrance of the building. On a wall in front of them was a large wooden board, which clearly indicated the locations of the vast number of legal offices within the building.

There was no need for such scrutiny, as they call knew the way.

Turning left in front of the bank of lifts, they passed the duty security reception desk. The duty officer just nodded as they walked past.

At the end of the corridor, facing them, they found the general office with a large wooden sign at the side of each door depicting the CPS. The department is fronted by two large oak wooden doors, with a half panel of frosted glass in each door. The doors were fitted with sizeable brass finger plates on each door, and large ornate brass door handles.

Sue entered, leaving the others outside. Sue walked in and met with a hive of activity. She walked over to a glass-panelled office. On the door was a sign, 'Office manager.'

Sue knocked and entered; the manager, Amanda Worthing, looked up, "Hi Sue, what can we do for you"?" Sue, somewhat embarrassed, replied, "Amanda SP is aware of what I'm about to tell you and do?" Sue coughed, "I'm going to inspect the contents of all female staff members' handbags and personal belongings and any other bags they have with them. We'll also search the briefcases, or shoulder bags, of the male members of staff?"

At 5.20pm. As members of staff began to make overtures, depicting the end of the day. Amanda and Sue came from out of her office. Amanda shouted, "Can I please have all your attention, with the knowledge of Mr Patterson, Superintendent Ford, and members of her MCU team, who will be carrying out a bag search?"

"There are two female officers and two male officers. Please form an orderly queue and open any personal handbags and shopping bags; this won't take long?"

A queue began to form, ribbonlike, down the middle of the office, between the central desks, giving up the low voices of expectation and obvious verbal complaints.

Unbeknown to members of staff, Phil and Pete nonchalantly walked about the major office on either side of the queue, slowly moving along the desks, showing interest.

The queue slowly meandered down the room, people talking to each other, obviously pondering, and somewhat complaining under their breath as to what was going on?"

Phil recognised Hazel Combes, slowly marking time with her colleagues. He walked away from the line to gain the attention of Peter. All he did was raise his eyebrows and look in Combes's direction.

He turned and left Pete to return casually to his usual place, again trying not to cause attention. Noticing that the queue had passed Combes's work desk, a position that Phil knew from his previous visit. Peter could see that Combes was slyly dropping back, not causing any suspicious thoughts to her colleagues of her actions.

It was when it got closer to the door that she realised the outcome and what she had or carried in her handbag. Combes realised she'd been used, what with all the nights out, presents, and the stayovers and weekends; she shivered with disgust and felt used.

In the beginning, she agreed with the concept, such an easy matter, unaware of the consequences of knowing the number of prisoners released that passed over her desk. Pick a name, address, and offence, write it down, and smuggle it out, then pass the information on to someone.

Hazel would print a list of names, a matter not so unusual and not at all suspicious, for it was within her job description. The information languished on her desk, and she could pass such details on to another verbally. When necessary. She could pick up matters. Provide name, address, the offence, D.O.B. and the date of the released prisoner. Never thinking she'd get caught.

Phil and Peter stood in proximity of Hazel Combes, after the nod from Peter. Jules and Jill walked to their location. She was one of the last to leave the office.

Jules walked up to Combes. "Are you Miss Hazel Combes?" Hazel spluttered, "Yes, yes, why? What do you want?" Jules took out her ID, "Miss Combes, I'm WDC Julie Forbes, and this is my colleague, WDC Jill Mercer, both of the MCU."

The office was now empty as most if not all, her colleagues were more interested in getting home for the evening.

Jules took hold of Hazel, saying, "Excuse me." As she did so, she took hold of her handbag and passed it to Jill. They then escorted her to the manager's office. Jules opened the door, and they were met by the manager and their boss, DCI Field.

Sue nodded at Jill, who, looking at Hazel, said, "Hazel Combes, is this your handbag?" She nervously replied, "Yes, yes, why?" Jill looked at her and cautioned her after no reply. Then said, "Miss Combes, will you please open your handbag and place the contents on the nearby desk?

Hazel Combes opened her bag, and certain objects fell onto the desk, including lipstick and compact, yet some items were hindered due to a piece of paper wedged within her bag.

Jill said, "Miss Combes, will you please remove the piece of paper and hand it to me?" As she did so, her purse, comb, and eye shadow palette fell onto the desk.

Jules, wearing rubber gloves, moved forward, and straightened out the piece of paper from her bag. Looking down written in black ink, and not typed, the name and address of a female prisoner, Lesley Webster, being released from Styal prison, Manchester, on Wednesday. Having served 8 years for infanticide.

Jules, looking at Hazel Combes, "Miss Combes, I'm arresting you for the theft of information contrary to the data protection act. What do you have to say?" She burst out crying.

Jill, who was also wearing rubber gloves, placed the piece of paper in an evidence bag, folded it over and placed it in her coat pocket.

58

On arrival at Derby Lane police station, Jules, and Jill both escorted Hazel Combes and stood with her in front of the bridewell sergeant. Jill explained, "Sergeant Lancaster, I arrested this person. The circumstances of this arrest are as follows: I, together with other officers of the MCU, attended the CPS general office. The accused was seen to make note of certain matters on a piece of paper.

During the search of staff, as they left at the end of the day. Noticing the suspect with her handbag discreetly walking backwards away from the office door and the search area.

We eventually detained Combes; we took her into the manager's office. In search of her handbag, we found incriminating evidence. In her bag, she had a piece of paper with the details of a prisoner due for release. The details Combes should not have in her possession, copied from details protected by the Data Protection Act. Which we believe her intention to pass to a third party?"

After accepting the charge, Combes was duly processed, including her home address, 45 Monk Street, Wavertree, Liverpool, L13 3AF. DOB: 26.07.2000 23yrs. The taking of her fingerprints, when completed, was taken up to the MCU office.

Eric was as good as his word, and on arrival to the general office, he'd laid on coffee and tea. Combes was placed in interview room 1. Accompanied by WPC Amanda Eccles, one of the female duty officers.

In the general office, they all sat down to enjoy their hot drinks. Sue who seemed concerned, was sat next to Eric. "Well, we have Combes, found with incriminating evidence.

"But let's not forget, she'll be missed by at least her parents or a potential boyfriend, for if you think about it, who else would it be for? Say he's in the chain of information?"

She looked at Lloydie. "Please prepare a duck (police jargon for a warrant) for Combes's home address." She looked at Jules, "You and I need to get at Combes. Time is of the essence."

Sue and Jules walked into the interview room. Amanda stood up and acknowledged Sue. She turned to leave. Sue smiled at her. "Amanda, can you organise hot drinks, perhaps get yourself a cuppa?" Sue looked at Hazel, "Would you like a hot drink?" She replied, "No."

Sue and Jules sat opposite Hazel, with tears running down her face. Sue opened a drawer in the front of the table, handing her the customary box of tissues. Taking one, she thanked Sue.

Jules opened two new tapes. Placing the new tapes into the recording machine. She switched it on, and after a moment, there was the usual bleep. Jules stated the time, day, and date, mentioning, all present. After which, she sat back and relaxed.

On completion, "No doubt, Miss Combes, you must realise that you're still under caution?" Hazel just nodded.

"You must realise that you were duly cautioned at the time of your arrest. I'm Superintendent Ford, and this is my colleague, WDC Forbes, of the MCU."

Sue looked at Hazel. "Miss Combes, I have to warn you that by law, you are entitled to legal representation, a defence solicitor?" Hazel just sniffled, "I know, what's the point?"

Sue looked at her, "Miss Combes, can you please explain your job within the CPS general office?" Looking at Sue, "Superintendent Ford, that is a rhetorical question, so if you wish, let's play the game. Somehow, you've caught on, hence the alleged search of personal properties conducted by your officers?"

Sue looked at her, "Then Miss Combes, have it your way. Are you the only person in the CPS general office with the facility that enables you to log on to the system, which permits you to run off and record the details of released prisoners?" She replied, "Yes."

Sue looked at Combes, "Is that the sole purpose of your job?" She burst out laughing. "No, of course not; I also deal with and implement the release protocol for prisoners. That on the day of release are secured in the knowledge that they have somewhere safe, and suitable to stay. Plus, enough money to support themselves in the community?"

She continued, "The releases are not always daily. Plus, we record and note the offences committed, and we prepare a list of prison departures subject to the sexual offender's act. So, you see, there are many reasons for the use of my computer portal for other matters?"

Looking at Combes, Sue said, "Can I please ask you to explain the piece of paper we found in your handbag that partly restricted some of your items from falling out onto the desk?"

She smiled at Sue, "Superintendent Ford, this is rather boring, you have your evidence?" Sue, in utter frustration, banged the palm of her hand onto the top of the desk. (A point she'd learned from Carter.) Both Combes and Jules suddenly jumped with fright. Sue shouted, "Combes, I do hope you're not trying to admit that this is your first such action in these matters?"

Sue looked at Combes, and after her next question, as to her residence status?

Hazel smiled, "Actually, I live in two places; I live with my parents and, at times, spend the odd weekend with my boyfriends."

On hearing the mention of a boyfriend, Sue looks at Combes, "How long have you known him?" Combes thought for a moment and replied, "About six months."

Sue felt a sudden intake of breath, for her mind was racing. She looked at Combes, still sat with a smile on her face. "Hazel, we have prepared a warrant for your parent's address. At that stage, your parents will be informed of your present situation?"

Sue, with a stern look on her face, "Hazel, who is the boyfriend? We need his name and address?" She smiled, "Well, it's Adrian Rice, 24, Wellington Street, Anfield, Liverpool 4." Sue looked at Combes," Hazel, what is his date of birth?" She replied, "He's twenty-three."

I knew it would come to this: for Superintendent Ford, I'm no fool; just look at me; in anyone's eyes, I'm somewhat of a rather 'plain Jane' and make no mistake. When you see Adrian, you'll appreciate what I'm saying. For Adrian is so handsome, why me?"

Sue looked at Hazel with a sympathetic look, "Hazel, we're not in the business of opinions, but it's important. Do you feel that your meeting was natural or stage-managed?"

Combes narrowed her eyes, "Superintendent Ford, we've all seen in the films where a prisoner in my position says, "What's in it for me?" Sue coughed, "Hazel, are we looking to make a deal?" she replied, "Yes."

Sue looked at Jules, "Interview terminated at 8.30pm. On completion, Sue looked at Combes, "Your interview has been ended; whenever a suspect calls *'deal,'* it brings the proceedings to a halt, and the tape has been switched off; I wish you to remain here, on my return can I suggest some refreshments?" "Yes, some water, please."

Sue called, "Amanda," And she opened the door, "Yes, sir?" Sue smiled, "Amanda, will you remain with the prisoner? I'll be back shortly." She replied, "Yes, boss."

59

Sue and Jules both left for the general office. On entering the office, Lloydie looked at Sue, "Boss, can we serve the warrant on her parent's address?"

Sue replied, "Yes, but before you go, I have another address, that of a boyfriend, Adrian Rice, 24, Wellington Street, Anfield, Liverpool. 4."

Looking at all her team, Sue looked at Lloydie, "Lloydie, we need more of the team; I suggest another four will do. That makes Pete and Phil, plus two, and Lloydie and Ian, plus two, call the extra four out."

Sue looked at them all. "This is going to be a long night. Your first job at each address is to retain all personal mobiles; I don't care if they scream the fucking rafters down, they need to know that we're not fucking around; all property will be returned, except phones with incriminating evidence?"

"I feel your biggest problem will be the boyfriend if he's in, but at the first sign of incriminating evidence, he's nabbed, then you're to get SOCO and get them to pull the place apart. It may be worthwhile to have them on standby?"

Charlie stood up, "Boss, what about me?" Sue smiled, "Thanks, Charlie, but as my APO, you're needed here. I may need to go out?" He smiled, "Shall I make the drinks?"

Sue said to everyone, "Off you go, you can drink all you want when we get the guv back. Divide the extra help up and arrange for them to meet you at the addressee's concern. Now you're all armed, but pay special attention to the boyfriend's address, for this is a setup, and Combes, is the patsy?"

Sue smiled at Jules, "Could I trouble you to pass a drink through to Combes, for I feel I need to call TF?" Jules turned and got on with it.

When all had left their various tasks, Sue was left with Charlie and eventually Jules.

Sue called the force control room. "This is Superintendent Ford. Can you please call Commander Frost, asking him to call me?" There was a curt reply from the force controller, "Yes, ma'am, will do."

Sue smiled within, thinking if Carter was only here…

She was suddenly brought back out of her daydream as her mobile suddenly activated. Taking out her phone, she uttered, "Ford."

"Superintendent Ford, it's Frost?" "Sir, just to inform you, we searched the CPS general office with the permission of Mr Patterson and his office manager."

Sue continued, "It was during the search of the staff's individual properties my officers noticed that the key suspect kept nonchalantly moving to the back of the cue, not drawing attention to herself, but obviously she feared being searched."

"On the eventual search of the suspect's bag, we found the incriminating evidence, a hand- written piece of paper with the details. – Lesley Webster, 32yrs. DOB 14.12.1991. 23, Aintree Lane, Aintree, Liverpool,10. Served 8 years for Infanticide. Guilty of murdering her 6-month-old baby, the body was found in a nearby canal."

TF said, *"Obviously, details of the next victim? Well, if you've found the primary offender, will she give us her accomplice, for she is just a pawn?"*

Sue coughed, "I feel she isn't that stupid as she's asking for a deal?" Sue held the phone at arm's length, for she knew what was coming. TF screamed, *"A fucking deal, she's only nib shit."*

Sue replied, "Sir, that's as well as it may be, but Combes may have been persuaded for certain information due to her unique role in CPS. Yet we don't know the key facts?"

"It was by per chance that DC Phil Watson, while stood in the CPS office with DC Peter Williams, waiting to discuss a forthcoming hearing in the crown court. That Phil noticed Comes discreetly making notes and placing pieces of paper into her handbag?"

"We presume, giving such information to the boyfriend to pass on to another, she may well be the pawn, but she knows all the mechanics of the system?"

Combes mentioned the boyfriend's present address. I feel that the boyfriend could be the main conduit to the perpetrator of all the offences. He hopefully will give us Carter?"

TF coughed, *"How long has it been?"* (She thought you must think I'm mad, for you more than most…) Sir, 5 days, he must be going nuts?"

60

Carter gasps for air, his eyes flashing open...He props himself up on his elbows on the bed.

"You were sleeping. It was ...just a...dream." His mouth was so dry. His tongue was so heavy he thought, "Christ, will I ever speak again?"

"I need water...?" He thought, "When did you last have a drink, early last night, or could it have been this morning?" As usual, he has no sense of time due to the cloak of utter darkness that impregnates his present surroundings.

Feverishly like some, unfortunately, a scarred person having been blighted with blindness. Carter spreads out both of his arms and, with hands, swishes over the bedcovers in a futile attempt to find the water bottle he last used and discarded on the bed.

He shouts, "Where the fuck are you?" In utter frustration, he shuffles over the mattress to the edge of the bed. Standing, he steadies himself, leaning against the bed, he gets his balance.

Using the mattress as a guide, he moves to the end of the bed. He leans against the bed. Carter had already worked out by shuffling the length and breadth of the cell that it was, 30 shuffles one way, by 25 the other.

He already knew it was 5 small strides and with an outstretched arm in front of him. Eureka the fridge.

He leaned down and quickly opened the fridge door, and with his fingers, he feverishly pulled out a chilled plastic water bottle. With a crack of the seal, he quickly opens it, placing the top onto the top of the fridge. Indicating to his captures his water intake?

With trembling hands, he places the bottle up to his mouth, spilling the cool, refreshing liquid everywhere in his eagerness to quench his thirst.

When finished, he relaxes back on the bed. He suddenly thinks he could do with a pee.

Using his computer-like brain, he remembers it's a further 8 strides to the bathroom. He stops at the doorway, shouting…" How much fucking longer is this going on for…?"

After leaving the toilet, he realised that there was a sink to his right and a towel placed over the taps. He thought how bloody considerate. Moving his hand, he felt what he thought must be a mirror, purely by shape. He called out, "Excuse the *pun*, but you are taking the piss; a mirror, what the fuck do I need that for, for I can see fuck all?"

Mumbling to himself as he shuffled back to his bed. He counted the steps and with his hands out in front of him. He met his target; before doing anything, he pressed the mattress he let out a small cheer. Done it.

He stirred in the bed for the umpteenth time; due to the cloak of blackness that covered everywhere, he was unaware if it was day or night. He realised that it was clinically known that if a person experiences total darkness. It can play havoc with one's sleep pattern.

He wasn't stupid, for he thought that by feelings given off from his mind and body, the darkness was causing both physical and psychological problems.

To keep his mind and body together, he remembered the article in one of the dailies about the release of Terry Waite, the Archbishop's envoy, detained for four years by some terrorist group or other whilst in Beirut.

He mentioned how he passed the time by in his mind writing a mental version of a book. He remembered laying back on his bed, the floor and dictating to himself, as well as aloud such a tone.

He had plenty of thoughts swirling around in his mind. Starting as a child, bathing in the love of his parents, for although they were in business, they always sought time to spend with him.

Unfortunately, he remembers the day they called him, and due to circumstances beyond their control, his parents reluctantly informed him that he was being sent to boarding school. He thought that his life had imploded. And yet that was where he met his best friend, Ian Radcliffe.

The outline of his book meandered through all his time at school and eventual university, and of course, GIRLS! That subject matter alone filled several explicit chapters monitoring his sexual behaviour and events that filled their four years at Oxford.

He, of course, remembered one Saturday night. He'd been at a party with his present girlfriend and, after an abundance of alcohol, took off to a nearby bedroom. Pushing all the coats off the bed. Set about making love.

Carter had been seeing her for a number of weeks, and on such occasions, it was always the same result. When making love, she wanted all her sexual feelings fulfilled and showed little in response. So, out of total frustration, he jumped up, dressed, and left to the sound of her shouting, "Carter, Carter, come back! What's the matter?"

On his way back to the halls, he walked into an old Oxford pub, where a mature but gorgeous barmaid called Sam. immediately noticed that he was trying to look for answers in the bottom of a beer glass.

After several drinks, she stated, "What's a handsome lad like you being so upset on a Saturday night?" She invited him to join her in a stay-behind. That was the beginning of a four-year affair and his full sexual education. He gained two degrees, a 2.1 in Politics and Contemporary History, and a 1st in sexual behavioural science…

Sam attended the graduation ceremony but, alas always knew that his future career would take him to Liverpool.

He realised that while trying to keep his mind fulfilled by the events of the so-called virtual book. That exercise was needed to sustain some sort of fitness regime. He started a regime of exercises. Sit-ups, press-ups, knee bends, he thought star jumps, were out of the question.

After such exertion, he'd fall back on his bed, remembering where he'd left the bloody water bottle.

61

Sue had remained in the general office, talking with Charlie. When suddenly, the door opened. Looking towards the door. Sue noticed both Peter and Phil stood in the doorway with broad smiles on their faces.

Sue said, "Don't fill the door looking like a pair of Cheshire cats; come in and tell all?"

Peter looked at Phil, and like a pair of kids, he pushed Phil, "Phil, go on tell the boss, it was your hunch that …?" Sue screamed, "For Christ's sake, don't behave like a pair of muppets?"

Phil smiled, "Boss, we have Rice!" Sue stood up and, walking over, kissed each on the cheek, "Tell all?"

As Peter walked over to the coffee thermos, he picked up four mugs. Turning them over, he began to pour coffee into them. As he topped them up with milk, he said,

"Boss, we arrived at Rice's home address. Met by our additional members of the team. Wills and Alex, to assist in the search?"

"Rice answered the door. I told him who we were. We explained the usual, showing him the search warrant. He tried to ask for information on the doorstep?"

"He tried to refuse access to the property. It comprised of a two-up and two-down terrace. A small vestibule, leading into a small lounge, basically set out, a small wooden frame, three-piece suite covered in blue corduroy material. A central hearth and fireplace, a TV, and a few pictures on two of the walls."

"At the rear of the room was a set of stairs leading to the upper part of the property. There is also a door that leads out to the back room, small kitchen, and back yard. That leads out via a door into an entry."

"We were all standing in the lounge; I nodded at Alex." He said to Rice, "Stand up and place both hands on the wall?" Alex conducted a thorough search of Rice. On completion, he told him to "Sit."
After ten minutes, SOCO arrived. We all dressed in our forensic overalls."

"Looking at Rice, we told him the reason for our visit. I explained that we're members of the MCU, and the other officers were from SOCO."

I asked Rice, "Are you the only person on the property?" He replied, "No." I asked him, "Who is here with you?" He replied, "I left my girlfriend in bed upstairs?" "I asked him her name?"

He replied, "Susan Sutcliffe." I went to the bottom of the stairs and shouted her name?" She replied in a quiet voice, "Yes." I told her who I was and that I was sending up an officer who would remain on the landing. For her to get dressed and remain in the room."

"I called CH, telling them who I was and that I needed a WPC to attend at this address?"

"Fifteen minutes later, the WPC arrived. I explained to her the situation. I asked that she go upstairs, where she'll find, DC Ashton, one of the team. I want her to go into the bedroom, search the girlfriend, and have a quick look around. When completed, bring her downstairs. I gave her a pair of rubber gloves. She smiled and left."

"Eventually, the WPC, carrying a cardboard folder, eventually, the girlfriend came down the stairs followed by the WPC. Wills, bringing up the rear."

"The WPC stated, "I found this on a bedside table, positioned on the right-hand side of the bed. Sutcliffe informed me Rice's side of the bed?"

Peter looked at Sue, "I cautioned and arrested Rice for Conspiracy. For being in possession of stolen goods, contrary to the Data Protection Act. I also cautioned Sutcliffe for being involved in Associate evidence."

"Back at Derby Lane, I recited the reason for the arrests to Sergeant Lancaster, informing him that they will both be detained in custody to enable further inquiries to be made.

Sue looked at her junior officers, Sue smiled, "I'm impressed now. I want Combes included for the same reason. All three are to remain in custody at Derby Lane. Pending further inquiries?"

Sue looked at them all, "Now, the three are all tucked up for the night; let's all sign off duty?" Looking at her watch, "Christ, it's 1am. Jules leave a note for Eric, informing him that the following officers, and name them, won't be in until 10.30am. Now be off with you."

There was a tired chorus of "Night guv."

Sue, while in the car on the way home, picked up the force radio handset. "WDS Ford to Ch." The duty operator's reply responded immediately. *"Ch to WDS Ford." "Yes, ma am."* "Will you please contact Commander Frost, asking him to contact me...?" Charlie knew what was coming. The reply... *"Ch to Superintendent Ford, Roger ma'am will do, Ch out."*

Sue looked at the handset, holding it up in front of her face as if she were about to squeeze the life out of it. Shouting, "It's not ma'am as in ham, it's boss as in TOSSER...?" Charlie burst out laughing, "The guv would have loved that..."

Charlie had dropped Sue off at home for the night after the "Good Nights." Sue entered her house; she had just taken off her coat when her mobile activated.

" Ford." *"Superintendent Ford, it's Frost."* "Sir, I'm sorry it's so late, but I thought I should bring you up to date. We have Combes, Rice, her boyfriend, and a girl found in the upstairs bedroom of his house by the name of Sutcliffe."

"Due to the lateness of the hour, I decided that they'll all remain in police custody until later this morning when they'll all be interviewed. I feel that Rice, if put under pressure, may reveal the details of the perpetrator?"

TF replied, *"Sue, I know you have not forgotten the time rule in the dealing of prisoners?"* In a temper, she took in a deep breath and, as controlled as possible, said, "No sir, they'll be up before the courts in the morning for a plea and remand in custody for further enquiries." *"Good, keep me informed."* He then closed the call.

Sue thought to herself, "I'm no fucking sprog?"

The following morning, Sue, on arrival at the office, signed on duty, followed by Charlie. She looked at Jules, "Have we prepared resumes for the detained prisoners?" Jules replied, "Yes, guv, they are appearing in the Maggie's' court this morning?" Jules smiled, "Phil and I are on our way to court asking for a remand in custody for further inquiries."

Coombes, Rice, and Sutcliff appeared before the Magistrate. The clerk of the court read out the names, D.O.B. and addresses. He then read out the charges, and they pleaded, 'not guilty.'

The prosecution solicitor read out the circumstances of the offences, asking for a further remand in custody for further enquiries into this serious matter.

They were remanded in custody for 21 days.

62

Carter opened his eyes and raised his head off the bed. He took a moment, not that in the ink-black room atmosphere, he had any form of reference…

He turns and sits on the edge of the bed, arms by his side. He pushed himself up, stood, and managed to gain his balance, and decided that he needed a pee. He realised that he may be getting used to his bearings, due mainly to all the counted steps from his bed to the bathroom.

He suddenly thought for it was like a bolt of lightning, *'You stupid bastard, you've concentrated so much on your bearings, dwelling on the mental dimensions of your prison?'* He'd failed to wonder if there was anyone in shouting distance. Or, if his abductor detected his desperate shouting, they may affect some sort of punishment. Or, at the very least, perhaps a passer-by, who may hear him call?

Laughing at his last thoughts, he nearly imploded, realising how his thinking process had reduced from a senior detective to that of a narrow-minded flop.

He thinks, *'I'm not dying.'* He screamed. "I'm not dying, so you can all fuck off." He stands and awaits any recoil. *'Silence.'* Not a single reply of resentment.

Thinking of the toilet, he shuffles to relieve himself of all the water he drank to save himself from dehydration. As he enters the area of the toilet, his hand catches on the door frame. An issue never experienced before, for he'd never thought of the construction of his prison before.

It was while he nonchalantly set about his task, he decided to sit rather than stand. He thought he'd been lucky at first. The last thing he wanted was the smell of pee on his clothing. It was while sitting on the loo having a pee, he suddenly recalled the sound from that frame? When completed, he turned and washed his hands. He tapped his damp fist on the wall in front of him. The returning sound was hollow.

He tapped further to his left, and as he did so, the sound was also hollow. Then, it suddenly changed from a hollow tap to a thud. Carter thought, studded wall. He went and tapped on all the maintaining walls, it was all studded.

He began to get excited. He thought, in fact his brain re-computed all the recent information. He now began to follow the wall around the room, tapping as he went and not the direct line back to his bed and base. Again, the sound of studded walls.

He suddenly found himself in a pool of sweat with excitement. Carter thought he needed a weapon. Again, his brain sparked to life. The bathroom sink. Realising that the sink was held on a metal frame.

With enthusiasm, he began to retrace his steps back to the bathroom. On arrival, he reached for the sink. He felt the edge of the sink, which he knew was attached to the wall, supported by two metal legs fastened to a metal frame.

Shuffling away, he returned to the bed; he felt for what he was looking for around the base until he found his leather loafers, as he was in stocking feet. Slipping them on his feet, he shuffled back to the toilet.

His mind was racing, thinking the toilet may be the best point of attack, for it may be at the end of either the building or a room within a room, hence all the studded walls.

On arrival at the toilet, he found the sink. For all intents and purposes, the sink lay on a load-bearing metal frame with two legs, one at each corner. Secured, he thought, perhaps to a metal plate or a stout wooden bracket.

He was weak due to the lack of substantive food. Food? He suddenly thought of his captor's routine, *'Every three days,'* their subsequent visits to his cell to replenish supplies.

He shouted, "Shit." If I only knew, they may have even come in the night while asleep, without him knowing. Or where are we in relation to the three-day cycle? His mind raced, thinking to himself. 'No.' His attempted escape had to be made right now, for there were so many variables.

Standing holding onto the sink At the front with both hands, he crouched down. He dropped his left hand down to feel the supporting metal leg. The sink wasn't very deep, and he felt one of the legs supporting the frame.

His mind was racing. Touching the leg, he thought it was not very solid; it was L-section metal, attached at the corner of the frame, with the leg secured to the floor. He sat on the floor, feeling a sudden rush of light-headedness due to the lack of decent food and his whereabouts.

Carter thought, get over it. He lifts both legs and kicks out at the support. The first reaction to his act was the feeling of dizziness, forcing him to vomit more than once on the toilet floor.

He continued with the stamping, but sudden cramps in his stomach forced him to curl up in a ball, with shooting pains to his head causing such headaches, yet he thought of the inevitable.

After a brief period, he continues: All the suffering, the leg gives way, and it breaks free at the floor. He kneels, takes hold of the supporting leg, and begins to pull it backwards and forwards until it eventually gives way.

It left him holding a piece of metal that was wider at the top, where it had been joined to the fame. He explored the leg of metal tapered somewhat at the end with an L-shaped foot, damaged from the force of his kicking.

After a while, he stood up. He shuffled over, feeling for the wall; he began to tap, hearing the hollow sound; he held the leg in both hands and stabbed out the metal leg, hitting the wall.

It took several stabs with the metal-like spear to break through the plasterboard, with the chippings of plater falling into the darkness. He knew what to expect that the hole would be some 5 inches in depth, and he'd find the outer plasterboard facing.

Carter continued a hole, which, in its infancy, stretched from one of the timber supports to another. Finding at the lower part of the hole a sawn timber noggin fitted between studs to brace the frame.

Carter suddenly thought for a moment that with all the noise of the banging, it may alert his captors. He waited. Nothing? Because of his detention, his emotions changed. His mind played tricks on him, stunting his initial enthusiasm, which heralded his escape plans. He may be detected.

He takes several minutes to pull himself together. It all depends on the second piece of plasterboard, thinking what lay behind it? He thought, well, there is no response to the noise of the banging; what is the worst they can do...?

Taking hold of the metal leg in both hands, he strikes at the outer and facing plasterboard. Pieces break off into the darkness when he feels a sudden rush of cold air.

Although the final hole is small, his eyes suddenly squint at the shaft of light, which appears immense due to his original bearings. He thinks it must be night; his brain recognises no natural light. He waits a minute, thinking, yet again, no reaction to all the noise.

He continues in his effort to enlarge the hole in the plasterboard. Stopping from time to time to listen to any evidence of his aggressors. Carter eventually stoops under and between the noggins, enough for him to get through and out of his hell hole.

Standing in a large cold room, yet still looking down and squinting at the lights coming from an outer window. Carter stood with his impromptu weapon in one hand, covering his eyes with the other, realising he'd been kept in utter darkness.

Eventually gaining confidence, he investigates his new location, the room; the most obvious smells, petrol, and oil, give his new location away. Plus, the worktops at the far end of the room were littered with assorted tools and vices. He recognises two vehicle ramps, yellow Curley, air compressed airlines. He also noticed the Sun page three pictures dotted around the walls.

He turns, recognising he must be in a large garage-type area; he thinks like those on small industrial estates. He returns to the hole, his means of escape realising that it is a room, off a garage. Perhaps a one-time office, so easy to convert into his prison.

Carter with hooded his hands over his eyes, squints through one of the windows. Through gaps in his fingers protecting his eyes from the unaccustomed lights, he recognises the lighting of a KFC restaurant, somewhat in the distance. He quickly equates in his mind the protocol for there are drive-through vehicles and walk-in customers.

He stands back, still no sign of his impending captors. Thinking should he eventually escape from this place, he should leave his calling card. He pushes back into his cell with the extra light. Enters, goes to the fridge, opens the door, and takes out a pack of sandwiches.

Holding them in one hand, he painfully scratches the back of his hand, and he walks over to the hole in the plasterboard, examines the back of his hand and looks for the obvious result. Blood.

It is there in abundance. Walking around the room Carter delivered droplets of blood in certain places. Under the toilet seat, under the sink, he rubs his hand under the pillow on his bed, the bed sheets. Plus, a discreet place between the two plasterboard hollows as he leaves.

He walks over to the roller shutter doors, thinking if this doesn't set some sort of alarm off... He pulls on the chain. No movement. In the gloom, he feels down and finds it's locked and secured with a padlock.

Walking gingerly over to the worktop surface, he takes hold of a large shifting spanner and returns to the padlock. With a heavy swing, he crashes it on the lock and smashes it. He quickly frees the chain, pulling on it, and the roller shutter door begins to open.

With a blast of air, free air, in his face, he makes off free.

63

After what seemed like a 10-to-15-minute walk, he stumbled. Carter eventually arrives at the KFC restaurant. He obviously thought that he must look somewhat dishevelled and unkempt. But he didn't realise how bad until walking into the restaurant and saw the signs on all the diners' faces.

He walked up to the counter; several of the young assistants began to stare at him, one turned and as she was about to enter the spiel, 'Welcome to…" On looking at Carter, she called, "Frank, Frank."

Frank, dressed in his KFC manager's uniform, walked from behind the kitchen area, "Yes, Amy, what's up?" At the same time, the manager saw Carter. He came to the edge of the counter where Carter was standing. "Look, pal, you can't come in here. Now get out."

Carter looked at him, and it was the look in his eyes and his voice. "Could I please trouble you to call 0151-709-6010 and then hand me the phone, for I'm a police officer…The manager was just about to say the words, "Get out of here?" When he decided to act on his request.

Minutes later, the manager took a mobile phone out of his pocket. After entering the number, he passed the phone to Carter. Apologising as he left.

An annoyed voice repeated, *"Hello, Merseyside police; how may we help you?"* The duty operator heard a low voice, "This is Chief Superintendent Carter…." The voice at the other end said, "Sir." "I want you to get hold of an unmarked police car, no blues, or horns. Task it to pick me up at the KFC restaurant located on Speke Hall Road…?"

The reply came, "Sir, yes, sir." Carter sat in a chair close to the manager. He looked up at him, "Would it be at all possible to have a coffee black no sugar? I'm afraid that I have no money, but I'll duly pay you when my colleagues arrive?" The manager smiled, "Just wait a minute; it's on the way."

He returned within minutes and handed him the coffee in a plastic container in a plastic holder. "I've put in some cold water, as it's rather hot straight from the machine?" Carter thanked him. The manager said," How about some food?"

Carter replied, "Thank you all the same, but I'm in need of medical attention first. But I must tell you that someone will call tomorrow for a statement; it won't be anything heavy. Are you on duty tomorrow?" He replied, "Yes, six to midnight."

Carter smiled and sat back. It was some ten minutes later that he saw two plain clothes personnel enter the restaurant. On seeing Carter sitting holding his coffee.

One of the officers approached him, "Sir. I'm DS Mike Jordan, and this is my partner, WDS Joyce Smith; we happened to be in the area and fielded the call." Carter, shielding his eyes, sheepishly looked at him, "Can I trouble you to pay this man for the price of a coffee, for I haven't any money?"

When settled, Carter thanked the manager for his help and hospitality. He looked at Mike Jordan, "No fuss, just take me to the Royal." As Carter stood up, he wobbled. Both officers took an elbow each; prior to leaving, Carter noticed the bewildered looks on all the faces of the diners. He was assisted out to their waiting car.

Joyce Smith was behind the wheel while Carter was placed in the back seat; Mike Jordan, securing him in place via his seat belt, shouted, "Joy, it's a blue light and horn job to the Royal, please." She made no reply but just did it and drove like the advanced driver that she was.

Jordan felt Carter droop in his seat. He took out his phone and contacted the Royal A&E, informing them of their visit with a sick officer. Carter whispered to Jordan, "Please ask CH to inform Superintendent Ford of the MCU to attend the Royal ASAP." He then collapsed unconscious.

At the Liverpool Royal A&E, with the blue lights and the claxon alerting their arrival, they turned into a vacant ambulance bay. Joy, leaning forward, switched off the warning system.

She then jumped out of the car and ran into the area where the victims were taken. She called, "We need a doctor for a sick colleague?" Two paramedics ran to assist her.

"What's the problem?" She shouted above all the noise, "We have a senior officer in need of medical attention, pointing at the car, "He's unconscious, held up by my colleague."

One of the paramedics, together with a doctor, ran, pulling a gurney at the same time. Pulling up at the side of the car, Joy opened the rear nearside door. Mike got out and left matters to the medical team.

Mike said, "Joy, you go in with him while I'll go to reception and book him in?" The paramedic shouted, "It's okay, you can do it later; we need both of you to explain matters to the medics?"

Carter was rushed into the body of A&E and taken through to the AAU (Acute Admission Unit). He was pushed into a curtained area. A doctor followed by a sister walked into the area and met the two officers. He said, "Okay, what seems to be the problem?"

Mike said, "I'm DS Jordan, and this is my partner, WDS Smith; we received a call via our force control room to attend at a KFC restaurant on Speke Hall Road, a rush job, but no blue lights or horns."

Joy Smith interrupted, "To pick up this officer, who informed us that he was DCS Carter of the MCU?" Mike Jordan said, "That's as much as we know, except we do recognise him. He collapsed when leaving the restaurant?"

The staff member with the doctor was Sister Chris Atkinson, a senior sister in A&E. "I also recognise your colleague, as he has a habit of calling in on us?" Looking at the young doctor, "He is special, and in about 15 mins. After messages have been sent, we'll have more scrambled eggs than we can cope with."

Mike looked at her, "He mentioned calling Superintendent Ford, but he was in and out of consciousness; I just thought he was delirious. An unwarranted call to a senior officer would get me in the sh...?"

" Chris said, "DS Jordan, you'll be in more shit if you don't call her. DS Sue Ford is his deputy in the MCU. She'll need calling, and while you're at it, call Commander Tony Frost, C.I.D.

After all was put into action, Mike Jordan returned to the A&E and stood talking with Chris Atkinson and Joy. At the same time, Carter was being dealt with.

Mike looked at Chris, "You seem to know our senior officer very well?" Chris, with a whimsical smile, replied, "I knew him when he was a lowly young DC working out of Eton Road, with a rogue of a DS by the name of Eric Morton, retired… She turned and smiled at Carter. As he lay receiving attention and walked away.

64

In the depths of her sleep, Sue heard a noise in the fog of a dream. She thought the firewall of her brain would filter it out, but no, it persisted. She sat up cursing, "That fucking phone?"

Getting out of bed, she shuffled to a low bedroom cabinet with four drawers, on top of which she'd left her phone. Through the haze of her sleepy eyes, she saw in green letters, *'Force control room.'*

Pressing the little green telephone motive, she called, "Ford." "Ma'am, it's the duty control room Inspector; we've received a call to the effect that DCS Carter had been taken to A&E." Sue looked at her phone, thinking, is he taking the piss? The problem was that no one knew of his abduction.

Sue said, "I'm going to put down my phone and call the Merseyside police force control room, and if this is a fucking joke, I'll find you and kill you?" A quiet voice said, "Ma'am." Sue closed the call. She immediately called the said number.

A quiet voice said, "Merseyside police, how may I help you?" Sue said is that the duty Inspector?" The same voice replied, "Yes, ma'am." She called, "Ho! Sorry, but if you call me ma'am again, you'll be…? He interrupted, "By the way, boss, your APO DI Charlie Watson is en route to pick you up, as it's a serious matter. And perhaps you may bump into Commander Frost?"

Sue whispered, "Inspector, I'm so sorry for doubting you, but you see, this matter is for restricted personnel only."

The Inspector replied, "Yes, boss." Sue stood in her droopy PJs. She jumped and screamed and excitedly ran to the bathroom in tears of joy.

After a quick shower, Sue stood fully dressed, with her holster and firearm clipped to her trouser suit belt. Her front doorbell sounded. Opening the door, she saw Charlie standing somewhat perplexed?"

Looking at Sue, he said, "Boss, what's up? I was just told to pick you up?" She smiled. I'll tell you in the car; just head for the Royal, blue lights only as it's late."

When in the car Sue suddenly turned to Charlie, "Wait one?" She took out her phone. She called Abby Remington, for it had been days since they'd last spoken, and agreed only to call her when you have good news?"

A tied voice answered the phone, "Yes, who is it?" Sue said, "Ms Remington…She shouted, "You've found Carter?" Sue replied, "Yes, but at present, he's at the Liverpool Royal, under observation; I've only just been informed myself."

"I can arrange for a traffic mobile to pick you up, or you may wish to drive yourself?" She cleared her throat, "I'll make my way down, thank you very much?"

Sue said, "On arrival park in an ambulance bay, walk into A&E, go to the information desk, I'll inform them of your arrival." Sue heard a quiet voice say, "Thank you so very much, Detective Superintendent Ford; I realise it must also have been a strain for both you and your team." She closed the call.

Sue turned to Charlie, "What the hell are you waiting for?" Charlie said, "What the hell is going on?" "They've only found the guv." He took off with the blues and twos sounding, he thought, sod the time.

Sue commented on Abby's reaction to the news. Charlie turned his head quickly to his left. "I suppose, boss, it didn't evoke the same reaction as it did in you?" Sue, smiling, looked at him," Detective Sergeant Watson, please concentrate on your driving?"

At the Royal. Charlie parked up, and they both quickly walked to the A&E department. On arrival, they were both met by Chris Atkinson. They both saw a concerned look on her face. She walked over and warmly welcomed them both.

"Well, yet again, we have the presence of that man, Carter. Sue looked at Chris, "Would it be too much trouble to inform your duty reception staff that a, Ms Abby Remington will be attending." Sue gave Chris a whimsical smile?"

They both turned and followed Chris to the *'AAU.'* On arrival, they were met by two people standing outside of the curtained bay. A man stood at one side and a female at the other.

On seeing Sue, they both came to attention. The man said, "I'm DS Mike Jordan, and pointing at Joy, said, "And my partner, DS Joy Smith, from night CID 'E' division."

Sue gestured for them to join her in a vacant office together with Charlie. Sue looked at both officers, "Well, what happened?" DS Jordan informed her. Sue looked at them both. "This is extremely sensitive information, and if this gets out, your arses will be in slings."

"Now, DCS Carter was abducted by some person or persons. He's been missing for some 8 days and just happened to walk into the KFC on Speke Hall Road. Why?" DS Jordan said, "Boss, it was as simple as that, the *'Why'* we don't know?"

Looking at the two officers, she thanked them, you may go." She then explained, "Please forward your statements to the MCU for my attention. It will all come out in the wash." They smiled and left.

On leaving the office, they were met by Tiny Frost. He smiled as the two officers left. Sue explained the situation."

He looked at Sue, "Have you seen Carter?" Sue apologised, "Sir, I thought it more important to deal with any rumour sources?"

The three walked to the edge of the bay. The doctor turned, "I don't know where this man has been or kept, but I hasten to say not in any usual domesticated environment?"

Sue looked at the doctor, "No doubt you are aware that your patient is a very senior police officer. He was unceremoniously abducted from his home address, and until his appearance at this A&E department, he had been missing some eight days?"

"It was only when he walked into a local KFC outlet that we were told of his whereabouts?"

The doctor turned, "Well, from a medical point of view, his blood pressure is through the floor, his heart is racing, and he could be suffering from dehydration, but, yet we've been unable to take a urine sample. We have sent blood types to the labs; as you can see, he is on two drips."

On a visual score, he is somewhat dishevelled; his hand, nails, and face are dirty; there is some sort of dust on his clothes, and he has a scratch on the back of his wrist; the wound must have been deep. He will be admitted."

Sue said, "Sir, I'm getting the night SOCO officer here. He can take his clothes for testing and a sample of blood from that wound; the guv wasn't that stupid. I'm willing to bet when we find where he was kept, there will be discreet blood samples left about the place?"

Just then, a nurse coughed," Officer, I found this lady waiting at the nurses station?" Sue turned, "Miss Remington, I am sorry, but I did leave a message that we were to be told of your arrival."

Abby smiled, "Why, I did think matters would take a bit of a knock on the finding of Carter?" Sue quickly introduced her to Tony Frost, after which she escorted her to the bay where Carter was standing.

Abby just stood and burst out crying; after what was about ten minutes, she turned. Sue quickly repeated what the doctor had said. She took her over and introduced her to Chris Atkinson.

"Carter will be admitted to the hospital, yet we have no ward, and he may well remain here for a few days. But we do need Carter to come round so we can ask him some obvious questions?"

"I do suggest that you go home and return later today with some suitable sleeping attire. Were you may find, Carter has come round and sitting up, making a nuisance of himself." Laughing, she begrudgingly turned, thanked everyone alike and left.

65

It was 10.30am. Sue walked smiling into the general office, with Charlie in tow. Met by Eric, as usual, sat at his desk. He got up to prepare a coffee for Sue.

Sue, while signing on duty, turned, and smiled, "Please forgive me, dear people, for looking at members of the late team, but due to the lateness of the hour when we left the office last night. I received a message from the control room: the guv has been found."

"Will you all join me in the conference room, for I feel that the information should be shared with the whole of the team?"

On her way towards the room alone at the time. Eric gently took her to one side, smiling, "Boss, how is he?" Looking at Eric with such an upset look on her face, "He's terrible, Eric, and let's leave it at that. For it took me all my time to stop…" He looks like he's been kept in a dog's kennel?"

Sue linked Eric's arm, pulling him to her, releasing him as they walked into the conference room. The whole team came to attention. She flapped her hands, suggesting they sit. As usual, she took her place at the top of the room. Unable to hide her feelings. She called out. "Look, I have some good news; the guv has been found."

The whole of the room erupted. Again, Sue flapped her hands in the air to suggest they all sit and settle down.

She explained matters, how it all came about. "Now we still have the three prisoners, Combes, Rice, and Sutcliff. I'm leaving for the hospital to see if the guv has come around and may hold any information that may lead to the perpetrator?"

"While I'm away, I wish that a member of the team contact DS Mike Jordan, and DS Joyce Smith, for we need statements from them, if ready, collect them. The KFC manager starts his shift at 6pm. I want someone to collect his statement?" She looked at Lloydie. "Can you arrange matters?" He replied, "Boss."

Returning to the general office, looking at Eric, I'm leaving for the Royal, he smiled at Sue. "I hope all is well with Carter?" As she walked to the desk to sign out, she said, "As do I."

Looking at Charlie, "Are you ready?" He smiled and followed her out of the office.

Downstairs in the yard, before leaving for the hospital, Sue took out her phone. "Yes, Abby Remington." Sue said, "We're about to leave for the hospital. Do you need a lift?" She replied, "Thank you, Superintendent Ford, but I'm just about to leave for the office, for I have an important meeting to chair, but I'll attend on my own, in my car, enabling me to return to work, should Carter, still be unconscious?"

Sue shouted, "Bugger, your meeting; Carter is being admitted and needs some usual sleeping apparel, although he'll now be in a gown. If he has come round, he will need other clothes?" The phone went dead.

On arrival at A&E. Both Sue and Charlie were informed that Carter had been moved to the ICU. Sue took a sharp intake of breath, placing both hands to her face, looking at Charlie in a shocked way.

The doctor informed them both that Carter had taken a turn for the worse in the night, that the effects of his abduction, wherever he'd been kept, and how treated.

The doctor looked at Sue, "I believe you are aware of such a ward due to his previous visits?" He smiled and turned away.

Sue immediately called Abby and, while trying to downplay matters. And yet maintain her professional being, for she was on her way to the ward as she spoke. She informed Abby of the location.

On arrival at the ICU, she pressed the doorbell to the ward. After explaining who they were and who she was there to visit. They were admitted, informed that he was in his local section, the goldfish bowel at the top of the ward.

After passing all the beds of sick and perhaps dying patients, the cacophony of noise given off from all the medical equipment was always the same, and yet it was the precursor of the metabolic sounds giving hope. They both came to where he was being kept.

They found a ward sister in blue scrubs. Smiling, "Well, he even has Jenny, the same nurse who has nursed Carter on previous admissions?"

The sister said, "You've just missed the doctors' rounds. The reason for Carter's placement in the ICU is purely prevention. At present, he is still unconscious, so we are awaiting blood results; he is showing signs of dehydration, and his hands show signs of excessive wear and tear.

At present, due to his clothes being taken from him in the night, for forensic reasons, he is just dressed in a gown."

Sue took out her phone and called Abby. "Abby, have you left for the hospital?" "Excuse the formality, "No, Sue, I had to go into the office first, on bank business; why?"

"Could you please bring in some sleeping apparel for Carter, as he's in a hospital gown, although as yet still unconscious, it's not too important, but when he comes round, he'll feel better in his own clothes and shaving apparel?" She replied, "Yes Sue, I 'll return to the flat before I come to the hospital?"

Sue looked at Charlie," Let's take a quick peep and leave instructions to be called on his return to consciousness?" They walked round to the door of his fishbowl. They were permitted entry. They both looked upon a man asleep on his back, with the hospital bedclothes pulled up to his chest, with his arms flat on top of the bed.

Sue looked at Charlie, "Could I trouble you to go tell the ward sister of our instructions, and please organise an APO on the door 24-7?" He looked at Sue and smiled, saying, "Yes, boss." He turned and left.

She looked about her there was no one about. She quickly bent down and kissed Carter on his forehead. "Now look here, Mr. Get off that arse of yours and out of that bed. I need you where I can see you all during working hours; I'm missing you?" She bent down again and kissed him on his cheek. Stood up and left.

Round the corner in the ward, she found Charlie stood, talking with the ward sister. She coughed, "Ready, Charlie?"

66

Back at the office, they both signed in. There was only Eric in the office, and he produced the magical mug of coffee. Sue sat opposite to Eric, with Charlie sat on the other side of the office.

"Well, the guv had been moved to the ICU, in the same fish bowel, and even the same nurse. He is unconscious, which poses a potential problem for the medical team. He presented with low blood pressure and poor reaction to a light in his eyes. The rest, one of which, you know, the essential urine sample nigh impossible ?"

She stood up, looking at her watch its 12.30pm. "Let's get Coombes up here, but in the meantime, I'm calling TF, for before we found the guv, I was asking for a deal?"

"Can you find Jules? Get her to produce Coombes, and I'll be back." She turned and left for her office. Charlie looked at Eric, who smiled, saying, "Yes, I know, but whatever you've heard or seen, please respect her privacy?" Charlie replied, "She's too good a boss, of course."

When in her office, Sue dialled TF's number. A rough bark answered, "Frost." "Sir, it's Superintendent Ford before she could say another word. *"Well, how's the bugger doing? Sat up in bed with pretty nurses serving him ice cream…?"* Sue replied, "No sir, just the opposite, he is still unconscious and has been moved to ICU?"

The roar turned to a shout, *"Why the fuck Ford, am I only hearing of this now?"* Sue looked at the handset, "Well, sir, I've only just been fucking told." She thought for a moment; I just can't slam the phone down on him, for I need to discuss Coombes?"

She coughed, "Sir, I need to discuss the prisoner, Coombes; she wants to make a deal?" TF thought for a moment, *"What has she to offer?"* Sue replied, "Well, sir, we know what we want, but it all depends on what she wants, and how far we're prepared to go?"

She continued, I think she'll give us Rice, the so-called boyfriend, but we want the bastard responsible for all the murders, plus the abduction of the guv, yet still lying unconscious, we don't know of any injuries occurred?"

"But as I've already said, "It's what she wants in return; so far, she is responsible for giving out information contrary to the Data Protection Act, conspiracy to murder. So, what can we give her if she gives us the perpetrator drop all charges?"

There was silence from the other end of the phone, a sudden splutter, *"Ford, see what she can give us and what she wants?"* He closed the call.

Sue got up, returned to the general office, and saw Jules standing with a file under her arm, and it so happened that she had the file recovered from Rice's house. She looked at Eric, "Anything from the hospital, no, then come on Jules, let's go and see what Coombes has to offer?"

Jules led the way to interview room 1. She opened the door to find a WPC sitting with Coombes. She stood up, "Boss, I'll be outside?" Sue smiled, "Go to the general office and get yourself a cup of tea or coffee?"

She looked at Coombes, "What about you?" She looked up, "I'm good, thanks."

Sue said, "Hazel you realise that you're still under caution?" She replied, "Yes."

Sue looked at Jules, who began to place two new tapes into the recorder. She switched it on, stating the time, day, and date, and the persons all present. The machine gave out a bleep.

Sue looked at Coombes, "Hazel, I again notice that you have no legal counsel?" She replied, "No." Sue said, "You do realise that you have a right to a solicitor, even as you know the duty solicitor?" She again refused.

Sue said, "So be it." "I'd like to return to the last-mentioned item when last interviewed. You wish to make a deal?" She smiled, "Yes."

Sue continued," Hazel, the problem with deals is that both sides wish to come away with something positive?" Sue leant back in her chair. "So, what do you have to offer, and what do you want in return?"

Coombes looked Sue, straight in the eyes. I can give you the murderer, so what is that worth?"

Sue looked at Jules, who she thought was about to fall off her chair in surprise. Sue had collaborated with Carter for years and had experienced such remarks, but is it true?

Sue, with a poker face, said, "Jules, just pass me that file?" Pointing to the one recovered from Rice's home. Sue thanked her. She took hold of the file and spread the contents out in front of her.

"Hazel, do you know what these pieces of paper represent?" She looked down, "Why yes, they look like the information I passed to my so-called two-timing bastard of a boyfriend, Rice?" Sue slapped the table, again frightening both Jules and Coombes.

Looking at Coombes, she shouted, "No, they are what one could call copies of death sentences passed on 9 people, of which 9 is all we know of, and of course, the 1 that survived an attack, you seem to think this is funny?"

Combes looked at both of her interrogators, "Well, officers, have you ever felt used. I mean, really used?"

"I met Rice at a party held in a club; many of the revellers were a mixture of solicitors and CPS staff. Yet there were other non-legal guests, friends of friends; it was someone's party. I forget the name of the host?"

"I was introduced to Rice, a handsome and alluring enough kind of guy, a league above the usual I meet and know. He was so smooth, and, during the evening, he made such a fuss of me."

"We had several smoothie dances, and the drinks were flowing. Rice asked me if I was part of the legal gathering, and when I told him, "Yes, and that I worked in CPS, he seemed to show an inordinate amount of interest in me."

"Oh! he was very subtle; it started with nights out fancy meals in good restaurants. It wasn't long before we started to sleep together. He'd invite me on occasions to spend the odd weekends at his house in, Wellington Street."

"One time, he'd bought enough goodies in for us to spend the whole time in without going out. We spent most of the time in bed, nipping downstairs to make the odd snack that we ate in bed."

Looking at both Sue, and Jules, Coombes said, "Officers, surely I'm not embarrassing you?" And burst out laughing.

"He was rather devious when he asked the odd question, implying interest in my job. On one such weekend, after more than a few drinks, and of course, intimate sex both on the floor in front of the fire and bed later."

During the odd bouts of pillow talk, he asked, and I told him the intricacies of my job, and I did. It was so casual. He was clever and never showed much interest; he just seemed to let it go over his head."

Coombes continued it was like a rant, she just let the words flow out. "It was one special weekend at his place, and we'd been out for a meal; we quaffed two bottles of red wine and several liqueurs with our coffees. We both fell into a cab home."

I didn't realise that Rice wasn't that drunk; he was just playing at it, and he suggested, "Honey, I have a friend who hates the whole social system, the total lack of effort by people in authority. Admitted stupid sentences handed out by the courts."

Coombes said, "Rice stated that this friend mentioned that he had a sister who got caught up in drugs, and the pusher was Terry Wilkinson, and it appears he never gets convicted?"

She continued, "You see, I just thought I was helping, and it wouldn't do any harm. Just get, Wilkinsons details, give them to Rice, and he passed them on."

Sue coughed, "Hazel, who was the person who wanted the information?" Coombes suddenly turned like someone recovering from a dream. "No, Chief Inspector, that's not how the game is played; what will you offer me?"

Sue looked at Jules, "Interview terminated at 12.30 pm on Wednesday, 7th March 2018.

Sue called, "Officer." The interview door opened. "Yes, boss." "Will you please take this prisoner down to the holding cells?"

Coombes screamed, "What the fuck. I've told you what I have to offer; I can give you Rice and one other; I'm not telling you the other name until you tell me what you can give me?"

Sue turned, "It's above my pay grade to make spontaneous promises; please don't worry, I'd like to give you the Crown Jewels for the predator. But even you know that matters would have to be put before my bosses and CPS."

Sue called the WPC, who stood outside, "Officer." The door opened, and Sue smiled, "Take her away." The WPC took hold of Coombes and led her away.

Looking at Jules, Sue said, "Please collect everything up and come through to my office when ready."

67

Sue was sitting in her office when there was a tap on her door. She called, "Come in, Jules." The door opened, and Jules entered, placing the recorder, the two recently recorded tapes, evidence recovered from Rice's house, and other papers onto Sues's desk.

With the phone in hand, she gestured for Jules to take a seat. She pointed to her phone with her free hand; she mouthed TF. "Yes, sir, it's Superintendent Ford; I've just completed a second interview together with WDC Julie Forbes of the prisoner Coombes."

"Yes sir, in a protracted interview, Coombes has clearly mentioned her role in the matter, implicating Rice and how he fitted into things; she even mentioned the role played by the perpetrator. At the end of which, willing to name him, but insisted what's in it for her?"

"Sir, I mentioned to her of the 5 offences, which led to 9 victims, that we know of to date and that all the original information had come from her. Suggesting that it amounts to one big conspiracy."

TF said, *"Ford, we need to organise a meeting with Simon Chapman and arrange legal representation for Coombes. The offences are too serious, as I don't want it kicked out for lack of a legal brief. Arrange it?"*

She slammed the phone down on the cradle. "That bugger forgets I have the guv out of commission, pretending to be ill?" Jules burst out laughing, "Boss, I'll leave it up to you to tell him?"

Sue sat back in her chair; taking up the phone, she dialled the general office. "Hello, Eric, any news?" She gently replaced the phone. Looking at Jules, Sue gently moved her head from side to side.

Taking in a sudden intake of breath and exhaling. Sue picked up the phone, *"Ask Phil to attend my office please, and produce Rice for interview. Thank you, Eric."* Looking at Jules, "Can I leave you to organise the typing up of Coombes's evidence from the tapes?"

Jules smiled, "Of course, boss, please don't worry about the guv?" Picking up all the bits and pieces, she turned to leave her office; opening the door she saw the smiling face of Phil just about to knock.

Jules was about to close Sue's door. Phil smiled, "Okay?" "Yes," she smiled, "But the boss was a bit fragile;" She nodded to leave.

Sue called, "Is that you, Phil, get in here and stop one of my top officers' powers of concentration?" As Phil entered, Sue burst out laughing. Looking at Phil, she gestured for him to sit.

"Phil, do you know if Rice has a legal rep?" Smiling, Phil acknowledged his boss, "Well, not up to now?"

Sue looked at Phil, "Well, the interview with Rice will be quick, yet legally, as you know, he should have the option?"

"I intend, after the usual introductions, to explain to Rice that we have a witness, which places him in the frame, and if he wants to help himself, that it would be in his best interest to give us the name of the perpetrator?"

Looking at Phil, she smiled, "I feel it will be the same as that with Jules's stint. I want a deal?"

The phone on Sue's desk suddenly rang out. Picking it up, she said, "Ford." It was Eric. "How would you like to attend at the Royal…That's as far as he got… Standing, she rushed round from behind her desk and, leaning down, gave Phil a peck on the cheek. "It's the guv he's come round." She continued running until she got to the general office.

Entering the office, she was met with a collective wall of smiling faces. Eric, Lloydie, Charlie, and the secretaries, to name but a few. Looking at Eric, she handed him a piece of paper. It's self-explanatory while explaining in her rush to sign out, "Call Abby, tell her the news if she hasn't already been told, offer a lift, you know the form."

"Charlie, where are you?" The equally excited reply came, "Boss right behind you."

Sue suddenly stopped, "For Christ's sake, let's just cool down. Lloydie and Phil, can I leave you both to interview Rice? You know the form. Has he got a legal rep? Does he want one? Tell him we have a witness, placing him in the frame?"

"Please don't mention Combes. And finally, the *'deal'* subject, may rear its ugly head; we need for him to implicate himself, suggesting he knows a name? But wants to deal?"

Running down the corridor, followed by Charlie, she called, "See ya." And disappeared.

68

The trip to the hospital was adrenalin-fuelled, for it was blues lights and claxon horns all the way. On arrival, they parked up. Leaving the car, they half-walked and half ran into the body of the hospital. Taking the lift to the first floor and ICU.

Outside the ward, they were met by a plainclothes APO officer, who, on seeing Sue, came to attention. He was just about to say, "Afternoon ma…" Charlie interrupted, "Paul, it's boss." Paul opened the door; Charlie remained with Paul after Sue continued into the ward. "Paul spread the word; it's "Boss when dealing with Superintendent Ford."

Entering the ward, she was met by the same sudden cacophony of noises. Alarms of equipment were being administered to severely ill patients.

Walking down the ward, Sue smiled at the relatives attending at the bedside of their loved ones, the same relatives as envisaged on her previous visits. Sue noticed all the pain etched in their eyes.

At the end of the ward, Sue came to the fishbowl, Carter's present residence. To be met by two doctors, Chris Atkinson and, of course, Carter's nurse, Jenny. All in conversation.

While she waited for the end of their meeting, Charlie eventually joined her. Seeing both Sue and Charlie. Chris Atkinson broke ranks from the group and welcomed them. Chris smiled, "Well, it would seem they've found some sort of life in that excuse of a man. The nurse, who had also broken away from the doctors, to continue with her duties.

Sue looked at Chris, "Who had, of course, been light in her original conversation with Sue, "Well, how is he?" Chris, with a stoic look on her face, replied, "He's very weak. His main problem, apart from severe dehydration, is his aversion to light, a form of photophobia. The doctors have managed brief conversations with Carter. They managed to ascertain that he'd been kept in a sheer black hellhole, the darkest of places, for a considerable time?"

Sue, looking suddenly upset, whispered, "Well, he's been missing for eight days." Chris suddenly hesitated, "He hasn't mentioned anything else, but if one had been kept in the complete dark, and I mean no access to light, either natural or electrical, it would cause several problems."

Sue said, "May we see him?" Chris smiled, "He's on 15-minute ob's, looking at his nurse, who smiled. Chris said, "You've got 15 minutes."

Walking over and opening the Perspex, convex-shaped door to complete the *'fishbowl'* effect on his area. Charlie stopped. Sue turned, "Charlie, what's the matter? He smiled, "No boss, you go look-see; I'll remain at the nurse's station."

Sue smiled and disappeared. Chris looked at Charlie, "How on earth does she keep it under control? Doesn't he know she loves the bones of the man?" Charlie looked at Chris and just smiled. Chris remarked, "You're all good people."

Carter's nurse, who couldn't help but hear the conversation, stated, "Can we include you in with the Supt?" Chris blushed, "It would seem, nurse, that you haven't enough to do?"

Standing at the foot of Carter's bed, Sue looked down on a site that she had witnessed on one or more occasions. Carter laid out flat, covered with the hospital bedding. The only difference from the past, she noticed a surgical cloth which had been placed over his eyes.

Walking down the side of his bed, passing his arms that were laid on top of the bed and not covered. As Sue strolled towards him, she gently trailed one of her fingers along his arm.

A weak voice said, "Nurse, is that you?" Sue whispered, "No, Carter, it's only me?" Voice recognition, she noticed a weak smile on the lower half of Carter's face.

"Sue, Sue, Sue, where have you been? It seems I've been conscious for ages?" Sue, in a controlled voice, squeezing his hand, "Guv, I have more important matters to deal with, apart from you?"

He raised his voice slightly, "Pull up a chair. I need to talk to you. Are we alone? It's no secret, but if alone, I can be that more graphic with my language?"

"Take out your phone and record the following, time, day, and date." Sue did placing her phone on his pillow close to his head so and, after a couple of seconds, stated the requisite details said, "Go."

"I have no idea how long I was kept in that fucking God-forsaken hole. I know it was a room with a double bed, a fridge that they replenished every three days and toilet facilities. All of which I detected by feeling alone?"

The room was in total blackness. No strip of light from any ill-fitting door or window, of which I didn't detect. The offenders even removed the bulb out of the fridge. You can imagine it drove me crazy. It so happens that on one visit to the loo, I accidentally knocked on the door frame; it wasn't immediate; in fact, it was while I was washing my hands. I thought it sounded hollow, perhaps a *Studded wall?*"

Sue leaned forward and touched his arm, "Guv…! He called, "Even in the hospital, you call me fucking guv. Lowering his voice, he moved his hand as if searching for hers. Finding it, he whispered, "Sue, in such circumstances, will you please call me Carter?"

The door to his cubicle opened. Sue turned to see his nurse smiling, "Sorry, officer, but I need to check his, ob's?"

He immediately complained, "Can't they wait? I need to give my colleague sensitive information?" A voice from behind Sue quietly said, "No, Carter, they can't; they're our only means of knowing how you're" doing?" Carter suddenly smiled, "Chris Atkinson?" As I live and breathe, would a kiss suffice and buy me some time?"

Chris looked at him, "You think that smile will...?" Carter interrupted, "Chris, it's very important; we are against the clock, trying to detect a psychopathic murderer?"

Chris looked at the nurse, "Can we make an exception? Can you work around matters?" She replied, "Sister, if it's alright with you, who am I to complain?"

Although Carter was unable to see any faces, he smiled, "Thanks, Chris."

Sue stood up and carried her chair to the far side of his bed to enable the nurse access to the various equipment. The nurse, looking at Carter, smiled, "I'll start with your temp, for you'll have to remain quiet for several seconds; all others are straightforward." On completion, the nurse said, "You can continue."

Carter took in a sudden breath. "Where were we?" Sue played back some of the tape. *'I thought it sounded hollow. Studded wall?'* "Right, with a degree of sheer excitement, I began knocking the wall above the sink in front of me hollow. The end wall was hollow. I returned to the main room and conducted knocking the walls, hollow."

"I felt for my bed, and sitting on it, I thought, what were their intentions, my death?" Bearing in mind the three-day cycle to replenish the fridge, perhaps they may have called in the night. My mind was going crazy. I decided now or never."

"I put on my shoes, thinking I needed to protect my feet, for I needed some sort of tool. The only thing was the metal legs that supported the sink. Perhaps I could kick them away. I returned to the toilet area. Feeling the legs, they were of narrow-angle metal, welded at the top of the frame, and screwed into the floor."

"I lifted my leg and kicked out. Being in a weak condition, I vomited on the floor of the bathroom and felt faint. It took several goes, but eventually, it gave way. I was left with a spear-type instrument."

"I returned to the main part of the room. I was wondering if it sounded completely studded. Was this room built especially? I decided to try in the middle of the wall facing my bed. I stabbed, and stabbed, at the wall, breaking through the plasterboard. I, of course, felt the outer skin of the wall."

It had all the wooden supporting framework, but eventually, I knocked through and felt the sudden surge of air; although I saw my first signs of light, I had to protect my eyes. The air, and this is important, was punctuated with the smells of petrol, oil, and grease. I thought, garage?"

"I wondered about, felt the obvious work benches, tools etc. I nearly broke my neck on one of the inspection ramps."

Carter suddenly stopped; he said, "Jenny, can I have a drink? My mouth is parched. Jenny took hold of a beaker with a straw in it resting on his table. She nodded at Sue, who was sitting closer to the table. She picked it up. She leaned over and placed the straw on his lips. He drew up the liquid and spluttered, "Thanks, Jenny." Sue said, "It's me, so get on with it." Carter just smiled.

On completion, he coughed, and Sue switched on her phone. "I suddenly thought, Carter, you need to leave DNA to prove you were detained in that evil room. I returned to that shitty room. However, the chances of getting caught were narrowing by the minute. I cut my hand on a sandwich packet and hopefully left smears and droplets of blood."

Sue suddenly said, "Carter, your mind must constantly be on the go; what a perfect source of evidence?" He smiled, "Through sheer desperation. I found a roller shutter door, broke the lock, and escaped."

Carter suddenly stopped talking for several minutes. "Sue, I really thought all the banging would attract the attention of my abductors, but no. They never thought…?"

"It was late and dark, as you know, except for the lights radiating from the KFC sign and restaurant. Wherever it was, I managed to stumble, for I needed to cover my face."

Carter ex-hailed, "Well, Sue, that's it precisely. It will need fine-tuning before I can include it as my statement of evidence. But will it come in handy to jog my memory? Of course, day, date, and approximate time all relate to when abducted. Plus, the day, date, and time of this interview?"

Sue, of course, completed matters, saying, "Vocal statement taken from DCS Carter, at 3.30pm. Wednesday 7th March 2018, while a patient in ICU at the Liverpool Royal Infirmary, witnessed by Superintendent Ford."

Sue looked about her, with no one about. She leaned down and kissed Carter on his cheek, saying, "I have a lot to be getting on with. See you tomorrow?" She turned, leaving to the sound of Carter calling, "Sue, Sue, please just wait?" There was no reply.

The next voice he heard was that of his nurse, Jenny. "Carter, are you alright? Superintendent Ford has just left?" "No, no." Came via the half-hearted reply?"

"Jenny walked up to Carter. Leaning over, she gently moved his eye protector back in place, "Now look here, Carter, it must be kept in place; your eyes need rest."

69

Carter's nurse was standing at the foot of his bed, busily making notes on a daily state clipped to a special desktop attached to the metal frame of his bed. Reporting and logging, and sometimes using her mobile phone, to carryout calculations of medicines, tablets, per mg's and drip volumes.

Sensing a movement behind her, Jenny, suddenly turned to see an attractive lady standing at the door to his area. Jenny walked to the door she opened it; the lady said, "My name is Abby Remington, a friend of DCS Carter?"

Her beauty surprised Jenny, plus the brown pig skin holdall she carried, containing some clothes for the patent.

Jenny smiled, "Carter is on 15-minute obs; I've just noted his latest. I will need to return in 15 minutes, and please excuse me, for it's important to record accurate readings for the medical staff." Jenny turned and left.

Abby put down the holdall and crept up to his bedside. She leaned down and kissed him on the lips. He murmured, "Oh! Olga, my gorgeous Russian domestic not again, you're tiring me out?"

Carter said, "Awe, Abby, it's the aroma of your perfume that gave you away." She slowly moved her hand down under the bedclothes, "We've got 12 minutes before your nurse returns; let me pleasure you in the interim?" Carter took hold of her arm, "Abby, Abbs, if I can't have the dog, then the tail is just useless. You have no idea how many times I thought of it, both here, laying in this bed and that pathetic hell hole in which I was detained?"

She removed her hand and placed one on either side of his face; half standing, she leaned down and kissed him hard on the lips. "Well, Carter, that will have to suffice?"

Carter, with his eyes protected, sighed. "Abby, Abby, Abby, you have no idea how I thought of such matters when one doesn't have the perception of time, not aware if it's day or night?"

"There are countless negative effects on our minds and bodies when one is kept in severe darkness and isolation. It affected my sleep pattern, and I suffer from hallucinations, and my mind is in utter turmoil. Carter whispered, "Lean closer to me?"

Abby leaned over with both arms gently resting on either side of his bed covers to support her weight. She whispered, "Carter, I'm here?"

He moved his head to feel for her ear. "Abby, I remembered that when Terry Waite was kept in total isolation, he, in his mind, with the aid of his memory, formulated the pages and chapters of a book, which he later published."

"I attempted the same. I lay on the bed provided, and although it didn't take long for the memories to flood in. It was you I turned to, the woman I'd recently met, and in this morass of manmade horror, clung to all the thoughts that I held dear, for you see, it was you, yes you, Abby, became my strength, and my rock."

"Abby, feasibly, it was one of the most stupid of ideas; through all the darkness, you, and the memories of all the erotic showers we shared, and our time spent together in bed, it all came flooding in; it was as if my memory became a receptor. Transmitting all my sexual feelings of you to my brain."

"The influx of information flooded my mind. At times, I nearly drowned in such thoughts, so you see the effect it had on me?"

On the rare occasions when my mind is reduced to your input. Other such notions entered, for as my mind speculated on the immense weight of the darkness, it tendered to dwell on my fate?"

"I tendered to wonder what such plans this psychopath has for me while he or another keeps supplying the water and sandwiches; that's fine. If matters continue and he never gets caught, he may well cease the replenishment of items, leaving me to die…?"

Abby could feel the sweat on his face; the whole act of his recollection was upsetting him. Abby took hold of his head with both hands, "Carter, Carter, please stop, for it's upsetting you, the memory of the matters you've had to go through. While trying to remain sane, to keep you in a reasonable state of mind?"

While she cradled his head, she took hold of a tissue from a box on his locker. She gently wiped off all the perspiration from his face. Abby commented, "Why, Carter, your seating…" He interrupted her, "Horses sweat, men perspire, and women only glow." She burst out laughing.

She leaned down and whispered, "Carter, Carter, I can't begin to imagine the terrible nightmare you've endured for the past eight days. In fact, I toiled with the brain-numbing insidious mind games, the constant needle-pricking shock waves continuously pounding the thoughts of where you're being kept and in what conditions?"

She began to cry. Carter, gently feeling around, took hold of her head, facing it down towards him; finding her lips, he kissed her passionately. "Oh! Abby, dear Abby, this infernal problem has been as worse for you to endure, all that time not knowing?"

"Well, my dear lady, it's all over. For I will get better, as will you, and we'll both run down the rabbit hole that is our flat, we'll disappear…"

Abby, with tears in her eyes, said, "Yes, Carter, about that... Carter, you need to rest; the whole of this is upsetting you. I must go. She leaned down and kissed him softly on his lips, turned and left. As she left his room she turned, and saw Sue, who had remained at the nurse's station.

As Abby walked towards her, Sue said, "Why the tears? What's up?" At that precise moment, Jenny walked towards them, holding a white envelope. Sue murmured, "What's that?" Jenny said, "It's marked, Carter. It was on top of his clothes when I was unpacking them." She handed it to Sue.

Sue, with such a cold look in her eyes, said, "What the fuck is this?" Abby interjected, "Superintendent Ford, it's personal and has nothing to do with you?" Sue replied, "Wait here?" She called, "Charlie."

"Yes, boss?" Came the reply, "Charlie, will you please go in and have a chat with the guv, I won't be a minute?" As he passed her, he heard, "Now, Miss Remington, we're going for a chat." She took hold of Abby's arm and led the way to an empty office.

In the office, she turned, facing Abby, waving the envelope; she again said, "What the fuck is this? Perhaps it's a *'dear John'* letter?" Abby spluttered and began to cry, "Sue, I just can't deal with this; it's killing me; seeing him lying there, I'm totally unable to think and believe what he's been through, and what happens after this episode?"

She continued through her tears, "There will be other occasions, for that man lying there is the head of a specialised unit in the Merseyside police CID. He's the man to get at if things with a case or the villains feel you're closing in on them. Take out Carter and stop or hinder a serious enquiry?"

Continuing, Abby, through her tears, faltered and stammered, "Tell me, Superintendent Ford, is this the first time this has happened to Carter whilst head of the MCU?"

Sue looked at her; she took a deep breath, "Er! Now, for you see that man lying in that bed, he wasn't asked, he was told, to take on the mantle of the newly formed MCU and build a team."

"He did so, and at first, all his colleagues were standing around to wait until he, or it dropped a bollock, well it didn't. Out of all the units countrywide, we have the best clear-up record. And it's all down to him, that man in there. You see, with what he's gone through in the last four years, it's a wonder that he hasn't been committed?"

"Abby whispered, "But it's likely to happen again; he may even be killed. I couldn't stand it, and I felt I should end things, as I'm likely to become nothing but a whimpering whatever, friend, partner, for Christ's sake, wife. No, no, no, I can't?"

Sue took hold of her shoulders, looking her straight in her eyes, "I think Carter is likely to be admitted for about six or so days, even more, if you take in the psychological effect all of this is having on him?"

Sue, looking at Abby, whispered, "Now, Miss Goodie, two shoes; if you think that I'm going to allow you to serve that fucking letter on him, your sadly mistaken. I'll lock you up for "Incitement to cause a riot."

"For should your lack of indiscreet timing have a worsening effect on Carter's mind and spirit. The man is special. The whole of MCU, plus *'Jane'* Commander Frost's secretary, Chris Atkinson, senior nursing sister in A&E, and others near and far, will cause you immense pain?"

When Sue had finished with her rant, Abby had got herself together. As they left the office, Abby looked at Sue; she smiled, "I suppose I can add you to that list, for working as close as you do with that man, it's inevitable?"

Sue turned, "No, Abby, my problem is, I love that man, guilty as charged, and if you say anything to anyone, least of all Carter, let me please remind you that I carry a gun." As she said it, she held her coat open, revealing the item clipped to her trouser belt.

Abby just shuddered. She looked at Sue, "Okay for me to just pop in and say goodbye?" She handed her the letter back. "I suggest that you file this under 'S' for its contents. I'm sure they'll allow you as long as you want?"

Abby returned to the fishbowl. Sue shouted to Charlie, "I'm sure you girls have been chatting long enough. Bye, guv, see you tomorrow." Carter shouted, "Bye, Sue, take care?"

70

When in the car leaving the hospital for the office. Charlie looked at Sue, "Boss, is there a problem?" Sue, looking straight ahead, replied, "Just drive?"

On their return to the general office, they both signed back in. Eric produced his magical mug of coffee for Sue. At the same time, she sat next to him. Eric whispered, "How is he?" Sue smiled, "Fine…Eric interrupted, "Chinas fine, now how is he?" Sue said, "Well Mr clever arse, could you please arrange a scrum down for noon? All hands, no excuses."

Sue got up and left for her office. Eric waited a while, then he looked at Charlie, for Charlie was always the next port of call when trying to ascertain any shit which may have happened involving his current principal. "Well, Mr, What happened at the hospital? A blind man can tell the boss has got her arse out of gear?"

Charlie looked around the room, and for that moment, they were alone. He coughed, "It seemed to kick off as Miss Remington was leaving, and there was a conflab between Abby, the guv's nurse, and the boss?"

"I then saw the boss waving a white envelope around, then she suddenly took hold of Abby, escorting her to a nearby office, and that was it. For whatever happened, it was behind closed doors?"

He continued, "A good fifteen minutes elapsed, the office door opened, and they both came out. It was obvious, however much Abby tried to hide it, that she had been crying. Abby returned to the guv's room. I'd been tasked to sit and talk to him. The next thing, the boss shouted, and we left."

At noon precisely, they all filed into the conference room. Suddenly, Tony Frost and Wendy Field, the press officer, turned up without them knowing Sue had called them both.

With the appearance of TF, the whole room came to attention. He gestured for them to sit. He was sat next to Sue. He looked up at her and smiled, "Well, Superintendent Ford, this is your show."

Sue stood and faced the team. "The guv? The light still blinds his eyes; for how long? It's up to the medics, yet he seems in good spirits. He has a constant visitor, Miss Abby Remington, a friend. Muted laughter was heard from the team.

After a brief pause, Sue resumed. "Right, we have got our work cut out for us. Coombes, Rice, and Ratcliffe were all detained because of information gained by Phil and Peter. I hear that during an interview with Lloydie, and Phil, that Rice, also wants a deal?" Sue laughed, "Well, bless my soul."

Sue looked out over the room, "Catching on to Coombes gave us Rice. Sutcliffe was caught up in the raid. Our main course of action was to establish where the guv was being kept. Then suddenly, he turns up like a bad penny at the KFC. For all those who are unaware, the guv had a friend called Penny?"

The room erupted with laughter. TF stood up. "We have the guv; we want the perpetrator. Both Coombes and Rice must know who he is?" He fidgeted whilst on his feet. "As you all know, we are nearly at the end of our rope for the time that we can hold the three suspects in custody."

Sue stood up, "While we discuss this matter, I want enquiries made in a radius of, say, about 50 yards from the

KFC, for on how the guv presented, I feel he couldn't have walked much further?"

"So, we know the guv mentioned a garage-type building with roller shutter doors." Lloydie stood up, "Boss, while you've been dealing with the guv and the information given to us by the medics?"

"Alex and Jill have made discreet enquiries in the neighbourhood. In and about the approximate given distance, and directly behind the KFC they found a car showroom. At the rear, they have their own garage, for obvious reasons. It has a roller shutter door?"

"The whole of the site is a business park. There are several other small units, a tyre repair workshop, a double-glazing supplier, wholesale furniture and carpet suppliers, and so on. There are two other garages, but they are located at the far end of the park, too far for the guv to have walked."

"The nearest location is the Toyota dealership, with the usual supply of cars in the showroom and the usual array of second-hand cars on the forefront. Boss it's the garage at the rear of the property that interests us?" He then sat down.

Sue thanked him. She looked at Alex. "While you and Jill were playing Mr. and Mrs., what did you see?" There was a titter from the team. Sue shouted, "Oh! Come on, children, let's get serious?" The laughter grew even louder.

Alex stood up, "Boss, it was on one occasion that both Jill and I drove through the estate. Due to haphazard parking, we just slowly drove along, not causing any raised eyebrows. When we noticed the roller shutter doors of the garage adjacent to the Toyota dealership open."

"We noticed the two inspection ramps, work benches, and all the usual equipment to enable MOT work. The most important of which, we noticed a large item of equipment that looked out of place, pushed against the neighbour's wall?"

Alex, who remained standing, smiled, "I've got pictures?" He smiled, "Jill thought they'd never come out; I used one of those cardboard cameras you get at weddings?"

After a raw of laughter, he reached into his inside jacket pocket, removed a brown envelope, and handed it to Sue. Opening it, she thumbed through the photos, and as she did so, she called aloud, "DS Alex Wilson, front and centre."

He turned crimson. Jill walked over, smiling. She linked his arm, pulling him into her chest, laughing, "Oh Al, I'll never doubt you ever again?" She gave him a quick peck on his cheek.

Sue walked over, "Alex this is so important, for it goes to the significant heart of the matter, giving credence as to the possible place of your guv's detention. On behalf of the team, thank you." She moved forward and kissed him on his cheek.

On this occasion, there were no cheers in the room, for everyone knew how important it was. Sue called, "Right, I need these pictures enlarged. Alex, will you take them to SOCO?" "Yes, boss" came the reply. She continued, "I want a plan and the enlargements on the whiteboards yesterday! Now let's jump to it."

It seemed as if all in one, the room burst into action; noise was abundant as team members burst into life. In all the excitement, Sue called, "Scrum down 5.30pm.

71

Sue walked into the general office; Eric was sitting at his desk. She looked at him, "Eric, can I leave you to organise all the secondary work? I'm off to see if the guv may have recalled some further recognition of his encounter and detention?"

Sighing out in the diary, both she and Charlie left for the hospital. In the car, Charlie looked at Sue, "Boss, how are you keeping?" She sighed, "Charlie, why don't you concentrate on the job at hand and stop worrying about me?"

Charlie smiled, "Boss, I know you'll never tell me, but you do realise it will eat away at you. The consent pressure of spending eight or more hours depending on our schedules. In the constant presence of the man, you...She screamed, "DS Watson, you have the one job, and one job only, to look after the guv, your principal. And recently to include me. Now do your fucking job."

He never took his eyes off the road, "Sorry boss, I made the mistake of crossing the line in the sand, never to be crossed, especially by a junior officer...I'll ask for a re-assignment forthwith."

Sue let out a great sigh, "Charlie, dear Charlie, only two people are travelling in this car that profess their love for the man. Unfortunately, there is only one that can express it. You, in so many ways, for you're prepared to take a bullet for the man. I, perchance, must just grin and bear it. Let that be the end of it."

Nothing else was said. On arrival at the ICU, Sue acknowledged the duty APO and continued passed the permitted visitors, some showing their grained-in masks of anticipation. Several looked up from their task at hand and simply smiled, identifying with a fellow visitor.

Sue stood outside the fishbowl, awaiting permission to enter to see Carter. Charlie peeled off and stood at the nurse's station. Sue just smiled.

Sue entered his location. Saying hello to Jenny, who stated, "I'm just off to 'hand over' held at the end of our shift." Sue burst out laughing, "Why Jenny, you seem to be here 24/7. I should have realised there must be other nurses?"

Sue walked past her, "Bye Jenny, see you tomorrow?" As she strolled through to his bed, not taking a particular interest, she mumbled, "Alright, guv, how are things?" She suddenly gasped, "Awe Guv, what a lovely surprise?" For there, sat up in bed, was Carter, wearing a blue T-shirt and sunglasses. He laughed, "On doctors' rounds, I met a psychologist attached to the end of the group.

"Her instructions due to the period spent with my eyes covered, owing to the terrible conditions I had been kept in. They are category 4 dark brown, only used in deserts and conditions of very bright sunlight. The doctor intends to reduce the prescription as time goes on."

He continued smiling, "In the meantime, she intends to interview me in relation to the conditions and the reason behind it?"

Sue realised that Carter showed the signs of a typical blind person, always staring to the front, occasionally turning to the sound of the vocal noise.

To lighten matters, Sue, looking at Carter, said, "Alex, together with Jill, while moseying round the business park, produced one of those pathetic cardboard type cameras, handed out at weddings. On a hunch, he took a series of photographs, for as they passed the potential garage, for the roller shutter doors were open."

"He took a series of photos. At present, they are with SOCO to be enlarged. But Carter, they show two inspection ramps, a series of workbenches, in fact, the items described by you, when first interviewed. But best of all, Carter, he noticed a large item stood in the garage, against a neighbouring wall, perhaps covering something...?"

Carter gently took hold of her arm. "Sue, do you think it at all possible they needed to cover the damage made by my escape?" Sue smiled, "Carter better still; it's well within your walking radios to the KFC?"

Sue sat back in her chair. "We're processing the photos, drawing up a plan of the area for the whole of the team to ingest. Carter, you more than most know of our problem. The culprit by now is aware of your escape and that Coombes and Rice are missing?"

"In the likelihood that the bastard has connected all the dots, he must realise that he's lost his formidable prisoner and possible negotiating chip. Plus, his organisational team, of Coombes and Rice, have both been locked up?"

Sue suddenly stood up; leaning over, she gave him a quick peck on his cheek. "See you tomorrow; in the meantime, hope to put matters to the two prisoners, for we must put them up before the magistrates, with a holding charge of Aiding and Abetting, for both being found in possession of prohibited information due to the data protection act. To be detained in custody due to the seriousness of the offence.

Carter gently moved his head, looking in the direction of Sue, "Well, should you need any help or assistance, you can always call on TF and me when visiting. He squeezed her hand, and she left.

72

A couple of days later, actions were being put into action. The important photos and plans of the area had been completed. The two prisoners had been put up before the magistrate's court and were both remanded in police custody for two months, to be detained at Risley remand centre.

Wendy Fields, the PR director for the police, had several meetings with TF, but the result was always the same, 'No press.' The only message she may be permitted to offer the crime reporter on the Liverpool Echo is to take him into her confidence. "You'll get the first bite of the cherry, a 5-minute start before all others when all is revealed?"

Back at the office, all proceedings were continuing with the usual day to day activities. At one of the scrum downs. Sue had instructed Lloydie to obtain a warrant. Marked, *'Abduction of a senior police officer.'* For a forthcoming raid on the garage. All matters had been carefully assessed, for one of the main problems being. The location of the garage. And the possible access is due mainly to the hindrance of vehicles.

A smartly dressed man parked his car in the Liverpool Royal Hospital car park. Locking it, he casually walked in the direction of the front of the hospital. He was dressed in an immaculate blue suit, a crisp white shirt, a red and blue striped tie, and black brogue shoes.

He straightened out his very smart jacket, carried a briefcase and a stethoscope in his left hand, and clipped an official ID card to his top pocket. He asked one of the security guards where to find the ICU.

On receiving the instructions and not wishing to draw attention to himself, he slowly made his way to the lift, following the signs for the ICU. Entering the empty lift, he pressed button one on the indicator panel.

The lift came to a quiet halt. The doors opened. The intended visitor exited the lift and again followed the signs for the ICU. Outside the ward, he acknowledged the APO.

In a quiet, educated-sounding voice, he said, "Good afternoon. I'm Mr. Raymond Ward, a Psychology Consultant from Aintree Hospital. To assist in assessing DCS Carter's potential for his return to work?"

The duty APO recited the instructions to the nurse on duty at the nurse's station. The electronic lock activated the duty APO pushed the door open. The Consultant casually walked up the ward to the nurse's station.

The nurse, without any further enquiry, pointed to the fishbowl. "That's Mr. Carter's location." He turned to his right and walked over, pushing the door open, to be met by Jenny at the foot of Carter's bed.

Jenny introduced herself. The visitor replied, mentioning the reason for his professional visit. Jenny smiled, "Carter is through there, pointing to his bed some several feet away.

He looked at Jenny, "Nurse, could I trouble you to assist? I need to see his chart?" Jenny led the way; Carter was sat up in bed with his headphones in place, listening to some music, unable to hear his intended visitor.

Jenny stood at the large board at the foot of his bed. "This is a recording of Mr. Carter's obs."

The visitor quickly assessed the situation; he noticed that Carter's bed was round the corner to the door and the nurse's station. Within seconds, he withdrew a 9mm black colt with a snub-nosed silencer from his briefcase. He brought it down sharply onto Jenny's head. Pole-axed, she fell to the floor.

Carter was totally devoid of his actions, for the sunglasses were that dark, plus the music in his ears, he remained sat nodding his head.

Knowing that time was of the essence, the stranger stood back and shot Carter thud, thud, twice in the chest. Making sure Carter remained upright, he quickly moved to the front of the bed and pulled Jenny to the far side of the bed to avoid early detection.

On completion, he replaced the gun into his briefcase; he took hold of the stethoscope and case, just turned, and casually walked out of the fishbowl. Looking at a nearby nurse, he casually stated, "Thank you, nurse," and looked in the direction of Carter, for the door was open. "DCS Carter, I'll see you again and forward my report. He left, saying goodbye to the same nurse at the nurse's station and calmly left the ICU ward.

It was while Sue was chatting with four of her junior officers, Lloydie, Ian, Peter, and Phil, discussing their plan of action. When the phone on her desk rang, simultaneously followed by Eric, who just happened to knock on her door, entering before Sue had the time to say, come in?

Eric walked in with a terrible pallor to his face. He nodded at Sue, indicating the direction of her phone.

Sue picked up the phone, "Superintendent Ford, how may I help you?" The reply just seemed to resonate in her mind, and for several seconds, it made no sense for Sue just dropped the phone. She screamed, "Charlie!"

Charlie didn't even have time to make her office; she saw him running down the corridor towards her. He shouted, "What's up, boss?" Through her tears, she shouted, "The hospital quick, the guv's been shot." Sue hadn't realised her statement had such a catastrophic effect on those who heard her call.

In the car and travelling at warp speed, Charlie drove on the blues and twos, down Prescot Road, Kensington, and finally Prescot Street, and the hospital.

Charlie mentioned, "What on earth had happened?" Sue, with tears in her eyes, said, "Carter has been shot twice to his chest, and Jenny has been knocked unconscious." Charlie looked at her in total disbelief.

Rushing into the hospital, they entered via the front door, running past both uniformed police officers and uniformed security guards alike. Both Sue and Charlie had their IDs on lanyards about their necks. One of the security guards shouted, "Wait, where do you think you're going?" Charlie shouted, "Get out the way, we're police officers."

Leaving the lift, they found the door to the ICU permanently open, with a plainclothes officer standing questioning all persons trying to gain entry. Before Sue could say anything, the officer called, "Alright, boss." And waved them through.

Entering the ward, they reduced their pace to a modest walk. At the top of the ward at the nurse's station, it seemed like controlled mayhem. Out of all personnel both police, and senior nursing staff Sue, noticed Chris Atkinson.

She walked over, and it was quite apparent that she'd been crying. She waved an arm, indicating for them to follow her to a nearby office; on entry, they found it empty. Charlie remained outside, and Chris shut the door. She leaned against it, spluttering, "Yet again, that bloody man of yours has an inherent way of attracting attention?"

She had no sooner said the words when she burst out crying; she gasped, "Please, Sue, can my outpouring like a little girl be kept in this room." Sue, who herself was still upset "Okay, Chris, what happened this time?"

Chris, who sat on the edge of the office desk, said, "Yet again, a man enters the ward, impressing the duty APO, and young nurse on duty at the nurse's station, telling her who he was and the reason for his visit."

"While in the fishbowl. The offender hit Jenny over her head and shot Carter twice in the chest."

Looking at Sue, she said, "TF is outside amongst the melee of people trying to get a grip on things." Sue said, "How is Carter?" Chris replied, "He was taken down to the trauma ward and, after he'd been stabilised, removed to theatre. At present, he's still in theatre. They are working on the removal of the two bullets. Young Jenny has a slight concussion after the hit on her head."

Sue looked at Chris, "Well, I'd better get out there and see if I can be of any help?" Charlie opened the door, and Sue walked out into the throng within which she saw TF. He beat a way through to her.

"Superintendent Ford, as you can see, all hell has broken loose. Now, can you cope if I hand matters over to the MCU?" Sue said. "Yes, I'll make a call and get some team members down; plus, while the guv is in theatre, we'll get a SOCO officer to discreetly check out the fishbowl."

Sue looked at Chris, "Would it be possible for me to use your empty office?" Chris replied, "Help yourself; in the meantime, I'll get things sorted outside. I feel the last thing you need is a multitude of medical staff?" Sue said, "Cheers."

Sue walked over to TF, "I'm setting up shop in an empty office; over the way, Charlie is setting up an APO 24/7 at the fishbowl for when Carter returns. Due to upsetting the predator, knowing they'd lost Carter out of that hellhole, I know they'll try again. At present, we need to stabilise the ward for the other occupants and their visitors.

TF smiled at her, "One thing about Carter…?" She looked at him. "Yes, sir, we all know.?" TF knew quite well what she meant, for he was always reluctant to see and speak to anyone except his Lordship.

73

Sue had set up shop. She got a SOCO officer in place within the hour. The word had spread, and it was all hands to the pump to assist wherever possible.

Sue rang Joe Purcell, the DSO (District security officer for the Royal), to collect all relevant CCTV footage of the areas covering the car parks, the front entrance to the hospital, the lifts, and the ICU.

One of the team interviewed the young nurse on duty at the nurse's station and waited to see how Jenny was fearing, for she may confirm the offender's description.

While this was all going on Charlie kept a watching brief outside of Sue's new location. Chris kept up a supply of hot drinks.

It was while she was in her new office she called Lloydie. "Look, Jim, how are you fixed with the warrant?" He replied, "I have it as we speak?" Sue said, "Take Peter, Phil, Alex, and Jules with you; have SOCO officers standing by. See if you can get hold of one of the specially trained blood sniffer dogs; you never know. Execute the raid ASAP."

Sue, when matters seemed under control, rang Eric, "Boss, hello, how are things?" Sue quietly replied. "I know that you all back at the ranch will be worried, but just to let you know, Carter is still in theatre. I will let you know when I have more positive news."

Eric thanked her, "Is there anything else I can do, boss." Sue whispered, "Less of the boss crap." Eric burst out laughing. "Now, where on earth have, I heard that statement before?" Sue, laughing, said, "Mr Morton, could

I trouble you to send down a couple of the team, for we need to sift through and view some recovered CCTV tapes." "Yes, Sue, leave it with me."

Before Sue finished the call, Eric suddenly shouted err… But before he could speak… Sue interrupted… "Err…, Yes, I know. What about Abby?" There was an awkward silence. Sue discreetly mentioned to Eric the argument she'd recently had with Abby. Over an intended 'Dear John' letter and how she'd managed to talk her out of leaving him. It all being related to how she couldn't put up with the undue stress?"

"Eric, if that's how she behaved on his abduction, how the fuck will she behave knowing that he's been shot. Eric, what the fuck do I do? It will break his heart, yet again; it's a case of the right tent but in the wrong desert?"

Again, there was another reticence in the conversation. Until Eric's quiet voice said, "Boss, you know what you must do? Again, it comes with the territory. Now, where have we heard that quote mentioned?" Sue whispered, "Yes, from the mouth of the dear man I need to protect." She sighed, "Oh Eric, I must go to his flat and break the news to her, better than over the phone, or if it gets out in the press?" The line went dead.

Sue walked out of her temporary office. She immediately saw Charlie, who was still standing outside the door, talking with Chris Atkinson. Chris looked at Sue and shook her head. Sue walked over and, as she did so, looked at her watch and saw that it was 3.30pm.

Chris said, "Sue, would you and Charlie like to join me in a cup of coffee?" Sue smiled. I'll be with you in a minute; I must talk with a member of the team?"

Sue met up with Ian, who had come to the ICU together with Niki, and Jill. "Ian, how are things?" Ian had a controlled smile on his face, "Well, boss, due to the fact you were on the phone, I didn't want to interrupt you, but SOCO think they may have a print?"

Sue made a controlled eruption of excitement. Ian stated, "Not so quick, boss. The SOCO officer stated there is a lot of elimination to do, for there are nurses, doctors, cleaners, and other members of staff who you know had access to the guv's fishbowl?"

Sue, trying to control her elation on the brief news. Took several second to take control of herself. "Ian, I'm off for a brief coffee with Chris and Charlie. After which, I'm off on a rather vital call. Sorry, I must leave you to organise matters with SOCO, plus you have the help of Niki and Jill, in the drawing up of a list of essential staff members who had reason to enter the fishbowl?" "Ian replied, "Yes, boss."

Sue then turned, straightened her coat, joined Charlie, and they both walked off to join Chris. In her office in the ICU, being a senior A&E sister had reason to liaise in both departments.

During their coffee, Sue mentioned she was rather worried about the time it was taking to deal with Carter?" Chris said, "Look, although Carter was taken post-haste out of ICU to the trauma team unit in A&E. It being the best place to stabilise him, which took some time, prior to his inevitable appointment in theatre."

Sue thanked Chris for their coffees, stating that she had to go and pass on some unfortunate news?"

74

When in the car, Charlie looked across at Sue, "Where to boss?" Sue, with not so much as a buy or leave, replied, in a low voice, "2, Keswick Mansion's. Charlie's head nearly came off his shoulders, and he coughed, "Where?"

"Sue looked at him, "Charlie, as a professional police officer in the APU (Armed Protection Unit), deafness is surely a hindrance?" He replied, "But boss...?" Sue interrupted; I want to inform Abby personally instead of over the phone in case the press get hold of matters?"

On completion of her conversation, she leant forward and picked up the radio handset. "Superintendent Ford to CH." The operator replied, *"Superintendent Ford, go ahead."* "Yes, could you arrange for a bereavement officer to attend at 2 Keswick Mansions, Sefton Park? Although it's not a bereavement, just a matter of an OMG (Oh my God) type message. I'm en route; inform the officer to conceal her vehicle. I'll ask if needed. *"CH out."* Came the reply."

On arrival, Charlie looked at Sue, "Boss, I'll wait in the concierge office; just shout if needed." Sue replied, "Fine, I'm hoping it won't take long, but due to her reactions in the past, I may call for help." Charlie, prior to parking up, looked over the far end of the car park and noticed the police vehicle; he flashed his headlights.

Sue, followed by Charlie, walked up to the main door of the flats and pressed number two on the shiny entrance panel. After several seconds, a quiet, business-like voice said. "Yes, how may I help you?" Sue took in a breath, slowly letting it out, saying, "Abby, it's Superintendent Ford. Can I come in to see you?"

The traditional buzzing sound came from out of the black holes of the speaker on the panel, "Pull the door?" Sue, aware of the procedure, pulled the door open and walked into the main reception area. She acknowledged the concierge and walked up to the front door of Carter's flat, leaving Charlie in reception.

The door opened, and Sue saw Abby, dressed in casual clothes, standing in her bare feet. Looking at Sue, she said, "What's happened? Please don't say he's been killed?"

Sue said, "May I come in?" Abby replied, "Why, yes, of course." Sue followed her into the lounge. Stood in the lounge facing each other, Abby said, "Sue, please take a seat,"

Sitting in one of the comfortable armchairs, she made herself comfortable, for the wearing of her sidearm was something of a hindrance. Abbey remained standing in front of one of the settees. Sue whispered," Will you not sit down?"

Sue looked at Abby. "I'm afraid there is no easy way to say this, but Carter was shot earlier this morning while in hospital. Sue could see all the blood drain from her face; it was as if she had imploded, eyes closed. She fell backwards, and the settee cushioned her fall to the floor.

Sue quickly called Charlie, "Get the officer." Minutes later, the officer ran in. She asked Sue the name of the patient. Sue replied, "Abby."

Sue and the officer quickly walked over to her. Bending over, the officer placed a cushion under her head. She then took hold of her hand, tapping it gently, she called, "Abby, Abby, are you okay?"

Abby suddenly came around. The officer said, "Just stay there." Sue said, "I won't be minute. She left for the dining room; walking over to the lovely drinks cabinet, she gently opened the door. Taking out a crystal goblet, she poured a measure of brandy into it. She thought I'd better take the crystal decanter with me, just in case.

Sue returned to the lounge she offered the glass goblet to Abby, "Down the hatch." Abby swallowed the brandy, in one and she immediately spluttered as her reaction to the taste and the sudden kick from the brandy, "I'm okay. Will you please continue?" They sat Abby down on the settee.

Sue took in a big breath, "Well, Abby, it's what we call a *'lone wolf'* type of criminal who blagged his way into ICU, informing the staff on the nurse's station that he was a consultant, asked to interview Carter, on his ability to return to work?" He did need to be interviewed on such a matter. The predator, presented smartly dressed, gave the appearance of a medical consultant?"

Abby, looking at Sue, said, "How does just anyone walk into a hospital, and giving a load of BS, walk up to a patient and shoot them, for Christ's sake?"

Sue looked at Abby, "Well, all the whys and wherefores' will be investigated by members of the MCU. But a hospital is a private place with access to the public 24/7. If you have the bottle and appear to talk sense..." At this very moment, it falls to me to inform you it will come out in the press?"

Sue suggested yet another drink; Abby held the goblet out. While Sue replenished it, on this occasion, Abby just sipped at the liqueur.

The colour returned to her face. "I suppose you're here..." Sue interrupted Abby. "Officer, thank you for your attention; you can resume your duties. She smiled, turned, and left.

Abby continued, "Here to not only break the news, but due to my last reaction, you thought it would be the straw that broke the camel's back, and I'd just walk out without any further notice?"

Sue, on seeing that Abby was returning to some sort of normality, returned to her seat. She looked at Abby. I'm here for damage limitation; the last thing Carter needs is that, after all this, his partner disappearing on him?"

Abby smiled, "Well, Superintendent Ford, rest assured, in the hours since we last spoke, I've had time to think, and I assure you it was a close-run thing. I suppose now, should I think of that course of action on all of this, people will think me a cow?"

Sue replied, "If you wish to be formal, Miss Remington, I have to say that Chief Superintendant Carter is my first and last priority, for you see, if he doesn't function, the MCU will take a hit, for he is the be-all and end-all, of the unit. So, do you see the position I'm in? The guv needs assurance in his domestic home life, and you're the key."

Sue stood up. DCS Carter may be out of theatre by now; I haven't heard. I suggest that you take yourself down to the hospital. He may well be in recovery, whatever. No doubt I will see you later?"

She turned. "I can see myself out." Sue smiled and left.

76

Sue, followed by Charlie, returned to the car. As Charlie drove off, he turned, "Boss, is everything okay?" Sue replied, "Just attending to some damage control? The hospital, please matey."

He smiled and drove off. While leaving the estate, Sue's phone was activated. Taking it out of her pocket, she said, "Ford."

"Boss, it's Lloydie. I just thought you'd like to know; SOCO found a print in that terrible place where the guv was detained. It's not the guv's; he was illuminated. Boss, I'm just pleased that you weren't with us on the raid?"

Sue leaned back, her head pressed back on her headrest, putting the phone on speaker, closed her eyes and whispered. "Lloydie, tell me?" "Why on earth, boss, can you not just accept that we have the guv back, although…?"

She shocked Charlie, sat next to her, but even more Lloydie, at the other end of the phone, as she screamed, "Lloydie…?"

"Well, boss, the guv was right; he was detained in a small specially constructed room, entailing wood studding, covered with plasterboard. It contained a double-sized bed, fridge, and bathroom."

He continued, "We found the hole and the metal angle-shaped leg he forced from the sink support in the bathroom. He must have stabbed and slashed at that plasterboard wall to make good the hole big enough through which he escaped."

"We found the hole blocked. Some item had been placed in front of it by some person, or persons unknown…? Why block either the unsightly hole or the means of a person's escape? We haven't yet made enquiries at the garage."

"SOCO officers, in their search, found several items of blood left in discreet places by the guv. Blood that matched the guv's blood group, ad hoc; therefore, it must be his. Plus, his clothes, taken when admitted into the hospital, show signs of plasterboard dust?"

Sue whispered, "What was the place like?" Lloydie replied, "Peter, Phil, Alex, and Jules joined me in the raid. We entered the building next to the garage and found a room within a room attached to the garage."

He continued, "The guv didn't know that there was a disguised door at the back of the room, allowing access into his prison, permitting his captor, or captors, entrance into the room to replenish the fridge of any food and water consumed."

Lloydie said, "Boss, the room was painted with black paint, no windows, or ill-fitted doors, which admitted any signs of natural light. The five of us stood in that room, and I asked Phil to close the door. I have to say that I couldn't see a hand in front of me. It was pitch black."

Sue spoke, "Can any of us begin to believe how one could spend eight days in those conditions? I wonder how much it may have affected the guv?"

Sue said, "I'm on my way back from the hospital. I've been engaged with the inquiry, consulting with SOCO and the team, plus I went on a brief message. I want you to plan for a scrum down, say 6.00 pm?" He replied, "Yes, boss."

At the hospital and on their arrival at the ICU, they met Chris Atkinson, standing by the nurse's station with a big grin on her face. Sue immediately thought it must be good news. It was.

Chris informed both Sue and Charlie that Carter was in the recovery room adjacent to theatre, in post-op, and if he behaves himself, he'll be back in his usual bed."

Sue looked at Charlie, "Will you please organise for an APO 24/7 on the fishbowl's door? No excuses, or I'll take it up with TF?"

After a welcome mug of coffee, Sue took out her phone and called Abby. Passing on the news, she could hear her excitement down the phone. Sue suddenly had a black thought. She suddenly thought, what if Abby wanted to leave Carter, unable to take the pressure of his job?

Sue gasped that she could assist in helping Carter get over her, taking her place in his life… She thought what a terrible Churchillian *'black dog'* attitude.

Sue's thoughts were suddenly disturbed by the sudden appearance of a porter and staff nurse pushing Carter, lying on a gurney, returning him to his awaiting hospital bed.

Seeing him settled, Chris looked at his notes. She looked at Sue. "Carter had a bullet that passed through his right lung, causing a pneumothorax. The second hit him in his chest, missing his left lung by 5mm, injuring his left shoulder.

Sue tried to hide her shock. She thought although she had seen similar injuries to him in the past, she could never get over them happening to Carter. Her thoughts were immediately filled with Abby.

On leaving the ward, they both thanked Chris for her hospitality. It was when they got to the ward door that they both bumped into Abby. Sue was immediately caught off guard, not wishing to show any chinks in her armour.

She brought her up to date with all that had happened. Sue apologised, "I can't stop for I have a meeting to attend at 6 pm. If you need anything, just call me. See you."

77

Sue and Charlie both signed back in after what had been a rather fraught day.

Sue took a welcome mug of coffee from Eric and, like Carter, sat next to him. It was a special place where, although at work, she felt so comfortable and relaxed, a brief respite from the job.

She thought how much she missed Carter; it was a special place, the time spent enjoying their morning coffees, Carter, Eric, and herself, a brief portion of time that she so enjoyed, no loved. A schedule of which he permitted.

The door to the general office opened it was Lloydie. He looked at Sue, "Boss, if you're ready, we're all in the conference room waiting for you?"

She got up and, accompanied by Eric and Charlie, followed Lloydie; as she walked, she felt a gentle hand on her left shoulder. It gently gripped her, and when she turned, she saw it was Eric; he just smiled and winked. Sue felt warm and got the simple message.

Entering the room, the whole team came to attention. Sue smiled with pride, realising how Carter must have felt each time he entered that room. Sue suddenly stopped and turned. "Ladies and gentlemen, we only stand for one person entering this room?" A voice from the middle of the room said, "We stand out of respect."

Sue blushed and continued walking to the front of the room and turned. "Thank you, just to let you know, the guv is back from theatre and back in his permanent bed in the fishbowl, in ICU. There was a ripple of laughter.

"The predator in shooting the guv twice, one bullet punctured his right lung, causing a pneumothorax, the second bullet, caught the left of his chest 5 mm above his lung."

Sue was quiet for the moment. Eventually, taking in a deep breath, she turned, "Lloydie, what have we got?" Lloydie, who was, stood next to Sue. "Boss, there are several items?"

He turned to one of the whiteboards, which had been set upon a large easel. Taking hold of a metal telescopic pointer, he extended it to its extreme length; they all noticed the small red LED-type light at the end.

Sue picked up her chair and carried it back to enable her to see the board. She turned it at the correct distance and sat down.

His first example was the two enlarged fingerprints placed next to each other. Pointing at print 'A,' He said, "Boss, this print was recovered by SOCO from the foot of the guv's bed; it's a right-hand thumbprint.

He continued, "Print 'B' is also a right thumbprint, again recovered by SOCO, retrieved from the fridge door in that hell-hole were the guv was kept . Can you imagine if one dropped to their haunches and supported their balance by putting their right hand on the top angle of the door? Or lazily leaned down and opened the fridge door by using his right hand, his right thumb caught on the door?"

"Boss both prints match, although found at two different locations approximately seven miles apart?"

"Boss, you will also notice a series of photos recovered from the hospital CCTV security tapes.

(1) Shows a smartly dressed man by the side of a car in the hospital car park. (2) Shows the same man making enquiries with a security guard, then seen entering the hospital.

(3) Shows the same man in the main hospital hall walking towards the doors that lead to the lifts.
(4) Shows the same man waiting by the lift doors.
(5) Shows the same man in the lift.
(6) The man in the lift leaves the said lift on the 1st floor.
(7) The same man standing outside of the ICU appears to be talking with the APO.
(8) Shows the same man in ICU.

Lloydie continued, "One of the photographs was shown to the nurse on duty at the nursing station. Who permitted the offender access into the ICU. She identified the man as being the same man who wanted to see the guv. He is the man shown in all the CCTV film prints."

Sue stood up and turned her chair, facing the team. She looked at Lloydie, "It would be too much to ask that our friend is known at MER/cro (Merseyside Criminal Records Office). Sue could tell by Lloydie's face. Sue said, "Sorry, Lloydie, that was so stupid of me."

Sue stood up, "Now our friend is in the wind, and since we detained Combes and Rice, his source of information has dried up, and our friend won't be happy. Without his source of information, he'd be unable to conduct his one-man vigilante campaign?"

"As far as I see it, we have the garage next door to the guv's location; that's a bloody big question: who owns the building in which they housed the guv? So, let's get at it; there's plenty to do."

78

Joe Purcell is the district security manager of the Liverpool Royal Infirmary. Stood up from behind his desk. He thought it had been some time since he met up with his security supervisor.

It was 3pm. The afternoon shift was about to sign on duty. Joe had a contingency of thirty security guards. Forming three shifts of eight men and two women officers. One of his main problems was the cover of A&E. It meant that he had to detach three men and two female officers on the night shift to assist in dealing with all the jetsam and flotsam within the department.

Joe entered the security office; on entry, he saw ten smartly dressed security officers. Each dressed in black boilersuit uniforms, tucked into their black boots, wearing black berets. Each guard was wearing blue Kevlar bullet and stab-proof vests, with the word SECURITY OFFICER clearly printed on the front and back.

All officers enjoyed a chat with their boss. During the conversation, Joe, looked at an officer called Robinson. "Ollie, how did you enjoy your leave? You look very tanned?"

He replied, "Great boss, the wife packed the car and picked me up on Friday, after my day shift... Joe suddenly thought, "Ollie, I forgot you were on leave; what was your patrol area on your last shift?"

Ollie replied, "I was covering the car parks at the front of the hospital, off Prescot Street and Hall Lane."

He suddenly thought, 'Body Cam.' "Ollie, when you signed off duty prior to leaving for your jollies, where did you put your body cam?" Ollie smiled, "It's in my locker, for I'm on control room duty, so I don't need the camera."

Joe thought there may well be a chance, "Will you go and fetch it for me?" Ollie replied, "Will do, boss, I won't be long." While he was waiting, Joe busily tapped his fingers on a desk.

Ollie returned carrying the piece of equipment. He held it out for Joe, who, on thanking him, took it and returned to his office. In the office, he fired up his computer. He placed the USB plug into his computer and placed the other end of the lead into the camera.

He pressed, *'play'* and a grainy screen cleared to reveal a picture of the car park. He could hear Olie's voice and the normal day–to–day sounds of cars and people needing directions.

Joe turned down the volume and concentrated on the picture. After some fifteen minutes, he suddenly saw the suspect standing next to his car. He turned up the volume he heard. "Sorry, could you please direct me to the ICU ward in your hospital?"

Ollie politely replied, "Yes sir, enter the front of the hospital, walk into the main hall, and at the top left-hand corner, there is a door. It leads into a corridor. There is a directional board stating lifts to the left, and ICU is on the first floor."

The man turned and left towards the front of the hospital. Joe pressed the rewind button, and slowly, the film rewound until he found what he was looking for. He shouted, "Got it." He pressed. *'Stop.'*

The picture revealed a blue Audi A5 saloon, reg L67 EFT. Joe took out his mobile phone from out of his jacket pocket. He called the police control room. 709-6010. The call was answered, "Merseyside police, how may I help you?" Joe said, "Could I trouble you to contact Superintendent Ford of the MCU to please call Joe Purcell, the DSO for the Royal?" The operator replied, "Yes, sir."

Joe replaced his phone on his office desk and waited. After ten minutes, his mobile was activated. He picked it up, "Joe Purcell." "Joe, it's Sue Ford; what can I do for you?"

Joe replied, "Superintendent Ford...Sue suddenly interrupted, "Joe, after all these years, please call me Sue." "Sue, I have something for you. Can you call at my office in the hospital?" Sue burst out laughing, "Oh Joe, that sounds interesting. I'll see you in twenty minutes."

Sue, who was in her office, stood up and set off for the general office. On entering, she noticed Eric, in shirt sleeves, working at his desk. He looked up, "Boss, can I help you?" Sue smiled, "Will you find Charlie? I'm needed at the hospital. It's not about the guv; it's Joe Purcell, who wants to see me?"

They both signed out for the hospital. Charlie looked at Sue, "What's up, boss?" Sue replied, "I have no idea, Charlie. It's Joe Purcell, wants to see me?"

On arrival at the hospital, Charlie parked up, locked, and secured the car. They both walked off in the direction of Joe's office.

Joe welcomed them both, asking, "Coffees?" When settled with their hot drinks. Sue said, "Well, Joe, what do you have for us?"

Joe turned his laptop computer towards them and pressed' *play*.' They both looked at the screen so attentively. It all happened exactly how Joe had seen it. The suspect's picture that they knew by heart but. Joe turned up the volume. They both heard the suspect asking for directions to the ICU?"

He then replayed the tape and stopped at the part where the suspect stood by the car. Better still, they both saw the reg. Sue suddenly took in a deep breath, "Joe, a reg, you, darling."

"Joe stood up and handed Sue, the tape from the body cam. "Take this. I hope it helps?"

Sue looked at Joe, "Will you please excuse me?" Taking out her mobile phone, she feverishly pressed the numbers for the force control room. "Yes, this is Superintendent Ford of the MCU. "Yes, ma'am, how can I help you?"

Sue managed to keep her feelings about any chauvinistic opinions to herself, for the duty officer had no idea of her mood swings in relation to such matters. On this occasion, there were more important matters to think of.

"Yes, can I trouble you to run this car reg through the PNC (Police national computer) Lima 67 Echo Foxtrot Tango?" (L67EFT) Five minutes later came the reply Sue so dearly wished.

"Ma'am, the motor car private is a blue Audi A 5 saloon; the registered keeper and owner of that vehicle is, Robert Spencer, 25, Station Road South, Liverpool 25. Nothing known." Sue smiled to herself, "Yes, thank you, officer."

Sue closed the call, placing her phone back into her coat pocket. She immediately turned to Charlie, "Derby Lane, as quick as..."

Sue turned and looked at Joe, "Joe, this day, you, together with the valuable information contained on the body cam worn by your security officer, may be responsible for leading to the arrest of the suspect, who tried to cause harm to Carter. In turn, may be responsible for some nine murder victims. Thank you, Joe."

She smiled, "Joe can I please send a junior officer to collect a statement from you, and the security officer on duty at the time?" He just burst out laughing, "Why of course, see ya."

79

On arrival back at Derby Lane, both Sue and Charlie approached the diary to sign back in the office. Eric looked up, "Well, by the look on your faces, you both look like the proverbial cat that's got the cream?"

Sue sat next to Eric to enjoy a well-earned mug of coffee. Eric looked at her and smiled. "Well?" Sue couldn't hold her excitement any longer. She blurted out. "Eric, you won't believe it; Joe gave me this." She produced the tape from the body cam footage.

After their coffee, Sue left along the corridor with Eric; Sue linked his arm in excitement. As they walked, they corralled all team members into the conference room.

When all assembled, she looked at Phil. "Phil, could I ask you to set this up for me? It's a tape from a body cam, and I'd like you to play the recording through the TV screen in the room?"

Ten minutes later, Phil was ready. They switched off the lights, and Phil, pressed the play button. Like before, the screen cleared, showing a man standing by a car. From the room, she suddenly heard a collective chorus, "That's him?"

Sue smiled and shouted, "Quiet." The film continued, together with volume, they all heard the tell-tale sounds of people and cars in what appeared to be a large busy car park.

It continued showing the subject approaching the security officer and recorded on camera. "Can you please tell me where I can find the ICU?" The security officer gave the necessary directions.

After which, Sue, looked at Phil. "Phil, please rewind the tape and press *'play.'* But this time, ladies, and gentlemen, pay particular attention to the blue-coloured Audi A5. It's parked up with our suspect standing next to it. You will briefly see the following number plate: L67 EFT."

Resuming, Sue explained, "The registered owner of the car is one, Robert Spencer, 25, Station Road South, Liverpool 25."

"Now I want him checked out with MER/cro; by the photo, he looks in his 40s, so that makes him born approx. 1978, which may assist us in identifying him?"

Sue continued, "It's 5.30pm. I want one of the team to do a drive past Spencer's home to check for a suitable position, to conduct obsie's?" She turned, "I want two teams of two, one to cover 10pm. to 3am. and the second team to cover 3am to 8am.

She mentioned to Lloydie that she was informing the control room of the operation and who to inform in relation to any suspicious circs?

"I want to know if he leaves his house in the vehicle, during the night to go anywhere, however local, he must be followed."

Sue, looking at Lloydie, said, "Is it names in a hat? For I'll make an overtime request for the individuals?"

"All items were sorted. Alex and Gill, 10pm till 3am. and Niki and Simon, 3am. till 8am. Both teams were told prior to going off duty. Anything suspicious all matters are to be reported to the force control room."

Sue signed off duty, "I'm off to see Carter, she looked at Eric, "Do you want to come with me?" He reneged. The office was empty. He smiled, "No, Sue, you go; I feel if his nibs is conscious, you can run your latest information passed him."

Sue looked at him, "Let's hope, no, let's pray, Spencer, breaks cover?"

In the car with Charlie, while he drove to the Royal, her mind was in neutral. She suddenly thought. 'Oh shit, I've forgotten to tell TF.' She took out her phone and contacted him. *"Frost"* "Sir, it's Ford." During the journey to the hospital informed him of matters to date. His reply was positive, and he closed the call.

Her mind began to go into free fall while imagining all the variations of the wheel falling off.

On arrival at the ICU, the duty APO nodded at both her and Charlie. He opened the door, not daring to mention the word, ma'am, for the warning had gone round to all and sundry.

Sue walked up to the nurse's station, showed her ID to the nurse, then asked if she could spend a few minutes with DCS Carter?" Charlie remained at the nurses, station.

The nurse smiled and suggested that she run it passed sister Atkinson. On seeing Chris, Sue walked up to the fishbowl. Chris was talking with a doctor. Chris smiled, "Well, I suppose you've come to see your colleague?"

"You've got fifteen minutes."

Sue entered the fishbowl and, to her surprise, saw Jenny. She gasped, "Jenny, how on earth are you?" Jenny smiled, "I'm good, thanks, although, at the time, I was scared stiff."

Sue looked at her, "Well, the question is, how is he?" Jenny replied, "I'm just popping out to get some drip bags for his Lordship?" Jenny smiled, "He is awake, but he must still wear the sunglasses. The eye bods have been to see him."

She walked into Carter's sleeping area to find him lying on his back, with both arms out of the bed, resting on his bedding in front of him. She noticed he still had a drip in his left arm. He still had his sunglasses. On hearing Sue's footfall, he looked in her direction.

He turned, "Why Sue, what a lovely surprise." She noticed that Carter had pulled himself up and was leaning against the pillows at the head of the bed. Portraying a weak smile, he adjusted his sunglasses.

Sue sat on the chair at his side. Carter, not thinking, offered his hand. She leant forward and took hold of it. It felt so soft and gentle. All her foreboding feelings began to rise within her, yet like on so many occasions, feelings that should be controlled.

"Carter, how are you?" He smiled, "Well, I've just had a visit from the Ophthalmologist surgeons. Both gentlemen checked my eyes saying that my natural vision is stronger, and it won't be long before I can ditch the sunglasses?"

80

Carter's dedicated nurse, Jenny, walked in. She smiled, "Have you met Miss Suesan Ford, a supposed police officer? Carter burst out laughing, "Don't you mean my nemesis?" Jenny smiled, "But surely Carter, don't you mean your Girl Friday, as on so many other occasions...?" They all burst out laughing.

After Jenny had changed the drip bag, she turned and smoothed his bed, and, in doing so, it meant she bent over so close to Carter. She turned and, smiling, she left. Sue thought, what a job, to look after Carter in bed?

She smiled, "Carter, are you in the mood to talk shop?" He said, "Well, if you don't mind, I'll just sit and listen, but in the end, I may feel tired, as my powers of concentration tend to waver?"

Sue began, "Now, Carter, you are fully aware of matters from the start. I must tell you that with the help of Joe Percell, we have the bastard on tape parking his car in the hospital car park. He asks the security guard, who is wearing a body cam, for directions to the ICU?"

"It all started when you walked into the KFC restaurant because of your verbal statement taken by me whilst you were in ICU. An investigation of the area took place in a radius of 50 meters from the KFC. Alex and Jill, while making discreet enquiries, used a cardboard camera to take a series of photographs."

Sue mentioned the hole in the wall of the garage; accordingly, the resulting means of your escape. Then, the next day, we found some large fixture had covered the hole.

Continuing, Sue mentioned the warrant executed by Lloydie, and members of the team. He explained the state of the room where you had been detained, the conditions, and the fact that he couldn't see a hand in front of him when the secret door was closed.

Sue noticed that Carter began to shiver; she could only think of his incarceration for 8 days in that hell hole, that even mentioning it was influencing him. Sue looked at him, "Carter, I won't continue, for I can see the effect matters are having on your memory."

Sue looked at him, "Carter, I have some good news for you. It came via Joe Purcell at the Royal. He realised that one of the security officers was on leave when your attack took place."

"Joe asked if, when on duty before the onset of his leave, what was his duty?" The officer replied, "I was on duty in the hospital car park, wearing my bodycam." Sue continued, "Joe, on a whim, asked to see the camera. He played the film, and low and beheld, the guard had taped the suspect?"

"Carter, the news gets better, for when checking the film, we saw that the suspect had parked a blue-coloured Audi A5, then asked the guard for directions to the ICU?"

"On a serious look at the tape, we found the reg of the car; we have the licenced owners, name and address, and location of the vehicle?"

On receipt of such positive news, Sue looked at Carter, hoping to see such a positive response, but his face was motionless; it remained blank. Sue said, "Carter! Did you not hear what I said?"

But Carter remained pensive. It was while Sue was trying to explain matters that Jenny returned to Carter's bedside.

Looking at Sue, Jenny gestured for her to leave from Carter's bedside and follow her to the entrance to the fishbowl.

When in position, Jenny looked at her, "Sue, he needs time; the period spent in total isolation and being confined to a small pitch-black room, in total seclusion for eight days, is having a terrible effect?"

Jenny, with a stern look on her face, "Add it all together; the lack of light and human contact has mentally weakened him. He also reported endless hours and days spent in complete solitude, we have temporally lost the jaunty Carter. The Carter that carries everything before him, the MCU, and all his team."

"My job permits me to flit in and out without detection, and at times privy to Carter's treatment, and it was on one occasion when interviewed by the duty psychologist, I realised his mind was so weak that the important factor was to be rest at all times?"

Sue thanked Jenny for her thoughts. "I must be off." Sue walked back to Carter's bed. She looked at him. "Carter, you have the look of a film star laying there in bed. I must be off will call shortly."

Sue leaned over and kissed Carter on his cheek; as she did, he took hold of her, "Sue, will you please ask Abby to visit me? I need fresh clothes, but I wonder if matters are cooling off?"

Sue, trying to be positive, replied, "No probs, I'll give her a call."

Prior to leaving, Sue gently took hold of Jenny and walked her out with her towards the fishbowl door in the ICU, "Well, what's his visiting pattern like? How often does Abby call?" Jenny shrugged. She laughed, "Well if he were mine, I'd never be away. I think with her working." her voice tailed off…

81

On leaving Carter, Sue collected Charlie from the nurse's station and left for the car. When in the car, Sue got on her hands-free phone and called Eric. He answered, and seeing the caller's name, he said, "Boss…" Sue interrupted, "What, on the bloody phone?"

Eric replied, "Sorry, Sue, how is Carter?" She replied, "Well, it's hard work, Jenny; is the perfect example of a truly professional nurse. Explained that the guv is slowly and painfully coming to terms with his situation."

"I experienced first-hand that while I excitedly explained information from and how we, the team, are proceeding about the case in general. I thought that I'd see the reaction of our typical Carter, but no, he seemed tired and drained."

Eric, trying to maintain a decent level of atmosphere, cried, "Well! Sue, what did you expect? I feel that it's not just the circs of this latest bout, but the man is tired. His home life is topsy Turvey. Since the loss of Helen and the children, there is no stability in his life?"

He continued, "TF won't get off his fucking back, he asked for a twelve-month sabbatical, it's granted, what happens?" Sue screamed, "That's my fucking fault, the first sign of shit, and the top floor fucking panic, *'Get Carter.'*"

Eric said, "Now, look here, Susan Martha Ford; you know that when Carter handed in his ticket (police jargon for a resignation), panic ensued. The Chief Constable, on your advice, suggested leaving the door open and that in the event of the MCU being tasked with a case like the psychotic cases of Gainsford and Hughes, he would be willing to return. He agreed. "

"You know he was, given the leave, to go off, yet to retain his job, on full salary, and retain his rank, and, well, you know the rest, they called him back because of the job. All about organ harvesting and the selling of human parts. And the lengths they went to obtain their clientele?"

Eric, on completion, whispered, "Sue, this is by no means your fault. You had only been in place a month, and bang! *'The shit hits the fan.'* TF and the top fucking floor panicked. But now, Sue, you've got it, as the working head of the MCU. And Carter will return to a good or excellent job maintained."

Eric said, "I'm at home at present?" Sue screamed, "For fuck's sake, boss, why didn't you say?" He replied, "Goodnight, Sue. See you in the office tomorrow."

While driving, Sue closed the call and then pressed Lloydie's name in her list of contacts.

"Yes, boss, can I help you?" Sue replied, "Er, yes, Lloydie, how are things going for the obsies teams?" Jim replied, "We made a sweep of the suspect's address. It's got good cover, so we're set fair for the two remaining teams?" He coughed, "I'm on call, and told both teams I'm there first call?"

Sue said, "Jim, I'm going to give you an order; it's never been done before, never needed; until the circs of this case, remember, the first call is me?"

Sue's next call was to the force control room, "This is Superintendent Ford. Will you please show me off duty at this time?" When outside her house, Sue looked at Charlie, "Goodnight, flash, see you bright and early."

When home and relaxed with a drink in her hand, she called Abby, *"Yes, Abby Remington.* Abby heard, "It's Sue Ford." Sue heard a sudden splutter in Abbey's voice, *"I wondered how long it would be until I received such a call;*

of course, it had to be you, for hospital staff and junior officers would know it's not in their remit?"

Sue replied, "No, Abby, it all stems around the fact that our job is bad enough, when alone, as police officers, when we meet a potential friend, partner, or wife. When during their relationship one comes against the wall of injury to their loved one."

"It all becomes significant on seeing their friend, lover, partner, or husband laying in a hospital bed." Sue shouted, "They don't fuck off and hide?"

Abby interjected, *"Superintendent Ford, how dare you speak to me like that? I'm not a child?"*

Sue interrupted, "No and as such, I'm sure that you knew from day one the employment of your possible suitor. He wasn't a music teacher, chef, or fucking driving instructor. No, he's a senior line officer in the Merseyside police CID, in fact, head of the MCU?"

"Most senior officers would retire to a comfortable office desk, but no, not Carter; he is a true leader and leads from the front. A shining example to his team."

"But I have to say as such, he is open to all the elements that the criminal fraternity conjures up in an effort to suggest, cut the head off the snake, and the team will Implode?"

Sue continued, "Abby, it's rather simplistic of me. But Carter needs you to get over his latest incident. May I suggest that due to this latest effort made by a predator to murder Carter, hoping it would diminish the efforts of the team?"

"Abby, can I suggest? If you feel you can't accept Carter's employment and all that has happened, I assure you that an armed protection officer is on duty 24/7, and there will be no further occurrences."

"In conclusion, Abby, if you want to relinquish your relationship with Carter, please do it when he has fully recovered, and he can deal with the situation. For at present, he is at his lowest ebb and needs all his strength to recover and not to be hit with a '*dear John'* letter."

There was a pause, *"Sue, do you not feel that putting matters off is worse? For now, he has the likes of you and the team for support. For if this had not happened, my relationship with Carter would be over, for as a senior officer in the bank, I've been transferred to another branch?"*

Sue said, "When?" A quiet voice replied, *"In three weeks at the end of the month."*

Sue thought, 'Shit,' Does that man not deserve some sort of stability? "Abby, can I ask that you retain normal visiting hours for, say, about 7-10 days? I feel that he may remain in the hospital, and hopefully, when released, you may still be around?"

"Abby, Carter needs fresh clothes; at least Mrs. M will see to the laundry; all you need do is to visit him and act accordingly."

There was a long sigh, after which Abby whispered, *"Okay, you do realise I do love every bone in that man's body, but it's my career?"* Sue replied, "What a fucking pity; you should have thought of that before you got involved?"

82

Jim Lloyd answered his phone on the second ring. "Boss, are you okay?"

"Yes, Jim." Came her reply, *"I'm only calling re the set-up with Spencer?"* Jim replied, "Boss, all is sorted. All we need do is sit back, and keep obsies?" *"Night Jim."* Came her reply, *"Let's see what transpires?"*

Sue's phone was activated at 8am. Sue was readying herself for work. "Ford." *"Morning, ma'am. It's the morning duty Inspector in the force control room."*

"WDC Wilson, has contacted the control room, the suspect Spencer, driving a blue Audi A5 motor car private, Lima 67 Echo Foxtrot Tango. He got in the car and just left his home address and headed for the city?"

After ten minutes Sue's phone activated again. *"Ma'am, WDC Wilson suggested they remain on duty and continue obsies for continuity of evidence until the suspect arrives at a possible destination?"* Sue replied, "Thank you very much. I'll inform my officers I'll be on duty at Derby Lane within the next 30 minutes." *"Ma'am."*

On arrival at Derby Lane, Sue entered the general office, signed on duty, and received the traditional mug of coffee from Eric.

Eric said, "Boss, Lloydie has just despatched Graham and Sheila to take over from Niki and Simon. The latest location appears, the Liverpool City Municipal Offices, in Dale Street."

"The object vehicle was parked in the official car park, off North John Street. The suspect, Spencer, was seen leaving his vehicle carrying a red coloured knapsack over his right shoulder. He returned fifteen minutes later to the object vehicle, minus the knapsack?"

Sue screamed, "Stop him now, and seize his vehicle, Lloydie; get on to CH to summon traffic mobiles to assist."

Lloydie called CH. "Close off Dale Street, North John Street, Castle Street, and James Street. The entire block. Due to a police operation?

Lloydie walked into the general office, "Ch has called for a partial closure to the required area."

Sue looked at Lloydie, "Jim before this all kicks off, I want Spencer brought here and his car to be taken to Lower Lane, Forensic Garage, and rip it apart?"

The target vehicle was stopped on Water Street. Spencer was surrounded by MCU cars fitted with blue lights flashing and claxons sounding. Niki and Simon in one vehicle. Graham and Sheila, in the second.

All four officers, being armed, approached. Spencer sat flummoxed in his car. Niki approached his vehicle and issued the warning, "Armed police officers, switch off the ignition, and get out of the car."

Spencer was detained, he was cuffed and placed in one of the MCU vehicles. There was utter chaos as it was rush hour; a cacophony of car horns sounded as Water Street had been closed.

Niki said, "We'll remain with the car. Graham, will you and Sheila remove Spencer? He's to be arrested and taken to Derby Lane. After the vehicle has been seized, I want the low loader to remove the vehicle to Lower Lane, explain matters, and sign off duty with the control room?" They both agreed and left.

On arrival at Derby Lane, Graham and Sheila took hold of Spencer and led him into the Bridewell, explaining the circumstances of the arrest to the duty sergeant, Derek

Lancaster. He was duly processed. On completion, he was removed to the MCU offices upstairs.

Lloydie removed the handcuffs and led Spencer off to a nearby interview room. At that moment, Peter, one of the duty bridewell officers, attended and assumed a position outside of the interview room.

Lloydie then walked back to the general office where he entered in the duty book, the circumstances of the arrest of the prisoner. On completion he turned and left for Sue's office. He knocked on her door, and he heard, "Come in." Jim opened the door. Sue pointed to a chair. "Boss, we have Spencer; he's in interview room one, with Peter, stood outside.

Sue smiled, "Good." She continued, "I've just had a call from the duty Inspector in the control room. All the relative persons, SOCO, bomb squad, and uniform personnel, on arrival at the official building, found a red coloured knapsack tucked away in an empty ground floor office."

"The knapsack contained what appeared to be a bomb, with all the look-alike parts. On further examination, it was found to be a fake. Although to all intense and purposes looked quite real, causing issues until verified."

Sue smiled up at Lloydie, who said, "All has been made safe, and all traffic is now flowing freely. So, we have Spencer, so let's proceed?"

83

Sue picked up her desk phone and called TF. Jane, his secretary, answered, *"Commander Frost's office."*

"Jane, it's Superintendent Ford. Does he have a minute?" Jane swooned, *"How is my favourite, DCS Carter, doing? The poor thing laid up in that hospital. Does he need an extra nurse to give him a bed bath?"*

Sue burst out laughing, "Honestly, Jane, can you not raise your mind above your navel?" Laughing, she said, "Now, is TF in or not?" A frustrated voice mumbled, *"Putting you through."*

"Frost." "Sir, It's Superintendent Ford. I thought I'd bring you up to date on the Spencer case and the issue in the City centre. Although it caused mayhem, Spencer has been arrested and is being held at Derby Lane. The knapsack contained what appeared to be a false bomb. His car is being held at the Lower Lane forensic garage. Plus, we're about to raid Spencer's home address."

There was a pause, *"Ford, I'm pleased to see that matters are all under control and the MCU is in safe hands. A testimony to Carter.* Sue replied, "Sir," and put the phone down.

Sue leaned forward, picked up a file and left for the general office. On her way, she mumbled, *'That fucking man is such a chauvinist pig, it wouldn't kill him to give a compliment?'*

In the office, Eric looked up from his work, "Who is a chauvinist pig?" Sue said, "I'll give you three guesses." Eric smiled as he held his hand under his chin, like the statue of the 'Thinker.' "Well, let me see now, the guv is in hospital. I wonder, yes, it's got to be TF?" They all burst out laughing. He turned, "Boss, coffee?" Sue gestured, "Please, but don't get up; I'll serve myself; while I'm at it, can you get hold of Lloydie?"

As Sue walked over to the coffee thermos and helped herself, Eric whispered, "Why can't you teach Carter?" A ripple of laughter went round the office.

Sue smiled and sat next to him. He smiled, "How are things?" She whispered, "Miss him like hell?"

The door opened, and Lloydie walked in, "Boss?"

Sue smiled, "Jim, will you get Peter and Phil to prepare a warrant for Spencer's home address? Then will you come with me to interview Spencer?" "Yes, boss."

As they approached interview room one, Peter opened the door. "Boss," Sue said, "Thank you, Peter. Will you help yourself to a brew, then remain outside the door?" He smiled, "Yes, thank you, boss."

As they entered, Spencer sat on the far side of the table, and Graham sat opposite. On entry, Graham stood up, "Boss."

Sue looked at Graham, "DC Evans, did both you and WDC Williams explain the circumstances of the arrest to the Bridewell Sergeant?" Graham replied, "Yes, boss, and he was duly processed. Spence was then brought up to the MCU for further enquiries."

After Graham left, Sue followed him outside in the corridor. Looking at Graham, "Will you please take Spencer's fingerprints, taken in the bridewell? I want them checked with the fingerprint department against the print found in the guv's fishbowl. And the print, from that hell hole, where the guv was detained."

After a comparison has been made, if positive, return them all to me. For I wish to use the evidence when interviewing Spencer?"

Sue continued, "I'm going to tell Spence that we will serve a warrant on his home address; I also want his car ignition key or fob from his property taken with the team. I want his car ignition key or fob submitted to the driver's lock or computer system and see if it fits?"

Graham replied, "Yes, boss."

Sue returned to the interview room, and Lloydie sat down opposite Spencer. Lloydie took out the recorder and placed it on the table. He unwrapped two new tapes. He placed the tapes into the machine.

Lloydie switched it on, and after a short bleep, Sue said, "Robert Spence, you are still under caution?" He just nodded. Sue said, "For the purposes of the tape, the defendant just nodded."

Sue then said, "I'm Detective Superintendent Ford, and this is my colleague, Detective Inspector Lloyd. It's 10 am. Wednesday, 7th May 2008, you were arrested and detained on suspicion of leaving a suspect device contained in a knapsack in the Liverpool Municipal buildings?"

"Spencer, the aforementioned charge is just a holding charge, for you will be eventually interviewed for the attempted murder of Chief Superintendant Carter of the Major Crime Unit and GBH on staff nurse Jenny Hughes."

Spencer made no reply. Sue said, "The defendant made no reply."

Sue looked at Spence, "Robert Spence, I have to say that you are entitled to legal representation. I'm prepared to suspend this interrogation to enable you to seek the services of a solicitor; if you have no solicitor in mind, we can always provide the services of a duty solicitor?"

Spence replied, "Why, I've done nothing."

While looking at Spencer, Sue opened a file. She took out 5 photographs and placed them facing upwards. Sue said, "For the purposes of the tape, Superintendent Ford has shown the accused Spencer 5 photographs marked DSF1 to 5."

Spencer leaned forward, looked down at the table, looked up at Sue, and smiled, "So what?"

Sue looked at Spencer. "Spencer, can you tell me who is the person in each of the photographs?"

He smirked, "Er, no, sorry."

Sue looked at Spence. "Let me explain the sequence of the photographs?"

"Spencer, the first photograph shows a man standing next to a blue-coloured Audi A5 registration number L67 EFT in a car park in the Liverpool Royal Hospital."

"The second photograph shows the same man who approaches a security guard."

"The third photograph shows the same man standing in front of a bank of lifts."

"The fourth photograph shows the same man at the door of the ICU ward. In this same photograph, it shows a man in plain clothes standing outside of the same ward door."

"The fifth photograph shows the same man at the nurse's station in the ICU ward."

On completion, Sue said, "Spencer, do you recognise the man in the series of photographs?"

He replied, "No."

Sue looked at Spencer, "Spencer, have you ever been in the ICU ward of the Liverpool Royal Hospital?"

He replied, "No."

Sue said, "Spencer, have you ever been in the area of the ICU known as the fishbowl, the area where DCS Carter lay recovering from a recent period of abduction?"

He shouted, "I've already said no."

Sue looked at her watch. "Spencer, you have frequently evaded my questions about your identity during this meeting, so I'm terminating this interview at 11.15am." Lloydie leaned forward and switched off the tape.

Sue continued, "Spencer, you will be taken down to the holding cells for your lunch. During the break, we are going to serve a warrant on your property. Spencer this being the normal protocol after the arrest of a suspect."

Sue called, "Officer." The interview door opened, "Boss?" "Peter, will you take Spencer down to the holding cells for his lunch?"

84

Sue was sat in the general office finishing off a sandwich, and a mug of coffee. The office door suddenly opened, and in walked Peter and Philip with beaming faces.

Sue looked up, "Well, gentlemen, you both look as if you're about to burst with excitement. Peter took several evidence bags from behind his back, and Phil did the same.

Placing them on the office desk close to Eric. Sue stood up. "Well, what do we have here?" Peter said, "We raided Spence's home address, 25, Station Road South, Liverpool 25."

"The property front door was opened by a lady called Rosemary Spencer. Wife of the accused. We both showed the lady are IDs and who we were. Phil showed the lady the warrant, signed by a duly appointed magistrate, which we had in our possession. He informed her of our intentions.

On entering the property, Jules, who had a file under her arm, accidentally dropped it? She panicked, apologising, while she bent down to recover the paper from the file strewn on the floor. On the inside cover of the file, secured under a paper clip, was a photograph of Robert Spencer.

Rosemary Spencer called out, "That's Robert, why have you got his photograph?" Jules blushed as she looked at Phil, "Sorry, sarge." Phil then looked at Rosemary Spencer, "Your husband is the reason for why we are here."

Phil said, "Jules, please remain with Mrs Spencer. He then stated, "Are you the only person present in the property?" She shouted, "Yes, why are you asking?" Phil asked, "Please inform us of the set-up of the property?" She mentioned in a complaining voice. "Front lounge, rear dining room, kitchen, three bedrooms, two on-suit bathrooms, basement, and garage."

Phil continued, "With the assistance of my colleagues and uniform officers, we are about to search your property. He nodded at personnel, and the search began."

Peter coughed, "In the basement, we recovered all the property in the evidence bags, components to make a bomb, false or otherwise. SOCO offices were present?" Peter smiled, "As requested, on our way, we took Spence's keys from his property. We found a black fob. When I pressed the *'door open'* button, there was a click that unlocked the car doors, the same when I pressed *'door lock.'* In the car, with the fob in hand, I pressed the starter button on the console, and it ignited. Proof it's his car."

Peter said, "In one of the evidence bags, we recovered paper evidence from the Insurance company and the DVLA, documents stating both owner's name and address, and reg of the car. *Spencer's."*

Sue suddenly stood up and cheered, after which she said, "After I've finished interviewing Spencer, send the evidence bags to the Chorley labs for forensic reports…?" Phil suddenly interrupted, "Boss we thought you may like these?"

Phil and Peter both took out an evidence bag containing a vanilla file from the inside of their jacket pockets. They both put on rubber gloves, and Phil handed a pair to Sue.

They opened them and placed some of the papers out on the table. Sue stood dumbfounded, fighting for her breath, pointing with a rubber-gloved finger… "Are those copies of printed emails?"

On close examination, Sue paused as she fanned out the papers, "Look, they show all the names, addresses, offences, and the time and dates of release…Where did you find the file?"

Phil smiled, "Boss, they were stashed down behind some books on a shelf in a sort of library."

Sue, looking at Lloydie, "Jim, after our interview with Spencer, organise a Traffic detail escort with the control room to escort one of our team mobiles, with two team members, to Chorley." Jim replied, "Boss."

Eric walked over to Sue and hugged her, whispering, "Congratulations, boss." And kissed her on her cheek.

"Jim, are you ready to resume battle?" He smiled, "Yes, boss."

Sue and Jim Lloyd both walked into the interview room. Peter, the uniform officer, stood up he smiled, "Boss." He turned and left.

They both sat down opposite Spencer. While Jim organised the recording machine, stating the time, day, and date, and all present. Sue looked at Spencer. "You do realise that you are still under caution. He replied, "What if."

Sue looked at Spencer, "I see that you still have no legal representation?" He replied, "How many times do I have to say I don't need one."

Both Sue and Jim reached down to the floor and brought up all the evidence bags. Spencer suddenly shouted, "What the fuck?" Peter opened the interview room door. "Boss?" Sue shook her head. She smiled, "All is well."

Sue looked at Spencer, "I informed you that while we had the lunch break, officers from this team would execute a search warrant at your home address. Duly completed, and the contents found were placed in evidence bags, which appear to contain items of interest."

She continued, "Spencer, you will notice that one can look into the bags and see the items recovered from your home."

She picked up three bags, "The following bags are marked DSPW 1-3 (DS Phil Watson) recovered from your basement. You will notice that they contain coloured wires, terminals, mobile phones, bulbs, and switches?" He replied, "No comment."

She picked up another bag, "Evidence bag marked, DSPW 1 (DS Peter Williams). You will notice it contains Insurance and DVLA documents for M/c private L67 FET a blue Audi A5. Showing the owner's details, Mr R Spencer, 25, Station Road South, Liverpool 25." He replied, "No comment."

Sue then picked up two similar bags, "Evidence bags marked, DSPW 2 and DSPW 3. Although similar, they are the initials of my two Detective sergeants.

I've produced them together, for they each show a vanilla file, which contains several emails. They show the names and details of released criminals. The names match murder victims investigated by the MCU."

Jim passed Sue yet another bag. "Evidence bag marked DSPW 1. You will notice that this bag contains a set of personal keys; removed from your property when detained at Derby Lane police station. On the same ring, there is a car fob, giving access to a blue Audi A5 L67 FET, allowing one to enter and start the car via a button on the car console." He replied, "No comment."

Sue looked at Spencer, "I'm about to show you again item marked DCIF 1-5, a series of photographs of a man in different situations in relation to The Liverpool Royal Infirmary. Are you that man?" He replied, "No."

Sue turned and produced a statement taken by Jules in an evidence bag marked WDCF1. Spencer, will you please take this and read it?" After five minutes, he looked at Sue, "So?"

Sue looked at Spencer, "Robert Spencer, you have continually made negative responses to all my questions and items of evidence produced. You will be taken down to the bridewell, where you'll be formally cautioned and charged with the placing of a suspicious device in a public building, contrary to The Criminal Justice and Public Order Act 1994, section 60.

Spencer said, "Do your worst."

Sue called, "Peter?" The interview room door opened, and Peter said, "Boss?" Sue calmly suggested, "Take him down to the holding cells where he is to be detained."

Spencer was taken away.

85

Sue walked into the general office, Eric looked up from his work, "Boss, are you okay?" She smiled, "Yes, Eric, we're just that little bit nearer to closure in the Spencer case. I know it, Jim knows it, Ian knows it, Peter knows it, Phil knows it, and Jules knows it. The only bloody person who doesn't seem to know it is one, Robert Spencer, of this fucking parish?"

On receipt of her mug of coffee from Eric, she turned, "I'm off to my office to call TF. When Jim returns get him to organise the trip to Chorley. Get hold of one of the 'Chuckle brothers' (Peter or Phil). One of them can accompany one other of the team."

I need the other brother to check the crime file, making sure we have all the relevant statements from the hospital personnel. I need this matter nailed." Eric looked around the office, and they were both alone, and he smiled. "Yes, Sue."

She beamed at him, turned, and left for her office. When she sat down, she picked up her office phone and dialled TF's direct number. TF should answer, but no, it had been re-directed through to Jane, his secretary.

"Commander Frost's office; how may I help you?" Sue hesitated, "Jane, it's Superintendent Ford. I need to speak with TF?" Jane unexpectantly gasped and, in a torrent of words, *"He's out of the office, but how is Carter? Oh, I do miss his visits to see the boss; he has such a lovely ass."*

Sue, without any hesitation, said, "Ask Commander Frost to call me." And slammed down the phone.

After the pathetic call, Sue stood up and stormed out, leaving for the general office.

As usual, Eric looked up, "Is everything alright, boss?" Sue, trying to keep her temper under control, replied, "No, just tried to call TF and had to accept the dribble from Jane about the guv. In a strop, I put the phone down on her."

"I want to make sure that all is in order with the Spencer case. We need to prepare a resume for Spencer's production at the Maggie's court tomorrow morning."

"Eric, will you please inform Lloydie that I'll see him in court tomorrow morning? I'm just off to see the guv to see if he may be up to reviewing matters to date. Can you get hold of Charlie for me?"

At that very moment, the phone on Eric's desk activated. He leaned over to answer it. He looked at Sue and mouthed, *'TF for you.'* Sue exhaled and walked over to his desk.

She noticed he had a smile on his face as he mouthed, *'You're in the shit.'* She snatched the handset from him. "Ford."

On completion of the call, she handed the phone back to Eric, smiled, "TF just wants to be kept in the loop."

Walking over to the day diary, she looked at Eric, "I'm signing out, but calling at the hospital to visit the guv on my way home."

At that moment, the office door suddenly opened, and in walked Charlie.

On arrival at the ICU ward, the duty APO, who immediately recognised them, stood to attention out of respect. They both produced their IDs, complying with protocol. The duty officer pushed the door open, and they both entered the ward.

As they entered the ward, the APO said, "Boss, we have yet another doctor wishing access. He showed an ID clipped to his trouser waistband. Charlie said, "Describe him, he replied, "Boss, that's him talking to the nurse at the nurses station?"

Looking down the ward, they both noticed a very pleasant type of gentleman, or doctor, a tall man dressed in a blue two-piece suit, white shirt, blue tie, and a fawn three-quarter length raincoat, in possession of a briefcase.

The nurse looked up and nodded at both Sue and Charlie, who both headed towards the fishbowl. Charlie, aware that Sue was armed, remained to talk with Chris Atkinson as Sue continued to visit Carter.

The enquiring doctor left from the nurse's station, walking towards the fishbowl.

Sue had entered and walked through to Carter's bed area. Whose bed was to the right, protected by the partial edge of Carter's curtains, which had been pulled back and secured traditionally, by the use of the end of a curtain to form the knot. Carter looked up he smiled, "Why, Sue, what a lovely surprise. Sue immediately noticed that Carter was not wearing his sunglasses.

Jenny Carter's attentive nurse was busy in a medical cupboard. The door to the fishbowl opened, and in walked the stranger. Chris murmured, "That's unusual. I don't recognise that doc…?" With that, Charlie ran to the fishbowl.

On entering, Carlie noticed that the stranger was standing between him and Sue. At the same time, Sue had leaned over to kiss Carter on his cheek. The stranger opened his briefcase and took out a handgun fitted with a silencer.

Charlie, who had removed his firearm from his holster, placed it against his right thigh; he shouted, "Armed police officer, drop your gun, or I'll open fire; I am an armed protection officer. I won't tell you twice. Now kneel on the floor."

Sue looked up from Carter, and she quickly assessed the situation. Sue withdrew her firearm and, leaning over Carter, holding up her firearm with a straight arm, called, "Armed police, drop your firearm, or I'll indeed shoot you."

She looked at the stranger who had dropped to the floor to his knees after a quick mathematical equation. Dropped the gun to the floor.

The stranger looked up at Sue, "Fair cop." Placed both his arms in the air. Sue, while Charlie, had the stranger covered. Replaced her firearm into its holster, took the stranger's arms and fitted him with handcuffs. She cautioned him.

Sue took out her phone and called Eric, "Eric, will you send three available team members down to the ICU? We have one for escort to Derby Lane." Eric replied, "Yes, boss, your suspicions were correct; there had to be other's?"

While Sue was on the phone with Eric, Charlie looked at a somewhat overwrought Jenny, who seemed to be shaking with all the commotion. Charlie took hold of her and placed an arm about her shoulder to comfort her.

Charlie looked down at her. "You don't happen to have a pair of rubber gloves that you can lay your hands on? She looked up at him," Seeing as we're in a bloody hospital, I think so? She whispered, "Yes." She walked to a nearby wrack holding three cardboard boxes marked S. M. L.

Looking at Charlie's hands, she smiled, "I feel L (Large) will suffice.

Putting on the gloves, he walked over and picked up the gun used by the imposter. The gun was a 9 mm model 17 magnum. He pulled back the slider and removed the bullet in the chamber. He then turned the gun over and removed the cartridge; minus the bullet in the chamber, he counted 16 other bullets.

With the gun made safe, he placed the gun and silencer into an evidence bag brought to the ICU by Alex.

Phil took hold of the offender. Phil said, "My colleague, Detective Superintendent Ford, cautioned you at the time of your arrest, you made, "Fair cop." He just smiled.

Wills took hold of him; "You'll be taken to Derby Lane police station to the offices of the Major Crime Unit, where you'll be detained."

86

After all the turmoil, Sue, laughing, looked at Carter, "One thing about you, Carter, you certainly know how to show a girl a good time?" She leaned down, intending to kiss him on his cheek; he suddenly turned his head and body, enabling him to kiss Sue on her lips.

She suddenly thought... Carter had interrupted her train of thought by taking hold of her, saying, "Thank you, Sue, you deliberately placed yourself in harm's way. He kissed and hugged her.

Sue stood up and, looking rather flustered, straightened her raincoat, coughing and spluttering, "Well, well, let's leave it at that."

In the meantime, Alex and Phil had removed the prisoner, accompanied by Wills, escorting the prisoner for transportation to Derby Lane.

Sue turned, looking at Carter, and smiled, "I wonder if this could be kept under wraps, for I'd hate Abby to hear about this, but I suppose it's inevitable, hey Ho!"

She turned to leave the fishbowl, and she noticed a smart-looking gentleman standing at the side of the door. On seeing Sue, he smiled, "Boss." Sue looked at him, "And who may you be?" He replied, "I'm DS Lucas, the guv's new APO, while in the fishbowl. Plus, you have my colleague on the ward door. Organised and sanctioned by Commander Frost." Sue smiled, "Thank you."

Outside on the ward, Sue bumped into Chris Atkinson, who had witnessed the commotion, especially Charlie's immediate reaction to the events and Carter's protection.

Looking at Chris, she laughed, "You have yet another APO posted to the ward?" Chris smiled, "Pray to tell, where on earth do you find all these gorgeous, handsome men? It's worth it, though, if there's a need for a certain person to be kept in cotton wool. That man is like the proverbial cat, who has nine lives?"

Sue looked at Chris, "The present count is 4?" She turned and left.

One of the young nurses in passing said, "Sister Atkinson, "I see that lady, visiting Mr Carter regularly; I've often wondered who she is?" Chris replied, "Well, on the record, she is his deputy, Superintendent Susan Ford, to all intent and purposes, a hardnosed police officer."

"But off the record, and I mean off the record, a woman who just happens to love and worship the ground he walks on." The nurse just smiled, "Oh! Sister, I thought that was you?"

Chris, in a loud whisper, spluttered, "Nurse Daily, I'm sure you have more than enough work to be getting on with?" In a pretend huff, Chris turned and walked away.

Later in the car with Charlie, on their way back to Derby Lane, Sue looked at him, "I know it had not been mentioned, but Carter and I always thought that   Spencer must have needed help, for when you look at some of the offences?"

"The logistics of such attacks, it must have been obvious, particularly when you look at the number of multiple victims, and the degree of execution, a point in question, the three victims in the baths at the rear of the builder's yard, and the poor victim squashed to death by all the pavement slabs, piled on top of each other?"

She continued, "We may well find there are others who assisted in these matters. When you get a group of people who may object that all the various social workers, probation officers, and so on even the police. Set up to act and deal with all the various aspects of life and failed. They take it upon themselves to act on their behalf."

"If one looks closer, you could include Adrian Rice. Combes's illicit boyfriend. Rice, who functioned as a conduit, allowed the information of released convicts to Spencer. That gives you Spencer, Rice, and another?"

On their return to Derby Lane, Sue, and Charlie both signed back in. Eric welcomed them both with a typical mug of coffee. They both sat down and explained to Eric yet another attempt on Carter's life.

The General office door suddenly opened, and in walked Lloydie and Peter, who had both returned from Chorley, together with Phil, Alex, and Wills, who had returned from the Royal.

Sue looked up, "Well, gentlemen, where are we up to with our suspect?" Phil turned, "Boss, after relating the circs of the arrest to the bridewell sergeant Derek Lancaster, on completion, the charge was accepted, although the suspect refused to answer any questions, or give his details."

Phil continued, "The offender has been duly processed, his fingerprints taken, and rushed off to the fingerprints unit for a prompt ID result. It could take anything up to an hour. We owe a load of favours."

Sue looked, "Well, help yourselves to a coffee while we await the prisoners, ID if known?"

She continued, "On receipt of the information, if not known, and he still refuses to give details, charge him with the 'Attempted murder' of DCS Carter, under section 1(1) of the Criminal Attempt Act 1981." She coughed, "Due to the serious nature of the offence, he has been refused bail."

"The same applies to a positive result with fingerprints, except, prepare a warrant, blar, blar, blar, blar."

Sue turned, "I'm off to my office to call TF and Simon Chapman of the CPS to inform him of the serious nature of the offence."

When she sat in her office chair, she picked up the phone and called TF. *"Frost"* "Sir, it's Superintendent Ford, just letting you know, one male was arrested for the attempted murder of Ch Supt Carter while recovering in ICU, in the Royal."

"DCS Carter's, APO, DI Watkins, and I were both on hand. The intruder was apprehended, and his firearm was neutralised. He was removed to Derby Lane by members of the MCU team."

The line fell silent, and eventually, TF said, *"DI Watkins had to give a full report of the incident to the Det Ch Supt of the APU (Armed Protection Unit). His version of events appears to differ from yours. You failed to mention that you threw yourself across Carter, placing yourself in harm's way. DI Watkins was behind the offender, and you were facing, as you were visiting Carter at the time."*

He continued, *"Ford, I'm putting you in for The Queens Gallantry medal for bravery,"* Sue was flabbergasted and replied, "But sir, it's only a thing that any of us would do. Sir, I'm about to call and speak with Simon Patterson about the prisoner's production in court tomorrow."

The next comment floored her from TF, *"Sue."* Hearing TF's casual comment, having dropped his chauvinistic attitude. Using her Christian name, she nearly dropped the phone. *"Sue, don't forget to keep Wendy Field in the loop?"* He closed the call.

87

After the total shock experienced during the call with TF, in which he staggered her when mentioning the two salient points. Sue picked up her phone and called Wendy. The reply was very concise, *"Wendy Field, how may I help you?" Sue replied,* "Wendy, it's Sue. I have just spoken with TF. Are you aware that there has been yet another attempt on Carter's life?"

Wendy replied, *"Yes, I received information via the force control room, I was also informed of your act of gallantry, and that TF's putting you in for a gong?"* Sue interrupted, " *Look Wendy please play that issue down, TF wants you to be kept in the loop."* After several minutes, Sue explained a watered-down version of the incident. On completion, *Wendy thanked her.*

"The offender will be appearing in the Maggie's court in the morning, and Ian will have copies of a resume of the offence for you to hand out to members of your press friends?"

Wendy burst out laughing, *"Look, it just happens that Ian is a DI in the MCU, and we happen to live together. I'll get into him tonight to get the low-down of the job?"* Sue laughed. She screamed, *"TMI, TMI."* And replaced the phone.

Sue got up from behind her desk and walked through to the general office. Opening the office door, she was met by a wall of sound, for in unison, Eric, Lloydie, Ian and Charlie all called out as one. "Boss, do you need anything?"

She replied, "Yes, a couple of matters. Ian, Wendy, is aware of the incident re the guv. Will you take her copies of the resume for her press friends? Lloydie, where are we in relation to the prints?" He replied, "Boss still waiting, I'm afraid?" Sue looked at him. "Do we have a warrant waiting to be filled out with the relevant information?" Lloydie replied, "Yes, boss."

Looking at Charlie, "Well, sunshine, collect a copy of the resume; we're off to CPS to have a chat with Simon Patterson."

Sue looked at Eric. "Well, boss, you are fully prepped with proceedings. He looked around the office, and he noticed that all presents were busy with other matters. He smiled, "Yes, boss and it would seem you have all matters under control?"

In the car, while travelling to the CPS, Sue looked over at Charlie, "Erm, Mr. When were you going to tell me of your version of matters in ICU? You do realise that your version given to your boss fluttered over to TF, and he wants to recommend me for a gong?"

Charlie looked at Sue, "Well, boss, I only reported it as I saw it?" Smiling, she looked at him, "Perhaps, you should have run it by me, for I'd have advised reducing all the potential, lifesaving, protection crap?"

He responded in a controlled voice, without a single loss of concentration. "Boss, there is a great deal of difference between a training scenario set-up, and the real thing. You can never self-impose the effect of looking down the barrel of a gun conducted in earnest."

"You never thought of the situation; without any thought at all for your own safety, you threw yourself in front of the guv." Sue, without thinking, as if in some sort of self-induced trance, whispered, "Well, if that's the only way to get a grip of the guv...?"

She suddenly seemed to self-implode with embarrassment. Charlie, without so much as a step change in conversation, said, "Boss, here we are, ready for Mr Patterson?"

Sue looked at him, and she was just about to say something when Charlie interrupted, "No, boss, there's no need for any explanation."

Later, sat in the CPS outer office, they overheard Mr Patterson's secretary introduce them via the intercom. His office door suddenly opened, and the tall-haired, smartly dressed gentleman said, "Superintendent Ford, welcome. Please come in and bring your colleague with you."

In his office, Sue said, "Mr Patterson, may I introduce…" Simon Patterson smiled, "Superintendent Ford, your colleague needs no introduction; we met when DCS Carter was his principal." They all shook hands.

Simon Patterson beckoned them to two spare chairs opposite his desk. "Please sit. Can I interest you both in a cup of coffee?" They both agreed, and his secretary served them two cups of coffee, both white with two sugars.

Patterson eventually sat at his desk, looking out from between two towers of files. Plus, directly behind him and to his right were two long wooden tables littered with court files and papers. The rest of the office looked like a well-equipped library. From floor to ceiling, there were shelves holding volumes of legal reference books and many others. The only gap was a large window overlooking Dale Street. Sue wondered what on earth happened with cases such as the Davenport papers; the floor would be littered.

Simon Patterson smiled, "Superintendent Ford, do you mind if I call you Sue?" She replied, "No, that's fine."

He smirked, "How may we help you?" Sue took in a breath and, letting it out slowly, she began. "Mr Patterson, I don't know if you're aware, but there has been yet another attempt on the life of DCS Carter."

Patterson suddenly sat bolt upright in his chair as if he'd received an electric shock. He looked at Sue," That's unbelievable. Is Carter alright?"

Sue explained, "Both DI Watson and I detained the offender. Hence, the reason for this meeting. The prisoner was arrested, his firearm removed and made safe. He was cautioned and removed to Derby Lane. At the police station, the circumstances of the arrest were submitted to the bridewell sergeant."

She continued, "The prisoner refused to answer any questions in relation to his details. He was fingerprinted as per the arrest protocol. His prints have been forwarded to the HQ fingerprint unit; we are awaiting results as to his identity if known?"

"Should we identify him via his fingerprints, then he will be charged under those details."

"At present, he's been charged with attempted murder and will attend at the Magistrates court in the morning. I have with me a resume of the circumstances of his arrest. Simon Patterson took it and began to read the resume. He then looked up at Sue, "Have you read this?" Sue looked at him, "Yes of course why?" Patterson smiled at her, "Well it would seem DCS Carter, would owe his life to you if matters had played out at the scene, what?"

Sue leaned forward and took the single piece of paper, from the CPS Lawyer. She immediately recognised that the resume information had been altered, and re-typed?" She looked at Charlie, who sat with hands covering his face to stop his spluttering, to refrain from laughing.

She spun round looking at Charlie, "What do you know about this?" Charlie replied, "Boss surely you remember the old rule, never ask a colleague to type your resume, for they are likely to change you fore names, to something stupid, like Cuthbert, of Montague, but equally funny when read out in court?" He stated there is no point in changing the resume as matters have been delivered to the court."

Sue blushing looked at Simon Patterson, "What can you do?" Looking at her he said, "Sue I'm sorry but matters have been put into action, I suggest you let your colleagues listen to your act of bravery." He smirked as he looked at Charlie.

Sue said, "Well, If he is unknown when addressed by the Clerk of the court, and the prisoner still refuses to give his details, may I ask that he be proceed, and he be detained and refused bail? The same, of course, will apply if he is a known offender to be detained without bail due to the severity of the case. We have a warrant awaiting service to search the offender's address, as per normal?"

On completion of the meeting, as they were about to leave, Mr Patterson's, office phone activated. He leaned down, picking it up. He just said, "Patterson." After a few seconds, he looked at Sue, "Sue, the call is for you?"

Taking hold of the phone, Sue said, "Ford." *"Boss, it's Lloydie; we have a result; our friend is no other than Brian Smedley, 23.12. 1988, making him 30 years of age, he resides at 27 Newton Street, Werst Derby, Liverpool 13."*

"He has previous for inciting trouble with all the tree huggers, blocking motorways, and major sports meetings; he may be on the periphery of matters. As we speak, a warrant is being sworn; Peter, Phil, and other members of the team are making for his address."

Sue let out a sigh, "Thank you, Lloydie; by the way, I'll see you when I get back at the ranch." And put down the phone.

Sue mentioned the details to Simon Patterson, who smiled at Sue, "Please just amend the resume, of his name and address, and D.O.B. That's all, and I'll see you both in court tomorrow.

88

Sue had only been sitting behind her desk for about fifteen minutes when there was a knock on her office door. She looked up from the file she was reading. She took in a deep breath she called, "Come in."

The door opened, and she noticed Lloydie standing in the doorway. "Lloydie, come in." Smiling, she stood up. "Scrum downtime already?" He replied, "Correct, boss."

Entering the conference room, the whole team came to attention; Sue looked around the room. "You all know what to do; neither the guv nor I can sort it out. I just give up."

A voice from the back of the room said, *"Respect. And we've all read the resume."* There was a sudden outbreak of applause. Sue waved both arms in the air, "Enough already."

When normality resumed, Sue stood at the top of the room, flanked by Lloydie and Ian; they both sat down, and Sue remained standing. "Other matters will be dealt afterwards."

Smiling down at the team, she said, "The prisoner detained in ICU after an unsuccessful attempt on the guv's life is one, Brian Smedley, 30 yrs. Of 27, Newton Street, West Derby, Liverpool 13." After the circumstances of his arrest were related to the Bridewell sergeant, he refused to answer any further questions. He was eventually identified after his fingerprints revealed his details."

"Smedley has previous form for the usual, a tree hugger, an activist that carries glue to stick themselves to motorways, in other words, a pain in the arse."

Sue looked at Lloydie, "Jim, I've been thinking, let's prepare a resume for both Smedley and Spencer, mention the two unsuccessful attempts on the guv's life. Mention to CPS that it's just a look and show, both to be detained in custody for further enquiries."

Walking over to one of the whiteboards, Sue wrote and pointed to all the names and details of the offenders. Sutcliffe will eventually be discharged; she was a by-product, found in the wrong bed, at the wrong time, when discovered during the search of Rice's home address?"

"Hazel Coombes will be charged with aiding and abetting in the supplying of information contrary to the data protection act. She's up for a plea or trial."

"Rice will be charged with Aiding and Abetting and Conspiracy. He is a silent partner in all of this, and his fingerprints are all over this. He seduces Coombes, managing to persuade her to retrieve valued information from her computer in CSU."

Rice then acts as a conduit, passing all the information wanted by Spencer and Smedley. The relevant victims were killed due to the insignificant sentencing, and they took it upon themselves to conduct their own punishments."

"Spencer and Smedley, both realise that the team are closing in on them, decide that the only way out is to kill the guv."

"There you have it." Looking at Lloydie and Ian. "Lloydie, I want you with me in court tomorrow.

Smiling, she looked at Ian, "I want you to take the new resume of evidence of Spencer and Ridley to your beloved Wendy for her friends in the press. Ian's face was a picture. The whole room burst out in laughter. I feel you may wish to ready yourself, for Wendy will try to retrieve all the relevant facts."

"Tomorrow, Ian, if you survive Wendy's interrogation?" The whole team burst out laughing. Sue smiled, "Ian, see to the evidence recovered from Ridley's residence; I want it examined and prepared for any future trial?"

Sue looked at her watch, "It's 7pm; let's call it a night and assume matters tomorrow, when bright-eyed and bushy-tailed.

Sue looked at Charlie, "Can you do me a favour, he replied, "Of course, boss anything?" I'm signing off duty and wish to visit the guv."

89

On arrival at the ICU, both Sue and Charlie ran the expected gauntlet of the APOs outside the ward and inside at the entrance to the fishbowl. The first acknowledged Sue correctly, "Evening boss." She replied courteously as the officer opened the ward door for her.

Sue walked up to the nurse's station, apologised for the lateness of the hour, but asked if she could have a quick chat with DCS Carter. A ward sister was sat next to a duty nurse. The nurse looked at the sister, who just smiled, "Why, of course, officer, he is in his own little bubble further up the ward."

Charlie looked at Sue, "Boss, I'll remain and have a chat with the duty APO standing at the fishbowl door."

Sue sashayed passed them both as she entered the fishbowl, nodding to Jenny, his highly accomplished nurse. She called, "I do hope you're not decent back there?" Carter replied, "It depends on who's asking?"

Sue entered Carter's sleeping area, which can be cordoned off by a curtain, allowing privacy on doctor's rounds. It was drawn back. He was sat up in bed with a book in his hand. "Why Susan Martha, what a lovely surprise. He pointed to a bedside chair, "Sue, take the weight off."

She sat and, looking at him, thought, *'Yes, it appears that the sparkle is beginning to return to your eyes, not all, but some nonetheless.'*

Carter looked upon her with excitement, "Well, well, give me, give me, what's the news?" After about fifteen minutes, Sue updated Carter with all the relevant details of the case. Carter smiled, "Well, boss, it would seem that I can take extended leave, for the team is in such good…?"

Sue looked at him, "This is only as long as it takes, Carter; you are, and always will be, the head of the MCU?"

Sue stood up and collected her bag and coat, ready to leave. Carter looked at her. "Erm Sue, I'd just…" Sue interrupted him, "No, Carter, I know what you're going to say, but there is no need."

Carter punched the top of his hospital locker, "Christ, Sue, you put yourself in the line of danger; we'll never know if he'd have fired… you'll have saved my life, at a possible fatal effect on you, I'm just trying to say, 'thank you', but saying thank you never seems to cover it, but thank you all the same."

As Sue left for the door of his private hidey-hole, he murmured, "Abby's left me; she told me yesterday, it would seem, my job and recent events were the cause. Plus, her career prospects are more important. Having received a promotion to area manager in customer relations."

Sue turned and stood facing him, placing her bag and coat on the end of his bed. Stood, with her hands on her hips, smiled, "Well flash, what on earth are we going to do with you?" He smiled, "That's it for me; I'm off to join a retreat or monastery, for where women are concerned, they can all fuck off."

Sue laughed, "Have you a discharge date, for I'll inform all eligible females to hide; she turned and laughed uncontrollably. As she turned, she passed Jenny and Chris Atkinson; as she passed, they heard, "If only." Sue and Chris both looked in the direction of the remark. To notice Jenny, turn as she walked back towards Carter's bed.

Outside at the nursing station, Chris looked at Sue, "He's due for release next week." Sue looked at Chris, "Can you give me a shout? I'll have Charlie on standby." Saying their goodbyes, they both left.

In the car, in between Charlie's frequent questions about the guv, Sue's mind wondered, *'What the fuck do these women want, for in Carter, you get the complete man, charm personified, I'd give my ticket in tomorrow if it meant a future with him?'*

Parked outside of Sue's address. Charlie looked at Sue, "Erm, boss; we've arrived. Sue spluttered, "Okay, thanks, pall."

Sue, when home, took off her coat and hung it up in the hall closet; whilst in the closet, she removed her firearm and holster clipped on her waistband. Placing them in a floor safe. When completed, she walked through to her kitchen.

She opened her fridge door and took out a can of lager. She pulled on the ring pull and opened the can. It didn't touch the sides. After the first gulp, she suddenly belched. She laughed, "Susan Martha, what would his nibs say?"

In the lounge, Sue began to play mind games. Well, Carter, if you were here, alone with me. I'd have to excuse myself, but I'd make up for it, for I'd take you by the hand and take you upstairs, strip you off, and we'd have the sexiest shower under the sun. Sue began to ponder on all the immoral ways.

Sue flopped down on her settee and cried her eyes out. She blubbed, if only to be given the opportunity, and began to scream hysterically, rubbing her fingers through her hair in utter temper; when stopped, her mind turned to the inevitable, Carter. Eventually, she'd fallen asleep, but the dreams continued.

Suddenly, the sound of her house cooling down and the sudden clinking sound disturbed her. Looking at her watch, it was 4.30am. She was cold and shivering. Sue stood up and began to stumble upstairs; at the top, she walked into the bathroom and began to strip off; she thought no to a shower, thinking that she'd be up in a few hours and would shower then.

In her bedroom, she got into her sleeping apparel, the only feminine item being her fluffy pyjama bottoms. The rest is composed of a gent's T-shirt and Carter's sweatshirt, typical of Carter, it being of excellent quality, was still unwashed. Yet, still retained his signature smells, although they were dissipating with time. Yet still enough to cling to. She pulled on her bed socks and jumped into bed.

She pulled up her duvet and curled up within it, yet not before placing a spare pillow by the side of her, the illusion of a bedfellow, next to her. If only Carter, there would be truly little sleep that night. She crossed her arms as if hugging him.

Sue should have felt relaxed, not tired, although she'd fallen asleep downstairs. Sue knew it wasn't a restful sleep, for her sleep pattern was littered with disgusting what-ifs of Carter. With a sly smile, she thought, I wonder if his skin is that smooth. Sleep eventually descended on her.

She woke to find herself in bed with the pillow in her arms. She looked down at it, and she burst out laughing, 'Well, was that as good for you?' Stripping off, she stood in the shower, and Sue lifted her arms in the air, flaunting her slim body, "All this could be yours sunshine; what else do you bloody want?" She felt a wreck and could if, remained in bed have slept for hours.

Stood in the kitchen, showered, and dressed, ready for the day ahead, with her usual cup of coffee in hand. As the doorbell sounded, she thought, 'Hey Ho!' at least one can dream.'

As she left her house, she immediately saw Charlie leaning against the car with arms folded. "Morning, boss," Sue replied and got into the car. She sighed, "Another day, another dollar." And they were off.

90

In the general office, after signing on duty, Sue looked at Eric, "Are all the children in?" Eric laughed, "Yes, ma'am, all waiting for the boss." As Sue turned to leave, Eric winked," Now go and be a second guv."

As she walked down the corridor, she called, "That will be the day."

Entering the conference room, she there experienced the usual, and it was the same usual reply. Standing at the top of the team, she turned and smiled.

"Now, children, you all know there is only one person you stand to attention for when in this room...?" A quiet voice from within the team said..." *We stand for whichever guv oversees us."* A cheer resonated throughout the room.

"Right, settle down; your guv is due for release from the hospital next week. Chris Atkinson will give me a call. She looked at Charlie, will you please make yourself available?" He smiled, "Yes, boss, I'm sure cover will be made available for you?" She huffed, and her voice tapered off...

Sue turned and looked in the direction of Ian Baxter, "Baxie, what did we find at the Smedley's address?"

Ian stood up. "Boss, we served the warrant; the door to the property was answered by a woman calling herself Amanda Smedley, who claimed to be his wife. Together with members of SOCO. The search revealed incriminating evidence."

He continued, "In a locked drawer, in the back bedroom of the property, which she claimed she had no key. I warned Mrs Smedley that under the terms of the warrant, we can gain entry by force."

"We forced the drawer; a search revealed plans, papers, and correspondence in relation to the address where the guv was to be detained. The papers detailed items and requirements for the construction of that terrible isolated room."

"The many different sizes of timber, plasterboard, plumbing equipment, copper pipe, boxes of 15- and 28-mm copper pipe clips, an electrical fuse box, wire, plugs, and switches, boxes of 100mm and 40mm galvanised nails, a double size bed, and fridge."

On completion, Ian looked at Sue, "Boss, all the evidence recovered from Smedley's address has been placed in several evidence bags and located on a table at the back of the room."

Sue looked over the team, "Well, we have all the relevant evidence on the three defendants; the two tomorrow will be up before the Maggie's court for a plea."

"See you all tomorrow, Charlie; when you pick me up, it's straight down to the courts."

They all signed off duty and left. Alone in the office with only the three of them. Sue coughed and, with a taint of embarrassment, gently turned to Eric, "Boss, I have a bit of bad news; Carter yet again finds himself in receipt of another totally unexpected 'dear John' from Abby."

Eric reached up and gently removed his glasses, then from his trouser pocket, took out a handkerchief (A garment not carried by most men); he blew a breath onto the lenses of his glasses; as each lensed dulled, he began to polish them.

He then looked at both Sue and Charlie. "Shit." Looking at Sue, he said, "Please, boss, don't take this the wrong way, but what the fuck do these women want?"

Sue turned and looked at Charlie as she went to leave the office, "Charlie…"

In the car on the way home, Sue took out her mobile phone; after pressing the contact category, she pressed a selected button.

Charlie, who sat in the driver's seat in close proximity, overheard, "Abby Remington."

There was a silence. Sue eventually said, "Miss Remington, I visited Carter earlier, during which he informed me of your situation, having told him while in the hospital of your decision. I thought we agreed that you'd wait until Carter was released and at home before telling him of your wishes?"

Abby replied, *"Well, I needed to organise my transfer, and unable to wait until his release?"*

Sue shouted, "You cold-hearted bitch, you certainly know how to kick a man when he's down?" She replied, *"How dare you talk to me like that."* Sue interrupted, "If I had my way, I'd lock you up, you spoilt cow." Sue heard, *"Er, er, DS Ford, I'm not one of your typical hicks. I'm a professional individual and should be treated with respect."*

Her reply was quite brief, "Miss Remington, I'll inform the duty APO at DCS Carter's home address that you must be accompanied, always, when entering his flat if you've not completed matters by 1pm. Tomorrow, then the remaining items will be placed into cardboard boxes and removed to a local charity shop. How do you like that?"

Abby whispered, *"Miss Ford, I've always thought that there has always been an Elephant in the room?"* She closed the call.

Charlie looked at Sue, and she looked at him, "No comment."

91

Events happened quite quickly; Chris had contacted Sue, as promised. Charlie was dispatched to collect his boss from the hospital. DI Kate Williams, one of the other team of APOs, was informed of her new asset, Superintendent Ford, and seconded to Derby Lane.

"Charlie knew what to expect, for Carter would have to run the gauntlet of pretty nurses in ICU. His charge for their thanks was a kiss on their cheeks. Charlie attended with the expected wheelchair.

Carter was assisted into the chair, he placed his holdall on his knee, and Charlie began to push his charge from the ward, but not until after all the tender kisses to the nurses.

The last two were the most important, Chris and Jenny. After his peck on Chris's cheek, she looked at him, "Carter, please look after yourself, for you've given enough to the job." It was then sweet Jenny's turn. Carter removed his holdall. Charlie knew what he wanted; he assisted him.

Carter placed a hand on each of her shoulders, and he looked down smiling, saying, "Jenny, Jenny, Jenny. What on earth can one say? You've put up with more than in your job description, and you are a wonderful advert for NHS nursing." With tears in his eyes, he said," How can one ever thank you?" He lowered his head and kissed her on both cheeks.

She looked up and whispered, "Please take care, Carter, always remember, if all else fails, there is always...?" She turned and walked away.

In the car, while on their journey home, Carter looked at Charlie, "I wonder what to expect?" Charlie never turned his head, concentrating on the road. "Guv matters have been dealt with. Miss Remington has left and taken all her belongings."

Charlie parked up in a convenient car space in front of his block. Assisting Carter from the car and into his wheelchair. Passing through the entrance of the flat, the duty concierge and the duty APO acknowledged him, and both greeted him with a warm welcome.

The duty APO assisted Charlie in lifting Carter in his chair up the two steps leading to the front door of his flat. Charlie stood to one side and pressed the RFID key fob on Carter's key ring onto the security reader.

Surprisingly, the door suddenly opened, and they both found Kate Murphy standing with a gaping smile, wearing her floral apron, brandishing her yellow marigold rubber gloves. Holding the door with her right hand, she pushed back a strand of hair from out of her eyes. "Carter, you're home at last?"

Charlie pushed him along the hall. Mrs Murphy beckoned with her head towards the kitchen. On arrival, she looked at them both, "Coffee?" They both smiled in agreement.

Charlie eventually looked at them both, "Well, I must be off." Carter, in his chair, busily tackled the hand wheels of the chair, propelling himself along the hall. At the front door, looking up at Charlie, he said, "Thanks, mate, for all…, well you know what I mean…?"

He smiled, "No need, guv, just let me know when you have to attend any outpatient appointments and your appointment with the police surgeon, for I'll pick you up." He smiled at Carter, it's a pity you couldn't have heard how a certain WDS dealt with a certain situation?"

As he opened the front door, "Carter, you know the inevitable: for your phone will ring off the hook, there'll be calls from TF, Sue, Eric, alike and loads of well-wishers. Please try to relax while matters pan out?" Carter looked at Charlie, "You mentioned relax; what the hell have I been doing for the past five weeks?" Charlie smiled, "Goodbye, guv, and he was off."

With the door closed Carter turned and pushed himself back to the kitchen. He stopped at the kitchen table, taking a sip of coffee; he looked up at Kate, "Kate give all?"

With a sad face, she looked at Carter, "Son, I know by certain steps, taken by a certain person…" Carter interrupted, "Christ Kate, I know she's packed up and left; she informed me while I was in hospital."

Kate stood with her hands on her hips and, with a broad smile on her face, said, "Ah yes, but do you know about what our Sue did?" Carter, with a blank face, just stared at Kate; she shrugged his shoulders, "What?"

"Well, Sue told her what she thought of her and of the timing of her decision-making. Sue gave her an ultimatum… Your visit to DCS Carter's flat will be under escort by the duty APO if not completed, by 1pm. All your belongings will be put into cardboard boxes and taken to the nearest charity shop."

Carter was speechless.

Kate Murphy spent daily visits to Carter's, instead of the usual twice weekly. Mainly due to Carter's limited access about his flat, in his day-to-day proceedings.

It wasn't for the cleaning, for the place was immaculate, or shopping, for the fridge, freezer, and cupboards were filled to the gunnels. But Kate thought, I must see to the preparation of easy microwave meals, for he can always revert to *'takeaways.'*

Kate Murthy thought if Tom, her husband (Carter's training sergeant), was still alive, he'd agree. But Kate had so much respect for Carter, for after Tom's unexpected death, only months after his retirement. He called quite unexpectantly one evening and unpretentiously suggested a situation that suited both parties. That was her Carter.

92

It was while Carter, was convalescing at home that he began to receive the calls as predicted by Charlie. TFs was just touching base, for Carter realised it was just a fishing exercise to ascertain his possible return to work. One such call he received from Sue. Her call was asking for a home visit to see him, stating that she'd have Eric in tow.

The intercom was activated for the front door to the block. Carter pushed himself down the hall to answer it. "Yes, just pull the door." Carter wheeled down to the front door of the flat. He opened the door and pushed himself into the raised reception hall of the flats.

Looking towards the reception, he saw both Sue and Eric. They both walked towards him, both displaying courteous smiles. He wasn't to know that on seeing Carter's demise, Sue fought to control her feelings, for the sight of Carter in a wheelchair completely knocked her for six. He showed his proficiency as he reversed back into his flat, welcoming his closest friends and colleagues.

Kate Murphy had prepared a display of coffee mugs on the breakfast bar. Together with assorted sandwiches and biscuits.

Carter smiled; please take off your coats and place them on the coat stand. He looked at them both, "Coffee?" In unison, they both replied, "Yes, please."

Kate looked at him, "Carter, why don't we go into the lounge, while I see to the drinks shortly?"

When in the lounge, Eric said, "Son, how are you getting on?" Carter smiled, "Apart from beginning to have an upper body like David Weir, fine." All three burst out laughing; when all was restored, Sue left to assist Kate make their drinks.

Returning carrying a tray with their coffees and assorted items for a casual lunch.

Although it wasn't by direct questions, Carter realised that by the tone of their enquiries, the conversation was leaning towards his possible return to work. They discussed his potential outpatient visit for the next day.

Carter looked at them both, "Unfortunately, the appointments cover not just my initial abduction, hence an appointment with a psyche. Plus, one with the NHS SS department, the physios.

Sue sat back, "Christ Carter, it will take ages; you know how slow these inter-department medical bods work?" Carter burst out laughing, "Ah, but they don't know of a certain Commander Tony Frost, who has a panel of police surgeons on his side, and Diane and Martin, my bolt hole in the country?"

Carter suddenly got up out of the wheelchair. He stood up, "Well, how about this? One good thing is that there are no problems with my balance and walking.

Eric and Sue screamed, *"Carter!"* Eric looked at him, "Why, Carter, shouldn't you at least wait for the *'All clear from the medics?'* Carter burst out laughing, "Well, I'll just have to jump back into that infernal machine tomorrow; my hands are red raw."

When matters resumed. Carter looked at Sue, "Well, Susan Martha, why don't you tell us of the *'Abby Remington'* circs?" Sue blushed, "Well, that stuck-up-nosed bitch, drops a time bomb on you whilst in bloody hospital; what an unfeeling cow?"

Eric smiled, "Have I missed something?" Carter looked at him, "Boss, did you not hear that Keswick Mansions was put under siege? Susan Martha here, threatened that all visits to the flat, will be under escort only. Conducted by the duty APO. That if her possessions were not cleared by a certain date, and time. They'll all be put in cardboard boxes and taken to the nearest charity shop?"

Eric burst out laughing, looking at Sue, "You are the guv's second in command. Does that give you the authority to speak and act on his behalf?" Sue sat looking at them both, "Well."

Carter looked at them both. "Well, Sue, let's put it this way: after all that occurred, the inevitable was bound to happen. Your actions intercepted all the shit that a *'knockback* can bring."

On leaving and saying all their goodbyes, Carter shook hands with Eric and gave Sue a peck on the cheek. Sue whispered, "Guv come back soon as I miss you."

Carter looked at them both, "I hope you don't mind, but I won't see you out, for they all know I'm in a bloody wheelchair?"

93

Carter and his trusted friend and APO Charlie, over the next couple of weeks, circumnavigated the many and varied obstacles associated with all the necessary visits to the many medical departments within the Royal. To prove he was fit to return to work.

At last, his final appointment with the police surgeon arrived; he presented himself for the usual, *'Please turn your head to the left and cough, then a quick check of his heart and lungs.'*

He had only been home a matter of minutes when his mobile phone activated. He took it out from his inside jacket pocket. "Carter."

"Carter, it's Jane, the boss wants to see you at 9am. Tomorrow. He shouted, "That was fucking quick?" She continued, *"But Carter you know what he's like, he wants his best boy back?"*

She continued, *"Now look here, Carter, when you attend, will you please put on that lovely blue suit, a white shirt, and that blue tie with the maroon lightning flashes on it? For you look so gorgeous?"*

Carter took in a deep breath, "Jane, our relationship ended some time ago; you made your decision quite clear when I handed in my ticket. You didn't wish to know a civvie. You mentioned something of an itch you wanted scratched, describing our relationship. But the inevitable put an end to our relationship."

A soft voice replied, *"Sorry, Carter, which was my mistake..."* Carter replied, "There you go." He closed the call.

Carter's next call was to Charlie, *"Guv, are you okay?"* "Yes, I'm fine; sorry to disturb you, but can you pick me up at 8.30 am. in the morning? TF wants to see me?"

"No probs, guv, see you then."

Later in the evening, Carter prepared for bed in his usual way. He showered, after which he threw himself under the duvet, expecting sleep to descend upon him, but no, he forgot that the mere thought of the name of Jane threw a giant spanner in the works.

He tossed and turned, although the images that flooded into his brain were somewhat forgiving. Carter played the *'what if game.'* He burst out laughing while he lay back on his bed, for the subject matter was, '*Jane*'?"

He was thinking about the original rules. The matters of the game referred to by TF when toying with decisions made by him. At the same time, dealing with one crime or another.

But in this case, the subject matter, in the rules of this *'what if'* game, is nothing but all the wonderful thoughts of Jane.

Eventually, after his shave and shower, he thought, should 'I' as he investigated his wardrobe, with the towel wrapped around him, 'No' I don't want her to think I'm easy?"

At 8.35am on the dot, the front door of his flat sounded. It was Charlie, for the duty APO would have let him through the front door. He opened his door to see the smiling face of Charlie, "Morning guv, is it shit, or promotion? It can only be the two reasons for TF wanting to see you?"

Carter, after saying, good morning to all the duty team. Looked at Charlie, "It may be as simple as my return to work after my spell in hospital and yesterday's medical?"

The routine was always the same. Enter HQ, show your ID to the duty reception officer, and walk over to the bank of lifts. Enter, press button 5 and your off. The door opens, and you leave the lift to the right. There you have it, TF's office with Jane, sitting outside at her desk.

On hearing the bell acknowledging their arrival, the opening of the lift doors, Jane knew full well who it would be. She casually turned and looked at them both, "Why, it's like buses...?" DCS Carter, and DI Watson, how nice to see you both?"

Carter thought, 'What, no sexual innuendos, not having to walk the sexual gauntlet. Jane must be playing it cool. Jane picked up her phone and dialled TF's number. Looking at Carter, she said, "Carter, will you please go in?" As he left for the door, Jane whispered, "Pity about the suit?" and winked at him.

In his office, TF, who looked immaculate as always, stood leaning on the edge of his desk, with his arms folded in front of him. After the distraction, Jane entered with a tray carrying there two coffees, she placed the tray on the table and left.

Carter was fully aware of the script, yet on other occasions it was via the phone. TF, who had returned to his chair. He looked out at Carter, "Do you wish to remain on operational duties, or could you drive your team from a desk with Superintendent Ford on point?"

He looked at TF, "Sir, do you wish to receive my resignation now, for a second fucking time?" TF burst out laughing, "Carter, Carter, no, no, it was the thoughts passed to me attested to by the medical folks. On the one hand. The judgements of the medics at the Royal, and of course the various police surgeons?"

He continued, "Both options are based on the amount of time spent over the years in hospital, and the medicals undertaken with the police surgeon?"

Carter looked at his boss, "This is no bull shit, but I can only work one way...?" TF interrupted, "Son, even the Chief and Jane, sat outside of this bloody office know this information. Like you, what's said in this room remains in this room...?"

He smiled, "Business as usual?" Carter stood and smiled. TF walked over, and they both shook hands; they were both aware of the total respect held in both camps.

He looked at his man. "No one knows of this conversation, and I know you don't like any fuss, so get DI Watson, to pick you up in the morning, but remember your on light duties."

Smiling, he turned and left TF's office. Outside, Charlie stood up. Carter said, "Off we go." As Charlie turned to leave, Carter mouthed to Jane, *'Call me later, please?'*

When in the car, Charlie looked at Carter, "Where to guv?" "Home, James, please, Charlie, and could I book you to pick me up tomorrow, no fuss? I don't want even Sue to know?"

94

Charlie, prior to dropping off his boss made a quick recce of his flat, although, at the time, there was an APO on duty in the front hall. For Charlie always remembered Carter's abduction, from his bedroom turned, "See you in the morning guv?" And left.

Carter raided the fridge, taking out two cans of Lagers, he left for the lounge. He had just sat down, and in the middle of pulling the *'ring pull'* off his can, he had only just taken a slug of beer when his mobile phone activated. He thought, 'Shit.'

"Carter." *"Carter, it's Jane. TF is out of the office, so I have some time for a chat?"* Carter took another slurp of beer, wiped his mouth with the back of his hand, and just stopped short of calling, "Ah..."

Breathing out, he whispered, "It was your attitude yesterday, so without throwing bombs at each other in the blame game, why don't you come around when you finish work to have a chat and some tea?"

He heard a sudden intake of breath, "Oh, Carter, that would be wonderful..." He laughed down the phone, "Please don't think that includes a shower?" She screamed down the phone, *"Spoilsport, I was just going to say that I'd call home for a clean pair of panties?"*

"No, Jane." Carter replied, "I feel that we will need to sort out some ground rules before we anticipate the rest of the evening?" He closed the call.

Carter only had to order the *'take out.'* For their tea, for the flat was immaculate, for under Kate Murphy's tutelage, the only thing he had to see to was the making of his bed, and a general clear up of the bathroom.

Timed for the meal to arrive at 5.30 pm, he thought if TF were running late, then he'd just place the meal in the oven.

The meal arrived, and Jane arrived at about 6 pm. He picked up the handset, saying, *"Pull the door."* A controlled voice replied, *"I know, I know."* He smiled to himself as he walked to the front door of the flat.

He opened the door and looked to the right to see an apparition moving towards him. Jane stopped in front of him. "Please don't think I dress like this for just anybody; she smiled and leaned forward and kissed him on his cheek.

Carter placed an arm about Jane and escorted her into his flat. When in the hall, he kissed her gently on her lips. She responded. When completed, she looked up at him. "Carter, now that is what I've missed?"

They both walked down the hall towards the lounge. She slipped off her coat and let it fall to the floor at the coat stand, realising the effect for Carter. She turned, and Carter called, "Christ Jane, but you look beautiful."

She wore a black low-fronted dress, which fell to an inch above her knee, black hose, and a pair of black stilettos. Her jewellery was conservative, with a plain gold-coloured necklace and gold-coloured studs in her ears.

He raised an arm, indicating that she had entered the lounge. She sat on one of the comfortable settees. He looked at her, "Wine?" She smiled, "Lovely."

He returned carrying a bottle of red wine and two beautiful wine glasses. He placed the items onto the coffee table and then proceeded to fill their glasses. On completion, he passed a glass to Jane, taking the other for himself. Sat next to each other, they picked up their glass, saying, "Cheers."

Jane leaned over towards Carter, to replace her glass back on the coffee table. The act of such a simple task was near impossible for him to miss, for her well-rounded breasts nearly spilt from out of her low-fronted dress and bra. Jane, with a wicked look, whispered, "Well, Carter, what are the ground rules you wished to discuss?"

He spluttered, "Well, this is our second time around; I have to say that the main offender in the capitulation of our relationship was your bloody boss, TF. He was pontificating in his office to both me, and Wendy Field. He stuck his nose in where there was no shit on the completion of the 'Michael Hughes case'."

"He wanted Wendy Field to reveal all and release the full story to the press. Before the case had even been tried, it meant he'd gain kudos with the Chief Con. And senior government officials in the Home Office, who had drawn up the theory of the MCUs."

"No, he wouldn't listen to me; he just wanted to ride roughshod over the case. I told him to go ahead, for he'd be responsible for the biggest legal fuck up that this force had ever comprehended."

"He backed me into a corner; I knew he hadn't run it passed the Chief, so I told him that he could stick his job up his arse. Well, there you have it, I walked, and you didn't seem to like it, the thought of me becoming a civvie."

Jane looked at him through the saddest pair of eyes he'd ever encountered. "Carter, it's because I've seen or heard of you being back on the job. God knows what may have happened if I'd met you as a civvie?"

Both sat looking at each other, somewhat surprised, for they both wanted to work matters out, yet having to think of the consequences. Suddenly, Carter stated, "It's the bloody 'what ifs' again?"

Looking at Jane, he said, "I feel it would be best served if we draw a line under the past, that's history, and deal with the present. I know we're no strangers to each other. So, one may see it as putting on a favourite item of clothing, knowing that it feels so comfortable?"

"Yet again, in our case, to re-gig our relationship, we will need to administer restraint from the start.

He noticed that tears had begun to well up in her eyes. Jane looked at him, "You've only just come out of hospital. It was TF who told me to ring you, asking you to attend at his office, and no sudden act on my behalf. But it wouldn't take much."

"Jane, looked up with concern in her eyes. "I'm so sorry Carter, can you ever forgive me, I've been a complete ass. He smiled, "Well, can I interest you in some tea, and see how matters play out?"

Fortunately, his *'takeaway'* hadn't spoiled, and he managed to serve a presentable meal. He had purchased a curry with all the trimmings. During the meal, Carter had asked Jane what she'd like to drink, and he offered wine, or beer.

95

The time eventually arrived, for they had both consumed several glasses of wine with the meal and in the lounge. A quantity of coffees, accompanied with equal measures of Baileys original liqueurs. They were both sat next to each other on the comfy settee.

Carter looked at Jane apologetically, "I just thought not commencing back at the office until tomorrow. Having only an APO in reception, we could spend the evening, and perhaps the night together, before I get back between the shafts."

Jane suddenly turned and tossed her arms about his neck. She whispered in his ear, "Oh Carter, I've been so silly in the past?"

She leaned up and kissed Carter on his lips, and he responded. "Carter, I do understand that you may have been suspicious for my reasons, but it was never you returning to the job; it was when given the opportunity to speak and see you, I just thought…?"

He stood back, looking at her, "Jane, you must know I'll find it so easy to return to our past relationship. I would love to salvage what's left of the evening. I thought it would have been that much better if matters had developed more naturally."

She took hold of his hand and led the way to the bedroom; he resisted at first and then saw the look on her face. Thought, "Oh well, why not? She must have computed my insidious attempt to dig myself out of the hole.

Both, in their desire and excitement, had within minutes rendered themselves naked while standing in the bedroom. It was obvious that they both must have thought, *'shower or bed.'*

Jane looked up at him, "Carter, for Christ's sake, make a decision?" He burst out laughing, "But Jane, when given two options, it means there has to be a third, shower then bed, then sex?"

Jane looked at him, "Carter, the difference is the width of a cigarette paper, now…" She hadn't finished her lecture on sex locations. When he gently took hold of her around her waist, lifting her, taking her giggling, and squirming into the bathroom. He switched on the shower, in the wet room and he walked in carrying his pray.

Jane began to scream, for she knew what to expect. For the first several seconds, the torrent of water ran cold until reaching the correct temperature.

Screaming, Jane called, "Carter, is this the way you wish to swoon me?" Through the torrent of water, he took hold of her and pressed her against his warm body, "No, but just you wait."

The water eventually began to warm up to the prescribed temperature, and he immediately began to feel her body relax while in his arms. He put her down and reached for the soapy shower hand glove.

Oozing with soap suds, he began to pass it over the length of her back. She clung to him with her head on his shoulder and began kissing his neck. After a couple of minutes, Jane turned and, with a smile of anticipation, looked at Carter as if permitting him to complete his task.

Knowing from previous history, Jane would not complain; in fact, the opposite, for his intended target remained a beautiful specimen of a woman.

He could feel her begin to riddle with intended excitement and standing back, allowing Carter, to have a full view of her beautiful body. As Carter began to soap her front, she started to stiffen up with anticipation.

Allowing him to lean down and kiss her breasts and nipples. She screamed, "Carter, please stop and take me to your bed. I feel that if we remain in the shower, although I'd certainly accept that if it were our only option, I feel, in bed it would offer so much more room to express ourselves?"

He gently wrapped her in a giant bath sheet and carried her off to bed. When she stood at the side of the bed, he lowered her down and opened the towel. He immediately looked down at her magnificent body.

He knelt at the side of the bed and began to kiss her, firstly on her lips, to which she duly responded. He then began to kiss the length of her gorgeous, warm body, and he concentrated upon some of her most pleasurable items, to which she responded, omitting gasps of delight.

Eventually, after a brief period, she took hold of him and pulled him down on top of her. At the same time, she permitted him access to her.

His actions brought an immense reaction; Jane, having foreknowledge of her sexual response to such matters, for caution, stuffed a corner of the duvet into her mouth.

The following morning, Jane leaned over and kissed Carter on his lips while still fast asleep. On receipt of the third kiss, he opened his eyes. She smiled down at him, "Why, Carter, you're nothing but a cheat. Were you feigning sleep?" He looked up at her, "I was pretending so that you may stray and begin to kiss me all over my body. In your attempt to wake me."

Jane burst out laughing, "Oh Carter, you have no idea what I'd get up to if your eyes had remained closed, feigning sleep. I'd have gone to such lengths when attempting to awaken you. For your body, oh my God, is a virtual playground for total sexual pleasures. When left to play, allowing one to transverse all the undulating shape of your physique."

After she explained her previous statement, Jane went to great lengths to prove to Carter, by pleasuring him in such wonderful ways. After which they both got up and entered the bathroom. Carter began to shave, and while his face was covered in shaving cream, Jane, while passing, leaned over and kissed him.

He turned and began to rub his face over hers and her breasts, and she began to scream. "Carter, what? I was only kissing you, and now I'm covered in shaving foam." He laughed, "It suits you." When finished, he carried her into the shower.

During which he kissed her, Jane said, "Carter, how am I expected to stand after such a kiss? She looked up at him, "Carter, do we both take part in a sensual shower, repeating matters all over again?" He smiled, "No, if you wish, you'll have to call and continue this evening, for I must dress and be ready for work." As he left, she shouted, "Spoilsport."

In the kitchen, Carter had prepared two coffees. Over which she looked at him over her mug, "Carter, will this cause a problem for you?" Carter smiled, "Well, if one drip-feeds the situation, eventually, people will learn to accept it."

96

Carter was pleased to experience Charlie's, timing for it was appropriate. Jane had already left before he rang the front doorbell of his flat. The entrance to the main door of the block was opened by the duty APO.

He walked out, faced with Charlie's smiling face, to his awaiting car. When inside, Charlie looked at him, "Well, guv, here we go again; you do realise that the team will go mad at me for no prior knowledge of your return?"

Carter looked at him, "Charlie, I wouldn't have it any other way; the less fuss, the better."

On arrival at Derby Lane, he walked into the general office to be met by a chorus of utter surprise, "Why, guv, didn't you tell us?"

As Carter signed on duty, he was met by Eric and his ritual mug of morning coffee. Eric, who was a seasoned campaigner, just looked at him. "Morning, guv."

Eric had no sooner said the words when the door to the office opened, and in walked Sue. She did a double take, "What the hell...?" Eric laughed, "Yet again, the guv wanted no fuss."

Sue, when over the shock after signing on duty, looked at Charlie, "I suppose we can always change his APO to one who will play ball with us. All present in the general office burst out laughing.

Armed with her coffee, she went and sat next to both Eric and Carter. As different members of the team entered, they all reacted the same. Eventually, Carter stood up, looking at Sue, he said, "Superintendent Ford, will you please join me in my office?"

Minutes later, when both were in his office, he looked at Sue, "Perhaps the other way would be better, for it would get matters all over and done with, not having to go over the issues all over again?"

He looked at Sue, "So Susan Martha, what do you have to tell me?" She sighed, "Not wishing to say the 'Q' word, but matters have been, so in the meantime, we have been preparing the committal file for the four major offenders. The fifth Sutcliff was discharged, *'No case to answer."*

Sue realised that Carter didn't want chapter and verse, for it was sufficient for him to be told how matters were progressing. Sue looked at Carter, "I hope you're not returning just because you're bored?" He burst out laughing, "No, Sue, I was given a full clean bill of health from the police surgeons, although to work, *'light duties,'* no pressure."

Sue looked at him, "Well, Carter, you more than most know that TF has them in his back pocket, and they dare not suggest a prolonged extension to your sick leave or a bout of convalescence?" They both burst out laughing.

At that moment, Sue got up, "I'll let you catch up on your paperwork?" He shouted for all to hear, "Yes, no one bloody does it when I'm off sick?" Sue sheepishly left his office.

Sue had no sooner left his office when his mobile activated; he looked down to see that Jane, was the caller.

He burst out laughing, "Well, I haven't had time to dry the pots?"

Jane murmured, *"Carter, I can't concentrate on my work after last night. I can't get you or the levels attained in our lovemaking out of my mind. It was fantastic. Will you please believe me when I say that I haven't sorted others after our affair?"*

After a short break in her conversation, Jane whispered, *"Carter, you are the first to know the amount of rubbish I spout when trying to tease you in the past. Suggesting how I could show you a good time, offering nights of sheer bliss?"*

"Carter, I now realise that I'm a mere novice when it comes to the pleasuring business. For I know if given another opportunity, that nights like last night would or could be cherished. For Carter, it's you." Jane said in a quiet voice, *"Carter, please allow me to call this evening for tea?"*

The next voice they both heard was that of TF's, *"Christ, when are we going to get some work done?"* Jane closed the call.

Carter began to wade through most of the paperwork and reports for they were self-explanatory, submitted by Sue, in relation to their present case.

After an hour he got up and walked through to the general office. Eric looked up, "Guv, can I be of any help?" Carter looked at him, "I'd murder for a cup of coffee?" Eric looked up. "Guv you only have to ask?"

When he sat with his coffee, he looked up at Eric, "Where are we in relation to the Smedley, Spencer, Rice, and the Coombes business?"

Eric explained, "Well, guv Coombes was the conduit, the wherewithal for the information to get to Smedley. Smedley is the main protagonist. Ably assisted by Spencer. Knowing that Combes and Rice had been arrested. The flow of information stalled, so it was you they went after."

"Rice met Coombes at a legal, CPS 'do' a smoothy dance, he realised the score, tempted Coombes, with nights out, special meals, weekends away, guv I don't have to explain?"

Eric, smiling, looked at Carter, "Guv, if you were a '*baddie*,' a job that you'd be good at?" The attractive secretaries in the office all burst out laughing.

Suddenly, the office door opened, and Sue walked in, "Well, what's causing all the uproar?" Eric smiled up at her, "I was just explaining the present case, the part Rice played in the swooning of Coombes, for information obtained from the CPS. The guv would be particularly good at?"

Sue burst out laughing, "You've got to be joking; he's passed it." All the girls in the office let out cries of complaint. One whispered, "If it was put to a vote…?"

Sue, who was playing Devil's advocate, thought, if only…

Carter, who had nearly caused his drink to evacuate down his nose on several occasions, looked at Eric, "Can you get hold of Charlie? I'm leaving for home." He looked at Sue. "Susan Martha Ford, should you wish to remain SOI 1, I suggest that you get matters sorted for tomorrow." There was a raw of laughter.

Carter signed off duty and left for his office. On arrival, he took out his mobile phone and called Jane. After several seconds, he heard her velvet voice, *"Carter, are you okay?"* He replied, "Why yes, I'm just informing you that I'm off home. It's my first day, and I need to conserve my energy!!?"

His comment was met with raw laughter, and Jane blurted out, *"What, after last night, I would have thought you'd need a week." She whispered, "See you later for tea, my treat."*

Jane was as good as her word; she pressed the intercom, and Carter just pressed the release button. In passing, she acknowledged the duty concierge and APO.

Carter opened the door to his flat. On seeing Jane, he took a double take, for she looked gorgeous, plus carrying her two brown-coloured takeaway bags that spoilt the picture.

In the flat, Carter, unloaded the two takeaway bags and left for the kitchen. On arrival he checked the meal and placed the curry and all the works into a low oven.

He turned and, in the hall, looked at Jane. He burst out laughing, "Please tell me you didn't go to work like that?" She smiled, "Carter we girls have our methods?"

Carter said, "But Jane, you look fantastic." She smiled at him, "Well, the secret is out; I've had blue lights fitted to the radiator of my car, and a claxon under the bonnet. I rushed home, showered, changed, put clean underwear in my bag, and rushed through to 2, Keswick Mansions?"

He kissed her on her lips. Before she had time to relish his kiss, he said, "I suppose a Fiat Punto needs all the help it can get?" She caught hold of him, "Well, Mr., we all can't afford a brand-new BMW fitted with all the trimmings…?"

97

After tea, Carter cleared away. He carried the remaining bottle of red wine through to the lounge, together with their two wine glasses. When comfortable, Jane looked at Carter. "Well, how was your first day back?" He laughed, "There was certain consternation, for no one had let it be known that I was returning to work?"

After their bouts of laughter, Carter got up, "Can I interest you in a coffee and Cognac?" Jane smiled, "Carter that would just complete a wonderful meal."

Again, while he walked through to the kitchen, he burst out laughing. Minutes later he returned to the lounge carrying a tray with their drinks. The night progressed, and it was during the evening that Carter had replenished their drinks yet again.

When he returned, Jane had laid up against some cushions with her legs and feet folded under her bottom. Carter sat and placed her legs onto his knee.

While they both sipped their drinks, Carter began to massage her toes with one hand. Jane whispered, "Oh, Carter, that's beautiful." He placed his glass down and began to concentrate on the job at hand. Carter gently, while massaging, let his hands move up her legs.

She suddenly jumped up, and while laughing, she called, "Carter, if you continue, I'll end up in a pool of water. She took his hand and tenderly manoeuvred him towards the bedroom.

On arrival, she undressed him. She then slipped out of her dress, revealing her erotic underwear, being so sheer he could see all her body.

Laying side by side, she looked up at Carter, "Mr. I've never known a man who when he looked, or looks at me, with those magnificent blue eyes. It can generate so much sexual activity within me. I feel that everyone can notice the ripple effect that it has on me?"

Jane began to kiss Carter all over. She removed his shorts and began to pleasure him orally, but having her mind on other topics, ceasing short of the inevitable. Although not one to renege, she climbed on top of Carter.

She impaled herself, letting out a cry of pleasure. "Oh Carter, I have in the past teased you at times, implying that this excuse of a female had unfathomable depths of sexual experience. Yet it is I who feel the novice in such matters."

"Yet you, Carter, do not need to jest with me, for you've no doubt heard the famous expression...' *Wise men speak because they have something to say. Fools because they have to say something?'* I feel so ashamed yet so safe."

Jane smiled down at him, "In my attempt to try and impress you, it is here that I feel the safest, with you inside of me. I cannot describe the ultimate satisfaction, whichever way we attain our sexual delights?"

On their joint climax, their bodies shook. Jane leaned forward, and she kissed Carter with so much passion, yet her body continued to shake, but she then began to cry. Carter placed his arms around her to offer her security.

Jane lay on Carter, her hip and her right leg resting over his torso, with her head resting on the nape of his neck. He pulled up the duvet and covered them both.

Prior to wishing each other good night, Carter looked down on Jane. "Please do not undersell yourself in the sex department, for you have an inevitable way of responding to me. Please do not worry." When completely comfortable they both, fell fast asleep within seconds.

Carter woke. He looked at his watch it was 6.45 am. Carter looked down at Jane and saw a beautiful woman asleep. He slipped out of bed, placing on his boxers. He left for the kitchen, knowing that the central heating was on, making the flat lovely, warm, and toasty.

When in the kitchen, Carter set about making a mug of coffee. There was no need for any help from contestants from 'Master Chef' He laughed, 'One teaspoon full of coffee, placed in a coffee mug and immersed in boiling water, *'Result.'*

It was while he was standing in the kitchen facing the kitchen worktop, about to take a careful sip of his perfect coffee of the morning. He suddenly felt a warm naked body leaning against him, with a hand that slipped under his boxers, with the Suttle undertones, "Guess who?"

"Wellll, what do we have, a lovely warm body pressed against mine with the feeling of a perfect pair of breasts on my back? Why, it could only be Ms. Jane Robinson, my beautiful lover."

Jane burst out laughing, "It must have been the location of my hand on your never regions. It sort of centralises one's thinking." They both burst out laughing.

Carter finished his coffee; looking at Janes's naked body, he blinked. "Lovely, I must shave and shower. He walked through to the bathroom. He began to immerse his face with shaving foam. As he began to shave, taking hold of his razor, started the first slide down the side of his face. He suddenly felt his boxers pulled down and a pair of hands placed on his crotch.

He suddenly let out a gasp of breath. "Jane, I nearly slit my throat, for Christ's sake." Jane leaned on his back, laughing. "I thought you were a highly trained, very senior police officer?" Carter replied, "Yes, yes, when confronted by a suspect holding a gun in my face, but when grabbed from the rear by a gorgeous woman, such matters are never covered in the training manual."

Carter continued under duress. But being a highly trained officer, he completed the task, although he needed the help of the preheated cold water of, the shower to recover his dignity.

While in the shower, Jane, through the torrent of water, looked up at Carter, "I will complete my mission tonight, for I know you have a busy day in front of you?"

On completion of the shower and whilst drying Carter looked at Jane, "Jane I feel that it won't be long before we may be on the same footing as before I submitted my notice after TF's dealing with the Sir Malcolm Arnold Ainsworth case?"

"That after my recent bout in hospital. TF suggested that I make an appointment with you to see him. To arrange a possible attendance at the Police Surgeon. That after our brief telephone conversation, I thought that after my time in his office, on leaving I'd find a way of asking you to call me, in an effort to re-ignite a bye gone relationship."

Jane walked over to Carter and took his head in both of her hands. "Carter, I'm so glad that we have been given a second chance, I have to say that during our break I never looked anywhere else, for all of my sexual innuendos, it was all show, and only directed at you."

"No Carter I'm in it for the long haul...He looked at her saying, "After the case we'll go away and sort matters out. When dressed they both kissed goodbye, Jane left, for TF's office, and Carter went to meet Charlie for his lift to the office.

98

On arrival at the office, Carter walked into the general office. Together with Charlie, they both signed on duty. Eric produced his traditional morning coffee, the first of the day.

On completion of his coffee Carter stood up, and left for his office, as he left, he looked at Eric, "Will you ask Sue to come through to my office?" "Yes, guv." he replied.

In his office while sat behind his desk, he looked at a few files, when there was a knock on his office door. He called, "Come in." The door opened and Sue walked in. "Morning guv is everything okay.

Carter beckoned for Sue to take a seat adjacent to his desk. He looked at Sue, "Where are we up to with the committal papers for, Spencer, Rice, Ridley, Combes, and Smedley?"

All submitted under their various charges, and of course the encapsulating offence of, Conspiracy. Sir they are up for a plea and sentence."

Carter looked at Sue, "Not wishing to evoke the Gods of crime I submit the 'Q' word and leave half chopping see you all tomorrow." Sue looked up at him, "Well sir, nobody deserves an early dart more than you?" Sue got up and left saying, "I'll send for Charlie, to meet you in the general office."

On arrival home, and after Charlies security swoop of the flat. Charlie smiled, "Sir, see you in the morning." He turned and left.

When alone in the flat, he walked into the kitchen and raided the fridge of two cans of lager. After taking off his overcoat, and jacket. He removed his shoulder holster, and firearm, placing them into the floor safe in his wardrobe.

Returning to the lounge he opened the first can, and it barely touched the sides. He placed the can down on the coffee table. He lay back and relaxed on the settee. He tried to blank out the intended committals. As he was about to open the second can, his mobile activated. He thought, *'Shit'* Not even home an hour, and the bloody phone goes off.

"Carter" He heard Janes lovely voice, *"Why Carter, why fore so official?"* He quickly responded, "Jane I'm so sorry I'm home, and I thought it was the bloody job?" Jane in an upset voice replied, *"Carter, are you okay, for being home so early, I thought for an awful moment you may have experienced a reaction after dealing with an operational issues, that you may have got involved, and injured that beautiful body of yours?"*

They both burst out laughing, Carter whispered, "No, Jane I was just fed up, and decided to half-chop?"

Jane said, *"It's all right for you, I must remain until TF goes home before I can escape home. For do you know under any other way, or circumstances, I'd be off home to smother you with my body?"*

Carter burst out laughing, "Well, I'll await with bated breath?"

Jane was as good as her word. At about 6pm she arrived at Carter's flat. She found him so laid back that she could pour him into the wet room. In fact, that was exactly how matters played out. For she quickly undressed, and lovingly, yet very gently removed his clothes.

When naked she placed an arm about him and tenderly escorted whilst kissing him on the nape of his neck into the wet room and shower. Under the torrent of water, she took hold of the soapy sponge glove, and began to soap his body all over in suds.

Jane had become an expert with such a soft yet especially useful item. She faced him and starting at his shoulders she as with a piece of velvet smoothed it down each shoulder, when at his chest in circles she covered him all over. Laughing she placed a soapy finger onto his nose, leaving a cluster of soap suds on it. He moved his lower jaw blowing up to remove it.

With that she turned him and began to soap his back, on doing so she placed her head on his back and whispered, "Carter I have you were I want you?" Laughing she adoringly moved the glove over his penis. "There I have you." While she applied her wears, she failed to realise that Carter had suddenly lifted a hand behind his back, and equally began to pleasure her.

She lifted herself on to her tip toes, and while resting her head on his back she said, "Christ Carter, you beautiful man. I suggest that we desist, dry ourselves, and resume matters in bed.

After the inevitable, when completed they dressed, and walked through to the kitchen for tea.

Epilogue

Eventually, after all the hard work completed by Carter and the team. It was committal day. All four defendants pleaded guilty, on the advice of their legal teams. Due to the weight of the prosecution evidence.

All the accused, Spencer, Smedley, Rice, were escorted by two male prison officers. Combes had the close assistance of a female officer.

The presiding Judge, Mr William Forsythe QC, had decided to deal with Combes first. He looked up at Combes, "Combes one could suggest that you were the instigator in this horrific case. For you employed in the CPS had a direct result on issues, for you were the supplier of all the pertinent information, supplying release dates of prisoners. It has been suggested by the officers dealing with these matters, that due to your evidence, it assisted with the eventual detection of your fellow accused."

"That in your case there are grounds of mitigating circumstances. You were tempted by the applied affection submitted by the accused Rice. Taking all matters into consideration, I hereby sentence you to 6 years imprisonment. Now take her away."

The judge then looked at Rice. "You were the main conduit of passing matters to your co-accused, Spencer, and Smedley. You groomed Combes over a period of time, by means of gifts, meals at pleasant restaurants, and weekends away, until you gained her affections. It was learning of her position in the CPS that you put your plan into action. I hereby sentence you to 12 years imprisonment. Now take him away."

The judge then looked at Spencer and Ridley the list of matters committed by you both amount to a list of such horrific issues, I feel it would be irresponsible of me to read out such issues to the body of the court. Yet it must be said that you both took part in some of the most ghastly, grisly, lurid, and macabre murders responsible for the direct killing of some 11 victims and others.

It is believed that after the arrest of Combes that your information dried up, so you decided to attack the head of the MCU, by initially abducting him for some eight days. He unbelievable escaped. Then while in hospital recovering Spencer while acting as a Consultant entered the ICU in the Royal Liverpool hospital, struck a nurse about the head, and shot the officer three times in the chest. While recovering in the ICU, you Smedley in a similar vein tried again to kill the officer, but on that occasion, you were detained during your futile attempt, by two brave armed protection officers you were detained, arrested, and removed into police custody."

The Judge looked up at the two remaining prisoners, Spencer, and Ridley. "I hereby sentence you both to, A whole life order, Now take the away."

The Judge sat back in his huge seat, he placed his fingers in an apex shape and talked over them. "Ladies and gentlemen of the jury and the court, there are few occasions that when I read certain items of the court papers, I find that I'm enabled to act in a positive manner."

"I take great pleasure in awarding a Crown Court commendation, to the senior officer, and team members of the MCU, who worked tirelessly through all the unbelievable crime scenes committed by the offenders, in these matters. I also wish to award a Crown Court commendation to Woman Detective Superintendent

Susan Ford, who placed herself in the line of danger when Ridley threatened to shoot, Chief Superintendent Carter while in the ICU of the Liverpool Royal hospital."

On their return journey to Derby Lane, Carters mobile activated, he looked at the screen and saw the initials TF. He looked at his colleagues, "Here we go." "Sir." "Carter placed his phone on speaker. "Where are you; I have Wendy Field in my office to compile a press release?" Carter replied, "Sir, Wendy will have all the information, and convictions. I'm putting in a leave request from now. DS Ford, will resume be in control of MCU in my absence."

Carter looked at Sue stating, " Susan Martha Ford, please close your mouth." Charlie, will you please take me home. Sue, when you get back to Derby Lane, please get Eric, to put in my leave 104 (police general form for leave application.) sign it and send it to TF's office.

On entering his flat Jane met him, "Well I've told TF I'm on leave with you, he can't stop it for your, his favourite boy."

Carter had made all the arrangements with Diane and Martin, on arrival at the farm, after all the hello's, they collected the two aging labs, and made there way to their cottage. They first relaxed by taking an invigorating walk with their two friends and began to lose all the tensions of the job to enjoy their holiday.